CW00428374

SIREN STORIES

Presents

UNHOLY WATER

A Halloween Novel

Jonathan McKinney

✝

Contents

CHAPTER ONE
Friends at the Royal Oak

The sky was grey and the air cool, as Aaron McLeary and Juliet Rayne walked down the hill from Rayne Manor, toward The Royal Oak, in the mysterious Lancashire town of Ecclesburn. The early autumnal evening, with its lingering daylight, was empty of charm or festivity, but for the rustle of dead, brown leaves underfoot.

'Of course love is a good thing,' Aaron said.

'I'm not talking about *love*, per se,' Juliet replied, gripping Aaron's hand as they walked. 'I'm talking about passion. I'm talking about desire.'

'Those are also good things,' Aaron said.

'You're sure about that?' Juliet asked.

'What would life be without passion, without desire?' Aaron asked. 'What would *our* lives be?'

Juliet squeezed Aaron's hand. 'Sure, but just because passion and desire make you and me happy, that doesn't mean that they're inherently *good*.'

'They feel good,' Aaron said with a shrug.

'But ... the theory I'm working on for class is this, okay? All of our negative behaviours begin with desire. Some people want food, so they eat too much, and they get sick. Some people want, like, a chemical hit, so they drink, they smoke, they do drugs—and again they get sick. And where it gets worse, is, when people give in to their desire for sex and they hurt their boyfriends, or girlfriends; or when someone wants power, which makes people do just terrible, awful things.'

'I don't think the issue there is desire, though,' Aaron said. 'Isn't it just, like, people following certain desires over others? Harmful ones, over harmless ones.'

'I have a whole chapter on that,' Juliet said. 'But that doesn't disqualify desire as the inciting emotion that leads to all the negative behaviour.'

'I think maybe it does,' Aaron said. 'I mean, say I was out without you, and I met some woman, and we hit it off. Say I wanted to have sex with her, right, and she wanted to have sex with me?'

Juliet wrinkled her nose and frowned. 'I don't like this example.'

'But I also want to keep things cool with us,' Aaron said. 'So ... I decide not to go off and cheat on you, because I wanna stay close and intimate with you.'

Juliet turned to look at Aaron, a quirkily mischievous smile on her face. 'Does that happen often?' she asked.

'All the time,' he said, matching her tone.

'Anyway,' Juliet said, 'I'm not saying that desire always causes disaster, but your example really confirms my point, and this is what I get to in the essay.'

'How?'

'Because desire needs to be constantly managed. That requires work. It can't be programmed. No matter how much we'd like to teach ourselves only to want things that are good for us, we can't. Desire awakens, every morning, like the sun, and with it comes the need to fight it. Because if we give ourselves over to absolute desire, we become monsters, who hurt each other, who damage each other, both inside, and out.'

'Sounds like a depressing view of the world,' Aaron said, as the couple, joined at the hands, reached the halfway point of Ragged Stone Road, where the road from their home met the south end of Lockwood Mews, the Ecclesburn high street.

'What's depressing?' came a curt and crisp, if friendly, voice.

Aaron turned to the voice. It was Robert Entwistle, the third member of the Rayne Helsingers. 'Oh, just Juliet's research essay,' Aaron said.

'For my psych class,' Juliet said.

'She basically thinks that, because we want things, we're destined to become demons,' Aaron said. 'You got everything?'

Robert patted the messenger bag that was hanging over his shoulder, down behind his hip. 'Stakes, crossbows, holy water,' he said flatly. 'We're all good. What are we looking at?'

'Nest of vampires,' Juliet said. 'They turned one of the barmen from The Royal Oak, and he set them up underneath the building, in the cellar where they keep all the beer kegs.'

Aaron nodded. 'The manager's losing his shit because, get this, he's got a function on tonight, and the vamps are smashing up the place.'

'Den wants the place open for business *tonight*?' Robert asked.

'He's not the nicest guy in the world,' Juliet said.

'And the fact that he *wants* to reopen makes him a bad guy, right Jules?' Aaron said.

'That's not what I said and you know it,' she replied.

'Anyway ...' Robert began, 'you know Father William, the new South African priest, down at St. Luke's? He's a total weirdo.'

'What do you mean?' Juliet asked.

'He's just really intense. He was blessing the holy water for me and his whole attitude was off. He was, like, all firm in the face, but occasionally he'd smile weird at me, and his voice was slow and serious.'

'Is he an old guy?' Juliet asked.

'No, young,' Robert said. 'Way younger than Father McMahon was.'

'So what's the deal?' Aaron said. He turned to Robert and joked, 'Did he fancy you?'

'I just got a bad vibe is all,' Robert said.

'Maybe you're just being a massive xenophobe?' Aaron said.

'Look, it's fine, as long as his holy water works,' Juliet said firmly. 'We don't want to get into a fight and lose because of bad sacramentals.'

A moment passed, while the three young vampire hunters considered this.

'We've still got some of Father McMahon's, right?' Juliet said. 'We should try out this new guy's water on a vamp, make sure it works, before we depend on it. If for any reason it's not the real deal, we use McMahon's stuff and find some more from somewhere else.'

'I'm sure it'll work,' Robert said. 'It's just that the guy was a bit of a freak. Doesn't mean he's deficient.'

'Juliet's right, better safe than sorry,' Aaron said, squeezing her hand.

Robert looked down at the couple's hands, joined, as they walked, and he envied Aaron bitterly.

For, Aaron didn't deserve Juliet.

Not as far as Robert was concerned.

But she wanted him, so that was that.

'Okay,' Robert said, 'we'll make sure the new priest's holy water works before we fall back on it. We shouldn't have to fall back on it. Jules, you said a nest; how many? Did Den say?'

'Five,' Juliet said. 'Four unknowns and the barman.'

'Five vampires,' Robert said, nodding with blasé professionalism. He brightened and looked up. 'Piece of cake.'

†

'Thank Christ alive that you're here,' said Den, the owner of the Oak, as he dropped his cigarette stub and stamped on it.

'And we thought you didn't like us?' Juliet said wryly.

'Jesus Christ can we just focus on the small matter of the five ... *things*, squatting in my bloody pub?'

'We're here aren't we?' Robert said.

'Where are they?' Aaron said, his hands on his hips in a ready for action stance.

Den turned his mean, narrow eyes to Aaron, and said, 'In the function room.'

'Where the pool tables usually go?' Robert said.

'Yeah, that's right. I discovered them when I came to open up this morning. Scared almighty hell out of me.'

'You're lucky that's all they did,' Juliet said.

'How did you know ... what they were?' Aaron asked.

Den shifted uncomfortably. 'Look. Everyone in Ecclesburn knows that ... they exist. Everyone knows. Doesn't mean we enjoy admitting it. And when I walked in there and saw them sleeping, naked, with'—he winced—

'blood, all down their fronts, and the poor Bradshaw girl torn to pieces—'

'They got Sara?' Juliet said, butting in.

Robert clasped the back of his head. 'Jesus, I should have known, she wasn't at uni today.'

Juliet reached out and rubbed Robert's shoulder. 'You couldn't have known, and it would have been too late anyway.'

'Did they get anyone else?' Aaron asked Den.

He sighed. 'No, just her, and my best barman.'

'What was his name?' Juliet said.

Den scowled tiredly at her, like he didn't understand the relevance of the question. 'Nick,' he said finally.

'I'm sorry for your loss, Den,' Juliet said earnestly, emotionally reaching out to him. He didn't seem particularly aggrieved beyond the fact that he'd lost an asset.

'Whatever,' Den sighed. 'Just get in there and ... do whatever it is that you do.'

Juliet looked up at the autumnal evening sun, hanging low. 'Sun'll set soon.'

'And that's what's keeping them in there, right?' Den said.

'They'll wait until the sun's twelve degrees below the horizon before they come out,' Robert said. 'Nautical dusk. It's the dinner bell.'

'Listen, mate, I don't care what the navy calls it,' Den said.

'The point is we have'—Robert pulled his iPhone out of his pocket and it lit up—'thirty-one minutes, before they come out here.'

'Hey, look at it this way,' Juliet said, 'if this was happening one week from today, the clocks would have gone back, astronomical twilight would've already started and you'd be dead right now.'

'Bloody nice, that is,' Den said.   'Listen I've got customers coming to set up for a party tonight from seven. That's'—he checked his watch—'Christ, twenty minutes.'

'You think you'll be open for business in twenty minutes?' Juliet asked, unable to disguise her bafflement at the notion.

'Well, the party itself doesn't start 'til eight,' Den said. 'The hosts are coming to *set up* from seven.'

'Yeah, no promises they'll be having that party tonight, Den,' Juliet said.

'They've already paid,' Den said, almost shouting, before taking out his Benson & Hedges and lighting one. 'And I've already spent the money.' He exhaled smoke at Juliet.

She blinked and stiffened her face, before turning her head and coughing. 'We'll kill your vampires. But we're not a bloody party planning committee. It can get messy.'

'Bloody well get in there then!' Den shouted.

Juliet smiled and held out her hand. 'Keys?'

†

Aaron and Robert were crouching behind the bar, hiding behind the big brass taps, amidst the crisps.

'Nice knife,' Robert whispered, nodding down at the large bayonet in Aaron's hands.

'Thanks,' Aaron whispered back, 'my mum sent it me.'

'Your mum sent you *that* knife?'

Aaron looked up from polishing it with his tee shirt. 'It was my dad's.'

Robert looked it up and down, impressed. 'You're looking forward to decapitating some vampires with it I take it?'

'I can't bloody wait mate,' Aaron whispered. 'I used to see my dad heading out hunting and he'd always have it strapped to his waist. I used to wonder when I'd kill my first vamp with it.'

Robert gave Aaron a nod. 'Enjoy pal.'

†

Juliet stepped silently over the wooden floor, toward the function room of The Royal Oak. She had been to the Oak for drinks, loads of times, so she knew where all the creaky spots were. She felt bad for the barman, Nick. And she felt a little guilt for never having paid him much attention while he was alive.

On the other side of the function room door, she thought, focusing her attention on the work at hand, were five vampires. Five undead killers. From what Den had said, she figured that Sara Bradshaw had not been turned; only eaten. But she was too experienced to take that for granted. So, in theory, there could be six.

She wanted to test their power level. If the four vampires were old and powerful, they would sense her presence through the door. If they were not, they might not. So, as she walked toward the entrance to their nest, her ears were curiously pricked, waiting for any sign of disturbance.

But all she could hear was the faint back and forth of Aaron and Robert whispering to each other behind the bar, as they lay in wait, which suggested the vampires were not aware of her.

Now right outside the door, she reached up and clicked open the upper lock. Then, she reached down and did the same with the lower, before standing again, making the sign of the cross, and pulling the double doors open.

†

'This is outrageous, Den,' said Elizabeth Reilly, the mother of the young woman whose birthday was to be celebrated in the function room of the Royal Oak that evening.

'Mrs. Reilly, I can't apolo—'

'Oh, save it Den, you greasy old bastard, and tell me when the room'll be free for me to go in and set up!'

'I have some ... last minute work ... being done,' Den muttered feebly. 'You weren't due for another fifteen minutes.'

'I like to be early. I really didn't expect that you'd be having work done on the night of my Mary's birthday celebration. This is really quite a disappointment, I shall have to go onto Trip Advisor if the work isn't finished *very* soon.'

Den, being exactly the greasy old bastard Elizabeth Reilly took him for, would have liked to tell her to go and take a long walk off one of the Barrington Cliffs; but, alas, the miserly penny-pincher valued her custom more than his own pride, so said only, 'Of course, Mrs. Reilly. Of course.'

†

What Juliet saw when she pulled the function room doors open made her stomach turn. She'd been fighting monsters for years at this point, so she'd witnessed more than her share of bloodshed in her meagre nineteen years and five months, and yet she was unexpectedly squeamish.

She swallowed, pushing the nausea down, and faced up to the horror.

The unclothed, lifeless body of Sara Bradshaw lay on the floor, between the vampires and herself. She'd had her blood drained, from multiple places, marked by sore puncture wounds.

The vampires themselves were awake.

With rapid reflexes, each of them twisted its head toward Juliet.

Ten dark and yet shining eyes, all on her.

The nearest of them lowered its head into its neck a little, like a cat on the prowl, ready to pounce. Two others, behind it, snarled like angry hounds. All five of them, however, began to move forward, toward Juliet.

The young vampire hunter smiled at her prey, and started stepping backward, turning into a run, as the creatures dutifully, predictably began to pour out of the function room, to chase her.

†

Robert's job was simple.

He was aiming his holy water launcher over the bar. Juliet would run past, luring vampires to follow her, and, when they went past, he would fire at them.

Simple.

Except ... he was in love with Juliet. Her wellbeing overrode every other impulse within him. Which meant that he couldn't relax. The plan was tight, the system had been tried and tested, and he didn't really doubt that it would work. But he was a bag of unresolved anxieties nevertheless.

Juliet ran in front of him, and he tightened his grip on the trigger, watching the vampires out of the corner of his eye as they neared his target.

†

'Hey, vamps!' Aaron shouted.

The front three ignored him and carried on pursuing Juliet, but the two bringing up the rear stopped.

They turned to face him, and snarled, lowering their heads, sizing him up with delightful hunger.

Aaron grinned excitedly and bobbed his head from left to right. 'Bring it,' he teased, lifting his flaming cross.

The vampires' eyes twitched cautiously, seeing the fire and the cross, but they didn't retreat. On the contrary, they began to step forward.

With his free hand, Aaron lifted his aerosol can filled with Butane lighter fuel, pointed it at the flaming cross, and began to spray. A thick, chaotic jet of bright yellow fire poured forward toward the approaching fiends, and hit the nearer of the two. The afflicted vampire began to blister terribly, the fire rapidly spreading over its dead skin.

But the second vampire retreated, and, while the first began to succumb to the flames engulfing it, Aaron walked right through the space where it had been as its ash fell to the floor around him.

Aaron grinned like a hyena, in pursuit of the fleeing creature, and the heat from the jet of fire set off the sprinkler system and the fire alarm, which blared a shrill, piercing siren.

†

The fire alarm made Den jump, and he dropped the cigarette he'd been lifting to his mouth, before turning to look at his beloved public house.

'Den ...' grizzled Elizabeth Reilly.

'I assure you, Mrs. Reilly, the function room will be ready for you in no time,' Den said feebly, turning back to the bitter woman.

'Is that not the bloody fire alarm?' Mrs. Reilly whined.

'Nothing to worry about, I'm—'

A window smashed, and Den turned sharply back to the pub. A man, pale and ghastly, had been thrown through his long ornate window. He landed lightly on the floor, and began to spin around to climb back up, when, with evening sunlight landing on him, he began to blister. Within seconds, he was ablaze, from head to toe. He writhed in agony, and in a few more seconds was consumed.

'Good God ...' Mrs. Reilly muttered.

Den looked up from the pile of ash on the floor to the broken window. Juliet Rayne was standing there, her shoulders back, smiling like she still had work to do. 'Get back to it!' Den shouted.

She ignored him, turned and focused on something, and leapt toward it.

†

Juliet tensed her entire torso, and put her fingers around the garlic-infused holy water vial attached lightly to her belt. The vampire facing her jutted its head forward like a werewolf, and snarled.

She pulled the vial off her belt and began to throw it at the creature, but, before she could, it collided with her, its momentum carrying them both onto the hardwood floor of the pub.

All of the equipment attached to the back of her belt hit the floor, and much of it crunched into pieces, or broke off the belt entirely.

The vampire on top of Juliet was heavy, and smelled of bitter blood, and rotten death. She kicked it off her, and rolled onto her front. She looked up at the floor before her, which is when she saw her mother's compass, sitting on the floor, out of her reach.

She started clambering for it, when the vampire started pulling at her feet. She dug her fingernails into the floor and fought with all she had to reach the compass.

The vampire climbed over her, pressing into her back with its feet as it went, and even kicking the front of her head when it passed her; and then it picked up the compass and clicked it open.

'Give that back, right now.'

The vampire grinned wickedly. 'Doesn't even work ...' it growled.

Juliet, outraged by the vampire's sheer audacity, ran at it. She ducked and swerved its two attempted blows, before pulling its neck backward and pulling it clumsily to the ground, forcing it onto its back.

She yanked the wooden stake off her chest, and plunged it into the creature's chest.

And, as it began to explode into dust, she picked up her mother's compass and reconnected it to her belt.

†

Robert watched, his heart pounding in his chest, as holy water landed on the vampire before him. Its skin hissed as a demonic steam rose into the air above it, and within moments, just a few seconds, parts of its skull were visible through the holes in its flesh. It collapsed onto the floor, and began to rupture sharply, its limbs contorting and cracking audibly as it writhed.

'I got—' Robert began.

A hand grabbed his shoulder and pulled him. He spun around to see the cold, stretched face of one of the vampires. Its face was distorted, in the demonic way vampires' faces changed before feeding, and its eyes were a bright, almost burning red.

'You killed my brother ...' the vampire snarled.

Robert reached down, grabbing the holy water cartilage from his weapon, intending to crack it open on the vampire's skin, but the fiend gripped his arm, preventing him. Its hand was locked so tight that Robert's wrist ached sharply.

The vampire looked Robert in the eye, grinned, and tensed its grip, when an arrow hit it, right in the temple.

'That one's yours!' shouted Aaron, who was standing in the place the arrow had been fired from. 'Here!'

Robert looked over at his friend while the vampire growled in pain, attempting to pull the arrow out of its head. Aaron was holding his late father's bayonet, which he threw handle-first toward Robert.

Robert, a little stunned, caught the blade, and then refocused his attention on the monster before him. He juggled the bayonet into his stronger left hand, and swiped it into the vampire's neck, completely removing its head.

Before either the head or the body landed on the floor, both had exploded into dust.

'I got first kill with the knife, mate!' he yelled lightly, in Aaron's direction.

†

Juliet tensed her back, feeling the active muscles in her torso, as she focused her attention on the final vampire. It was standing not six feet from her, looking utterly cornered. Aaron and Robert were free from their own scuffles, and were now surrounding the creature, which seemed to know that it was done for.

'Don't kill me ...' the vampire said.

Juliet recognised him, as the Oak's barman who she'd never got to know.

'My name is Nicholas Gibson. I haven't done ... anything.'

'You want to though, don't you,' Juliet said, lifting her head, revealing her neck to the vampire. The fact was, she *wanted* to bring out the creature's murderous side, because it made killing it easier on her.

'You don't ... understand ...' the vampire said. 'I didn't ... choose this.'

'Look, I'm sorry, but you're a killer now,' Juliet said. 'It's what you are.'

'Do you think it's right ... to execute someone for something that happened to them? Not for something that they actually did?'

'You're not a someone.'

'I *am* someone. I'm Nick Gibson. My mum's called Val, and my dad's called Darren. I have two big sisters, Sarah and Anna—'

'Stop it,' Juliet said.

The vampire stepped toward her. 'I'm a *person*. You don't ... kill people, who've not done anything wrong. That's not *right*.' The vampire took another step. Its face—its true, demonic face—was hidden. It almost looked like a sweet, normal guy. He'd been handsome, with poofy, curly hair that stood up on the top of his head, and Juliet couldn't help but feel sorry for him.

'I'm sorry, mate,' she said, empathising with the undead fiend. 'I know it wasn't your choice.'

'So don't hurt me ...'

'Jules ...' came Aaron's reprimanding voice.

'Don't hurt me,' said Nicholas, the vampire, taking another couple of steps toward Juliet. 'I swear to God, I won't hurt anyone. I'll be ... I'll be a *good* vampire. I'll drink ... animal blood, I'll help you guys hunt the bad ones. Please, I'm strong, I can help you guys. I don't wanna hurt anyone—'

There was a crunchy sticking sound, and the vampire's eyes widened for a moment, before it's entire body exploded into tiny little grains of sandy dust. As the sooty flecks fell to the floor, Juliet saw Robert standing behind it, with a sharp wooden stake in his hand, where the vampire's heart had been.

Juliet looked into the eyes of her friends—Robert's first, and then Aaron's—and she felt a little silly. She had been emotionally manipulated by an undead, soulless fiend. 'It ... almost had me ...' she muttered.

Aaron shrugged. 'Not to worry, babe,' he said.

Robert seemed to be taking it more seriously, as he eyed Juliet with concern. 'Promise me something, Jules ...' he said. 'Promise me you won't hesitate like that on your own.'

'If I was on my own, it would never have happened,' Juliet said, a little irritated. 'It only resorted to begging for its life because we had it surrounded.'

'Yeah, well, still,' Robert said. 'It's Regs. You show mercy, you die.'

'I know!' Juliet said.

'Come on Rob, you dick, she gets it, we weren't in danger,' Aaron said, walking to Juliet and throwing his meaty arm around her neck in what was, she supposed, intended to be a comfort. All it did in actuality was make her feel trapped under a hard, clammy log of skin.

She tensed her neck and climbed out from underneath the unwanted physical affection. 'Come on, you guys, the job's done. We need to do a last sweep and go tell Den that his precious bloody pub's clean.'

Robert didn't look satisfied. 'I'll go check the cellar if you guys want to go and sort payment out,' he said, still a little off, like he wanted to be alone.

'Nah, it's cool, I'll do the sweep,' Aaron said. 'You two are the negotiators.'

Juliet looked at Robert, and he looked back at her. She could tell that he was rattled, and being overly protective; and she didn't appreciate the lack of confidence. 'Fine,' she said.

As Aaron walked past them, heading for the door to the beer cellar, Robert stopped him. 'You're out,' he said, nodding down at Aaron's holy water belt. 'Here.' Robert offered Aaron the flask off his own belt.

'Cheers, bro,' Aaron said nonchalantly, taking the flask and heading away.

As he left through the Oak's creaking heavy doors, Juliet and Robert waited in silence.

'Come on,' Robert said.

'You think I'd hesitate in a one on one?' Juliet asked, as Robert headed for the door.

'No,' Robert said, holding the door open and looking at the floor.

'Sure feels like you do,' Juliet said, walking through the door into the mild October evening.

†

Aaron stepped down the steep, worn steps into the beer cellar. The three vampire hunters had taken out the five creatures they'd been hired to take out, so the sweep was really just a precaution. But vampires multiply. A nest can be cleaned out, but if you miss one, the nest will return by the next sunrise.

Sometimes, they would find a final vampire, loitering in the darkness somewhere. It was rare, but it could happen.

The cellar was pitch black so Aaron grabbed his iPhone and switched on the torch. He lit up the room in front of him. There were kegs lined up against each wall, big barrels with little wires running out of them, up the walls.

It smelled of stale water.

He shone the torch in another direction, revealing dozens of stacked boxes. There were bottled beers, bottled alcopops, piled up. Aaron contemplated taking one of the boxes of beer as a secret payment for services rendered, when he saw, behind the boxes, two tiny red lights, among the black, reflected by the light from his phone.

He squinted into the darkness, and made himself silent, which is when he heard a low, wicked growling.

†

'Two hundred,' Juliet told Den. 'Forty per vamp. That's what we agreed on the phone.'

'That was before you set off my bloody fire alarm,' Den snarled, keeping his voice low so as not to alarm Mrs. Reilly, who was trying to earwig from six feet away. 'I'm going to have to mop up the sodding water from the sprinklers before *she* can get in there, and she's already up my arse about getting in. One hundred and fifty. No more.'

'Oh, that's fine,' Juliet said. 'We'll just spread the word that your pub's an undead haven.'

'We know exactly where to put the right rumours,' Robert said.

Juliet smiled. 'The Royal Oak will be frequented by vampires, every night, in super high numbers, and we won't do a thing to help you, and neither will any other hunters anywhere in the North West.'

'The hunting community's a well organised machine, Den,' Robert said. 'And maybe we'll even head into Undertown and let the people *there* know—'

'Fine,' Den sighed, looking down at the two impudent, young freaks, reaching for his wallet. 'Two hundred.'

'Many thanks,' Juliet said, still smiling faux-politely as she waited for Den to flick through his notes and hand them over.

Robert meanwhile looked over his shoulder, back at the entrance to the Oak. As the sun set behind the eastern horizon, casting the small town of Ecclesburn into nautical dusk, Robert wondered what was taking Aaron so long. A sweep ought to take seconds.

'Here,' Den said, and dumped a wad of notes into Juliet's outreached hand.

Juliet flicked through them, took a ten pound note and handed it back to Den. 'A Carlsberg, a Guinness and a large red wine. When you're ready.'

Den narrowed his eyes, unappreciative of Juliet's chirpiness. 'That's more than a tenner,' he said, and barged past her to go back into the pub.

†

Aaron was desperately weak. A forced fatigue had replaced his initial confusion. And he wasn't even in pain, now. Rather, he felt ... empty. Profoundly, overwhelmingly empty.

He felt like he could drink a ... a river.

No, not a river.

He needed to drink, but not water. Not juice. Not beer.

He was thirsty for ... something else.

And then, the creature that had been supporting him, that had been lifting him, dropped him, and he fell to the floor. He felt like a sack of flesh, utterly devoid of energy. He simply could not move.

And still he thirsted.

And then something rich, wet, and thick, landed on his tongue.

It made him inhale, and it made his eyes widen, and it gave him strength. He looked down, at the arm in front of his mouth, and plunged his teeth into it. That same rich, thick wetness poured down his throat and, with each gulp, where he had been empty before, he was now full; where he was weak before, now he was strong.

He gripped the arm more tightly, and drank again.

The dense, bittersweet fluid overwhelmed him. It made his mind dart upward, out of the building, into the sky, up into the night.

The *night*.

His time.

The night belonged to him. He didn't know what that meant, but he felt it.

And as he lapped thirstily at the source of life pouring down his throat, he almost didn't notice the sound, in the dark, in the distance: the sound of the cellar door opening, and footsteps descending toward him.

His *mind* wasn't aware of the sound, but his *senses* were.

Each step, making those new senses jump, and scratch, and jolt.

†

Robert made his feet as quiet as he could. As he neared the bottom of the steps, which led around a corner and into the Royal Oak's beer cellar, he raised his flickering cross, glowing orange where he had lit it. In his other hand, he held poised his Eagle Jet Torch Gun Lighter.

On the one hand, he wanted to call out to Aaron. This was the course of action that seemed *normal*. The thing he would do if he believed Aaron was okay. And so, that was the thing he *wanted* to do. And yet ... this was also the course of action that might get him killed.

Nevertheless, he wanted to know, one way or another, and so he shouted, 'Yo ... Aaron!'

Silence.

This did not bode well at all. If Aaron was okay, he'd have shouted back. The only consoling thought Robert had was that, maybe, Aaron was laying in wait somewhere, ready to attack a final monster, waiting for a moment to strike.

Either way, there were certainly monsters in this cellar.

'Aaron, where you at man?' Robert shouted, and then made himself silent.

Still nothing.

And then there was something. It was like a licking sound. Like a ghastly, inhuman smack of something wet landing on something wet. It gave Robert a dreadful sense of urgent anxiety, and, when he realised that no one was coming toward his corner, he inched around it.

The first thing he saw was a series of beer kegs. They were lined up against each side of the wall, each with a wire running up and out of it. They created a grimy boulevard: a path that ran toward the end of the cellar, and at the end of that path was Aaron.

He was being cradled by a figure, which saw Robert flashing his light at it, and raised its horrible head.

It snarled.

And then the figure ducked down, and shot upward, carrying Aaron. Robert ran forward, his finger on the trigger of his jet torch gun lighter, and looked up. The slanted runway, through which beer barrels were no doubt regularly lowered, led up and out into the night, coming out right outside the Royal Oak.

'Aaron!' Robert shouted upward.

But it was no good. He was gone.

Robert ran through the cellar, shining his torch into all of its dark places, to make sure that there were no more monsters waiting to kill him, when he started to notice something odd.

His holy water flask—the one he'd given to Aaron—was lying on the floor.

He picked it up, to find that it was empty.

The floor was wet, and made his shoes soak. It smelled like the air in St. Luke's.

'Aaron?' shouted Juliet, from upstairs. 'Rob?'

'I'm ... I'm down here, Jules,' Robert said.

'Where's Aaron?' came Juliet's voice, accompanied by the sound of her shoes running down the stairs. 'Aaron?'

Robert looked at the floor, trying to figure out what had happened with the holy water, when Juliet ran past him toward the hatch through which Aaron had been taken.

'Aaron?!' she shrieked.

Robert was so distracted trying to figure out what had happened that, just for a moment, he didn't prioritise the safety of Juliet. As soon as he realised the danger she was in, he shook off his confusion, and ran to her.

'There was at least one more, down here,' Robert said, gripping Juliet's upper arms, while she looked around frantically.

She looked at him. 'Where is he?'

'He's gone. They took him. He's gone. We have to get out of here.'

'No! What the fuck, Rob? No! What do you mean, get out of here?'

Robert gripped her arms more tightly. 'Jules! We have to go. We have to go, now!'

Juliet's eyes flitted about wildly in the dark, and finally settled on Robert's, which is when she started to break. She looked like a small girl, scared and alone, and Robert wanted with all his heart to comfort her, to make her feel safe, and to make her feel better.

'We have to go,' Robert whispered. 'Now.'

CHAPTER TWO
The Various Plights of Jack Turnbull

Jack Turnbull was a man of stale promise. Like so many people, his potential far outreached his accomplishments. As a child, he'd had vision. An instinctive ear for music, a keen mind for poetry, and a perceptive, contemplative soul. Back then, he had longed most nights for a future career akin to that of Robert Smith, of the Cure, or of Morrissey, of the Smiths. He would be a deep, glamorous singer-poet.

Or so he thought.

In actuality, nearing forty years of age, he worked in a boxy office with air as stale as his promise, for a slightly below average document management company, creating records and entering data, for a boss five years younger than him, with no particular opportunities for promotion.

None of this weighed particularly heavily on him, most days, but it created in him a latent sense of impotence, of waste, and of claustrophobia.

One of the ways he would alleviate this sense was by filling his time with base pleasures, which is how he found himself sitting at the bar in the Crow's Feet, at the north end of Lockwood Mews, the high street in Ecclesburn, as he did most free nights.

The Crow's Feet had the best ales and the best lagers in the town—even making the shortlist for CAMRA's National Pub of the Year three out of the last four years—and, outwardly, that was the reason he drank there.

'Another Roosters, Jack?' said Becky Brannigan, the flame-haired barmaid, with a tempting smile.

Jack adored her. For, inwardly, *she* was the reason he drank there. 'Please, Becky, love,' he said, before gulping the last inch of the hazy gold ale in his glass.

She leaned toward him and took the glass out of his hand, their fingers touching for just a moment. It was enough to make Jack take a sharp intake of breath, before she turned to pour his beer.

He watched her, admiring her, desiring her, when the door chunked and creaked open. It took Jack by surprise a little, because he'd been so lost in adoration, and when he turned to see who it was he sighed inwardly.

'Hey, Becky,' said the incoming Gilbert Smith, as he took a seat at the bar next to Jack. 'Alright Jack, mate.'

Jack rolled his eyes. 'A'do, lad.'

'How are we all?' Gilbert said, rubbing his hands to emphasise how cold he was, despite the fact it was quite mild out.

'Fine,' Jack said.

'Fantastic, thanks Gil,' Becky said, while she put Jack's beer down in front of him.

Jack handed her a fiver.

She smiled and spun away toward the till.

'I just made the absolute best homemade curry, ever,' announced Gilbert, the showy twat. 'My parents were *amazed*.'

Jack took a breath and let out a long, already weary sigh, as Becky handed him his change, and leaned on the bar in front of Gilbert, waiting pleasantly for him to order a drink.

'I burn my beans on toast!' Becky joked. 'I wouldn't even know where to start with a curry!'

'Oh, it's *easy*,' Gilbert said. 'You have to start by chopping your onions and your garlics, right? And, if you want you can use chopped tomatoes, instead of chopping your own, and—'

'Are you having a drink, lad?' Jack said over Gilbert, cutting him off deliberately.

Gilbert looked a bit surprised, but not offended. 'Oh. Are you paying, Jack, mate?'

Jack gave Gilbert a dry smile. 'Sure.'

'Oh. Cheers mate. I'll have a Foster's, please Becky.'

She reached down for a glass and Jack was again distracted from his thoughts by her raw, physical beauty.

She poured. 'I definitely couldn't make a curry from scratch,' she said, looking at Jack first, and then at Gilbert. 'I do love a good curry, though.'

Jack let his eyes lower to her hips, pressing into her black shirt, which left just a half-inch of skin above her trousers.

'My dad's in town the weekend after next, and we're planning on trying out Kashish,' Becky went on as she finished off Gilbert's lager.

'At Junction Twelve?' Jack said.

'Aye, that's the one, have you been?'

Jack shook his head.

'I ... I think *I've* been,' Gilbert said.

'Is that right?' Jack asked.

'Yeah ...' Gilbert said, nodding, his eyes narrow like he wasn't sure. 'I think I went, like, last year or something.'

'Apparently the naans are huge, and you get loads of sauce,' Becky said.

'*That's* right,' Gilbert triumphed. 'That's right, huge naans. Yeah, loads of sauce. I remember now.'

Jack sipped his ale and scoffed to himself. He found Gilbert so irritating.

'I had something really mad,' Gilbert continued, 'like ... I had a ... I had this fish dessert ...'

'Fish dessert?!' Becky said.

'No, not fish dessert,' Gilbert said. 'What am I saying. It was a main. A fish main. But it was something mad, like ... I think it was ... yeah, it was, like, a shark.'

Jack laughed into his beer. 'It was *like* a shark, or it *was* a shark?'

'Yeah, yeah, it was shark. It was a shark vindaloo. It was mad. But it was really good, really excellent.' Gilbert nodded, playing the expert.

'Vindaloo?' Becky said, mildly aghast. 'That's one of the really spicy ones isn't it?'

Gilbert grinned. 'Oh, I bet you only eat a korma, don't you?'

'I like korma!' Becky said, playfully defending herself.

'*That's* not a curry,' Gilbert said. 'It's not a curry if it's not spicy!'

'I don't know how you can eat it that hot,' she said. 'I mean, it's not enjoyable, and you can't taste anything, just heat.'

'I can taste it really well,' Gilbert said. 'I just happen to like it. That's all.'

'Shark vindaloo, eh,' Jack said, grabbing his Golden Virginia and Liquorice Rizlas off the bar. 'I'll have to go and try it.'

Gilbert looked at Jack, a little concern showing in his eyes. 'Well, I'm pretty sure it was, like, one of the specials. I don't think they're still serving it actually.'

'Damn,' Jack said, rolling a cigarette, 'you made shark vindaloo sound so good, I was hoping to give it a go.'

Gilbert didn't seem to know how to judge Jack's demeanour. He certainly didn't seem to realise he was being mocked, but, much to Jack's disappointment, neither did Becky.

'I'm going out for a smoke,' Jack said flatly, unable to pretend he wasn't irritable.

As he pulled the heavy door open to head outside, he heard Gilbert about to begin waffling again, so he shut out the sound and let the door land behind him as he stepped into the evening.

He lit his cigarette and contemplated checking his phone. He couldn't be arsed. He'd no doubt have a shitload of texts from Rita, and he didn't want to have to explain why he hadn't replied. Easier, he decided, if he left the messages unread.

He looked back inside the pub and was filled with childish resentment as he saw Becky leaning forward over the bar toward Gilbert, occasionally laughing, occasionally stroking her hair behind her ear.

Gilbert.

Gilbert was such a dick, so full of shit.

Jack had always felt that he possessed what he called a "Bullshit Radar". And Gilbert was the sort of guy who set it off, pretty much all the time. Jack didn't believe for one second that Gilbert had ever been to Kashish, or that he'd ever had a "shark vindaloo", or even that he really *enjoyed* vindaloo.

That, he figured, as he exhaled smoke out into the autumnal air, was bullshit.

And the problem with bullshit is: it stinks.

The pub door creaked open inwardly, so Jack turned to see Becky holding a phone out at him.

'It's your mum,' she said.

'My mum?'

She nodded.

'My mum died twenty years ago,' Jack said.

'Sorry, she said she was your—'

Jack took the phone. He wanted to snatch it because he was irritated, but even in his irritated state he admired Becky too much to snatch from her.

'Yeah?' he said into the phone, before taking another drag on his cigarette.

'Jack,' came Rita's voice.

Jack exhaled and pulled the phone away from his ear and said to Becky, 'I'll bring it back in, I won't be long,' so Becky nodded and spun back inside.

'What's up, Reet?' Jack said, hostile right away.

'You have to come home, Jack,' Rita said. She sounded drunk, even to Jack, who was on his fifth beer. 'Tilly's being an ugly-hearted little brat.'

'Don't call her that,' Jack said.

'If you want to tell me what I can and can't call her, maybe you should spend more time here at home and less time in the pub, like some pathetic old git, ogling young barmaids, and—'

'What's Tilly doing?' Jack said, his irritation growing as he took another drag.

Rita snapped out of her momentum. 'She's talking about Halloween again. And she won't sleep. Every time I close the door on her, she pretends to be asleep, and then before I'm downstairs I hear her little goblin paw feet tip-tapping across her floor, over to her computer.'

Jack sighed. 'You have to stay with her until she's actually asleep.'

'Why don't *you* come home and try it, if you're so good at it!'

Jack clenched his teeth and summoned patience. 'Is she on her computer now?'

'I've left her to it.'

Through the phone, Jack heard the clink of a bottle connecting with a glass, and the inevitable pouring sound that followed.

'I've told her you're coming home to deal with her,' she concluded.

'Fine,' Jack said, throwing his cigarette on the floor, and pushing the door back into the pub. 'I'll be there in twenty minutes. Try not to pass out before that.'

He pulled the phone away from his ear, and could hear the weak sound of Rita shouting at him through it, so he cancelled the call and walked back to the bar.

'Why did she say was your mum?' Becky said lightheartedly, sensitive to Jack's bad mood.

'Because she's a drunken idiot,' Jack said, handing Becky the phone and picking up his pint. He took four big gulps, emptying half of the glass.

'So who is she really? Your step-mum?'

Jack gave himself a break, before downing the second half of his beer. 'She's my ex-wife's mother.'

Becky cringed. 'Awkward!'

Jack gulped down the rest of his beer, and slammed the thick glass onto the Guinness-themed bar mat. 'I've got to go,' he said.

Becky's demeanour, once warm, inviting, and tempting, sank. She looked at Jack seriously, her face straight and cold. She made eye contact with him in a way that wasn't warm, inviting, or tempting, and said, 'Be safe.'

Jack simply nodded.

She cheered up again, as though switching her charm back on, flinching only to say, 'Take a few cloves before you leave.'

'I will,' Jack said, avoiding Becky's eyes.   Then, he looked at her and said, 'See you.'

'Bye, Jack mate,' Gilbert said. 'See you at work.'

Jack just grunted at him, grabbed his coat and headed outside.

The air was chilly but not frosty. He resented the mild air, which would no doubt make him sweat before he completed the walk home. He stopped to take a handful of garlic cloves from the dish that sat on the table with the ashtrays.

As he set off, he pocketed all but one of the cloves. He took the remaining one in his hand, and began crushing it between his palm and his thumb. Once it was in pieces, he began rubbing it over his forehead, down his cheeks, across his neck.

He took particular care to rub the clove pieces over his neck.

Next he pulled up his sleeves and spread the pungent lumps over his wrists.

The walk home from the north end of town was short, but unpleasant. There was no one around. Not unusual for a Wednesday night in Ecclesburn. Satisfied that the garlic was sufficiently applied, he pulled his tobacco and Rizlas out of his jeans pocket and began to roll another cigarette.

†

Rita Smith was *very* drunk.

But, she was still in pretty good control of her movements and her ability to speak. She smiled proudly at that thought, and lifted her glass to her mouth, and drank.

The taste was harsh, but sweetly soothing, as the sound of Jack's key in the front door reached her in the kitchen.

She waited.

She heard his boots stepping into the house and the door closing shut quietly, in the sanctimoniously hushed way Jack always closed the door when Tilly was supposed to be asleep. Finally, he walked into the kitchen, as Rita took another sip.

'Is that my Couronnier you're draining?' he said, eyeing the bottle on the table in front of her.

Rita glanced hazily from Jack to the glorious, golden liquid in the half-empty bottle. 'Is that your caw-ronny-what?'

'The brandy.'

Rita let her head fall back a little as she looked up at Jack. 'I don't know what it is, but it's bloody nice,' she said, unable to disguise a contemptuous cackle.

Jack narrowed his eyes at her, like he was tolerating her. It made her furious. Not that anyone cared about *her* being upset, being affronted, she thought. Jack didn't care, and Tilly certainly didn't care.

Rita gripped her glass and brought it to her mouth before drinking again. 'Little madam's still awake, I'm pretty sure,' she said, letting the glass fall onto the table, causing the brandy to almost spill over the side.

Jack turned to leave the kitchen, but stopped, resting his hands on the doorframe as he turned to Rita. 'Hey. Don't call her "little madam".' He turned out of the door, and said, almost to himself, 'How many fucking times do I have to tell you ...' as he made his way up the stairs.

†

Tilly Turnbull heard her dad's footsteps as they climbed the stairs toward her room. Without a moment's hesitation, she switched off her computer screen and ran toward her bed, climbing in, rolling over and closing her eyes.

The door opened, letting in light from the landing.

Tilly opened one eye, curiously, and then closed it again, as she felt the heavy weight of her father sit on her bed, making her mattress lean in his direction.

'Tilly darling, I don't buy for a minute that you're asleep right now.'

Tilly didn't know what to do, so she faked a snore.

Her dad laughed. He didn't sound angry. 'Till, baby, stop dicking around.'

Tilly cringed and bit the bullet. She opened her eyes, and rolled onto her other side, facing him. He was a little unsteady, his head bobbing about in occasional, drunken tics. But he was her dad, and the look in his eyes was good, and pure, so she smiled. 'Alright, dad.'

'Why you still awake baby?' he said, blinking and steadying himself.

Tilly rolled her eyes to one side, avoiding eye contact.

'Come on, little one,' he said. 'It's way past bedtime. What's keeping you up?'

Tilly looked at her father curiously. She wondered: is he concerned? Or is he just trying to coerce her into acquiescent sleepiness. He seemed to have genuine love in his eyes, so she said, 'You know I have a busy mind, father.'

He smiled from ear to ear. 'I was the same. Always wanted to sneak downstairs and watch TV.' He inclined his head, like a playful detective interrogating a suspect, and said, 'I didn't have a computer in *my* room, though.'

'Fogie.'

'Fogie?'

'Um ... old guy?' Tilly said.

'Oh, thanks,' he said. 'So ... what were you doing on your computer babe?'

Tilly smiled, and looked away from her father's eyes again.

'Was it anything to do with Halloween, by any chance?'

Now, Tilly looked back at her father with an inquisitive squint. 'What do you know?'

'Well, your gran told me you'd been talking about it?'

Tilly stared at her father, irked instantly by the mention of her grandmother. 'Laura wants to go trick-or-treating. I'm indifferent, to be honest.'

'Is that right?'

She smiled guiltily. 'Mostly.'

Her father pursed his lips, unable to hide his dismay. 'What time would you be back home by?'

'That hasn't been thrashed out yet.'

'Look, talk straight, baby. Do you wanna go, or not?'

'Yeah ...' Tilly said. 'I want to go.'

'Okay, listen,' her dad said, shifting on the bed, focusing on her. 'As long as it's safe, you can go. If it isn't safe, you can't go. Do you understand that?'

Tilly wasn't at all sure about her father's grasp on what being "safe" and "unsafe" meant in Ecclesburn, so she looked up at him and said, 'Okay.'

'Is this a Harry thing?' he said, again jutting his head about, indicating his discomfort as well as his inebriation.

Tilly smiled. 'A Harry thing?'

'Sure. You know? Is it ... is it important because he's going?'

Tilly let her head rest on her pillow as she contemplated the best thing to say to *that* question. 'It's really just about hanging out and having fun with Laura. Harry'll be there, probably, but he's not the reason.'

'Okay,' her dad said, nodding. 'I get it. Listen. If I can work it, you can go. But'—his face sank into pure earnestness—'you go early, and you get back before sundown, or you don't go. You get me?'

Tilly looked up at her father. 'Thanks, daddy. You know, I don't think grandma will be thrilled.'

Her dad rolled his eyes. 'Your gran's smashed. She won't remember any of it.'

'Even so,' Tilly said, enjoying the mischief of her father.

'Listen to me,' he said, suddenly serious. 'I'm your father. She's your grandmother. What you do, where you go ... that's up to me, not her. You understand?'

Tilly wanted to be a good daughter and placate her ardent parent, but her fidelity to truth was too strong, and the truth was: she didn't believe him. 'You want to go downstairs and tell her that?'

He looked at her, surprised. 'You cheeky madam!'

Tilly looked at her dad facetiously. 'Didn't you just tell grandma not to call me that?'

Her dad's eyes widened. 'How did you hear that from all the way up here in bed, hey? Hey?' He went to tickle her underarms, and she squirmed from him, laughing and shrieking, until, finally, they settled. 'I'll talk to grandma,' he said. 'And remember, my word is your gospel, okay?'

'Okay, daddy,' she said.

'You going to go to sleep now, little one?'

'I will, daddy.'

Her dad leaned down and kissed her forehead. 'Good night darling.'

'Good night.'

He stayed, sitting on Tilly's bed, stroking her hair. She had intended to return to her computer, after her father had left, but, lying there, with his big fingers stroking her cheek, she found herself actually becoming drowsy. She found herself actually fading into a soft and warm sleep.

She let herself relax, knowing that her computer would be there in the morning, and finally drifted off.

†

Jack walked into the kitchen, grabbed a glass tumbler from the cupboard and sat down opposite Tilly's grandmother Rita. She was absolutely battered. Rita was a woman who had spent her adulthood learning to disguise drunkenness, and yet sitting there in Jack's kitchen it would have been obvious to a blind man that she was not far away from inevitably passing out.

Jack lifted his bottle of Couronnier away from her and began pouring a large measure into his tumbler.

'You just have to sit with her for a moment and she'll fall asleep,' he said. 'It's not complicated—'

'Bah!' Rita shouted, jutting sharply toward Jack. 'She needs to learn some *respect*. She's a liar, Jack. You know it.'

Jack sipped his brandy, enjoying it. 'And?'

'Little girls shouldn't be lying to their parents, and—'

'You're not her parent.'

'She shouldn't be lying to her grandparents either,' Rita said, steadying her head, which was starting to bob. She rolled her eyes. 'If I'd have pulled the things she pulls...'

'She's a kid, Reet. She doesn't *pull* things. She's just ... interested.'

'I'd say you're too soft on her if I thought you'd listen.'

Jack sipped his brandy again, eyeing Rita curiously. He figured he'd take this opportunity, while she was completely drunk out of her mind, to see if she'd open up a little. 'Is that the only reason you're ... upset?' he said, choosing at the last minute to say "upset" and not "angry".

Her eyes rolled again, and then she sharpened her glance, staring at Jack. 'I take it she was working tonight?'

'Who?'

Rita laughed, and the laugh became a cough. 'You know who. Your little Irish lady friend down at your little piss hole.'

'Hey ...' Jack said, 'if you mean Becky, she's not Irish.'

'Her father is.'

'She's not her father though is she?'

'No,' Rita said, eyeing Jack. 'No, she isn't her father. Did she ask you about Halloween?'

Jack cocked his head, confused. 'Did she ask me *what* about Halloween?'

'About going out with her friends?'

'What are you talking about?' Jack asked.

'I told you. Tilly was talking about Halloween. I thought you were going to talk to her about—'

'Ohhhh ...' Jack said. 'I thought you meant'—he stopped himself—'well, it doesn't matter what I thought.'

'You thought I meant your little Irish tart!' Rita said, her painted eyebrows raised joyously.

'No I ... hey, don't bloody well call her that!'

'So Tilly?'

Jack took a moment. 'She wants to go out. I told her she can go as long as she goes early and gets home before dark. And I told her I wouldn't tell *you*.'

Rita sipped from her brandy, her face sour. 'You and her ... you're always keeping your little secrets from me.'

'I told you, didn't I?'

Rita's face sank. She suddenly looked almost sober. 'Is this a good idea?'

'What do you mean?'

'You know bloody well exactly what I mean. Is it a good idea to allow a twelve year old girl out on her own? In *this* town?'

Jack lifted his glass and swilled the brandy around circularly. 'She's going to have to learn how to survive Ecclesburn eventually. Right?'

'She'll have to survive, to learn *how* to survive,' Rita said.

'I don't like this. She's a kid. She wants to go out with a bunch of other kids, and she said she'll be back before the sun goes down. I don't see why it has to be an issue.'

'It's an issue, Jack, because children are'—Rita closed her eyes and focused—'tempestuous.'

'Cut the'—Jack stopped himself. 'What do you mean?'

'She'll stay out late. She'll lie to you. She'll make plans with her friends, and sneak about, and while you're safely in your dirty, little pub with your dirty, little barmaid ... Tilly will die.'

Jack put his glass down. 'You think my going down the Crow's Feet is going to get my daughter killed?'

'I think your staying in this ... hell, will get her killed,' Rita said. 'Yes. I do.'

Jack breathed in deep and let the breath out slowly. 'Well. There it is.'

Rita leaned forward. 'The fact you don't take it seriously is *beyond* me. Say that happens. Say the worst happens. You're going to risk leaving me without my only granddaughter? Is that it?'

Jack shook his head. 'Wait. You're ... you're not worried about *her*? You're worried about me leaving you *without* her?'

'I lost my daughter, Jack, I don't want to lose my granddaughter too—'

'Angie isn't *dead*, Rita, she just ... fucked off!'

'She's still lost, Jack. And yet you keep us here in this ... unholy place. Why?'

'If you're careful, living here is perfectly safe and you know it.'

'Perfectly safe?' Rita said incredulously. 'Is that a joke? There's a funeral—a young person's funeral—every other week. People go missing all the time.'

'And yet ... I've lived here since I was born,' Jack said. 'You treat yourself, you protect yourself, and the ... *others*, they keep away. They leave you alone.'

Rita pushed her glass across the table, as though finished with it. 'You really haven't considered me at all, have you?' she said, squinting hazily at him. 'You haven't considered how it will affect me, if something happens to Tilly.'

'Nothing's going to happen to Tilly.'

'You'll go on as normal,' Rita said. 'You'll go to work, you'll go to the pub. I'll be the one stuck in this house, rattling around, surrounded by the ghosts of my daughter and my granddaughter.'

Jack wanted to argue. He found it outrageous, how she was framing the potential death of his daughter as some kind of inconvenience to *her*. But, ultimately, Jack knew how it would go. There was no point arguing with Rita. He drank, and sighed. 'What is it you want? You want to leave Ecclesburn?'

She eyed him carefully, and her face seemed to lose the hostility a little. 'What would it take? What would you have to do?'

Jack looked away from her. The fact was ... he didn't *want* to leave. He looked back at her. 'I'd have to sell the house. Buy a new house. I'd have to look for work, in a new area, and—'

'Let's start there,' Rita said, leaning forward.

Jack drank. 'You want me to look for another job?' he said thickly, as his mouth stung from the brandy.

Rita leaned back, as though composing herself. 'Start by finding a new job, out of town. You can ... commute, at first. After that, we can look for a house, nearer to the job.'

Jack was playing along, but the truth of the matter was that he had no intention of looking for a new job. He was comfortable in his current job. And then there was ... Becky. Not that he could tell Rita that a woman over ten years younger than him was a factor in his thinking. 'Look, it's late,' he said. 'I'm going to bed. You ... you can finish the Couronnier if you want to.'

'Think about it, Jack,' Rita said. 'The clocks go back on Saturday. The nights are about to get longer.'

Jack stood, and made his way to the door, stopping before leaving to say, 'I know that.' And after a pause, he said, 'Night, Reet,' and left.

CHAPTER THREE
Undertown

The door to Rayne Manor clicked unlocked, and then creaked open. Hollow and empty, the young, orphaned vampire hunter Juliet Rayne walked inside, followed by her fellow demon slayer Robert Entwistle. But while Juliet had expected to return to her home with two of her men—she found, in the early morning hours of Thursday the twenty-sixth of October, that she would return with only one.

For Aaron McLeary was gone.

The man she loved was gone.

She was barely able to comprehend this. She knew that the role of the vampire hunter carried with it obvious risks. She knew that. She had been made horribly aware of that, five years earlier, when she lost her parents. But she and Aaron and Robert had fashioned themselves into something of a profoundly well oiled machine, and she had grown ... complacent.

Robert shut the door behind her. 'Jules ... are you going to be okay tonight?'

Juliet looked out of the window, at the navy black sky on the other side. 'What time is it?'

Robert took a moment and said, 'It's just after one.'

'Oh.'

Robert said nothing.

Juliet walked toward the old, ornate coat rack her parents had owned, and rested her jacket over it.

'You should sleep,' Robert said. 'I'll sleep in the hall, on the wing outside your door ...'

'Why?'

'Because I'—Robert stopped himself, and refocused. 'In case you need me. For any reason.'

'Okay,' Juliet said. She knew that her voice was coming out like the voice of a robot, but she hadn't the energy to care about it. 'You sleep. I'll sleep. I'll see you in the morning, I guess.'

And, sheepishly, feebly, she wandered up the crescent shaped staircase, up to the east wing of the house, toward her bedroom.

†

The sky was clear and blue, and the air was sweetly frosty, after the sun came up. Robert was frying onions, mushrooms, beans, sausages and bacon in the luxuriously wide kitchen of Rayne Manor. His primary concern was simple: Juliet was in pain; therefore, comfort Juliet. Yet, he couldn't pretend he wasn't also aware that that there was some potential for him to benefit selfishly from her pain, and that thought kept trying to entice him.

For, he realised, with Aaron gone, she might begin to fall in love with *him*.

He cared about her too much to *entertain* the thought, and yet, no matter how resilient he made himself, it wouldn't go away.

He decided, summoning the better parts of his self, that no matter what, he would put away what *he* wanted, and that he would focus only on what *she* needed, like a good friend.

The door creaked open, and Juliet zombie walked toward the breakfast table. 'Hey,' she said, as emotionally distant as she'd been the previous night, before taking a seat at the table.

'How you doing?' Robert asked.

'Hungry.'

Robert turned and gave her a sympathetic smile.

'We have work to do,' she continued.

Robert raised his eyebrows openly.

'I have to find him,' she concluded.

Robert's heart sank. 'Jules ... he's ... he's gone. You get that?'

'I have to find him,' she said again.

Robert looked back to his frying pans, and stirred the onions and mushrooms, and turned over the meat. 'I wanted to talk to you ... when you're ready ... about the holy water.'

'The holy water?'

'It didn't work,' Robert said.

'You killed one, you doused him,' Juliet said, confused.

'That was the stuff I already had,' Robert said. 'The stuff that was blessed by Father McMahon. The *new* stuff, the stuff that was blessed by the *new* priest at St. Luke's. *That* didn't work.'

'We were going to test out the new holy water ...' Juliet said, as though vaguely remembering something from longer ago than the previous evening.

'We forgot,' Robert said, lifting the lid off the bread bin and taking out four slices.

'We forgot,' Juliet echoed, her horror at the absurdity of it clear through the mask of composure she was obviously wearing.

Robert dropped the four slices of thick white bread into the toaster. 'When I went down into the beer cellar, in the Oak, there was holy water all over the floor. I think that ... I think that Aaron threw it on the vamp that got him, but it didn't work.'

'Oh.'

'The new priest,' Robert went on. 'Father William. The South African guy. I got a weird vibe off him. I think there's something wrong with him. I think that's why his holy water didn't work. I wanted us to skive classes and go see him today.'

'I need to find Aaron today,' Juliet said.

'No,' Robert said, shaking his head. 'No, Jules. Aaron's gone. If you don't want to come along to see the priest, I understand. But—'

'I'm heading into Undertown today,' Juliet said. 'Soon as I've eaten and showered.'

'Undertown?' Robert said, aghast. 'Jules you can't be serious.'

'I'm super serious,' she said, her face flat and hard.

Robert continued shaking his head while he tried to process what Juliet was saying. He couldn't get his head around it at all. He looked up to speak, when the toast popped up with a sharp flick.

'That's what I'm doing today,' she said.

Robert sank again, and went to the fridge for the butter. He set it by the two plates he'd prepared, and then started stirring the mushrooms, onions and beans again.

'You can go investigate the priest if you want to,' Juliet said.

Robert buttered the four pieces of hot toast, and then began portioning off the food from the frying pans. 'I made it ... the way you like it,' he said, kind of feebly.

When he'd filled the plates, he carried them over to the breakfast table and set it in front of Juliet.

'I see that,' Juliet said, tucking in hungrily.

Robert picked up his knife and fork and began cutting off the end of one of his sausages. 'I don't understand what you mean,' he said. 'Going into Undertown. Do you ... do you want to get yourself killed?' He was genuinely curious.

'I'm going to get Aaron.'

Robert dropped his knife and fork noisily onto the plate. 'Aaron's *dead*, Jules. Right? He's dead. You can't *go and get him*.'

'I've been thinking,' Juliet said, ignoring Robert's harsh tone. 'About that vampire last night. He had a point, don't you think?'

Robert's appetite abandoned him. 'What?'

'The vampire, who said it was wrong of us to kill him, because he hadn't killed anyone yet.'

Robert shook his head.

'If I can get to Aaron before he wakes, before he goes out, before he kills anyone, I can bring him home. He can be a good vampire. He can help us kill other vampires. Bad ones. Like before.'

Robert watched her calmly eating her breakfast, trying to figure out what the hell she was talking about. 'There are no good vampires, Jules.'

'You know that? For sure?'

Robert's mouth hung open. He didn't know what to say at all.

'Because the stakes are kinda high, don't you think?' Juliet said. 'Aaron's out there. He'll be ... sleeping now. If I leave him with the monster that killed him, he'll become one, no question.'

'It's too late, Jules ...' Robert said softly.

'But if I can *kill* that monster,' Juliet went on, biting into a mushroom, 'and get Aaron to come home, I can save him.'

'You can't.'

'You don't know that I can't,' Juliet said.

Robert was a little floored. Her tone seemed sharp and almost psycho. 'I do, Jules. I do know that.'

She narrowed her eyes and pointed her fork at him. 'You just believe that because that's what we were taught. You've never *tried*. You've never tried to reform a vampire, and neither have I, so you don't know if it's possible or not.'

'They're ... evil,' Robert said. 'They don't have souls. They're killers. It's what they do.'

'*We're* killers. We kill them. We kill animals, and eat them.' She nodded down at the bacon and sausage on her plate. 'Some people are veggie. Maybe Aaron can be—'

'What?! A vegetarian vampire?'

Juliet stopped, looking for words. 'No. But he'll need blood, right? Doesn't mean he'll need to kill to get it.'

Robert, lost for words, finally ate the end of sausage he'd had on his fork since he'd sat down. 'What do you plan on doing in Undertown?' he asked, as the realisation settled over him that he was not going to dissuade her.

'Why, are you coming with me?'

Robert ate some more of his breakfast, and said, 'Yes. I'll come with you. But I think it's a bad idea, for the record. Now tell me, why are we going there, of all places?'

Juliet brightened, almost smiling at Robert. 'Well, we're not going straight there. We have one job to do first.'

†

'Okay,' Robert said, looking up at the Royal Oak. 'What are we doing here?'

'I need something,' Juliet answered, her hands on her hips as she too looked up at the pub, lit by the autumnal morning sunshine. 'After you.'

Robert took the offer and headed in through the door.

The inside smelled of cleaning detergent and fresh air. It was actually quite pleasant. Robert saw the top of Den's head as he crouched behind the bar. After walking closer, Robert saw that the moody landlord was pouring water through a selection of the beer taps and catching it in buckets.

'He hasn't come back,' Den said, not looking up.

'We didn't expect him to,' Juliet said.

Den shook his head. 'Then what are you doing here? You destroyed my place of business, I paid you, the end.'

Robert looked to Juliet for the answer.

'Who came for the body of Sara Bradshaw?' Juliet asked.

'What the hell, Jules?' Robert whispered.

She scolded him with her eyes and turned back to Den.

'Why?' Den asked without standing from his buckets.

'Was it the Lancs Incinerators?' Juliet asked, peering over the bar at the top of Den's head. 'The Clayton Cleansers?'

Den finally stood, towering over the two young vampire hunters, and rested his hands on the beer taps. 'You're a right pair of ghouls, aren't you?'

'Says the man who kept his business open to the public the day after a gang of vampires killed his most popular barman,' Juliet said.

Den didn't look impressed.

Juliet looked around. 'Look, who came for her body Den? It's important.'

Robert looked at his friend, at the woman he loved, with her long, blonde hair, falling down around her shoulders in its enchanting way, and wondered what she was doing.

'The sodding ... Clayton Cleansers,' Den said. He seemed to resent even using their name. 'Pair of weirdos they were and all—'

Juliet, though, marched out of the door, into the street, pulling her iPhone from her bag as she went.

'Um, sorry,' Robert said to Den, and hurried after her. By the time he got outside, she was already waiting on the phone.

'Yeah, Jim, hey,' Juliet said into the phone. 'Where do the Clayton Cleansers operate from?'

Robert felt a chill in the cool morning air as he listened, so he pulled his coat together in front of his neck and listened.

'Okay, great. Send me the postcode?'

Robert eyed Juliet uneasily.

'Thanks,' Juliet said into the phone, before turning to smile at Robert. 'That's fantastic.'

'What are we doing Jules?' Robert asked, as Juliet put the phone back in her bag.

'Heading to Clayton-le-Woods,' she answered him cryptically.

†

Robert was incredibly uneasy as he followed Juliet down the bridle path that ran along Bryning Brook, just on the outskirts of Clayton-le-Woods. The air was just as chilly as it had been in Ecclesburn, but, walking there by that narrow stream of murky looking water, Robert felt just as murky himself.

'Where's the entrance to the place?' he asked.

'Right along here,' Juliet replied. 'We go in through a borehole, built into the—'

Before she finished, they saw it. It was a brick wall, built into the side of a green hill. At the centre of the wall was a dark, thoroughly uninviting rectangular passageway.

'We go in there, huh?' Robert asked, tightly gripping his bag.

'Don't worry, Jim says it's vamp proof,' Juliet replied, poking her head forward as she approached the hole.

Robert followed her in, and started making his way down the steep, stone steps. 'What are we *doing* here, Jules?' Robert whispered, almost whining.

'Visiting the Cleansers, I told you already.'

'Right, sure, but ... why?'

'I need something. You'll see.'

They reached the bottom of the stairs, and made their way through a brief, narrow corridor, before entering a wide, dimly lit indoor reservoir. Brick pillars rose to the ceiling, out of the water that covered the floor. The pillars looked *old*. Like, *ancient* old. But planted in the water were a series of modern looking stepping stones, that led across the reservoir floor, toward the other side, toward another orange-lit hole in the wall.

'Come on,' Juliet said, starting to hop across the stones.

Robert followed, muttering obscenities under his breath. Once across to the other side of the reservoir, he continued to follow the object of his unrequited love through the next passageway, which led into a brighter room. Ducking under the narrow doorframe, he found the Clayton Cleansers.

They were two. One male, one female. And equally odd. They were pale, tall and thin, dressed all in black.

The female of the two lifted her head, and said, 'Never shall I lower my eyes.'

Juliet looked to Robert, waiting for him to answer.

'Before any challenge or foe,' he said dutifully.

'Never shall I bend my knees,' the tall, thin woman said.

'Before any lord or chieftain,' Robert said.

The woman smiled now, somewhat eerily. 'Never shall I bow my head.'

Robert sighed. 'Before any god or wight.'

The woman's eerie smile gave way to one more serene. 'Welcome, Celtic pagans,' she performed, speaking formally, as though on some official duty. Then, she tilted her head and lost the decorum entirely. 'Who are you guys?'

'Which one of you is Anna-Marie Gregory?' Juliet asked.

The man and the woman looked at each other, confused.

'I am,' the woman said. 'Although I go by Iris. Iris Oceanheart.'

'Fair enough,' Juliet said, before turning her attention to the man. 'And you're Connor McLean?'

He nodded, and then looked uncertain. 'Mars Lothlorien Moonshadow,' he said.

'Christ ...' Robert sighed under his breath.

'Iris, Mars, I'm Juliet Rayne, and this is Robert Entwistle. We're two thirds of the Rayne Helsingers.'

'The vampire hunters?' Iris Oceanheart said. 'You're ... young?'

'We're not the first to use the name.'

'Oh,' Iris said. 'So you're a Rayne. Your parents were—'

'That's right.'

Connor McLean, apparently also known as Mars Lothlorien Moonshadow, suddenly seemed giddy, his long legs buckling as he sauntered towards Juliet. 'It's ... it's an honour, Ms. Rayne,' he said, grabbing her hand and shaking it limply.

'Miss,' she said, correcting him.

'*Miss* Rayne, of course. Come in, please. You are very, very welcome. Let us soothe you, with refreshments, and guide you with words of prophecy from the spirits.'

'Listen, we're not here for a bloody palm reading,' Juliet said, 'I need to see the body of Sarah Bradshaw.'

Mars's face sank into confusion.

'The girl whose body you took from the Royal Oak in Ecclesburn, last night.'

'Why?' Iris asked.

'Okay, I'm gonna be straight with you,' Juliet said.

Robert's ears pricked up.

'I need her ears,' Juliet concluded.

Mars shook his head, confused. 'What do you mean?

'I mean I need to cut off her ears, and take them,' Juliet said, reaching into her bag and pulling out Aaron's new bayonet, the one his mother had sent him.

Mars took a collection of frantic backward steps, while Iris stepped forward. 'You can't be serious?' she said.

'Jules, Iris Oceanbrain is right, you can't be serious,' Robert said, gripping her arm.

'Get your hand off me,' Juliet demanded sharply.

Robert was taken aback, and did as he was told.

'It's Ocean*heart*, FYI,' Iris said.

Robert ignored her. 'Jules, what the hell are you talking about, you need her ears? What are you on?!'

Juliet stepped forward, toward Iris. 'Where is it?'

'What?' Iris said nervously.

'The *body*!' Juliet said. 'Where is it?'

Iris calmed, and steeled herself. 'I won't tell you.'

Juliet lifted the bayonet. 'You will.'

'Iris ... just tell her,' Mars said.

'No!' Iris said. 'That young woman's body must rest, so that she may enter the Summerland—'

'She's dead, and wherever her spirit's going, she doesn't need her ears,' Juliet said. 'I do. So tell me where she is, or maybe I'll take yours, Oceanbrain.'

'Juliet!' Robert shouted. 'We're leaving. Now.'

'You can leave,' Juliet told Robert without looking. She reached up and grabbed Iris's floaty black shirt, and lifted the knife to her ear. 'Tell me where the body is or I swear to your gods and mine that I will take your ears.'

Iris's nose twitched, and her eyes moistened. 'She's in the back,' she said as a tear fell down each of her cheeks. 'She's on the table in the back.'

Juliet let go of Iris and marched out of the room.

Robert followed. By the time he reached her, she was already leaning over the corpse. Robert felt awful when he saw the dead body of the young, innocent Sara Bradshaw. Iris and Mars had washed her, and perfumed her, and covered her out of respect—while the woman *he* was with was about to *desecrate* her. 'Jules this isn't right, this isn't you.'

She ignored him and began cutting. When she'd cleaved the first ear, she walked around the table and began on the other.

Robert winced.

When Juliet finished, she wrapped the ears in a white towel, and put them in her bag, along with the dagger.

'Are you satisfied?' Robert said.

'Very,' Juliet said, her face hard and uncaring, as she walked past him back into the room where Iris and Mars were waiting.

Robert followed behind her, making his way past the anxious pagans, and toward the door that led out to the reservoir. And as Juliet made her way through the door, Iris said, 'When choosing your path, keep in mind: one direction leads forward into challenge and growth; the other moves backwards into comfort and stagnation.'

Juliet turned. 'Did I not already cover the fact that I didn't come for a bloody palm reading?'

And with that, Juliet and Robert left, newly in possession of the two severed ears of Sara Bradshaw.

†

'What's going on?' Robert asked, as Juliet drove them back to Ecclesburn. 'I'm in pieces about what happened last night, same as you, but—'

'You're not serious?' Juliet snapped. You think you know how I'm feeling?'

'He was dear to me too, Jules.'

'Were you sleeping with him?' Juliet asked. 'Were you planning the rest of your life with him? Were you in love with him?'

Robert's head swayed with the car motion, and he let the question pass unanswered.

'You don't know what I'm feeling,' she said. 'You don't know what it's like, to love someone, and to not have them. So don't judge me.'

Robert looked out the window, at the misty, sunlit fields. He wanted to protest. He wanted to explain that he knew *exactly* what it was like to love someone and not have them. But he couldn't. 'You're acting way out of character, that's all.'

'I was never gonna hurt those pagans, if that's what you're upset about. I'm just doing what I have to do.'

'Why exactly?' Robert said, getting louder. 'Why the hell do you need the severed ears of a dead girl?'

Juliet sighed, like she was trying to avoid answering the question. Finally, her shoulders slumped. 'I needed a tribute.'

'What?'

'Payment. I needed a tribute.'

Robert banged his head gently against the car window. 'Who for?'

'For the Cacolamia.'

Robert banged his head again. 'Jesus.'

'You with me?'

Robert rested his head against the cold glass. He pictured the various ways that the two of them might be killed, going into Undertown, visiting the Cacolamia, and, while the thought frightened him, it didn't frighten him as much as the idea of Juliet dying in any of those ways *alone*. 'I'm with you,' he said. 'But ... if you ask me to help you hurt anyone, you're on your own, Jules.'

'I'm not going to hurt anyone,' she said. She sounded offended.

Robert said nothing. He simply let his head sway, while he contemplated the growing prick in his conscience.

†

The journey into Undertown was one that Robert was only anecdotally familiar with. He'd heard stories of villagers and townsfolk who had disappeared forever into the Hidden Borough, and he'd met a few people who had, according to their terrifying and exotic stories, gone the other way and come *out*.

Undertown was a word unused by civilised Ecclesburnians. But it was a word *all* had heard, at least as a rumour.

And, as Robert stood at the side of the woman he adored, looking up at the entrance to an abandoned kids' centre once called the Play Shed, the fear plaguing his mind was the possibility of going into—and never returning from—that place which *he'd* rather not utter the name of.

'You're sure this is where the entrance is?' he asked.

'That's what my dad always said,' Juliet replied. 'Apparently before it was a play centre it was a school.'

'Why would anyone put a school or a kids' centre on top of the entrance to a place like Undertown?' Robert asked, somewhat rhetorically.

'According to my dad, the elders who founded Ecclesburn made a deal with the, um ... *things*, that lived down there, to make it easy for some of their inhabitants to get access to'—Juliet winced—'food.'

'Despicable.'

'And the thing is,' Juliet said, turning to him, 'the creatures down there were never going to rise up. It was an unnecessary tribute. But the elders kept the place open until they were disbanded in the nineties. So the hundreds of kids who died were sacrificed, and it was for nothing.'

'Absolutely vile.'

'I know right? Anyway, come on. Let's go.'

†

The inside of the abandoned building was a blend of once colourful but now greying, dusty old slides and swings.

They were padded for safety. There were rope bridges and climbing frames and little areas with fun-sized football goalposts and basketball nets.

Robert followed Juliet through the various sections, eerie and forgotten, up the many levels. Inside and up close, there were cobwebs with little spiders sitting in them, guarding mummified flies and other bugs.

'We have to go all the way up there,' Juliet said, pointing up at the massive climbing frame that went up about five or six levels. 'All we have to do is go down the big slide.'

'That's it? Just go down one slide and we make it through?'

Juliet pulled her phone out of her bag and checked the time. 'It's supposed to spit us out down there,' she said, pointing at the bottom of the long, snake-like tunnel slide. 'But if we go down between twelve thirty and twelve thirty-three, it'll spit us out ... *there*.'

'There as in Undertown?'

'Bingo.'

'Fantastic. Okay, so what time is it now?'

Juliet clicked her phone on again. 'Twelve twenty-nine. Let's go.'

She began to climb, and, after a sigh and a prayerful sign of the cross, Robert followed. The climbing frame that led up to the top of the slide was easy enough to ascend. There were little rope rungs for his hands and feet, pressed against a faded blue wall.

He lifted himself up over the final edge, and joined Juliet in cautiously peering down into the mouth of the slide.

'You ready?' she said.

'Not even remotely.'

And then, with a brave nod, Juliet checked her phone again, put it in her bag, and dived down.

'I could literally just get the hell out of here right now,' Robert muttered to himself, before holding his breath, and diving in.

The slide was actually fun. Robert couldn't help but enjoy it, as his stomach turned excitedly. He let out a muted cry, which turned into a full scream of joy.

The last part of the slide was steep, and then it turned, straightening out, before ejecting him. Only, instead of instantly hitting the cushioned padding, he began to fall.

He was not sliding anymore. He was *free falling*. His scream of joy gave way to one of sheer dread and panic. After what felt like a hell of a long time, he splashed awkwardly into a body of icy cold water.

The water slowed his descent helpfully, and he organised his limbs, looked upward, and began kicking his legs. He hadn't been expecting the water so he hadn't held his breath, so, as he neared what looked like the blur of a grey sky, he started struggling to breath.

He kicked his legs again, and made a final push, escaping the water at last. He gasped for breath, and continued to kick his legs to prevent from sinking as he glanced urgently in each direction for Juliet.

'Over here!' came her voice from behind him.

He turned, still bobbing above the water, which smelled absolutely vile now he was out of it, to see her, climbing out of the water and onto what looked like a street.

He began swimming over to her, trying not to swallow any of the putrid, bitty water as he went. When he reached the end he was already growing tired from the swim, so he grabbed onto the curb of the street while the water lapped over it and ran down a little gutter that carried it back into the river.

'Good God, Jules,' Robert sighed, as he climbed out and lay down on his back.

Her face appeared above him. 'We made it!' she said, looking around. 'We're actually here.'

'Yay,' Robert cheered ironically.

'Pick yourself up. Come on. We have less than eight hours.'

'Okay, hang on, I—' he stopped. 'Wait, what?'

'We have to be back by twelve minutes past eight,' she explained.

'What do you mean?'

She looked down at him. 'We can only return to Ecclesburn tonight. Between eight twelve and eight fifteen.'

'So we're stuck here until then? What if we don't make it out during the window?'

'Then we're here another twenty-four hours.'

Robert felt energy return to him in spades. He sat up, and climbed onto his feet, while his soggy clothes clung to him. 'Okay, you could've told me that before I followed you here.' He looked around, at the bleak and grimy town in which he'd landed. 'God, was this place designed by Tim Burton?'

Juliet's bag was open on the floor, and her head was in her sepia map, still as dry as it had been in Ecclesburn, but for some murky drips running off her hands. 'Okay,' she said, and looked up and down one of the streets. 'This way.'

'Good,' Robert said. 'Let's go. Now.'

She smiled, and took his hand, and they began to depart.

CHAPTER FOUR
Gingerbread

Aliester, the centuries old vampire and Baron of Undertown awoke from his sleep, disturbed by his senses. For he sensed ... newcomers. Not *children*. Not some poor, unfortunate souls, lost forever to his domain. He sensed ... *purpose*. He sensed *intention*. Whoever it was that had entered his small kingdom, they had *chosen* to come.

He pondered it, wondering if it was an act of hubristic aggression. Some misguided offer of war. Or perhaps it was not an attack at all, but a rescue mission. Some sad, pathetic parents, come for their spoilt brat of a child.

But no, he felt, as he lay in his bed.

He sensed neither an attack nor a rescue.

He smiled and shrugged it off, choosing to return to the dark peace of his sleep. For come the night, after his rest, he would discover the nature of the intrusion.

He was content in that knowledge, and so he drifted back to sleep.

†

The swift walk from the street by the Undertown River to the storefront of Elspeth the Cacolamia's Emporium was the strangest ten minutes of Robert Entwistle's young life. There had been dozens of gawkers. Disheveled, deranged-looking watchers, marching up the grey streets as though going about their business—each taken aback when they saw the two pristine vampire hunters.

The town seemed to mirror Ecclesburn. All the roads were in the same places, only they were kind of decrepit. There was a sky, of sorts. A blackish grey thing that might also have been a very high ceiling. And the air was *foul*. Fouler even than the water had been.

There was no sunlight, which made Robert particularly uneasy. Walking around at night in Ecclesburn was dangerous enough. Walking around the mysterious underworld *beneath* Ecclesburn, where monsters and witches and ghouls walked the streets freely, was practically suicide.

And yet, no one had bothered them. Plenty had watched, but none had pestered, or attacked. It was as if they were intriguing, untouchable citizens of some upper class; aristocrats, walking under the protection of the state.

That thought bothered Robert too, so he pushed it away. 'Super,' he said, looking at Elspeth's sign. 'Shall we?'

Juliet gave a steely nod, and pushed her way through the black, macramé door curtains, while Robert followed.

'All hail, Entwistle ...' came a low, almost beguiling voice from the back of the room. And then she stepped forward. Elspeth the Cacolamia. A long, pale woman wearing a gothic black dress, swaying snakelike as she walked. 'For thou shalt be king hereafter.'

'Huh?' Juliet said.

'It's, um ... from Macbeth,' Robert said, explaining context without coming close to understanding the meaning.

Elspeth smiled as she sat on an ornate lofted chair, resting her hands on its wooden arms. Then, she looked at Juliet. 'And the noble Lady Rayne. Look at you. Here in my Gingerbread House, not to cast me into my oven, but to'—she turned her head curiously—'trade with me? Am I to be your Cassandra?'

'I brought ... I brought a tribute,' Juliet said.

Elspeth's eyes widened. 'Oh?'

'The ears of a woman, slain by ... vampires.'

'Was she to turn?'

'No. The vampires just killed her.'

'Still, a worthy tribute, young Lady Rayne.' Elspeth gestured with a glance at her table, holding multitudes of jars, boxes, little vials and other trinkets. 'Set it down for me over there, and tell me what it is you want.'

Juliet did as asked. She lifted her head and walked toward the table, then took the ears out, still wrapped in their towel, and placed them down.

Elspeth closed her eyes, as though enjoying a stirring song. 'What was her name?'

Juliet looked at Elspeth, confused, and then down at the ears. 'Oh. Um, Sara. Sara Bradshaw.'

Elspeth smiled, eyes still closed. 'Did you know her?'

Juliet cringed a little. 'Yes.'

'She was from our town and she went to the same uni we do,' Robert said.

Elspeth opened her eyes and gave Robert a look of almost baffled fascination. Then, she turned to Juliet. 'So, you desecrated the body of one of your friends?'

'It's ... it's not like we were baes or anything,' Juliet said.

Elspeth laughed slowly. 'Very well. You miss your soulmate, don't you? It is in your eyes.'

Robert rolled his eyes at the notion that the simple, almost dimwitted Aaron, of all people, had been Juliet's soulmate.

Elspeth narrowed her eyes and climbed off her throne, walking toward Juliet. 'Zeus split you from him, long before you were born, but in life you found him, didn't you? And now, you have lost him again.' She tutted twice, sharply, waving a finger with each reprimand. 'Foolish little girl.'

'His name's Aaron,' Juliet said. 'And he may be lost, but he isn't gone.'

'No, he is not gone,' Elspeth said. 'What was his full name?'

'Aaron Stuart McLeary.'

'What star sign was he?'

'Leo.'

Elspeth looked at Juliet. 'And you?'

'Um ... Gemini.'

Elspeth was practically beaming. 'You enjoyed his clarity?'

'Actually ... yes.'

'And I'm sure you fought sometimes?'

'Yes?'

'You enjoyed it?' Elspeth said.

'Maybe.'

'But he didn't?'

'He'd get upset,' Juliet said. 'He was'—she shook her head—'he's sensitive.'

Elspeth narrowed her eyes, suddenly an authority. 'Take back your ears,' she said. 'There's no road for you here, love.'

Juliet blinked, confused, looking at the ears on the table, and then back at Elspeth. 'No. I want—'

'I know, sweetheart. I see it. It's all over you. But just because you *want* it, doesn't mean you should *have* it.'

'Jules ...' Robert said, 'listen to her.'

Juliet stepped forward. 'The ears. I was led to believe
that the ears would suffice. Now, if you need something
more, that's fine. I can do more. But I'm not going home
with just ... a warning, and a bloody horoscope.'

'More?' Elspeth asked, suddenly intrigued. 'What more?'

Juliet took a moment, thinking it through. 'What do you
want?'

Elspeth placed her hands on her hips. 'A kiss.'

Juliet didn't wait.   She   marched   toward   Elspeth
purposefully.

'Not for me,' Elspeth clarified. 'For your king.'

'My ... what?'

'For Robert Entwistle,' Elspeth said, opening her palms
to him and stepping backward.

'You want me to kiss Rob? Fine.' She looked at him.
'Right Rob? For Aaron? That's okay, right?'

Robert couldn't help but step backward, and his rear end
collided with Elspeth's table. 'Um, what?'

Juliet advanced on him. 'It's life or death. Come on.'

Robert's cheeks came to life, as he switched from a smile,
to a grimace, to a wince, and back to a smile. 'But—'

Juliet stepped into Robert's stride, and put one arm
around his back, and the other around his neck. Then, she
snapped away, focusing on Elspeth. 'Lips?   French?
Tongues? What?'

Robert felt like he might explode. It was too much. He
wanted to pull her forward, into him, forever. It was
excruciating. It was agony. She was right there, pressed
against him. The thing that stopped him, the thing that
made sure he would *not* pull her in, in the almost obsessive
way he wanted to, was his love for her. The love that
compelled him, to do whatever *she* needed—regardless of
what it meant for him.

'Actually, I think I've seen enough of this Scottish play,' Elspeth said. 'Put the man down, Lady Rayne.'

Robert's heart was still in his mouth, his blood still alive and hot and humming, when Juliet casually dropped him and went to stand in front of Elspeth, while he remained locked in his delirium.

'You've seen enough, as in, you'll help me?' Juliet said.

'I will,' Elspeth said.

Robert, meanwhile, merely tried to compose himself, to regain his sense of control.

'Fetch me the pewter flagon,' Elspeth said, gesturing with her fingers at the table while she ripped a sheet out of a pad of paper that lay next to her huge seat. She set the sheet on her lap, took a huge, feathered ink pen out of a compartment built into the arm of her chair and waited.

Juliet came to her and gave her the embellished jug.

'You, mighty king,' Elspeth said, gesturing at Robert. 'Bring me one white candle and one red, and a cup.'

Robert snapped to attention. He glanced across the desk, locating first the white candle, then the red, and finally a cup, off one of Elspeth's shelves, above the table. He collected them into his hands and brought them over to the inscrutable Cacolamia.

Elspeth smiled at him, as he imagined a cat might smile at a mouse it pitied and hadn't the energy or motive to kill yet. 'Thank you, my dear,' she said, taking only the cup. 'Light those.'

Robert felt the urgency to do as he had been told. He looked to the table for a box of matches, but found what looked like a Zippo, only nearly twice as big. He flipped it open, and snapped the flame on. It was like a torch. 'Um ...' he muttered to himself, to focus, as he lit the two candles and placed them on the table.

'Write his name, here,' the black clad witch instructed Juliet.

Elspeth waited, while Juliet scribbled.

'Now, picture his face and repeat after me.'

Juliet closed her eyes and nodded.

'I call upon thy forces, thou hast bound,' Elspeth said.

'I call upon thy forces thou hast bound,' Juliet repeated.

'For an object of mine, needeth be found.'

'For an object of mine needeth be found.'

'Whether be it lost or broken.'

'Whether be it lost or broken.'

'Seek it out, as mine charm be spoken.'

'Seek it out as mine charm be spoken.'

Elspeth gripped Juliet's head with both hands and moved her face closer. 'Keep your eyes closed,' she said. 'Keep his face, in your mind.'

Robert watched Juliet as she pictured *him*. To see her go to such lengths, to do so many reckless, even corrupt things, just to find him—it shattered into pieces all the comforting narratives Robert had told himself to sooth his pain; how Juliet was only with Aaron because he was safe, and to get the dull-headed tough guy archetype out of her system.

None of those narratives could be true, he thought, because if they were she wouldn't go to such lengths now to get him back.

The thought festered, creating a painful swelling in his chest and in the pit of his stomach, which made his skin hum as he looked at the earnest frown of her closed eyes.

'Aaron Stewart McLeary sleeps, in the world above,' Elspeth said. 'He is in the Grosvenor Family Crypt, that lies between the cemetery at St. Luke's Parish Church, and the Cleve Woods.'

Juliet opened her eyes, and smiled. 'Thank you,' she said.

†

Tilly Turnbull's school playground was bustling with the slap of shoe soles and leather on concrete as the boys played football, chasing each other around and shrieking at one another. Tilly didn't hate the football. It fascinated her young mind. So much value placed in something so ultimately valueless.

It made her wonder: is value in a thing inherent, or is it only given by the valuer.

The former didn't seem to make any sense but, if the *latter* were true, then football was as valuable as any other thing that humans found valuable in the world.

That thought seemed too ridiculous, so Tilly chased it away, and forced herself to pay attention to her friend Laura, who seemed super focused on something.

'—whole group is going, and Mark's going, and if you don't agree, I won't have an in with the group, and I therefore won't have an in with—'

'Woah, slow up a little,' Tilly said, lifting her gaze away from the weird sport to her friend. 'If I don't agree to what?'

Laura looked confused for a second, and then smiled like a smart arse. 'Oh, *I* see. Taking in a little football, were you, hmmm?'

Tilly made a very prim and proper face. 'I'm absolutely positive I haven't a clue what you mean.'

Laura took a few steps toward the white chalk line on the concrete, which marked the sacred border of the game. 'So you weren't admiring any of the boys just now?'

'Actually I was pondering whether sport has any inherent value. You know, because, if it does, what does that say about the nature of value?'

Laura was still smiling, but shook her head now. 'Don't give me any of that. You were watching Harry.'

Tilly gave Laura her most unimpressed, catty face.

'You were!' Laura shouted. She grabbed Tilly's hand. 'I'll shout over to him?'

'No!' Tilly begged. 'Come on. Don't be a total bellend.'

Laura's smile beamed. 'This is perfect. Harry's friends with Mark. I like Mark. You like Harry. And I have the...'

'I don't like Harry, Laulau,' Tilly said. 'I mean, sure, he likes all the good TV shows and he's a nerd in the right way, but ... he's skinny, and his hair's all floppy, and—'

'Suppose I'd spoken to all the football team guys in 8B,' Laura interrupted.

'What, all'—Tilly did a quick count in her head—'three of them?'

'You know, for someone so disinterested in football, you sure counted quick how many 8B boys are in the football team.'

Tilly looked away from Laura's eyes shiftily. 'Is school spirit a thing? It seems like a thing. The reason I knew that? It's a school spirit thing.'

'Suppose I'd spoken to them,' Laura said, ignoring Tilly, 'and they'd told me that all of the football kids in year eight are going out, after dark, tonight. Also, a whole bunch of girls.'

'After dark?' Tilly asked.

'That's right.'

'That's crazy.'

'It's happening.'

Tilly was absolutely resolute. She did not buy it. 'There's no way that twenty kids are going out after dark, in Ecclesburn. No way.'

Laura nodded, her eyes wide. 'Oh yeah they are.'

'Wait, so what does this have to do with me exactly?' Tilly tilted her head a little, curious. 'You said, if I don't agree, you won't have an in with the group?'

Laura took a deep breath. 'Well. We're going to Cleve Woods.'

Tilly just blinked. 'That's insane.'

'Look, you know how boys are,' Laura said.

'Do I?!'

'Sure!'

'I don't think I do.'

'They like to be all brave and stuff,' Laura explained. 'So the plan is we meet at eight, at'—she took a piece of paper out of her cardigan pocket—'the Grosvenor Family Crypt.'

'We're meeting at a crypt?' Tilly said, her eyebrows raised in sheer disbelief. 'In *Ecclesburn*?'

'Well, no, we're meeting just north of it, in Cleve Woods, see. But the crypt is like the guiding star. But, we meet at eight, and we find the spot in the woods where the Cleve Witch was burned, and—'

'And what?'

'And we'—Laura shrugged—'we get high, and try to get off with Mark and Harry. Some of the boys are gonna bring lager.'

Tilly made a disgusted face. 'Gross. I'm not drinking lager.'

'Well I figured you'd bring leaf for Harry's vaporiser,' Laura said with a shrug. 'Point is, we go, we take a load of selfies, we get close to Mark and Harry. You can't tell me you're not interested.'

'I'm still getting my head around the going out after dark in Ecclesburn thing,' Tilly said. 'Remember Liz Smith and Scott Riley? Or the Llewellyn kid from year nine? People go missing in this town. And you wanna deliberately go to, like, the scariest site in the whole bloody village and ... hang out?'

'Kids are out after dark all the time,' Laura protested. 'The Llewellyn kid's parents moved, that's all. I'll give you the Liz and Scott thing, but they caught the guy who did that, and—'

'Why do you need me to come?' Tilly repeated sternly.

Laura took a deep breath. 'Okay. Your house is up that end of town. I'll need to get picked up, after. I can't get picked up from Cleve Woods. So let's go from yours, and we can meet the others, and be back in time for—'

'Laulau, what the hell makes you think I'm gonna be able to go out to Cleve Woods after dark?'

'Well, you said yourself, your dad spends most nights in the pub and your gran's always getting drunk.'

'Drunk, not paralytic.'

'Well, let's just get her from drunk to paralytic then,' Laura said, smiling mischievously. 'At the very least, we'll get her so wasted that we can sneak out and be back before she knows it.'

Tilly blinked at Laura. 'So your plan was to use the fact that my dad and my gran are total winos? That was your plan?'

'Well, it's not just that. I want you to come. It'll be weird if you don't.' She rolled her eyes dramatically. 'I'm not even sure I *want* to go if you don't come, and this is *just* the chance with Mark that I've been waiting for.'

'Ugh, you can quit that,' Tilly said. 'Quit it!'

Laura smiled. 'So do we have a plan? Can I tell Mark and his buddies that we're coming? Because you should come with me when I tell him.'

'I'm not walking into the bloody football,' Tilly said, like Laura had suggested sticking her hands in frogspawn.

'Well let's wait and cheer them on then,' Laura suggested. She looked around, at the boys chasing the ragged ball. 'It can't be too difficult to figure out the rules, right?'

Tilly sighed and her shoulders dropped. 'If they're running that way'—she pointed—'they need to kick it between those coats. If they're running *that* way'—she pointed the other way—'they need to kick it between *those* coats. It's not like they're playing Xenonauts.'

'What?'

'It's not complicated,' Tilly said simply. 'Look, if Harry scores, or if Mark scores, we'll cheer. It'll make them all proud and interested. Right? And then, at the end, I'll come with you to tell them that *maybe* we'll come tonight.'

Laura smiled and bobbed her head from side to side excitedly. 'Yay!' she squealed happily.

'Come on, you great, big arse. Let's see if football does have any inherent value, shall we?'

'Whatever,' Laura shrugged. 'I just wanna admire the boys.'

†

'You have had my hearty welcome,' Elspeth the Cacolamia said to Robert, holding a tray of what looked to him like a selection of cooked meats. 'Now, good digestion wait on appetite, and health on both.' She smiled like a devil offering forbidden fruit.

'Um, what?' Robert muttered, confused. 'Wait, is that from Macbeth too? It sounds Shakespearey.'

'My dear, precious king, you are to wait here with me four more hours—'

'Jesus is it still four hours?'

'So'—Elspeth jabbed Robert with the tray—'obey me. Eat. Strengthen yourself.'

'Um, Jules ...' Robert said.

Juliet, however, was busily tucking into something that resembled an oniony burger patty within a floury white bun, dripping with a dark red sauce. 'Mmm, it's good,' she said, her mouth full. 'Try it.'

'I'm good,' Robert said politely to Elspeth.

The witch didn't move. She simply held the tray of meats in front of him.

Robert smiled awkwardly and took the least offensive looking meat product he could find. A kind of pure, plain chicken nugget thing. He nibbled the front and was relieved to find it *was* chicken. At least, it seemed like it. It was tasty, too, and quite sweet. 'Mmm,' he said, nodding. 'That's good.'

'Her name was Henrietta Boffin,' Elspeth said, as Robert swallowed.

A terrible horror settled over him. '*Whose* name was Henrietta Boffin?' he asked, dreading the answer.

'The cat you are eating.'

Robert felt sick. Like he wanted to vomit. He couldn't help but think of his own beloved childhood pet cat. 'I'm so sorry Poppit,' he whispered to her memory. He looked to Juliet, who seemed equally disturbed, eyeing her burger through nervous eyes.

'Is this cat too?' she asked, wincing.

'No,' Elspeth answered. 'That was Alex Mack. She was a pig.'

'It's a hamburger? Oh thank God.'

Robert put the rest of his cat nugget back on Elspeth's tray and walked to Juliet, before moving his mouth to her ear. 'Are you *positive* we have to wait until after eight o'clock?'

'Sorry,' Juliet said. 'But yeah. Just ... ask her for something normal.'

Robert smiled, forcing bravery. 'Fine,' he huffed. 'Just so you know: I don't love it here.'

†

'Okay,' Tilly whispered to Laura, putting her phone down on her computer desk, 'my dad's confirmed he's going down the pub.'

Laura bobbed up and down on Tilly's bed giddily.

'And my grandma's already had nearly a full bottle of wine,' Tilly said. 'She usually starts to lose her memory about a half way through the second bottle.'

'Okay, good,' Laura said, nodding her head like she was buoying herself up. 'So how do we accelerate the drinking?' She rubbed her hands together. 'What makes her drink faster?'

'What drives her to drink?' Tilly said. 'Me, usually, I think.'

'You make her drink more?'

'Well, when I ignore her, or when I do stuff she's told me not to do, she says I'm the reason she drinks. It's totally false. I've seen pictures of her, when my mum was still around, when she was little and stuff, and, guess what:

big glass of wine in grandma's hand. So she was drinking *way* before I came along.'

'Enough depressing family history,' Laura said. 'Go get in her face and do something you shouldn't.'

Tilly pursed her lips thoughtfully. 'Okay, hang on.' She marched out of her bedroom, walked across the landing, and headed into her grandmother's room.

Laura followed. 'What are you doing?' she asked quietly.

Tilly went to the vanity table. 'Grandma just had this Mac lipstick delivered. She *hates* it when I steal her makeup.'

'Perfect,' Laura said.

Tilly found the lipstick and started slicking it on liberally. When she was finished, she leaned forward and kissed the mirror, leaving a defiant pair of red lips on it, while Laura giggled behind her.

'Okay, now to flaunt it,' Tilly said.

She ran out of the bedroom, over the landing and down the stairs, running through the hall and into the kitchen. Her grandmother didn't look up from her iPad. Tilly spotted the wine bottle, now completely empty, but her glass was still full.

Tilly went to the wine rack and pulled out a bottle of Yellow Tail Merlot—the same wine her grandmother had been drinking. 'Grandma, I'm taking this wine upstairs for me and Laura.'

The bitter old woman looked up now. 'You little brat, you'd better be'—she stopped, and squinted at Tilly's lips. 'Are you wearing my lipstick?'

'I found it and it looked nice so I figured I'd try it on, and I think I look absolutely fabulous, don't you?'

'Is that my bloody Mac lipstick, you little shit? Have you and your little brat friend been into my room and taken my bloody Mac?

'When I saw it I knew that I had to try some.'

Tilly's grandmother slid her chair back and climbed to her feet, pacing around the table toward Tilly, who put the wine down and ran around the table, keeping it between them.

'Was that not okay?' Tilly taunted.

'You deserve a smack, you little shit,' the grandmother barked. 'Your mother would have been smacked just for the attitude, let alone for stealing my makeup.'

'And you have no idea how much I appreciate that you've learned to be so enlightened in the years since she was little,' Tilly said, still running around the table to get away from her grandmother.

Tilly's grandmother stopped, and squinted at Tilly disbelievingly. She reached for the wine, opening it and topping up her glass. 'Where do you learn to talk that way?' she said bitterly. 'Not from me. Your mother never spoke that way.'

'Well, there are these things called *books*, Grandma. You read them, and you learn interesting new words and interesting new phrases.'

Tilly's grandmother gulped her glass until it was empty, and then refilled it with the wine Tilly had left on the table. 'You've no idea what a disappointment you are,' she said, not looking at her granddaughter.

Tilly shrugged. 'Well, I'll leave you to your wine, I suppose. Never mind. I *was* hoping to drink it myself, but, alas, I will bravely accept defeat.'

'Do whatever you like,' the grandmother said, sitting back down and refocusing on the iPad, with her glass in her hand.

Tilly walked quickly and quietly out of the kitchen, to see Laura waiting with a big smile, trying not to laugh, at the bottom of the stairs. Tilly shushed her, putting her finger to her mouth, and the girls went back upstairs to Tilly's room.

Once inside, Tilly closed the door and said, 'That ought to just about do it. Her head will be flat, on the table, in ... I'd say ... about thirty minutes.'

'Amazing,' Laura said.

CHAPTER FIVE
Cleve Woods

'I don't want to,' Robert said.

'We have to,' Juliet answered him.

'I know we *have* to, I'm just communicating that I don't *want* to.'

The thing that Robert definitely did not want to do was jump into the Undertown river. For, "river" seemed to Robert a generous way of putting it. Because it looked and smelled more like the bottom of the toilets at Glastonbury, only *huge*. Like a figurative mob in the sky had been relieving itself en masse, right on top of it.

'I could get used to the cat nuggets,' Robert said. 'And it's not as dangerous here as I was expecting. Really, we don't have to dive in. We don't.'

Juliet wrinkled her nose at him in a teacherly way, and said, 'It's the only way. We jump in, we head for the light at the bottom, and boom. Ecclesburn. Now come on. I'll go first. You follow.'

'Oh lord,' Robert sighed. 'Okay. Go.'

Juliet nodded, took a deep breath, and dived in.

'Oh, lordy, lordy lord,' Robert said, before taking a deep breath of his own, and diving headfirst into the "water". It was, at least, a watery texture. He splashed in and kicked his legs, keeping himself vertical so as to keep his downward momentum.

He'd never been good at opening his eyes under water. When he was little, he'd always been baffled by the other children who could do it with ease. It always stung him. But, now, with his safe return home dependent on it, he was forcing himself to look.

Juliet's promise was true. There was indeed a light. A distant, bright circular light. Robert started to worry, seeing how small the light seemed, fearing that it might be too far, that he might pass out from the lack of breath.

Sensing that he was beginning to panic, he tried to focus just on kicking his legs. Juliet was a way in front of him, so he kicked, and kicked, and kicked. And, as he did, the light got bigger, closer. He kicked more, and more, and more, but all the kicking started to take a physical toll on him, and he started feeling the intense need to gasp for breath, which of course he could not.

He began to feel lightheaded, and still he kicked.

He began to fear not just that he might miss the window and be stuck in Undertown, but that he might even drown. He worried, as still he kicked, that he might end up as just another Ecclesburnian who simply went missing, and never came back.

He kicked and kicked and kicked, and as his lightheaded state began to escalate into sheer drunken delusion, he pushed through something like a slimy film lining, and found himself hurtling down hard plastic, before rolling out and landing on his back. He breathed. It was glorious. It was one of the sweetest sensations of his entire life, just taking a breath.

And as he opened his eyes, as his mental state started to correct itself as he breathed in and out and in and out again, he saw Juliet standing over him, a wet, muddy mess.

He was back in the abandoned Play Shed, at the bottom of the huge snake slide.

Juliet held out her hand for him. 'Rob, that was ... amazing.'

He reached and took her hand, accepting her momentum and pulling himself up onto his feet. 'Never again,' he said. 'Never, ever, ever again. I mean it.'

Juliet smiled. 'Okay.'

Robert dragged something thick and clumpy off his face and flicked it onto the floor. 'I need a shower. And a cuddle.'

'No time!' Juliet gasped urgently. 'Come on, we have to go and save Aaron.'

Robert's head dropped, and with it his sense of optimism. 'Oh right. Wait, he's the monster. Save him from what?'

Juliet's smile turned, a little sad. 'Himself.'

†

Back, in the murky mirror village of Undertown, the vampire lord Aliester stepped out of the shadow of one of the ghoulish town's decrepit houses, toward the river.

He was followed by Lionel Casimir, the Death-Bearer, and three of his servants, who were bickering and tittering with each other.

But he was ignoring their quarrelling.

For his attention had been entirely seized by the strangers from above. The daughter of Thomas and Amelie Rayne, and her male companion, who had come into his domain, not to attack, and not to rescue, but to ... what? 'Curiouser and curiouser,' Aliester said, his cruel eyes narrow and contemplative.

†

'Ugh, what am I doing here?' Tilly said. 'I don't belong here. I don't like people. I shouldn't be here.'

Laura's eyes were glazed over with the acceptance of the cool kids, as the two girls looked up at the Grosvenor Family Crypt.

'It's open,' Tilly said curiously.

Laura rolled her eyes. 'Boys are so lame.'

'What, the boys opened the crypt to scare us?' Tilly rolled *her* eyes now. 'Jesus, that *is* lame.'

'Come on,' Laura said, grabbing Tilly's hand and pulling her around the crypt.

'Fine,' Tilly said, following Laura's lead, stepping past the crypt and over the crunchy October leaves toward Cleve Woods. 'I'll set aside my incapacitating misanthropy so that you can try it on with a boy.'

'You'll do what?' Laura said, as they entered the woods, before seeing the kids. 'Oh. Never mind.'

Tilly saw a small bonfire flickering away, and a whole bunch of the children from their year. There were large groups of boys with too much hair gel, sticking to each other; there were girls in twos and threes; and a few of the girls had paired off with boys, and were sitting with their sweethearts either talking or kissing.

'I'm not kissing Harry,' Tilly said. 'But, listen. I *will* sit with him for a while if you get a chance to sit with Mark. Because I'm a good friend.'

'You're an *amazing* friend,' Laura said. 'Speaking of which—I have something for you.'

Tilly blinked. 'Oh?'

Laura reached into her rucksack and pulled out a paper bag. She looked up, and started to open the bag. 'I got us friendship necklaces.'

'Um ...'

Laura slid them out and held them out to Tilly to examine. 'Mine says "best", yours says "friends".'

'Oh, I see,' Tilly said awkwardly.

'Do you love it?' Laura said.

'Honestly, I'm not really a necklace person,' Tilly said. 'I don't like feeling things on my throat.'

Laura sighed huffily. 'You have to wear it or we won't be jewellery buddies.'

'Well, now I've got *two* reasons not to—'

'Tilly!' Laura yapped. She poked her shoulder. 'Don't be a misery.'

Tilly took a deep breath, and took the necklace, and started clipping it around her neck. 'There, see.'

'Thank you,' Laura chirped merrily. Then she clipped her own on, as her eyes fixed on the bonfire, where the two boys were standing chatting to each other. 'Oh, Maa-ark,' she shouted daintily. 'Haa-rry.'

The two boys looked over. They both smiled widely. The kind of smiles you can't fake.

Tilly and Laura looked at each other, pretending not to care.

'Whatever, but I think they're happy to see us,' Tilly said.

'Totally,' Laura said, mirroring Tilly's nonchalant tone. Then, she grinned like a cheshire cat, letting her inner excitement out. She grabbed Tilly's hand, and the girls set off for the bonfire toward the boys.

†

Jack took two large gulps of the pint of Broken Dream he'd ordered, while Becky watched him for a response. He was thoroughly enjoying himself. There was no one else in the Crow's Feet, save for a couple of younger fellas playing darts in the back. So Jack was enjoying the company of the object of his crippling adoration, all to himself.

'How's your day been?' he said pleasantly.

She tilted her head a little. 'Um, really good. Thank you. I, um, well, you know I go to uni in Lancaster, right?'

'Right, of course,' Jack said, while shuddering. *He'd* started uni in 1997. Twenty long, damned years ago, when Becky would have been—

He stopped the thought, undoing the troubling maths in his head.

'Well, everyone else is so much younger than me, so I feel kinda weird being there,' Becky said.

'Right, I guess they're all fresh out of school, is that it?'

'Exactly. It's like, I feel like ... would it seem totally vain if I said I feel like I'm too mature for them?'

Jack took his time answering, not wanting to over stress the point. 'No, not really.'

'But, like, the last couple of days, the classroom's been getting emptier and emptier, in my theatre class, and—'

'Theatre, as in ... acting?'

'Yeah,' Becky said. 'I love it.'

'When did you first get into it?'

'Well, it's just an opportunity to act, really. I'm not, like, a big theatre nerd. But, as I said, I do love it. We're performing our production of Vinegar Tom, next Tuesday. On Halloween.'

'Vinegar Tom?'

'Yeah, I'm playing Alice.'

Jack sipped his beer. 'I don't know it.'

'It's about these women, in the seventeenth century, who are investigated for being witches. It's kind of about, like, society's modern patriarchal oppression of women as well, though.'

'Is it good?'

Becky nodded.

'And you're playing ...'

'Alice,' Becky said. 'She's one of the women who the witch-hunters go after.'

Jack smiled warmly. 'Are you ready?'

'I reckon so,' Becky said, though she didn't seem sure about it. 'It's obviously making me nervous now it's so close but I'm excited. There's'—she twitched a little, nervously—'there's still tickets left, if ... if you'd like to come?'

Jack wasn't sure, but it felt like Becky wanted him to come because she was into him.

That was definitely how it *felt*.

He smiled and said, 'I'd love to.'

†

Juliet looked up at the open Grosvenor Family Crypt as Robert caught up behind her, panting. 'Shit!' she hissed.

'It was ... to be ... expected,' Robert said, catching his breath.

'I guess,' Juliet said, when she noticed sounds, coming from Cleve Woods, in the distance, past the crypt. 'Do you hear that?'

'It sounds like, kids?' Robert said. 'It can't be kids though, right?'

'I hear music too. Come on, we have to go. If Aaron rises, and stumbles on some poor, helpless kids, that'll be it, I'll have lost him. That can't happen.'

'Jules, the bad thing would be the dead kids, not Aaron. Aaron's already dead.'

'I know,' Juliet said, grabbing his hand and pulling him around the crypt towards the woods. 'That's what I meant. I mean, I meant that too. Let's go, now.'

And off they went, as Robert shook his head in disbelief.

†

'Her name was Elizabeth Leach,' said Mark, the boy Laura liked, as he held a can of Carlsberg and stood in front of the fire. 'She was put to death in 1645, right *here*.'

'Was she ... burned?' Laura asked, twirling her brown locks through her fingers as she looked at Mark.

'Hanged,' he said, grinning and enjoying himself.

Tilly wasn't so impressed, but she was enjoying the story, and Harry had given her his coat, which didn't suck either. 'What did she do?' she asked.

'She used to lead little children, from Ecclesburn, down over there,' Mark said, pointing down at the brook a few yards on. 'She'd drown them, and drink their blood. She believed it would keep her from getting old.'

'Bull. Shit,' Tilly said.

'Well, it didn't work, obviously,' Mark said.

'No, I mean the *story* is bullshit,' Tilly said. 'She probably just had it off with men she wasn't married to. Or maybe she was a lesbian.'

Harry smiled at her, enjoying the way she was challenging his mate.

'Do you guys notice how in witch stories,' Tilly went on, 'they're always obsessed with getting old? The witches, I mean. They're always trying to stay young?'

Harry and Mark looked at each other, and then back at Tilly.

'Like, Stardust. Boom, the witches want to stay young. Hocus Pocus, boom, they want to stay young. American Horror Story, boom, stay young. That episode of Buffy, where the witch is the cheerleader's mum? Boom, stay young. And'—she raised her eyebrows at Mark—'*your* lame story just now? Boom, stay young.'

Mark took a moment, and then looked at the floor, doubting himself.

'I think it's not that women are obsessed with staying young, at all,' Tilly said. 'I think it's that *men*, who've *written* all those stories, *think* we're obsessed with staying young.'

Tilly was in her stride now. 'Like, when the bad guys are men, it's never, oh, I want to stay young, is it? No, it's like, oh, I want to take over the world, or, oh, I want to destroy all the Mudbloods, or, oh, I want to watch the world burn, or, oh, I want to take over the Pride Lands. But, when the bad guy's a woman? She's obsessed with youth. Or, she wants to make a coat out of dogs. So, y'know, youth and fashion. That's what we get.

'And, frankly, I think it's bad enough that poor Elizabeth Leach suffered the cruelty of being hated by her community, and that she was bloody hanged, literally murdered by an angry mob, without gonad-brains like you making up dumbass stories that cast her as some kind of vanity-obsessed monster.'

Harry was still smiling. 'So, who do *you* think Elizabeth Leach was?' he asked her, cocking his head to the side, curious without being demanding. 'If she wasn't a witch, I mean.'

'Um ...' Tilly started. She was suddenly nervous. She'd sort of forgotten that people were listening to her. And with Harry focusing on her, handing her his respect by asking the question, she was floored. 'I'd guess, like, as I said, she was a woman who liked having'—she stopped. Watching him, she suddenly didn't want to finish the sentence. 'You know.'

He looked at her, and it made her feel like he was looking at the actual *her*. Not the personality she performed, day to day, but the person inside.

She didn't like it.

But before she could really settle into that dislike, she was startled, by the sound of blood curdling screams.

†

Jenny and Tom were running. They were running as fast as they could. Jenny had screamed, at first, when she'd seen him.

It.

When she'd seen *it*.

With its demonic face, and its terrifying bright red eyes, and its awful sharp fangs.

Jenny had screamed, but Tom had chosen first to run. He hadn't been a coward. He'd made sure Jenny was holding his hand, even when it slowed him down, but Jenny couldn't focus on that, or anything else. She just wanted to run to her friends, to her people.

For, when she'd seen him—it, when she'd seen it—she'd still had the taste of Tom's tongue on her own. She'd still been high on the excitement, of being out late at night, and of kissing a boy she liked. But, now, she just wanted the safety of numbers. It felt like the most urgent need she'd ever experienced: to be with people, and to not be on her own.

But, of course, no matter how logical and necessary her need had *seemed*, it was about to put the lives of more than thirty children at risk.

Because the creature was following her, and it was fast, and it was gaining on her.

In that moment, being *chased*, being chased by a thing that wanted to harm her, to hurt her, to kill her, she knew real fear, and she would never unknow it, as long as she lived.

†

'What the hell's going on?' Harry said. His voice sounded lower than normal. Protective, suddenly.

The sound of footsteps and panting was getting louder and louder. It was so dark, out in the woods, that Tilly couldn't see what was happening, or who was coming, but the screams had been enough to startle her half to death.

The two figures ran into the clearing, lit by the bonfire. It was Jenny Lewis and Tom Howard. They ran straight into the group, like their lives depended on it, and stopped, grabbing people's hands, and pulling them.

'What's wrong?' cried one voice.

'What the hell?' cried another.

'Is this a prank?' asked a third.

Harry grabbed his iPhone and switched on his torch, before walking toward the clearing, where Jenny and Tom had run in from.

'We've gotta go, we've gotta get out of here, we've gotta go now!' begged Tom Howard.

There was a terrible growling, like a huge, angry dog, only more unworldly. It made Tilly's blood run cold, though she knew full well what it was. That certainty was confirmed when she saw him. A great, big guy with a bumpy, demonic face, all lit up by Harry's torch. He looked young—or, he looked like he'd been young, in life.

The monstrous figure grabbed Harry and lifted him up, moving his neck toward his mouth, and at that moment Tilly would have admitted being frightened for him.

As the creature prepared to plunge his sharp fangs into Harry's neck, a rope landed around his head, and jerked him backward so sharply that the monster dropped Harry, who began crawling away as fast as he could.

Tilly noticed the screams now. She'd been unaware of them before. Almost all of the children were howling. Tilly figured the best thing she could do would be to shepherd away those who hadn't already made a run for it.

†

'Aaron!' Juliet cried, holding tightly the rope to which he was tethered. Her eyes were moist with tears at the sight of him. 'Aaron, d'you hear me?'

He looked *evil*.

His eyes were a murky bright red, and his face had transformed, in the way vampires' faces do when they prepare to feed. He was wearing the same clothes as he'd been the night before. The same unseasonable denim shorts, and the same tight black tee shirt.

He growled at her, tensing his neck and tugging it from the noose around it. But Juliet's grip was strong.

'Aaron, man, it's me,' Robert said, holding holy water as a warning sign. 'Do you know who I am.'

'I know ...' Aaron snarled. Then he flashed his red eyes at Juliet. 'Let. Me. Loose.'

'No, darling, I won't.'

'I'll *kill* you.'

'Don't,' she said. 'Don't say that. You wouldn't.'

He looked at her, and his eyes started to soften. The red dulled a little and a bit of his ocean blue started to return. 'You have no idea,' he said, looking at her neck.

'Do you want me dead, Aaron?' she said.

'No!' he shouted.

'Then, come home with us,' she said. 'We'll work it out. You haven't ... you haven't done anything yet, you haven't killed anyone. Right?'

'I was going to. I was going to tear that boy's veins open. I *need* to. You don't understand. I need it. I need it now.'

'In the morning, we'll go to the butchers, we'll get pigs blood,' Juliet said. 'I'll say we're making black pudding. Loads of it.'

'Now.'

'We ... we can't get you blood now. The place will be closed. We ... we can't.'

'Now,' he said, again, as his eyes reddened. He gripped the noose and yanked it, but it held firm. 'I'll kill you for it. You don't understand.'

'You said you don't want me dead,' Juliet said. 'No. I *don't* understand.'

'Aaron, mate, come home,' Robert said.

'No. Blood. Now. Please. I can't ... I can't *feel* like this.'

Juliet stepped toward him, a little.

'Jules ....' Robert cautioned.

'Kill an animal,' she said. 'Drink an animal's blood. That'll do the job. Right? It doesn't *have* to be human, right?'

Aaron loosened his grip on the rope, a little. 'It's not the same. It's not the same.'

'How do you know?' Juliet said. 'You've never had human blood *or* animal blood before.'

'I just know. You don't understand. You can't.'

'Aaron, man, if you kill people, we're going to have to stop you. We're going to have to ... to kill you.'

Aaron glared at Robert. 'You'd have to *try*.'

'If I wanted it, you'd be dead now, man. See this?' He waved the holy water. 'This isn't the faulty stuff you tried on that vamp, last night. This is Father McMahon's. You'll be dead in moments if I want it.'

Aaron turned to Juliet, and his eyes softened again. 'Let me loose. And I'll kill an animal.'

Juliet smiled. A proper smile. The first proper smile since she'd gone down into the Royal Oak's cellar. 'Thank you. *Thank* you, so much. It's going to be okay. Everything's going to be alright.'

Robert couldn't help but roll his eyes, as Juliet made her way over to her fallen lover.

†

Tilly let Laura run in, and then slammed the house door closed. She grabbed her phone out of her bag and marched into the kitchen, where her grandmother was still asleep, folded forward over the kitchen table. 'I need to text everyone, to make sure they all made it,' she said.

'Oh god, oh god, oh god,' Laura muttered. 'It's really real isn't it?'

Tilly started adding all the kids she could remember seeing in the woods into a Facebook Messenger group. 'What's really real?'

'What the grown ups say. About Ecclesburn.'

'Of course it's real,' Tilly said, before heading out of the kitchen towards the stairs. 'Come on.'

The girls ran up the stairs, and into Tilly's room. Quietly, Tilly shut the door and sat on her bed, while Laura sat on Lilly's desk chair.

'I just can't believe it,' Laura said. 'I can't get my head around it. He was ... he was a ... he was a *monster*.'

'Say it like it is,' Tilly said, still adding people to her Messenger group with her phone. She looked up. 'He was a *vampire*. And he nearly killed Harry. He was going to bite his neck and drink his blood and kill him.'

'I don't believe in vampires.'

'And yet,' Tilly shrugged, and got back to her phone.

'I don't understand you,' Laura said. 'You're not surprised. Why are you not surprised? Harry nearly died. We saw a real vampire. Vampires are *real*.'

Tilly couldn't think of anyone she'd missed out, so she named the group "vampires", and looked up. 'Why d'you think we're not allowed out after dark? Why d'you think they tell us to rub bloody *garlic* on our necks? Why d'you think everyone goes to church when they're not religious?'

'Well, I know the grown ups think all that stuff is real, but I just figured it was them being strict and weird.'

Tilly typed her message: 'Did u all make it home ok?? Xx'

Then, she looked out of her window, at the night. 'As if going to church would help,' she said to herself, as Laura's phone pinged with her message.

†

Aaron pressed the young roe deer down, into the ground, and plunged his teeth through its furry neck, into its flesh, and tore. He pulled hungrily at the flesh, ripping it out in messy clumps, while the deer whimpered. The flesh was bitterly sour, so he spat it out, and *listened*.

He could hear blood pumping all over the deer's body, from its heart, lower down, in its chest, enclosed within its lungs.

Growling hungrily, and overcome with need, he plunged his hand through the deer's frame, pushing past its lungs, and ripped out its heart, which was still beating and gushing blood. He sank his face into it, and sucked it dry, gulping and snorting as he swallowed and slurped.

Fifteen feet away, Juliet and Robert watched.

Juliet was horrified, but relieved to have her man back. The sight of him ripping open a living deer was never going to go away, but it was, she decided, a necessary evil. And not entirely unlike the whole process of eating meat, which she was fine with.

'What the hell are we doing, Jules?' Robert said.

'Better the deer than a person,' she replied.

But Robert could only sigh, and lament. 'That's not what I meant,' he said sombrely.

†

Elspeth the Cacolamia was sweeping the floor of her Emporium, smiling as she waited for her sweet, innocent visitor to reveal himself. It was cute, she thought, observing his sense of theatricality. His lofted sense of his own potency also, to conceal himself. 'Can I help you, m'lord?' she said.

'You had visitors,' spoke the proper, elegantly rich voice of Aliester, the vampire, who stepped through her macramé curtains. 'Two.'

'I have had many visitors today.'

'These were from above,' Aliester said.

Elspeth smiled and focused on her latest guest. 'What of it?'

'I would very much like to discuss with you the nature of this visit,' Aliester said. 'If you are amenable to this request?'

Elspeth opened her arms and gestured to the back of her shop. 'Please, my lord, enter my home, and be my most welcome caller.'

Aliester followed her through the gloomy yet tidy corridors of her home, behind the store front, and into a warm room with a sturdy wooden table sitting in the middle of it. 'Do not try to bewitch me, Cacolamia,' he said. 'I will have your truth.'

Elspeth sat on one side of the round table, and the vampire who ruled Undertown sat on the other. She watched him, amused by every ounce of him. 'I have no need to bewitch you, my lord,' she said. 'Nor any desire.'

Aliester joined his hands on the table and leaned forward, scrutinising Elspeth with his eyes. 'Then tell me. What were the upsiders here for? Tell me,' he repeated, sharper this time, 'do they mean to wage war against me, to reclaim Undertown itself from me?'

'Vampire dust is a powerful charm,' Elspeth said, a touch of menace to her tone. 'Did you know that?'

Aliester said nothing. He merely watched.

'For instance, fifty grams of vampire dust, mixed with a little chilli powder and cumin, makes an excellent aphrodisiac for women,' Elspeth went on. 'When mixed into one's frying batter, that is. It produces a magically charged erotic high that a man, undead or otherwise, could only imagine.'

'I would like you to arrive at your intention, Cacolamia.'

Elspeth dropped her shoulders and frowned at the apparently dim creature. 'Did I stutter?' she said, her voice plain and unperformed now. 'I want vampire dust. Get me some.'

'You expect me to sacrifice one of my brethren for you?'

Elspeth narrowed her eyes, pulled a pinch of powder from the pocket on the thigh of her dress, and threw it onto the table. At once, a terrible fire raged where the powder landed, and the vampire stood and kicked his chair backwards. 'Get me the dust of a vampire,' she said again, stepping around the table towards him, readying another pinch of the incendiary powder. 'Get me the dust of a vampire or perhaps I will take yours.'

'You wouldn't dare,' Aliester said, pulling his cloak from behind him as he stumbled away. 'My hordes would burn you to the ground, along with your store. I respect you, Cacolamia, but my tolerance only runs so far.'

'I have your product and you have my price,' Elspeth said, before pointing at the door.

Aliester lifted his head in a noble fashion. 'Very well, though I expect fewer parlour tricks when I return.'

Elspeth turned her face to the fire. 'A bheith go fóill,' she said, and the fire obediently calmed itself. She smiled at Aliester, lifted her eyebrows, and said, 'Off you trot.'

†

Robert rocked in his creaky old chair, and clicked on his phone to check the time. 3:07am. Juliet would be awake in three hours, and, after that, he could probably get some sleep. He knew that Aaron would not be asleep. *Aaron* had slept all day. Whatever the recently turned vampire was doing, he was behaving himself, and that was a blessed relief.

For, Aaron hadn't come upstairs once in the four hours Robert had been sitting, waiting, watching.

Through the wall, Robert could hear Juliet snoring. A perfect, occasional wheeze that brought out all of his most primitive protective instincts. He was not a man of primal tendencies, particularly. He was a contemplative young man. Cerebral, even. Not particularly strong, or sporty, by the standards of vampire hunters—although he was stronger than most ordinary nineteen year olds. But, physical inferiorities and all, when he considered the possibility of the new vampire Aaron wandering up the stairs toward Juliet's room, with the lust of blood on his mind, Robert was filled with something that he knew to be inherently *manly*.

He would not allow her to come to harm.

He would not. He would not. He would not.

It gave him a strength he'd never known before, this realisation, this responsibility, sitting outside her bedroom, like a guard dog, waiting for a wolf to scare away.

He cleared his throat and forced his eyes open, keeping himself awake.

Three more hours.

Easy.

†

Aliester threw the satchel full of vampire dust onto Elspeth's table, and stared at her. 'Five of my brethren,' he said. 'This ought to ... satisfy you.'

Elspeth the Cacolamia circled the table, staring down at the satchel. Slowly, she unclipped the fastener, and lifted the lid of the bag open, taking a look inside. She smiled. 'Yes,' she said, before eyeing the vampire. 'Please, sit.'

Aliester sat. 'So. Tell me. What were the upsiders here for.'

'They are vampire hunters,' Elspeth said, sitting down. 'From the world above. They kill your people for money, and out of necessity.'

'I do not believe I asked who they were. I believe I asked why they were—'

'They came because one of their plucky number has fallen to one of *yours*,' Elspeth said. 'One of them, is now one of *you*.'

'A hunter has become a vampire?' Aliester said, reaching with his feelings to the world above, to the newly risen vampire there.

'They were three, and the intricacies of their interiors are *so* delightful. The leader is a she. The fallen is her lover. But the third is a he in love with the she.'

'The Rayne Helsingers,' Aliester said, with a laugh. 'You are talking about the Rayne Helsingers?'

'A deliciously dark triangle of desire,' Elspeth said.

Aliester smiled broadly, and scoffed to himself a few times. 'So why did the two that remain come to you?' Aliester said, lifting his head.

'They would find the fallen.'

'So that they might slay him?' Aliester said, as though stating the obvious.

But Elspeth smiled devilishly. 'No,' she said, shaking her head. 'Their desire is not his death. Their desire is his reformation.'

'The humans want to reform one of my brethren?' Aliester said. 'To make him weak, and fleshy, and soft within?' He scoffed and shook his head, vexed by the notion. 'No.'

'I promised you my truth, my lord, and this is it. The lady Juliet Rayne would find the vampire formerly known as Aaron McLeary, so that he might be'—she almost laughed—'saved.'

And Aliester laughed again. 'And, this other, this third, who loves the woman. What is his name?'

Elspeth took her time, swaying her entire torso from side to side as she sat. 'His name is Robert Entwistle. His desire for her is strong, m'lord. His desire for her is stronger than hers is for her fallen lover.'

'This, Cacolamia, is wonderful news,' Aliester said, leaning back into his chair. 'Truly, wonderful.'

Elspeth leaned over the table and reached for the satchel. 'Shall I add a spoonful of your offering to some frying batter, my lord?'

Aliester smiled, allowing his eyes to drop from Elspeth's own, to the contents of her dress. 'Why not?'

Elspeth's mouth twitched, a brief, demonic smile. 'No teeth,' she said, and left for her kitchen with the satchel.

CHAPTER SIX
A Blood Quest

Juliet stirred in her sleep, moaning at the hazy, blurry-edged vision playing out in her dreams. There was a man, and a girl. The girl was in a state of undress, but the man was clothed. She was on a bed, and he was standing. And, though they were clearly in a bedroom, it looked ... historical.

'M'lord ...' said the girl, humble and frail.

'Aye, sister?' replied the man, eyeing hungrily the curve of her thigh.

'T'is the direst cruelty, that we must part,' she said, reaching out for him. 'You leave me almost dead for breath.'

Juliet, watching in her sleeping state, felt that the girl was speaking not simply out of desire for the man, but also out of fear.

'I would leave you wholly dead for breath, if you petitioned me so,' the man said.

The girl smiled shyly. 'I've no ambition to be a devil meself, m'lord.'

'Wait a dozen seasons,' the man said. 'Then see.'

'But ...' the girl said, rubbing her thigh where he watched her, 'I fashioned you a charm of mighty force, m'lord. As a gesture of me thankfulness. That you might take still the world you fancy so.'

'Aye?' the man said. 'I pray thee, sweet sister, what is it?'

The girl leaned down over the side of her bed and lifted something. She held it out for the man to take. 'It is lodestone, m'lord.'

'And the charm?'

'T'will draw you, m'lord, to any devil more vindicative, more cunning, than yourself, m'lord.'

The man raised his head proudly at this. 'D'you suppose there are any more vindicative or cunning than I, sweet sister?'

'No, m'lord. T'is me own fancy that you shall ne'er be overwrought by another. But *this*, m'lord'—she lifted the object in her hand—'this, shall make my fancy absolute.'

'How so?'

'As I said, m'lord. T'will draw you to any more cunning, that you might emboss him. That you might front him. And that you might slay him.'

The man no longer seemed insulted. Rather, he seemed pleased. 'I give you thanks, sister. But ... I wonder. If he is indeed more cunning than I, how shall I best him?'

The girl smiled. 'T'is enchanted in more than one way, m'lord.'

'Pray, speak.'

The girl wrapped the object up in her quilt. 'I mustn't leave this about while I utter the charmed words.'

The man raised an eyebrow.

Once it was away, she said, 'When you find him, you must only speak these words, m'lord: "Nocturnal terror, come by night; thou art in error, to know my sight; for, enemy, thou'd never best; thine sturdy foe, now evanesce".'

'And this shall undo the devil more cunning than I?' the man said.

The girl nodded. 'Allow me one command, m'lord,' she said, as though making a request.

'Aye.'

'Ne'er teach another the words,' she said gravely. 'For t'will slay thyself, suppose there's n'other more cunning.'

And at this, the man smiled wickedly, and a new voice spoke.

'Others may have claimed my fame, but only I am worthy of it,' the voice said. It was ... *everywhere*. It surrounded Juliet. It seemed to speak directly to her. 'And now, just as I consumed the lifeblood of your mother, I shall consume the lifeblood of you.'

Juliet blinked awake.

She looked around.

It was still dark, and she was heavy eyed.

She rolled over, and went back to sleep.

†

Jack poured boiling water over instant coffee, enjoying the smell as his cup filled, creating a brown froth at the top. He was feeling good. Songs were playing by themselves in his head, which was not the norm. He felt like he could run around the block that morning, if he had the time.

Rita wandered in, her bare feet slapping on the hard surface of Jack's kitchen floor. 'Do me one,' she said.

Jack smiled and spun around to face her. 'Absolutely,' he said with an earnest grin.

She withdrew when she saw his smiling face, like she'd seen a slimy bug. 'We have to talk about your daughter,' she said.

Jack sighed. 'What now?'

'She's been in my make up, and she was *so* ill mannered yesterday. Jack, I mean it. It was like she was ... goading me.'

'That's kids,' Jack said. He wasn't in the mood for negativity. 'What did she do?'

'Oh, she was just disrespectful,' Rita said, sitting down at the table. 'She ... it felt like she was *mocking* me.'

'I'll talk to her,' Jack said, grabbing a cup for Rita and filling it with her coffee and sugar. Then he went to the fridge for the milk. 'Listen. I wanted to talk to you about Halloween.'

'Oh yeah? She's finally mentioned it to you then?'

'What? Oh, Tilly, no. Not Tilly. I, um, well ... I need to go out on Halloween.' He poured water from the kettle into her cup. 'Can I pencil you in to watch her?'

'Why not?' Rita said sarcastically. 'You do every other night.'

'Not every night,' Jack said, pouring the milk in.

'Whatever,' Rita said. 'Fine. Halloween, fine.' She looked up sharply. 'Wait, no, you have to talk to her. She wants to go out on Halloween. You *know* this.'

'She knows she can't go out after dark,' Jack said with a shrug. 'It won't be a problem.'

'Talk to her. If *you* can get her to show a little respect, then, sure, you have a deal. I'll watch her on Halloween.'

Jack smiled, a great, big smile. 'Fantastic.'

'Don't be so bloody cheery, you tit, it's too early,' Rita said, eyeing him suspiciously. 'It doesn't suit you.'

Jack's smile didn't fade at all. 'Sure. No worries. Cheeriness, over.'

Rita looked at him again like he was a filthy creature, and simply said, 'Give me my coffee.'

†

'Did you know that the inventor of the printing press was Catholic?' Laura asked. 'He was called Gutenberg. Johannes Gutenberg.'

Tilly rolled her eyes at her friend as they made their way out of the vending machine rooms to the playground.

'Or maybe it was Yohannes,' Laura said. 'I'm not sure.'

Tilly stepped out onto the hard concrete. 'What are you going on about?'

'He was a Catholic guy,' Laura said simply. 'The first book ever printed was the Catholic Bible.'

'So?' Tilly demanded.

'So ... it's not like people *just* started believing in this stuff. People have been believing in this stuff for ... you know, forever.'

'And?'

'And ... I think that makes it more, I dunno, believable.'

'When your printing press guy, however the hell you say his name, when he invented that thing, people probably believed the earth was flat,' Tilly said. 'Who cares about him, *or* what he invented?'

'I'm just saying that in the light of recent developments, a certain familiarity with religious stuff might not be the worst thing.'

'*Religious* stuff has nothing to do with any of it,' Tilly argued. '*Religion* is just a—'

'Hey,' came Harry's voice.

'Hey,' came Mark's, which was slightly more melancholy.

'Mark, are you okay?' Laura asked, stepping close to him but stopping at a safe distance.

'I'm fine,' Mark said with an unconvincing shrug.

'No, you're not,' Harry said.

'Yes I am, you gaylord,' Mark said.

Tilly couldn't help but raise her eyebrows into an unimpressed stare, which was aimed first at Mark, but then at Harry, to see how he'd take the insult.

'No, you're *not*,' Harry repeated. He widened his eyes and looked at Tilly, as though Laura wasn't even there. 'So. Vampires.' He grinned. 'Can you actually believe it?'

'Yeah, whatever,' Tilly said, performing her disinterest. Then, she remembered that people had been in danger, and focused. 'What should we do?'

Harry shook his head. 'About what?'

'About ... the vampires?'

'What can *we* do?' Harry said, smiling, like he was enjoying the back and forth.

'I'll tell you,' Mark said. 'I'll tell you what we can do. We can stop going on about ... about, bloody ... vampires. That's what.'

'Did you know that the inventor of the printing press was a Catholic guy called Johannes Gutenberg?' Laura asked Mark helpfully.

Mark didn't look impressed. 'What?'

'We're not sure how you say his name,' Tilly said.

'No!' Mark shouted, so loudly that a couple of nearby kids turned to look at him.

Laura took an instinctive step away from him.

'No, we're not talking about ... all that,' Mark continued. 'We're not.'

Harry flicked his curly fringe off his head. 'He's not handling it well at all,' he said. 'And, *I'm* the one who nearly—'

'Shut up,' Mark hissed bitterly. Then, he straightened his face out, like he was putting away all the memories he didn't want. 'Laura,' he said, with a smile.

'Yeah, Mark?' she answered him.

'Did your parents answer about Halloween yet?'

'You have *got* to be kidding?' Tilly said.

'Why?' Mark hit back, turning again to Laura. 'Look, we're pretty sure that, whatever that was, last night, it was some kind of stunt, some kind of prank.'

'No,' Harry said, 'we're not.'

'Like, the'—Mark made sarcastic speech marks with his fingers—'vampires ... they didn't even kill anyone.'

'Your concern is touching, Mark, really,' Harry said.

'Doesn't it seem a little convenient to anyone else that, in *this* town, where they have us under a curfew, we *break* curfew and find ourselves attacked by an actual vampire who doesn't kill *anyone*?'

Harry caught a nearing football under his foot and kicked it back to the boys it had come from. 'Maybe we got lucky?' he said.

'Or maybe it was something cooked up by our parents to scare us out of doing it again. Think about that. Isn't that more likely? Than the idea that, bloody ... *vampires* exist?'

'Well,' Laura shrugged, 'the grown ups *are* psychos.'

'My dad's not,' Tilly said.

'Come on,' Mark said, his voice rising in a kind of whiney way. 'The plan for Halloween is still good. Right?'

Harry turned to Tilly, as though curious for her response. He threw up his eyebrows in his admittedly cute, boybandy way. 'I don't wanna die, or anything,' he said, 'but ... we could be safe, and still have fun?'

'I don't think I can actually believe that, the day after we almost die, after sneaking out after dark, we're literally the very next day talking about doing it again.' Tilly looked at each of her friends in turn. 'Are you guys suicidal? Or just stupid? I mean, if we had some weapons, something we could use to—'

'We didn't almost die,' Mark protested.

'No. *I* did,' Harry said.

'Whatever,' Tilly said. 'Look. I propose we focus on what we ought to do about the fact that there are real vampires in this town. We have to do something, to, I dunno'—she made fists and awkwardly swung them about in the way she imagined a boxer would—'fight them or something.'

Mark simply rolled his eyes, while Harry winced at the absurdity of it.

'I think *that's* suicidal,' Laura said.

Tilly noticed Jenny Lewis and Tom Howard standing together, side by side like girlfriend and boyfriend, but not holding hands. They were pressed together, as though they were trying to get warm from the cold. 'Hey, Jenny, Tom, come over here!' Tilly shouted.

They turned to face her, and their faces sank. Slowly, they shuffled over.

'Hey,' Tilly said.

'How are you guys doing?' Harry asked.

Mark simply watched them suspiciously, obviously assuming they were in on the "prank"; and Laura simply watched Mark.

'We've been shitting ourselves all day,' Tom said.

'How've you guys been dealing with it?' Jenny asked the group.

Laura cleared her throat. 'Mark thinks it was a prank.'

'It wasn't,' Tom said, staring into empty space.

Jenny shook her head. 'No. It really wasn't.'

'We worried you lot might have told someone,' Tom said. 'We were just discussing this St. Luke's thing, now.'

'What St. Luke's thing?' Harry said, rolling his head to flick hair off his forehead.

'They just told us in form,' Tom said. 'We're going to St. Luke's this afternoon.'

'Why?' Tilly asked. 'All Saints' isn't until next week?'

Jenny shrugged. 'Mrs. Richardson said it's "overdue". And she says there's a new priest.'

'I've gotta say, I don't really fancy going there,' Laura said. 'St. Luke's creeps me out at the best of times. After last night, I really don't wanna be going that close to Cleve Woods. Like, ever.'

'But,' Tilly said, making her voice cheeky, 'a certain familiarity with religious stuff might not be the worst thing, right Laulau? And you can ask this new priest whether it's Johannes or Yohannes Gutenberg who invented the printing press.'

'What?' Tom said.

'It's nothing,' Laura said. 'But, d'you know what, Tilly, you're right,' she said in a cordial, grown up kind of way. 'I think we should steal a bunch of Bibles. Find something in there about vampires. Right?'

She turned a full circle, looking to each member of the group for some kind of approval, landing finally on Tilly.

'I don't think you're supposed to steal Bibles from the church,' Tilly said.

'Yeah and I'd be surprised if there's anything about vampires in them anyway,' Harry added. 'My mum's crazy religious. She just goes on about how evolution's a lie mostly.'

'Ugh,' Tilly couldn't help saying.

'But that's what we should do, right?' Laura said. 'Full recon mission at the church. See what we can shake loose from the crusty old priest. See what skeletons he has hiding in his closet.' She looked around again, circling the other way, but finding the group no more agreeable. 'Right, you guys?'

'It's not like we have a choice,' Harry said, flicking his hair off his face again. 'We have to go. We may as well make it interesting.'

And, as Tilly wondered what "make it interesting" actually *meant*, the school bell started chiming obnoxiously, a shrill and constant whistle. And, one by one, the children in the playground started filing back into the old, stale school building.

†

Juliet tightly clutched her mother's compass as she walked onto the landing of the Great Hall of Rayne Manor, from her bedroom. Robert was asleep, now that he was certain Aaron was sleeping too. Juliet's agreement with him had been simple. She would wait, and let him sleep a few hours, and then together they would go to the butchers in Ecclesburn town centre for some pigs blood.

Simple.

But Juliet was so curious, so filled with desire, that there was one part of the deal she could not keep.

She was not supposed to visit Aaron, deep within the cellar of the mansion. And yet, she couldn't help herself. She knew the fundamental risks. She understood that Aaron was sleeping, and to wake a sleeping vampire was a terribly unwise thing to do. But it didn't matter. She had lost him, and now he was found, and she dearly wanted just to see him.

Just to see him.

With this in mind, she wandered down the crescent shaped staircase, and into the Great Hall. She continued, heading for the door that led down into the cellar.

She stood on the safe side of that door and noticed that she was not afraid.

She wasn't sure if it was the number of vampires she had faced, or the fact that this time it was the man she loved, but one way or another, she felt nothing.

Nothing, but need.

Nothing, but desire.

She swung the cellar door open, crossed the threshold, and then softly pushed it closed again, holding it firmly so that it wouldn't creak. Then, she began down the stairs, using her phone as a torch. At the bottom, stepping into the room, she flashed her phone at the bed she had prepared for Aaron, but he wasn't there.

Now, she *was* scared.

'Aaron ...' she whispered. 'Are you awake? It's me. It's Juliet.'

There was nothing. Not a sound. She used her torch to scan the room, but it was a labyrinth. There were little, old corridors, secret stone safes, cubby holes, and various other pockets for someone to get lost in.

'Aaron ...' she said, stepping forward again.

'Jules.' The voice was by her right ear, so close it set off a startled panic in her entire upper body, and she gasped and stepped away from it.

'Jesus, Aaron,' she said, reaching for breath, shining the torch at his face. 'What the hell?'

'The hell ...' Aaron muttered, as though hearing the words for the first time, as though thinking about them for the first time. 'Yes. The hell.'

'Okay, Aaron, I wanted to come and see you, because, we're going into Ecclesburn today. We're going to get you some blood.'

Aaron's eyes closed softly. 'Some blood.' Then, his face began to change, and he opened his eyes and stared at Juliet malevolently. 'Yes. Some blood.'

'Now, now, now,' Juliet said, stepping backward, as her upper back hit stone. 'Aaron, listen. You don't want to hurt me.'

'Some blood, the hell, to hurt you,' Aaron said, his face contorted and confused.

'Aaron!' Juliet hissed, still gripping the compass, squeezing it tight. 'Focus. You're Aaron McLeary, and I'm Juliet Rayne. You're going to be fine, and you don't want to hurt me.'

Aaron looked pained, like guilt was overwhelming him. He nodded, brief little signals. And finally his face changed back, until he looked like himself again.

'I love you, Aaron.'

He opened his eyes and they met hers. 'I l—' he began. 'I ... lo—'

'It's okay, I get it, I hear you,' she said.

His face hardened. It didn't change, to its demonic form. It simply hardened, the way a man's does when he is angry. 'I *want* you,' he growled.

'I want you too,' she said, her voice cautious. 'I have some jobs to do, remember. To get you what you need.' She chose not to say the B word again.

He simply growled, long and slow and menacing.

'Remember who you are,' she said. 'Aaron McLeary. You don't want to hurt me.'

And again the anger seemed to dissipate in him and be replaced by that same terrible pain.

Juliet didn't waste any time. She made her way for the stairs, and started up them backwards. 'You're Aaron McLeary, and I love you, and it's going to be okay.'

He jumped, as though startled. Then, he turned his face at her, and started advancing.

She took a few steps up. 'You don't want to hurt me.'

'I ... don't.'

She took a few more steps up. 'You don't want to hurt me.'

'I don't.'

Juliet felt her back hit the cellar door, and reached behind her for the knob. 'Keep a safe distance, sweetheart, the sun's up.'

Aaron hissed, and stepped away from the bottom of the staircase.

Juliet pushed open the door and fell backward, into the sunlit safety of the Great Hall. 'Oh God, God in heaven, what am I doing?' she said, as her voice began to break. And then, sitting on the hard wooden floor, she began to weep.

She wondered when, or rather *if*, she would ever stop, and, still clutching her mother's compass, the compass that didn't work, she longed, deep, deep down, for her mother to come back to her, to cuddle her, to tell her that everything was going to be okay, and to tell her what she should do.

†

Robert's phone woke him up as it buzzed noisily on his bedside table. He blinked away the overwhelming desire to return to his sleep, and sat up, finally taking the phone and switching off the alarm.

There was a text message waiting for him. Just one, from Juliet. It read: 'Come downstairs.' It had been sent at 11:55am. Five minutes ago.

He threw off his duvet and climbed out of bed, racing out of his room and toward the landing that overlooked the Great Hall. When he started for the stairs, he found Juliet standing in the hall, by the door that led to the living room.

'I made you something to eat,' she said. She seemed a little off. A little timid, by her standards anyway.

'Thanks ...' he said. He walked toward her and followed her into the living room, where a wide plate stacked high with what looked like toasted sandwiches sat upon the large oak dinner table.

'I wanted to reciprocate,' she said. 'You made me an amazing breakfast, yesterday, and then ... well, you went above and beyond for me.'

Robert picked up one of the sandwiches. They had rashers of slightly burned bacon in them. 'Thank you.' He looked down at them. 'How many did you make?' he said, counting.

'I just kinda kept cooking. The hottest ones are these, at the top.'

Robert took a bite. Though burned, the bacon was good. He felt like he could eat all of the sandwiches, he was so hungry.

'Here, sit,' Juliet said, pulling a chair out for him. 'After you've eaten, go shower, and we'll head into town for the blood.'

'I want to go to St. Luke's today, as well, if ... if that's cool with you?' Robert said. 'I mean, yesterday we kinda got sidetracked, but I need to figure out what's going on with the new priest, and why the holy water didn't work.'

'Sure, of course,' Juliet said. 'Blood first though, yeah?'

Robert sighed, but tried not to let it show. The truth was that he was cheered by the care she'd shown him, and the possibility that she was beginning to appreciate him the way he wanted her to. The thought suddenly soured, though, when he considered that what he was feeling was immature desire, that it was the way a child wants to be loved. Not, as he wished to feel, the way a *man* wants to be loved. 'Sure,' he said. 'Yeah. That's fine.'

†

'We've got to make Halloween happen, I think,' Laura said to Tilly, as the two girls sat next to each other about halfway deep into the coach that was taking them from Cardinal Manning Catholic Secondary School, to St. Luke's Parish Church.

'It happens somewhat by itself, no?'

'The Mark and Harry part, I mean,' Laura clarified.

Tilly sighed.

'I mean, last night was going so well,' Laura went on. 'Before all the weird stuff.'

'Can I ask you something?' Tilly said, shifting to look at Laura. 'What do you see in him?'

'He's toasty gorgeous,' Laura said with a shrug. 'He looks like Bradley Cooper.'

'But he seemed so pissy before, about the whole vampire thing. He just came off to me like a little, whiney baby. Bradley Cooper wouldn't have reacted like that.'

'Hmmm,' Laura hummed thoughtfully. 'I don't care about that. I mean, he saw a vampire, it's not weird that he's spooked. Anyways, what about you? What do *you* see in Harry?'

'I don't believe I ever confirmed I see anything in Harry. I've got nothing against him, and I do like talking TV with him, I guess. But you're the needy one here, not me. I'm more concerned with what we ought to do about the undead monsters who want to kill us, than I am with kissing boys.'

'You're a big, fat liar, Matilda Turnbull,' Laura said, smiling as she gently pushed into Tilly with her shoulder. 'I can see right through you.'

'Yeah, I think maybe you're just seeing yourself.'

The coach slowed and turned, making both of the girls turn to look at the looming church steeple and its mean, brown entrance, all decorated with ornate stained glass windows with long, sad-looking saints painted on them.

'Come on,' Tilly said. 'Let's get this shit show over with.'

†

'Pigs blood?' said Eric Knight, the butcher.

'Yeah ...' Juliet said awkwardly. 'We're ... we're making black pudding.'

'For how many?'

Juliet and Robert looked at each other.

'It's a big party,' Robert said.

'Well, you know, we sell a fine black pudding,' Eric said. 'An *award*-winning black pudding, no less.'

'That's ... so great,' Juliet said, 'but, see, we wanted to make it fresh.'

'Is it for your lad, Aaron?' Eric asked pleasantly. 'He's a Scot, by heritage, isn't he?'

'He is, yeah,' Juliet said.

'His family's coming down,' Robert lied, regretting it immediately.

'Lovely,' Eric said. 'You'll be needing plenty of supplies then?'

'Really, we just want the blood, today,' Juliet said.

'Well, I don't sell pigs blood.'

Juliet and Robert looked at each other again.

'And, I don't use fresh blood to make my black pudding.'

'What do you use?' Robert asked, his curiosity taking over.

'Well, dried pigs blood powder,' the avuncular butcher said. 'Imported, from Holland.' He seemed proud.

'Shit,' Juliet said.

'It's really just as good. It's not important that the blood be fresh. I mean, of course, you get some butchers who produce fresh blood pudding, but you'll find they're a little overzealous. I've served black pudding made from powdered blood for over twenty years, and, if—'

'Who are they?' Juliet said. 'These ... butchers who use fresh blood?'

Eric looked just a little bit hurt. 'Honestly, Miss Rayne, my love, why don't you try some of my pudding. I promise you'll not—'

'Mr. Knight, I think I've been pretty clear. I don't want to buy black pudding. I want to *make* black pudding. And I want to make it using *fresh* blood. Not powder.'

Eric's avuncular nature evaporated, leaving behind a touchy, bothered old man. 'Well, as I said. I don't sell fresh pigs blood.'

Juliet took a deep breath and bottled it, as another customer jingled through the door.

Eric took the opportunity to cheer himself up, smiling at the old lady. 'Hello, Mrs. Hudson,' he said, before casting a dismissive eye to Juliet. 'If there's nothing else, Miss Rayne?'

Juliet let the breath out, and said, 'Fine, whatever,' before grabbing Robert by the coat sleeve and pulling him out of the shop. As she walked into the cool October afternoon, she looked like she wanted to cry. 'What are we gonna do now?'

'Well ...' Robert said, as his mind started thinking of solutions his heart wanted to block. 'We'll have to contact the fancy butchers who use fresh pigs blood. Ask them where they get it from, and then contact them.'

Juliet nodded, trying to be strong. 'Right.'

'But first, St. Luke's.'

Juliet's eyes widened desperately, and she turned to Robert. 'What? No. Please, we need to sort out this blood problem.'

Robert closed his eyes and tried to contain his impatience. 'Jules, the reason this happened is because Aaron relied on holy water that didn't work. Now, we still have the small business of hunting the vampires in this town that we *aren't* keeping as bloody pets, so—'

Juliet slapped Robert, hard, on the cheek.

He stopped, feeling the side of his face, now stinging. 'Woah. Not okay, Jules.'

She was shaking. Tears formed in her eyes, and she softened. 'I'm sorry,' she said. 'I'm sorry. Please, Rob, I'm sorry.'

Robert's chest was tight, and he wanted to scream at her, that what they were doing was crazy, and wrong. But he didn't. 'Okay,' he said. 'Look, I'm sorry I called him a pet. I didn't mean that.'

Juliet nodded, still being strong.

'Listen, why don't you go and Google the fresh blood thing, and I'll go to St. Luke's?'

'You're not going to help me?'

'It's just Googling, and making a few phone calls.'

'I guess ...' Juliet said, though she didn't sound convinced. She tilted her head a little, and stepped toward Robert, putting her hand to his cheek where it was red from her slap. 'Please, help me, Rob. I don't think I can do this on my own. And, if I can't get blood sorted by sundown, I'm going to have to come up with a plan for him for tonight.'

Robert loved her so dearly, so completely, that he could barely stand the idea of telling her no, to anything. But then he thought about the slap. He thought about the ears she'd taken from the late Sara Bradshaw. And he thought about the deer they'd sacrificed, so that their former friend could drink its blood. All of those thoughts pushed him to do the thing he hated doing.

'Sorry,' he said. 'No. No, I need to sort the holy water thing out. I'll be back to help you when I've got something to go on. Okay?'

She did her strong nod a third time, only this time her mouth quivered and broke into a sob, and her shoulders drooped, as she began to cry. 'I'm so sorry.'

He stepped toward her and wrapped his arms around her, while she nuzzled into his chest, weeping, and apologising. He shushed her, and rubbed her hair tenderly. He hated it. He despised every moment of it. To be so close to her, but so irrelevant. As she took comfort from him, *he* wanted to be the one for whom she went to such lengths. *He* wanted to be the one she would compromise herself for.

'Okay, listen,' he said. 'I'll help you, until Aaron's blood for tonight is sorted. After that, I'm going to the church.'

†

Tilly was scrolling through her Instagram feed as she shuffled into the church, the line in single file.

'Put that away!' hissed Mr. Willis at her, once they were inside.

'Yes,' came a slow, malty voice from the middle of the room.

Tilly looked up, to see the new parish priest of St. Luke's. He was a tall, pale, dark haired figure of a man, who looked like he needed to eat a few burgers. He was wearing the traditional black suit with the creepy collar, and he grinned at the children in a way that made Tilly's blood run cold.

'You will have no need of your telephones here,' he said, with a thick accent that Tilly didn't recognise—though it reminded her a bit of the characters in Neighbours. He stepped towards the children, cleared his throat with a cough, and said, 'For, this saccharin, old church, you will find, is a place of endless fascination, for those who are graced with eyes to see, and with ears to hear.'

Tilly dead stared at the guy, and said, 'For God's sake I am so sick of creepy ass shit in my life right now.'

CHAPTER SEVEN
Father William Izzard-Sinnett

'My name is Father William Izzard-Sinnett,' the disturbing, lanky priest said, addressing the five dozen pupils, watching him silently. 'You may call me Father William. I look forward to getting to know each and every one of you.'

'Father William's busy, getting used to the parish,' said Mr. Willis, Lilly's form tutor. 'So, you're all to get into two groups per form, and report to your tutors for your activity schedules. We're going to do rubbings, glass colourings, a brief gospel study, and finally Father William wants to give you a talk.'

'Jesus this is going to be slow,' Tilly said, leaning toward Laura.

'I know,' she agreed. 'And because the groups are based on our form groups, we can't even double up with the boys.'

'Come on,' Tilly said, nodding in the direction of the party of children gathering near Mr. Willis.

Laura waved daintily at Gemma Read, one of the girls in their group, and bounced toward her for a chat, so Tilly took the opportunity to look around. She didn't like St. Luke's particularly. She was fortunate enough to have a father who wasn't religious—a rare enough thing in Ecclesburn—so she wasn't forced to come to this place every Sunday like so many of her friends.

But none of that was to say that she didn't find the building kind of eerily fascinating. The founders of Ecclesburn had built the church, hundreds of years ago, so it felt *old*, in a way that was almost unique in the town, which had had multiple renovations, just in the few years Tilly had been alive.

Laura dragged over Gemma Read, pulling her by the hand. They seemed electrified by excitement.

'Is all this true?' Gemma asked.

'All what?' Tilly asked.

Gemma leaned forward. 'You saw a vampire?' she whispered eagerly.

Tilly blinked a few times, unsure of what to say. 'I guess there's no reason we shouldn't talk about it?' she said, looking to Laura.

'That's the way I see it,' Laura said.

'I think the others might deny it,' Tilly said, focusing now on Gemma. 'They're all a bit freaked. Especially Jenny and Tom. They got chased by it.'

Gemma's face turned a little pale. 'Woah.'

'Listen,' Tilly said. 'I think we should do something. You know, figure out how to ... fight them. But everyone else is all casual. I'm right, right? We shouldn't be able to live with ourselves if we know they're out there, but do nothing about it?'

'Well, you know what people say, right?' Gemma said. 'There are people who *do* fight them. Here, in town. Vampire hunters, they are. I heard my parents talking about it once, when they thought I was in bed.'

Tilly couldn't help but be intrigued. 'Vampire hunters?' she said, imaging who they might be; what exotic, extravagant lives they might lead. 'Who are they?'

†

'God I hate Google,' Robert sighed, reaching for his glass of water, as he sat at the desk in the wide, oaky study of Rayne Manor.

'You're better at it than me,' Juliet said over his shoulder.

'Basically, most of this is about buying dried blood, like Mr. Knight said. That's no good. And the problem with fresh blood is that it coagulates, like, within a couple of hours.'

'What does that mean?'

'Um, it becomes, like, almost a solid,' Robert explained. 'So, no good.'

'Rob ... I really don't want to be bringing live animals to the house every night.'

'Neither do I, but it's gonna consume our lives, getting enough blood for him, and getting it, like, an hour before he needs it? Every day? It's a crazy commitment. It'll take over your life.'

'So, what? I should just go in there and stake him? Because he's inconvenient?'

'No, I'm not saying that, I'm just saying ... it's gonna take over your life, is all.'

'That's fine,' she said, turning away so that she could pull a chair over and sit down. 'When you meet the person you love, more than anyone else in the world, nothing is too much trouble. You'd understand if you'd ever been in love.'

The words struck Robert, in the gut, and in the chest.

'So, what do I have to do?' Juliet said, oblivious.

'Well,' Robert said, swallowing his pain, 'we're going to have to make friendly with one of the farmers on the outskirts of town. One of the slaughterhouse guys. We find out when they slaughter their pigs, their cows, and we go buy some fresh blood.'

'And we have two hours to get it back from there to Aaron? We could take him, if they do their slaughtering after sundown?'

'Oh, sure, we'll just explain that we're bringing our quirky vampire friend for an all you can eat bloodbath buffet?'

Juliet rubbed her face, as though trying to alleviate the stress right out of it. 'He'll just have to get used to feeding on their schedule,' she said.

'The thing is, they won't slaughter animals every day, but Aaron'll need fresh blood every day. So ... we'll need a schedule set up, for, like, seven different farms.'

'Jesus,' Juliet sighed. 'Okay, so ... let's start making a list of farms, and making a note of when they kill their animals, and then start making calls. Yeah?'

'Jules ... I think that can wait, right now.'

'What are you talking about?'

'Sun'll go down in a few hours. Aaron's going to get hungry. If we don't find something for him to eat, he'll kill. You know he will. And, if he does that, we'll have to ... do that thing you don't want to consider.'

'Oh, bloody shitting pissbags,' Juliet moaned. She ran her hands through her hair, still trying and failing to get rid of the pressure within her. 'Okay. So ... I guess, let's go animal hunting?'

†

'No one knows who they are,' Gemma Read told Tilly. 'But plenty of other kids have heard about them, it's not just me. Like, Chrissie Jones swears blind her big sister was in the year below them, at Cardinal Manning.'

'The vampire hunters went to our school?' Tilly asked.

'Well, obvs,' Gemma said. 'It's the only school in town.'

'Yeah, all the unsolved missing persons cases really keep the classrooms from getting overcrowded,' Tilly quipped.

'But the point is, you don't have to fight monsters, because there are people out there doing it already.'

'I wonder ...' Laura said, speaking slowly, as though deep in contemplation, 'maybe it was them, last night? Maybe they caught the vampire that was about to kill Harry?'

'The vampire was going to kill Harry?' Gemma said, her eyes curling with sadness at the thought. She made a heart shape with her fingers and thumbs and pulled it front of her actual heart, lowering her bottom lip in a show of concern. Then, she cheered, a naughty glint in her eye. 'Thank God it failed, right girls? Harry Fox equals yum.'

'What do you think, Till?' Laura teased. 'Is Harry yum, or just ... meh?'

'Laulau, one day, you will realise that all boys, underneath the nice outer layers, are emphatically *meh*.'

'They do have nice outer layers,' Laura said, taking the opportunity to stare adoringly at Mark through the crowd.

'But vampire hunting is serious,' Tilly said, putting her hands on her hips, trying to make herself tall. 'And I bet, wherever they are, Chrissie Jones's big sister's vampire hunting buddies would agree. Only a terribly shallow loser would put boys ahead of fighting monsters.'

†

'Okay, listen,' Robert said from the passenger seat of Juliet's Audi A5 Cabriolet as they headed into town, 'I chose World of Pets for more than one reason.'

Juliet kept her eyes on the road. 'Okay?'

'It's right over the island from St. Luke's.'

'Oh, bloody hell, Rob, you said you were going to be *with* me.'

'Look, you don't need me with you to pick out a couple of rabbits, right? Just, go in, coo at the pretty ones, and try and go for ones that're at least kind of old.'

'Great, so I'm the angel of rabbit death, all by myself. Fantastic. What are you even going to do when you get there? Are you just going to say, "Hey, creepy priest, why didn't your holy water work?"'

'I've got a plan, alright. Jules, I wanted to do this yesterday. But what did I do instead?'

Juliet didn't want to answer, so she stalled. 'You, you—'

'I followed you into Undertown, swam in some excrement, and ate a cat called Henrietta Boffin. *That's* what I did.'

'You didn't eat *all* of it,' Juliet said.

'And now, instead of investigating why my friend got turned into a vampire, I'm coming with you, arguing with grouchy arsed butchers and going to buy the least offensive vampire feed we can find.'

'Okay! I get it. Christ!'

Robert let the moment pass, watching Juliet as she drove. 'Thank you,' he said finally, as Juliet entered the World of Pets car park. 'Listen, when you're done, come and find me in the church. And, I promise you, for the rest of the evening and first thing tomorrow we can go about making contact with some farmers.'

Juliet did the brave nod again, the one Robert was growing accustomed to. Her vulnerability was like Kryptonite to him, so he was happy that she'd been combative, or he wondered whether he'd have had the strength to actually leave her to do something by herself for fifteen minutes.

'Thanks,' she said, straightening herself out, as she parked. 'I'll be fine. I'll see you in St. Luke's.' She smiled. 'Go find out what the deal is with this new priest and his crappy holy water.'

Robert gave her an approving nod, and almost put his hand on her knee, before he caught himself. After letting himself relax a little, he said, 'Cool.'

†

Tilly was paying no attention to the rubbing she was supposed to be doing. Mr. Willis didn't seem to care. He was focusing on the losers who were busily getting stuck into the activity and pretending to love it, so as to gain his favour. Tilly didn't judge them for it. She could see the benefits. She just couldn't be arsed.

She was far more busy looking around, and wondering: why do the people of Ecclesburn run to religion to deal with the existence of vampires? She was of the mind that, should God exist, and should he be the Catholic God and not one of the other gods, if he's at all interested in providing protection from vampires, why doesn't he just squish them all?

She directed a thought at him, accepting that he did exist just long enough to hear her: 'if you can hear me, explain why vampires exist, and why people think you give a shit about it'.

She waited, her eyebrows up, but no great spiritual answer came.

'Oh well,' she said to herself.

She glanced around again. The whole church seemed to be going through a process of renovation, just like the rest of Ecclesburn had done. Tilly caught herself reflecting sadly upon this, and the realisation surprised her. She wouldn't have considered herself at all conservative, but with the church being the one part of the town that hadn't been modernised, she lamented briefly its former self being replaced.

'And what is your name?' came that creepy-as-all-hell, almost Australian voice.

'Um ... Tilly,' she said, looking up at the towering figure. She quizzed him with her eyes. 'Where are you from?'

'East London,' he said with a squinty smile.

'You don't sound like you're from London?'

'East London, Eastern Cape.'

'Huh?'

'South Africa, young miss,' the priest said. Then, he looked curious. 'What's Tilly short for?'

'Matilda. Turnbull.'

'A fine name. Named for the famous, fictitious child-witch?'

There was something about the way Father William looked at her that made the question seem highly passive aggressive. Tilly was aware of the fact that she'd have been terrified of him, had she not been surrounded by her friends and teachers. Nevertheless, she chose to be bold in that safety. 'Matilda wasn't a witch, dude. She was telekinetic.'

Father William laughed, and then coughed, and began to crouch down to her level. 'I will take you at your word on that,' he said, eyeing her with such interest that she wanted to wear a mask or run and hide. 'Dude,' he added ironically.

'Anyway, no, I wasn't named after her.'

'It is probably for the best,' Father William said, still crouching. 'From memory, I seem to recall that she was something of a needlessly defiant child.'

'Oh, I'm plenty defiant.'

Father William laughed, and turned his head, examining her even more curiously. 'Oh, I'm sure.' Now, his smile faded, and his eyes intensified sharply. It was almost like he was trying to *scare* her. 'Stay your wandering eye, and return to your rubbing.'

Tilly chose not to be intimidated. She stared back at him, just long enough for him to understand she wasn't frightened of him, and then said, 'Churches are boring anyway.'

†

Robert pulled open the great, big church door and entered to the familiar smell of centuries of incense smoke having penetrated all of the wood, and the cushions. Robert loved the smell. It was the thing that made him feel safer than anything else in the world. Sometimes, he'd come to St. Luke's just for the smell.

He was disappointed, though, to see school kids all over the place. It looked like they were on a field trip. Their familiar blue school blazers evoked memories of his own time at Cardinal Manning, which he had left behind only a little over a year ago.

He spotted the new priest, Father William Izzard-Sinnett, who was wandering slowly among the children, watching them the way a wolf watches sheep.

It gave him a chill.

He shook it away, and made his way over to him. 'Father William?' he said.

The priest looked up. 'Ah ... young Mr. Entwistle, isn't it? Back, so soon?'

'Yeah ... I was wondering, if you have some time, whether you're free for a bit of a sit down and a chat?'

Father William looked at Robert in such a way that Robert couldn't decide whether it was reflective of the priest's curiosity, or his *suspicion*.

'I am required to deliver a message from the Lord to the children, shortly. But ... I believe I am prepared. I can spare you a half hour?'

'Perfect, thank you.'

Father William's face relaxed, just a little. 'Please, follow me.'

The tall, odd priest led Robert down toward the front of the church, past the altar, and out of the main part of the building, into much more homely corridors. There were pictures of Christ on the walls, and of the Virgin Mary, and various other, less important religious characters.

'Would you like tea?' Father William offered. 'I love the tea here.'

'I'm good, thanks,' Robert replied, taking his phone out and quickly texting Juliet: 'In the back of the church with the priest, wait for me.' He clicked it off and slid it back into his pocket.

'Very well, young man,' Father William said, heading into a quaint living room. The priest sat down into an armchair, and gestured towards a sofa to Robert, who also sat. 'What can I help you with?'

Robert took a deep breath. 'Well, I'm thinking about becoming a priest.'

†

When Juliet reached the front door of St. Luke's, she wondered how she was going to even open the door. She had in her arms a big, brown and white, nicely ventilated rabbit carrier, containing two chirpy-yet-fragile bunnies. 'Hmmm ...' she said thoughtfully.

'D'you need a hand, love?' came a friendly enough male voice from behind her.

Juliet stepped back so she could turn around, albeit awkwardly. She didn't recognise the man, who threw a cigarette on the floor, stepped on it, and walked over. He stank of smoke.

'Here, let me help you,' he said, opening the door for her.

Juliet shifted the rabbit carrier a little in her arms, easing the pain in her fingers a little. 'Thank you,' she muttered over the top of it, making her way in.

'T'aww, they look like happy little bunnies,' the smoker said from behind her.

Juliet gritted her teeth, and tried to turn around. He was standing in the door, still holding it open. 'What's that?' she said, pretending she hadn't heard him.

'Your rabbits. They look happy.' He leaned down and poked at the box. 'Hello there. Hello.' He looked up. 'What are their names?'

'What?'

'Their names, what are they?'

'Oh. I, um, I haven't named them yet, actually.'

'They look old, didn't they already have—'

'Look, I'm sorry, but they're quite heavy, and I want to find my friend. Thank you for helping me with the door, but'—she nodded her head inside the church.

'Oh. Of course.'

'Thanks.' Juliet turned to enter the church.

'Just, remember.'

Juliet sighed and stopped again.

'You should find out what their names were before. They're fully grown. You shouldn't rename a rabbit.'

'Okay, will do!' she shouted over her shoulder, as she made her way into the church and started looking around for Robert.

†

'Is that so?' Father William said. 'How long have you been feeling this way?'

'Ever since I left school,' Robert lied. 'I've always felt quite close to God.'

'Yes?'

'But over the last year I've been feeling ... called.'

Father William took the word "called" very well indeed. He smiled, and crossed one leg over the other. 'Go on.'

'Well, I was hoping you could give me some pointers. How does a young man ... go about becoming a priest?'

'Well, you must understand, it is a lengthy process. One cannot simply go to some seminary and *become* a priest.'

Robert nodded.

'A man must enter first into a period of reflection and discernment, along with his parish priest, and the bishop of his diocese.'

'Okay, so that'd be you, and ...'

'Bishop Powell. If, after the period of discernment, the three of us discover that you are indeed being called to serve God's church, you will enter the Propaedeutic Year. After that, again, if all goes well, you will enter the Formation Course.'

'Should I be writing this down,' Robert asked.

'No, I shouldn't say so,' Father William said. 'You have already taken the first step, which is to come to the wisdom of your parish priest. I shall make contact with Bishop Powell, and together we shall pray for guidance in this matter.'

Robert smiled, faking humility. 'Okay.' He memorised the name "Bishop Powell", and climbed to his feet. 'I want you to know, Father William, I feel very deeply about this. I think it's right.'

Father William smiled in his unsettling way, and joined Robert in standing, coughing a little. 'That is a good start. We will see what the bishop feels, and, in due course, I will arrange a meeting with him, so that you may meet him in person. Now, is there anything else, young Robert?'

'Actually, yeah. Could I trouble you for some more—'

'Ah!' Father William said, smiling broadly. 'You want some more holy water, don't you?'

'I do.'

'Of course, young man. Do you know, I had heard tales of the sheer volumes of the sacramental required by the people in this parish, but I hadn't actually believed it could be true.' He tilted his head curiously. 'Tell me, what do you intend to use it for?'

Robert winced. 'Do you ... not know?'

'I've heard rumours, of course.'

'Here, in Ecclesburn, we're kind of ... overly cautious.'

'There are of course good Christians who believe that ... the vampire, is a sort of Anti-Eucharist.'

Robert's eyebrows shot up, surprised at hearing the V word come from the priest's mouth.

'Vampires consume blood in order to secure an undead eternity,' Father William explained. '*We* consume the blood of our Lord in order to secure a living eternity, with him.'

Robert had never thought about the connection before. He couldn't help but feel a prick of interest. 'Fascinating,' he said earnestly.

'Well, as I said, there *are* Christians who are quite zealous about it, but not where I come from. I've never really believed in literal tekkies.'

Robert gave a confused look. 'Trainers?'

'Tokoloshes,' Father William said. 'Evil spirits. In the flesh. Not my cup of tea. Nevertheless, please, if it quietens your spirit, take the sacramental liberally from my font, in the church.'

'Thank you, Father William,' Robert said. He had been thoroughly disarmed. Father William had seemed strange and unsettling when Robert had first met him, but this meeting had been another matter entirely. 'God bless you,' he said, playing the good Catholic for good measure, as he made his way out, and away.

†

Tilly was taking the opportunity afforded to her by a short break between boring sessions to have a look around the church. There wasn't much going on. The scary priest had disappeared somewhere, and her teachers seemed to have lost interest and were outside smoking every chance they got.

As she wandered from one area to another, she spotted a young woman, sitting on one of the pews at the front of the church. It looked like she was looking at her phone. Tilly made herself quiet and walked quickly down the centre aisle, toward her, leaning her head as she went.

Before she got to the front, a door opened to the right of the altar and a young man came out. He was quite handsome, in a kind of moody, romantic way, and he was followed by Father William.

Instinctively, Tilly ran down between the benches, a few rows back from the young woman. Then, in order to hide, she knelt on the little cushion on the floor, made the sign of the cross, and closed her eyes.

'I got your text,' the young woman said. 'How was it? What happened?'

Tilly opened one eye. The priest had disappeared off somewhere, leaving the young couple alone at the front of the church.

'I'm not really too sure,' the man said. 'I thought for sure he'd be weirder than he was. I see you got the, um, the rabbits.'

'I feel like an absolute monster,' the woman said. 'They're so cute.'

'Don't think about it,' the man said, and paused. Then, he said, more quietly, 'Anyway, we should go. Sundown's in a few hours. The priest said I can take as much holy water as I want.'

Tilly's eyes were still closed, but she couldn't prevent an eyebrow from rising.

'Okay,' the woman said. 'You can carry these rabbits.'

Tilly opened one eye again, and watched as the couple made their way down the centre aisle, until they passed her. Then, Tilly saw Laura, who passed the couple, and came to join Tilly.

'Do you know who that was?' Laura said, her eyes wide and bright.

Tilly shook her head, still being instinctively quiet.

'That was Juliet Rayne.'

'The rich girl who used to go to Cardinal Manning?' Tilly asked.

Laura nodded, still excited.

'The guy she was with said they were allowed to take holy water,' Tilly said.

Laura's eyes had never been wider. 'Holy water?'

'Yep. Now, tell me. When did Chrissie Jones's sister graduate sixth form?'

'I don't know, but I like where your mind is going,' Laura said.

Tilly smiled. 'Let's go ask her, hey? And then, we can find out when Juliet Rayne graduated. Because I'm betting pretty heavily that it was the year before.'

'So. Exciting.'

'I know right? Come on, let's go.'

†

'Oh, hey,' Chrissie Jones said to Tilly and Laura.

The girls looked at each other, confused, and then back at Chrissie. 'You seem ... angry?'

'Well, did you both, or did you not, go out after dark with the football players and their mates last night?'

'Um ... yeah?' Tilly said.

'Fine,' Chrissie said. 'I figured, surely, if you guys *did* go, you'd have told me about it. I mean, Laulau, you *know* how many times I've talked to you about Alfie. And, I bet he was there. And, like, why wouldn't you tell me about that?'

'Um, we're sorry?' Tilly said, failing to come off as even mildly genuine.

'Look, it wasn't nailed on that *we'd* get to go,' Laura said, 'so, like, I couldn't open it up too much, and, like, well, I...'

'You what?' Chrissie asked, folding her arms.

'I really wanted to go.'

Chrissie gave an angry smiley nod. 'That's fantastic.'

'Listen, Chrissie,' Tilly said, 'we're super sorry that we didn't invite you, but ... well, have you heard about what happened last night?'

'Oh God, did Alfie get off with someone? Was it Grace?'

'What? No. No, I mean, have you heard about what happened, with the'—Tilly looked both ways and leaned forward—'with the vampire.'

Chrissie's face conveyed absolutely nothing. It was almost pure, in its utter vacancy. 'Huh?'

'We saw a vampire,' Tilly said. 'It had these bright red eyes, and a big, bumpy forehead, and huge fangs.'

Chrissie wasn't buying it. 'Oh. Sure! Of course.'

'Look, believe it, or don't. I don't care. What I want to know is, when did your big sister leave Cardinal Manning?'

'Mandy? Last summer. Why?'

'She left *sixth form* last summer?' Tilly said.

'Yeah. Why?'

'No reason,' Tilly said cheerily, before pulling Laura's arm.

Laura resisted, and turned to to Chrissie. 'Look, if I get a chance to make it up to you, I will. We're talking about doing something on Halloween. Come to that.'

'Laulau, come on,' Tilly said.

'No, listen, it's fine you guys,' Chrissie said, brighter now for the mention of Halloween. 'Nice necklaces, by the way.'

Tilly gave Chrissie an impatient smile and pulled Laura away, before pulling her jumper up over the necklace. 'Okay,' she said, 'we need to find out when Juliet Rayne left Cardinal Manning, and I definitely wanna snag some of that holy water too.'

'Right,' Laura said, as the two girls walked back to their group.

†

Robert sighed and sat back in his office chair, tired and stressed from the day, when Juliet came and placed a bottle of San Miguel next to him. 'What's this for?' he said, picking it up.

'Just for helping me,' she said.

Robert drank. It was just what he needed. Cold, fizzy, and strong enough to alleviate *some* of the pressure within him. 'Thanks.' He looked out of the window, at the fading sunlight landing on the Barrington Cliffs in the scenic distance, and said, 'Not long now.'

'I know.'

'There's a slaughterhouse in Cockerham. We can go every day. Aaron'll only need about two wine bottles' worth. It should be fine.'

Juliet nodded, her face tense.

'Where are the, um, the rabbits?'

'In the cage, downstairs, by the cellar door.'

'Think of it like the bacon you made this morning,' Robert said, though even he didn't really buy it.

Juliet rested on the table next to Robert, and buried her head in her hands. Slowly, painfully, her shoulders started going up and down, and she began to weep. After a moment, the quiet crying turned into long sobs with awful gasps, all while she covered her face.

Robert reached out his hand and held it over her knee, not touching her. Just making himself *ready* to touch her.

'Can I ask you something,' he said, 'without you getting upset?'

Juliet opened her hands from in front of her face, and dried her cheeks with the fluted black lace sleeve of her dress. She looked confused. 'What?'

Robert withdrew his hand and rested it on the arm of his chair. 'I wanted to ask you something. Something I've been wondering. Something that confuses me. That's always confused me.'

'Okay?'

'What do you ... I mean, I don't always fully understand, what do you see in Aaron?'

She didn't react. She just carried on looking at him, waiting for him to make sense.

'You don't seem suited, to me,' he said. 'You didn't seem suited in school, and you don't seem suited now.'

'What are you saying? You think I'm not good enough for your friend, is that it?'

'Jesus, Jules, no. You have it ... you have it all backwards.'

She looked at him, still confused, but Robert couldn't help but wonder if she was beginning to understand.

'You're smart, and sharp, and, like, aware of things,' Robert said, avoiding eye contact now. 'You have a depth, that I, just, never really felt Aaron had.'

'Present tense, please.'

'*Has*, that Aaron has.'

'You think I have a depth?' she said.

The scrutiny was too much, her eyes, looking at him, observing him in his vulnerability, so he let out a long breath, scratched his head, and climbed off his chair to go and rest against the wall, a few feet further away. 'What do you love about him?'

It was Juliet's turn to look uneasy. 'I, um ... I love that he ... he keeps me safe.'

'Okay?'

'I don't just mean that he, well, you know, that he keeps me safe physically. I mean, he keeps me safe emotionally. You know?'

'Not really?'

'Well, after my parents died, he was there for me. You know? He dropped everything, he skived school, he got into trouble with his parents, and he was there for me. Always.'

'Okay. What else?'

'I'd be dead, a bunch of times over, if it weren't for him. Like, I trust him with my life, when we're hunting, and he's literally *saved* my life more times than I could count.'

'Anything else?'

Juliet looked bleakly at Robert, and her eyes moistened again. 'I failed him. I shouldn't have let him go down into that cellar on his own. I should have remembered what you said about the holy water. I should have been able to anticipate ... what was going to happen.'

Robert took a few steps toward Juliet, but stayed at a safe distance. 'Okay. Now, tell me why you love him, but you're not allowed to mention what he's done for you, or why you've let him down.'

Juliet looked like she didn't have an answer, which is just what Robert was expecting, *and* what he was hoping for.

Her gaze dropped to the floor, and she looked so sad.

Robert wanted to move the conversation on, so he looked out of the window, at the gloomy evening, and then headed toward the office bookshelf, glancing at the titles only a moment, choosing quickly a few that he thought a vampire might enjoy. 'Come on,' he said, 'it's time.'

CHAPTER EIGHT
The Rayne Helsingers

He didn't know who he was, but the name Aaron McLeary didn't seem to fit anymore. It seemed so ... pedestrian, so mundane, so empty. For, the creature he was now was not the same as the creature he was before. He could, for instance, hear sounds he'd never heard before, and see sights he'd never seen before. He was aware of pain he'd never felt before. Not psychical pain, of course. For, now, he could feel his incredible invulnerability. He could feel the power within him, the intense, overflowing *rivers* of power, which would allow him to heal in a moment an injury that would, in life, have taken months.

It seemed so cosmically ironic, then, when he considered in the next moment his intense *vulnerability*. For, if one of the humans were to merely cover him in holy water, or put a sharp piece of wood through his heart, he would vanish from the earth, forever.

Forever.

On the one hand, he had an eternity. On the other, he was in greater danger of death than he'd ever been.

This seemed unfair, somehow.

It was the vampire formerly known as Aaron McLeary's second night waking as an unholy fiend, and the painful, desperate clawing from within him for blood made him contemplate killing Juliet and Robert, just so that they might fight back and kill *him*.

For death, he realised, was infinitely more appealing than the *hunger*.

He felt attacked, even though no one was in the room. He felt like there were tiny, microscopic demons, underneath every millimetre of his skin, screaming at him like the devil, to *kill*, and to *eat*. Begging him to kill, to commit murder.

'Blood ... is life,' he said aloud, by accident.

He curled his fingers into fists, and allowed his face to reshape. He was growing accustomed to the change. It was like what picking up a knife and fork had been *before*. It signalled intent. To eat.

To *eat*.

The act had never carried such importance. It was simple, before. You get hungry, you eat. Now, though. Now, it was connected to his very core, the part of himself that truly *was*. You *are* your hunger, and you *are* your eating.

Memories from his life were returning to him. Memories which, when they were lived, had seemed incredibly unimportant. He remembered, for example, his philosophy teacher talking about existential nihilism. It had *all* seemed so dull then, but now? Now, it made sense, as though someone had shown him how the universe itself works, and fits together.

'Existence is meaningless,' he said, plucking words from the memory as easily as low hanging apples from a tree. 'Life ... has no intrinsic value. No value. Life has no value.'

With that thought echoing around his head, he heard the cellar door open, and footsteps, making their way down toward him.

†

'Stay behind me,' Robert whispered, carrying the two squirming rabbits and a bag over his shoulder, as Juliet followed him down the stairs.

'You don't need to whisper,' Juliet said. 'He's a vampire now.   He can hear your heartbeat, let alone your whispering.'

'Oh yeah,' Robert said, as he stepped into the cellar.

Juliet followed and flicked the light on.

'Aaron, mate?' Robert said. 'Where are you?'

'I am here,' came Aaron's voice, at the far end of the room, behind a low stone wall. 'Please, put out the light. I mean you no harm.'

'Oh, you mean us no harm?' Robert repeated, almost mocking Aaron's new, loftier way of speaking.

The light in the room dulled. Robert turned around to see Juliet stood with her hand on the dimmer switch.

'Did you bring ... food?' Aaron said. 'You brought something, didn't you.'

'You can't ... smell them, or whatever?' Robert said, squeezing the rabbits into his chest.   'Or hear their heartbeats?'

'I can.'

Robert caught Aaron peering at him in a way he'd never done when he was alive. It was like he was inspecting him. 'So you were just clarifying that they were in fact food, then?' the frightened young man said, to the creature that used to be his friend.

'I see you,' Aaron said, stepping a little closer to Robert. 'I see your desire. It dances upon your skin like Afro-Brasileiros swaying a lambada.' His face turned, becoming not demonic, but hostile. 'I *see* you.'

'Aaron ...' Juliet said. 'Talk sense, baby. Please.'

Aaron's attention switched to her, and, as it did, Robert's attention sharpened. 'Aaron, we have blood,' he said, feeling the rabbits, hearing their shrill squeaks. 'We have fresh blood.'

'And I hear the pain of you,' Aaron said, eyeing Juliet like *she* was the food. 'It is deep, deep within your chest, and within your gut. Isn't it?'

'I just ... I just want you back again,' Juliet said, nearing him.

'I see it now,' Aaron went on. 'I can *feel* it. The darkness. The void in you. But it is not what you think it is. It is not what *I* thought it *was*. It is your solitude, isn't it? The thing that drives you, that makes you come to me again. Not for *me*. Not for *us*. But for *you*.'

Juliet was in tears again now, and holding them back a lot less ably than she had before. 'Aaron, baby, please.' She reached out for him.

But he growled, and turned to Robert. 'Give me the fucking rabbits,' he said, snatching the bunnies out of Robert's hands without him barely even noticing it.

There was a muted squeak, and then the sound of lapping, like a dog at its bowl. Robert watched as his friend drank blood from a grey and white bunny rabbit while clutching to its brown companion, and he couldn't help but want to throw holy water over the fiend and have done with it.

'Come on,' Robert said, taking Juliet's hand and pulling her toward the stairs. She was stunned, like a woman who'd fallen out of another world, having lost everything she held dear. Robert ushered her up the stairs in front of him, and then turned to Aaron. 'Here,' he said, reaching into the bag over his shoulder. He pulled out everything inside, except for one vial of Father McMahon's holy water, and tossed it onto Aaron's bed. 'I brought you your phone, and some books. The phone's charged.'

Aaron dropped the grey and white rabbit, and proceeded to bite into the brown. He said nothing. He offered nothing. Neither a word, nor a gesture, of thanks, or of anything else.

'You're welcome,' Robert said ironically, and began up the stairs, and away.

†

It was late. After eleven, and Tilly was still awake. She'd had an exhaustive evening at her computer, diving into the world of online vampire hunter communities. She had made a few contacts, and she'd even sort of made a friend. She had found out about a number of weapons people use to slay vampires, and, perhaps most interestingly of all, she'd found out a lot about Juliet Rayne.

Yet, her eyes were heavy now, and sore from staring at her monitor.

She blinked a few times, and started going through her windows and applications, saving her notes, closing her conversations and her tabs, and finally shutting the computer down.

She yawned, and climbed into bed, stopping only to play "The Unforgiving", by Within Temptation on Amazon Music, on her phone. She turned the album down so it was just a quiet, soothing sound, and slowly drifted off to sleep.

†

Many hours had passed, and all Aaron could think of now, was the sunrise. True, he was safe. He was safely underneath Juliet's grand home, where he had once, in another life, lived. The sunrise would not touch him. And yet he was *aware* of it. His senses were already reacting to it. It felt like the sensation you feel before you sneeze, when the humming in your nose grows, and then explodes.

Only, there was no explosion.

There was just the humming.

It made him want to hide, even further and more securely than he *was* hiding, so he made his way to his bed and covered himself, while his mind went to the words he had spent the night reading.

Aaron couldn't help but wonder if Robert had been taunting him. For, before, Robert would have never given him *The Symposium*, by Plato, to read. Robert would have assumed Aaron had no mind for it. The two of them, though they had been friends, had never been intellectual equals. Aaron had never desired to be, for that matter.

And the book itself, a conversational treatise on love, and desire, seemed to Aaron now like a bite of the thumb—as though Robert was bragging, that he, in the world above, got to spend his days, out in the cool October sun, with the woman whom they *both* loved, whom they *both* desired.

For that was clear to Aaron. It was as clear to him as it was clear that his body was dead. Robert was in love with his Juliet. He'd never seen it before, though it seemed so obvious now. And Aaron was fairly certain that Juliet, though her love for Robert was profound, was oblivious to it as well. He would hold onto that, and bide his time.

And as he closed his eyes, to rest, those trumped up Socratic ideas went round and round in his head:

Love is desire.

Desire is created by lack, and so one cannot desire what one already possesses.

Therefore, one can only love what one does not possess.

'Neither of us possesses her now ...' he said quietly, toward the Robert in his mind. 'Neither of us possesses her yet.'

†

Tilly Turnbull was in a world of her own, as she ate her Frosties at the breakfast table, with her oddly cheerful father and her typically grouchy grandmother. Her mind was busy with speculative thoughts about vampires. For instance, how do you kill them? And what is with the connection to Catholicism? Tilly had always taken for granted that religion was nonsense, and she didn't enjoy that assumption being challenged.

Yet, vampires were real. That was now a confirmed fact. Juliet Rayne and her friend had taken holy water from St. Luke's. That was a fact too. So, with her suspicions about Juliet Rayne being a vampire hunter being confirmed, she would have to accept that holy water, at least, was an effective weapon against vampires, which meant: religion must have some clout in the fight against the undead.

She sighed at the thought.

'What are your plans for half term, Till?' her father said, looking up from his phone, his eyebrows raised and his tone pleasant.

Tilly eyed him with scepticism, curious as to his chipper mood. 'I dunno,' she said.

'Well, don't waste it in your room on your computer the whole time,' he said.

Tilly felt mildly affronted. She didn't like being told what to do. She looked at her grandmother, who was oblivious, reading something on her iPad, and then back at her father. 'I might go and see the new Thor, I guess. And just ... hang out with Laura. I haven't really thought about it.'

The truth of course was that she was planning to investigate vampires. Not that she could share that with her family over cereal.

'Well, it's a beautiful day out. Just don't waste it sitting in your room, or in a dark cinema.' After this second piece of unsolicited advice, Tilly's father smiled to himself and got back to his phone.

She wanted to tell him to get lost with his suggestions, but she let it go, and was about to get back to thinking about vampires, when her phone pinged.

It was a text from Harry: 'hey hows u? what u up to?'

Tilly sighed, and texted back: 'nothing why?' After she sent it, she regretted it. She'd intended to be dismissive, but reading it back she realised it came off like she was leading him to ask her to do something.

He replied: 'u wanna hang out with us?'

She scratched the back of her neck and thought about the best way to let him down, when another text arrived, from Laura this time: 'till we have to hang out with the boys today, u in?? xx'

'But my incapacitating misanthropy ...' she whined to herself, under her breath. She sighed, and text Laura: 'fine ok. whats happening?'

Her phone pinged: 'we're going back to cleve woods xx'

Tilly accepted it. She figured it might actually present her with an opportunity, to investigate the scene, so she sent a thumbs up emoji to Laura, and then started typing a positive response to Harry.

†

'Wait, why did you tell him you wanted to be a priest?' Juliet asked, as she and Robert set out in her Audi for the near thirty mile trip to the slaughterhouse in Cockerham.

'I want to know what's up with him, that's all,' Robert replied. 'I thought, if I can figure out how *he* became a priest, I might uncover why his holy water doesn't work.'

'Do you think he's ... y'know, one of those, um, paedo priests? I know it's horrible even considering it, but he might be. Right?'

'I don't think so,' Robert said. 'I mean, I'm not gonna rule that out. But if that's the case, that'll become its own thing that we need to do something about. So, and I know this doesn't sound great, I'm hoping it's not that because I really don't feel I have the time or the energy to get into something like that right now.'

Juliet didn't respond at first.

Robert watched her, deep in thought.

'I get it,' she said finally.

'But it might just be that he's kind of a big phoney,' Robert said. 'I want to understand how it works. Since school we've used Father McMahon's holy water with no issues at all. And I've never thought about it before. It was just a weapon. Now, I wanna know how it works, and ... well, I'm not completely lying about considering the priesthood.'

'Jesus, you actually *do* want to be a priest?' Juliet said.

'Not really, but ... well, there must be power in it, right? For some reason, holy water kills vampires. Why?'

'They're evil ...' Juliet shrugged, and then her face sank. 'I mean, um, not evil. They're, they're ...'

Robert understood that she was thinking about Aaron, so he swerved it, partially to spare her feelings and partially because he wanted to talk about the holy water thing. 'For whatever reason, there's power in the Catholic church. Power to hurt vampires. That's still what we do. It's still our mission. Right?'

Juliet paused again, and said, 'Yes, it is.' She sounded uncertain. 'But, I can't really get my head into it right now. You're not wrong, though. Long term, I have to get back into it. I'm hoping Aaron will help us, eventually. That he'll, you know, *want* to help us.'

'A vampire who hunts other vampires ...' Robert said, thinking it over. 'Like Angel, or Blade. Or Evelyn from Void City, or Jander Sunstar from—'

'Rob, would you bloody well *stop*? When I want a sodding nerd out I'll say so.'

Robert, a little stunned, took a breath and started over. 'Well, for one thing, I want to know every bit of dirt on Father William Izzard-Sinnett. I wanna know about every skeleton in his closet. I know it'll be tricky, with him being from so far away, but I wanna try. And, for another thing, I'm curious about sharpening myself, as a hunter. So, I told him I want to be a priest.'

'Don't you want to, like, find someone to spend your life with? A woman, I mean. Do you want to be alone your whole life? Sounds like hell to me.'

Robert pursed his lips awkwardly while he tried to choose what to say. 'I'm just looking into it. That's all. It's not like I'm going to chop my, um, well, what I mean is, it's not like I'm going to ... castrate myself, or anything.'

'So what's your next move?'

'The bishop of our Diocese is called Basil Powell. I want to go and see him, after we're done at the slaughterhouse, if that's okay?'

Juliet nodded.

'But I don't want to show my hand too much,' Robert said.

'You don't want the bishop to rat you out to Father William?'

'Exactly,' Robert said. 'Say I go and start asking the bishop if there's anything weird about Father William—say I even start sniffing around for *information* about Father William, if it gets back to him, and if he *is* a bad guy, I could be in trouble.'

'What are you gonna do, then?'

'I'll just have to be subtle. I told Father William that I feel very deeply about it. About becoming a priest, I mean. He said the next move is for him to pray with the bishop, but I figure if I go and see the guy, it won't seem out of character, given what Father William thinks about me.'

'I'm sorry I'm not much help,' Juliet said.

'It's fine. I'm going to start a case file at home, later. I want to know where Father William grew up, I want to know his friends' names, I wanna know where he studied, I wanna know his letter grades and aggregations scores—if they have those—and I want to read anything I can get my hands on that he's written.'

'Jesus,' Juliet said. 'You're a massive stalker.'

Robert flinched a little. 'It's a good cause. Think about it. This whole thing that's happened to Aaron, it's because Father William's holy water didn't work. How many more people might suffer the same fate because of this guy?'

Juliet didn't speak. She just turned her face toward Robert, and she looked angry.

'Eyes on the road, Jules.'

She looked back at the road in front of her, but her anger didn't diminish. 'I hadn't thought about that. It's kind of his fault, isn't it.'

'You see why I've been stressing over this?'

Juliet hummed thoughtfully. 'Look, I'm not interested in revenge, or anything like that, but I am angry. I'll try not to pull you away from what you're doing so much. Like, it *is* important, that you get to the bottom of it.'

Robert smiled, and looked out at the road. 'Thank you.'

†

It was the last Saturday of October in Ecclesburn, and the sun was out. It was frosty though, so Tilly was wrapped up warm as she walked by Laura's side along Lockwood Mews toward the north end of town. St. Luke's was half a mile out, and Cleve Woods was just beyond that.

'Do you know what happened to Juliet Rayne?' Tilly said, her head still full from the previous night's Googling.

'Her parents died, right?'

'Her parents were killed by vampires.'

Laura nodded sombrely.

'She wasn't much older than we are,' Tilly said.

'How did you find that out?' Laura asked. 'I mean, I doubt the Ecclesburn Post had a story in it about vampires and stuff?'

'There's, like, loads of vampire hunter communities online. It's kind of bizarre, actually, how out in the open they are.'

'Are you sure they're not nuts? I mean, just because vampires do exist doesn't mean that every muppet on the Internet is an actual vampire hunter?'

'Well, I spent the night messaging this woman, Sophie O'Hara, from Cheshire. She's, like, twenty-five. She was super suspicious at first, but after I told her about the thing that happened Thursday night she opened up.'

'And she told you about Juliet Rayne?'

Tilly nodded. 'She's kind of legendary, apparently. Juliet, I mean. Her parents used to fight vampires. They were called the Rayne Helsingers. Juliet and two of her friends took it over when the Raynes died. They slay vampires, mostly here in Ecclesburn, but they go all over Lancashire sometimes.'

'Listen, Tilly, I'm not doubting your new grown up friend or anything, but be careful. Don't go meeting these people. It might be some gross, sweaty old dude with a pic off the Internet of some twenty-five year old woman.'

Tilly rolled her eyes at her friend. 'I'm not stupid.'

'So who are these friends? The two friends Juliet Rayne hunts with?'

'I don't know. Sophie just said two guys.'

'You want to go and become one of them, don't you?' Laura said. 'A vampire hunter. A ... what did you call them?'

'The Rayne Helsingers.'

'One of them.'

'No, not really. I mean, the Rayne Helsingers? That's totally lame. But yeah I do want to hunt vampires. Definitely.'

'Tilly, why?' Laura asked, reaching the end of her patience. 'You said it yourself, Juliet's parents were killed. And I bet they knew what they were doing. You're a kid.

If you go out at night looking for vampires they'll kill you. In, like, five minutes.'

'It's about power,' Tilly said. 'You just need to be prepared. Like, yeah, I get it. If I went out tonight and hung around St. Luke's cemetery, I'd get killed. But if I get safe, if I figure out why religious stuff has power over vampires, and if I learn to use that power, I can do some good. Like, vampires kill people. That one on Thursday was going to kill Harry. We can't just let them go around killing people.'

'Given how you're always whining about your incapacitating misanthropy, it's a bit weird hearing you talk about how you want to risk your life protecting everyone else's.'

'Well, just because I don't like being around people doesn't mean I want them to *die*,' Tilly said.

'Just promise me you won't be stupid, please,' Laura said. 'I love you. I don't want you to die. People die here. You know it, I know it.'

'You're the one who wanted to go to Cleve Woods in the first place. And you want to go out with the boys on Halloween.'

'Look, going out with the boys is one thing. And I'll admit I'm not a hundred per cent sure I wanna be out after dark. Even in a group. Even if there's a chance I can get off with Mark. But going out looking for vampires is another matter entirely. That'll definitely get you killed. Think about it. Think about Thursday night. Harry's strong, but that vampire picked him up like he was a bloody rag doll.'

'This is why I'm saying we need to be *prepared*.'

'We?'

'Well, you were the one who said that maybe there was something to the whole Catholicism thing. Back when I pooh-poohed it. We could be partners.'

'I'm all for being safe, Till, and I'll read about vampires and use garlic and holy water and crosses or whatever, but I'm not going out looking for vampires. Sorry.'

Tilly tightened her lips thoughtfully. 'Okay. Listen, I'm not saying we should go out tonight with stakes and crosses or anything.'

'Good,' Laura said, nodding, as the two girls approached the entrance to St. Luke's. 'Now, let's go see what the boys are doing.'

†

'You want to do what?' said the confused "Senior Abattoir Operative", whose name was Bill.

Robert and Juliet looked at each other.

'Is Oliver Chapman here?' Robert asked. 'Because he said we were fine to come and get what we need.'

'Ollie's on cushy shifts. No weekends. I'm in charge today.'

'Okay, listen,' Robert said, 'it sounds a bit weird, but we just want some fresh blood for black pudding. We need ... quite a lot. Mr. Chapman said we were fine to come and get some, every day.'

'Every day? Are you pair caterers?'

Robert sighed. 'Um, we own a B&B. I mean, we *run* a B&B. It's ... it's new. We're really putting our best efforts into the breakfast part. So we're advertising ourselves on the back of the fresh blood black pudding. We can pay. Mr. Chapman said you throw away gallons of blood, that it's not a problem?'

'No, no, I mean, it's fine. What do you want? Pig? Cow?'

Juliet grimaced a little. 'Um, can we try both?'

'I don't see why not,' Bill said, smiling amicably.

'Fantastic,' Juliet said, before swinging her bag in front of her and pulling out two empty wine bottles.

'What are these?' Bill said, his eyes wide. 'You're putting the blood in *these*?'

'I, um ...' Juliet began.

'The Internet said it was the best way to keep the blood from coagulating,' Robert lied.

'Oh!' Bill laughed. 'Is that right? What a world, eh.'

Robert and Juliet smiled, humouring him.

'Well, this way,' Bill said, before turning toward a great, big set of silver doors.

†

Jack Turnbull was in an excellent mood. It was a cool, sunny October Saturday, he had a perfectly poured pint of Peroni sitting in front of him, he was watching the build up to Manchester United v Tottenham Hotspur on the big screen in the Lord Nelson, and to top it all off, the best part of all, Becky Brannigan was texting him.

He sipped his beer and listened to Jamie Redknapp on the TV, who was waxing lyrical about the difference Nemanja Matić had made to United's first team this season, when his phone pinged with a picture from Becky. It was her, in full costume for her play. She looked absolutely beautiful, glowing as she smiled. The costume was believable. She looked like she was from the eighteenth century, in a green peasant blouse with a leather waist-cinching belt, and with her wavy red hair down.

Jack smiled from ear to ear, and typed: 'You look great, very authentic.'

While he waited for her to read and reply, he looked at the photo again. He was proud, and thrilled, and excited. Just the fact that she'd sent him a selfie, smiling at him, presenting herself to him, it electrified him. Every little indication that she was thinking about him—every text, every emoji, every photo—it all came together and made him feel like he was living, truly living for the first time in years. For the first time in as long as he could remember.

His phone pinged: 'What are you up to? Xx'

'I'm in the Nelson.'

'Are you free later? Xx'

Jack's heart skipped a beat. 'Sure, what time?'

'I have rehearsals until 3. It takes about thirty minutes driving back, so say 3:30? In the Nelson? Xx'

He started typing, 'It's a date,' when he had second thoughts, deleted it, and sent instead, 'Sounds great, see you then. Have fun rehearsing. Xx'

Smiling, and full of absolute joy, Jack sipped his Peroni, and focused on the TV.

†

'That's the one, right,' Juliet said, as she parked at the side of the road. 'Number twenty?'

'Yeah,' Robert replied, undoing his seat belt.

The two of them got out of the car, and made the way up the short drive toward the front door of Bishop Powell's house, before ringing the bell.

They waited in silence, while a blurry shape moved inside, through the frosted glass window.

The door opened inwardly, revealing a smartly dressed, middle aged man.

'Bishop Powell?' Robert said.

'Yes?'

'My name's Robert, Entwistle. And this is Juliet.'

'Ah, you're our young would be Father Cristóbal,' the bishop said with a curious glint in his eye.

'What's that?' Juliet said.

'Oh, all in good time. Come on, please come inside.'

Chapter Nine
The Devil's Children

The inside of Bishop Powell's home was much like the rectory at St. Luke's, where Father William lived. There were religious paintings, and statues—the conventional iconography of mostly historical Christian art. But one thing screamed out at Robert as he made his way through the fresh smelling carpeted corridors and into the clergyman's living room:

This was the home of a vampire hunter.

There was a striking emphasis on the cross, particularly. Crucifixes of every sort were all over. And Robert had counted three holy water fonts already. *And* there were even fresh garlics, cut in half, hanging off the walls and resting on tables in little ramekins.

Robert and Juliet's eyes met, and the understanding past between them, that Bishop Powell was one of them.

'Father Izzard-Sinnett was quite impressed with you, young Robert,' Bishop Powell said as he led them to a sofa, before sitting in an armchair opposite. 'Please, sit.'

Robert and Juliet sat down, both of them sitting courteously upright.

'Does he know you're coming to see me today?' Bishop Powell said.

Robert looked down at the open Bible on the table between them, and then back up at Bishop Powell. 'Um, no. Is that a problem?'

'No, I shouldn't say so. I just like to know how strong the lines of communication are between the priests in my Diocese, and those who are under their pastoral care.'

'Oh,' Robert said, a little confused. 'Well, I went to see him yesterday, and we talked for a while, about ... everything. He's already spoken to you?'

'Yes,' the bishop said, giving little away.

Robert felt like he was being inspected, so he resolved to go in big with his story. 'I want to be a priest,' he said. 'That is, I believe that I'm being called to be a—'

'Called by whom?' Bishop Powell said.

Robert was caught a little off guard by this. 'Um, well, by God.'

'The reason I ask is that, it is Christ who calls. It is the Holy Spirit of Jesus Christ who calls young men to the priesthood. Tell me. How is your relationship with the Lord?'

Robert felt Juliet's eyes watching him. Her scrutiny seemed to affect his ability to lie. Nevertheless, he committed to it. 'Strong.'

Bishop Powell narrowed his eyes as he examined Robert, and then turned to face Juliet and smiled. 'And who might you be?' he asked, turning his head in an oddly familiar way.

'Juliet,' she said.

He turned his head a little more, opening his manner. 'Juliet ...?'

She shook her head, confused.

'What's your surname?' Bishop Powell said.

She took a second, eyeing him suspiciously, and said, 'Rayne.'

Bishop Powell leaned back into his chair, staring at Juliet in a way that made Robert wonder if the old man knew her. 'I thought there were three of you?' the bishop said.

Robert and Juliet looked at each other, and the pretence between them began to fade. Robert looked at the bishop and said, 'What do you ...'

'Forgive me, and allow me to properly introduce myself. I thought you knew. My name is Basil Powell. Like the two of you, I am a hunter. Or, at least, I was.'

'We saw the sacramentals,' Robert said, leaning forward now.

'And, we're not blind,' Juliet said. 'What with the garlic, and all ... but, who *are* you? We thought we knew who all the hunters were.'

'I told you, I am Bishop Basil Powell. But, in my youth, I was a Helsinger. Just like the two of you.'

'*What?*' Juliet said.

'Oh yes.   And, Miss Rayne, I'd like to take this opportunity to give you my sincerest condolences. Your mother and father were fine, fine people.'

'You knew my mum and dad?' Juliet said, her voice more tender and childlike now.

Bishop Powell smiled. 'I did.'

And while the shock of this settled among the two younger vampire hunters in that informal and cosy living room, the bishop slapped his hands on his thighs to stand, and said, 'Now, who wants tea? And a crumpet, perhaps?'

†

Tilly was feeling very uneasy. She was in Cleve Woods, with a bunch of the girls and almost all of the football players. Chrissie Jones had been invited, which was of interest to Tilly because she wanted to quiz her about her big sister, to see what she knew about Juliet Rayne; but Chrissie was following Alfie Rees around, and decidedly *not* taking questions.

That was frustrating, but it was not the source of her unease.

No, her anxiety was rooted in the fact that she was sitting alone with Harry. She had agreed to it only because it had coincided with the opportunity for Laura to go off with Mark. And it wasn't that Harry made her feel unsafe, or anything like that. He was actually quite nice, really. She did feel safe enough with him—although the main reason she felt safe was the sunlight shining through the leafless trees.

It was just that he seemed interested in her.

The thought was like some kind of hell. He might want her to talk to him, to open up to him. They'd talked plenty on Facebook about TV shows and movies and books and stuff, but ... right now he looked like he might want to know all of her deepest hopes and dreams.

She was not really an open book, emotionally.

She could cope well enough with the idea that he might grow resentful of her, and even that he might get angry with her for being all closed off or something; but what she really hated was the possibility that he might depend on her and that she might let him down.

She didn't want that.

She just wanted to be left alone.

People, she thought while she sat with him, tend to want things from you, and if you can't give it to them, if you can't be it for them, they get hurt.

Who needs that on their conscience?

Much easier to keep to yourself.

'Can I be dead honest?' he said, flicking his hair off his head.

'Okay?' she said, stuffing marijuana and tobacco into the heating chamber of the gun-shaped vaporiser they'd customised together over the summer.

'I like you, Tilly,' he said.

She smiled awkwardly, while she screwed the heating chamber into the vaporiser. 'That's nice. Gimme the battery.'

He handed her the battery. 'You're not like other girls.'

'Please don't say that,' Tilly said, giving him hard eyes while she attached the battery to the vaporiser. 'I am like other girls.'

'I just meant that—'

'Whatever you meant, you should know, I don't want to hear that. I don't want you to throw girls under the bus in some attempt to make me feel special, or whatever. Got it?'

'Okay, fine,' he said, shaking his head while he tried to calibrate. 'I meant that I like you more than I like other girls.'

'Well that's not much better,' she said, waving the vaporiser for emphasis. 'I mean, like, what do you have against girls, Harry?'

'For Christ's sake, I just meant that I'm, you know, I'm into you. Like, I like you.'

'Oh. Right.'

'I'm not saying I have a problem with girls or that I hate girls or anything like that.'

'Okay.'

He winced a little. 'So, is that okay?'

'What, that you like me?'

'Well ... yeah?'

'Well, it's a free world, right?' Tilly said. 'I mean, you can like who you want to like.'

He looked a little hurt, like his vulnerability tank had been emptied.

'What do you expect me to say?' Tilly said.

He flicked his hair again. 'Do you ... feel the same? Like, if I'm wasting my time, that's, like, totally cool. I'll back off. No harm done.'

'I, um ...'

'It's really okay,' he said, though his eyes said different, as he stared at nothing on the floor.

'Okay, look,' Tilly said, straightening out, focusing on him, 'I don't *not* feel the same.'

Tilly watched as the double negative unfurled itself in Harry's head.

'I'm just not sure that I'm really the girl for you, Harry.'

He smiled and looked at her, tilting his head a little, like he was examining her, or admiring her.

She wasn't sure which. Either way, she hated it. 'Stop it,' she said. 'Stop looking at me like that.'

'Okay, okay,' he said, 'I think you're cool, alright? All I really wanna do is get the opportunity to spend more time with you.'

Tilly took a deep breath as she tried to settle her nerves. Finally, she laughed a little, and smiled at him. 'Spending time, I can do.'

'Okay. Awesome.'

Still smiling, she held up the vaporiser. 'Leaf?'

He nodded, smiling back at her.

She held the gun-shaped vaporiser, pointing the barrel upwards. The two children leaned forward, their faces a mere couple of inches from each other, and Tilly pulled the trigger.

A steamy blend of cannabis and tobacco mist shot out as though from an aerosol.

Tilly and Harry closed their eyes and breathed it in through their noses.

They opened their eyes at the same time, and Tilly shook off the chill that flashed through her upper body, and relaxed.

She sniffed. 'Now,' she said, sitting forward, forgetting herself, 'we have to do something about these vampires. Right? I mean, there are *vampires* in our town.' Her head seemed light and stress free. 'And they're not all that badass, really. Like, throw some holy water on them and, boom, job done.'

Harry's smile widened, and his eyes glazed a little with the cannabis. He shook his head, like he was impressed, or enthused, or something. 'Does holy water really work?'

Tilly reached out and grabbed Harry's hand, pulling it closer to her. 'That's exactly what confused *me*. But, apparently, yeah, it does.'

'How would we go about'—Harry looked like he was searching for the words—'finding them, or whatever.'

'Finding vampires? I, um, actually ... I'm not sure.'

'Like, is there really anything concrete, about what kills them and what doesn't?' Harry asked.

'Okay, so I've been looking into it, after what happened Thursday, and, yeah, there's all of these communities, online, and—'

'Communities?'

'Of vampire hunters,' Tilly explained. 'The North West is crawling with vampires, apparently. And there's hunters all over the five counties.'

'So the whole North West is like Ecclesburn?' Harry asked. 'With, like, people dying and going missing every five minutes?'

Tilly was suddenly at a loss for words. 'I don't know.'

'Because if it is like this all over the North West I'd expect it to be, like, common knowledge, or something? Not something we all have to pretend we don't know about.'

'You might be onto something there, Harry Fox,' Tilly said, noticing now that she was still holding onto his hand. She looked down at it, and then up at him, and smiled, unexpectedly awkward.

They looked into each other's eyes, and Tilly realised she was in one of those moments she'd seen in movies, right before two people kiss. So, without any hesitation at all, she pulled her head back and up, and said, 'Definitely, you're onto something there, no question, no doubt about it.' She cleared her throat, and resettled herself.

He mirrored her, sitting back a little, but he still looked at her in that curious, almost intrusive way.

She smiled, a simple smile, and blinked the moment away.

'Something we can look into,' Harry said.

'Absolutely,' Tilly agreed, while she tried to remember what the hell the they were talking about. She held up the vaporiser. 'More leaf?'

He shuffled towards her a little, flicked the hair off his forehead with his fingers, and nodded. 'More leaf,' he said.

†

Bishop Powell set a long, oval plate full of buttery crumpets on the table, and returned to his seat. Robert was feeling particularly uneasy about how to proceed with the rest of the conversation, mainly because he was pretty sure a Catholic bishop with a history of vampire hunting would rather disapprove of what he and Juliet were doing regarding Aaron.

Trying to reform a vampire.

It was anathema.

And yet the bishop's secret past presented a big opportunity, to learn, to discover why the church had such power over vampires. Power, perhaps, to be wielded.

'I think it is a good thing, that you are feeling called by Christ, to serve his church,' the friendly bishop said. 'You must understand, the devil's children—the vampires—they are not his only method of attack against our Father's people.'

'You believe the devil literally exists?' Juliet asked, turning her head a little, her cynicism escaping her.

Bishop Powell looked baffled. Then, he turned to Robert, for unity. 'Well, of *course*, dear,' he said, looking back at Juliet. 'Aren't you ... I mean, haven't you slain many of his children?'

'I've ... slain vampires, yeah. But I've never really considered, like, Satan, or whatever.'

'Well, I'm sorry to say that he has considered you, my precious child.'

Robert cleared his throat. 'We're not really well versed,' he said, playing the intermediary, 'in the church's understanding of what vampires are, or where they came from.'

'But you use our tools to hurt them?' the bishop replied.

'My parents taught me how to kill a vampire when I was still in primary school,' Juliet said.

The bishop's eyes curled with sorrow at the loss of innocence, though there was recognition in him, as though he was not surprised.

'They explained it, and it's always worked,' Juliet went on. 'Fire, decapitation, holy water, the stake through the heart, and daylight.'

The bishop nodded. 'And the crucifix?'

'We've had mixed fortunes with the cross,' Robert said. 'So we've tended not to rely on it.'

'How interesting.'

'We've never had a problem with fire, or the stake, or'— Robert couldn't prevent his face flinching just a little— 'holy water. Well, until recently.'

'Oh?'

Robert checked Juliet, whose eyes were wide and hard, telling him to be quiet. He calmed himself, and faked nonchalance. 'We recently had a fight, and we had some holy water that didn't work.'

'Is that right?' the bishop said. 'Blessed by whom?'

'Father William,' Robert answered.

Bishop Powell seemed unsettled now. 'Let me get this ordered in my mind. You went to Father Izzard-Sinnett for holy water, and when you used it against one of the devil's children, it—'

'It might as well have been Dr Pepper,' Juliet said.

Robert frowned at Juliet, and then turned to the bishop. 'It was ineffective.'

'Oh dear. No one ... was lost?'

Robert could feel Juliet's tension, by his side, so he continued his dishonest indifference. 'No, nothing like that. We were prepared. Everything was fine.'

'What a relief,' Bishop Powell said, though his manner didn't seem at all relieved.

'Have you ever encountered faulty holy water before?' Juliet asked.

'Of course,' the bishop replied. 'It does not speak well to the content of the blessing priest's heart, I am afraid.'

'You think something might not be right about Father William?' Juliet asked. 'Because, that's what we—'

'I'd like to say, right up front,' Robert said, talking over Juliet, 'that when I met with Father William, yesterday, I found him to be a very earnest, sincere man. True, the first time I met him, I got a weird vibe. But, yesterday—'

Bishop Powell laughed a little. 'A weird vibe?'

Robert winced. He felt somewhat guilty. Father William had been good to him. 'I don't think he's a bad guy, is all I'm saying.'

'Young Mr. Entwistle,' Bishop Powell said, 'I have known William Izzard-Sinnett since he was a young boy. I knew his parents. I have prayed with them. I am not lightly suggesting that there may be a corruption within him, but if his sacramentals are not bestowed with the power of God, there *is* a reason for it. God sees all. He is not freely deceived, as we are.'

'We'd never really thought about it before,' Juliet said. 'We just kind of went to Father McMahon, got the holy water, and went ahead and used it. We'd never really thought about *why* it worked, or considered that it might *not* work.'

Bishop Powell took some time, examining both of the young vampire hunters with his eyes. He was curious, but still warm. 'I would like to pray about this. I do not believe that it is a coincidence, Mr. Entwistle, that your sense of calling coincides with this revelation about Father Izzard-Sinnett.'

'Can I ask you,' Robert began, 'does ... does Father William know about vampires? He claimed not to.'

'As far as I know, no, he doesn't. But if he has been deceiving you, and deceiving us all, then we simply cannot be certain of anything. Now, please, I really would like to pray on this a while.' He stood, prompting Robert and Juliet to do likewise. 'I'm on Facebook. Find me, message me, if you like. I will pray for you. For the both of you.'

Robert wasn't really satisfied, but Bishop Powell was being pretty clear. 'Okay,' he said. 'Thank you, Bishop Powell. God bless you.'

The bishop smiled, though his face remained perturbed. 'And you, dear children.'

✝

'Well, what did you make of all that?' Juliet said, as she drove the two of them onto the M6, heading south out of Lancaster.

'I don't know,' Robert moaned, as his head fell back onto the headrest.

'The more I listened to the guy, the more skeptical I became, personally,' Juliet said. 'Like, I'm not denying that holy water works, and that we've seen crucifixes burn vamps until they blister, but, like, do you really believe that vampires are the devils's children?'

'I don't know.'

'Like, if that were true, why would Aaron agree to eat the deer, or the rabbits. Why wouldn't he just charge at me and kill me. He said he doesn't want to hurt me. If he was, like, a child of the devil now, why would he say that?'

'I don't *know*.' Robert sighed as he thought about it, over and over in his mind. 'I don't know how any of it works, and that's the problem. Aaron seems ... *different*, but not like a different person altogether. You know?'

Juliet took her time, her eyes on the motorway in front of her. 'He's just ... he's just having to come to terms with the change he's gone through. The change he's *going* through. Like, his whole life is in complete ruin right now. He needs blood, and it's colouring everything for him. It's like ... it's like puberty.'

Robert looked at her, doubting her. 'It's not like puberty, Jules.'

'Well, one minute you're content with what you've got, right, and the next your flooded with all these *desires*. They make us change. They make us selfish, and toxic, and hungry. But we don't kill teenagers, do we?'

'Teenagers don't kill, fulfilling those desires.'

'And Aaron doesn't have to either.'

'Okay, so your take on all this, is that vampires aren't the devil's children. They're just ... a species whose desires make them kill. They're just ... natural predators. Of humans?'

'Exactly. They can still feel guilt. They can still feel empathy. Aaron does, I'm sure of it. Vampires can still ... function, in society. They just need ... help.'

'So what the hell have we been doing this last few years?'

'Well, I'm not saying that they don't become irredeemable, over time, the more they kill, the more human blood they drink,' Juliet said.

Robert wasn't buying into Juliet's theory, but he wasn't ruling it out either. 'So, here's my big thing on this,' he said. 'If vampires can feel guilt, and empathy; if vampires can function in society, and live their lives and not harm anyone ... isn't it wrong to kill them? Isn't it morally wrong?'

A silence passed as Juliet contemplated it. 'It's not ... morally perfect. I think we can agree on that.'

Robert stared out the passenger window glumly. 'I never thought about it,' he said, turning back to face her. 'I always just took it for granted that they were evil, and that was that. They were demons. They were soulless. They were irredeemable.'

'Me too.'

'I mean, it's definitely easier that way. Right? And, like, it's not exactly a reach to get there. They literally kill humans, every chance they get.'

'I know.'

'And I'm still not convinced that Aaron's guiding principle right now isn't self preservation,' Robert said. 'You know? Like, he was going to kill that boy, in Cleve Woods. I mean, shit, if we hadn't stopped him, he'd have killed a whole bunch of them I reckon.'

'I know that.'

'Is it justifiable, saving a creature so intent on killing, so intent on killing innocent children in cold blood?'

'I don't know if it's justifiable or not,' Juliet said. 'I mean, what's justifiable and what isn't is relative, anyway. Depending on your point of view.'

'Okay, well, from our point of view, is it justifiable? I mean, it's a gamble. If something happens, and Aaron gets out, and hurts someone. If he kills a child. It'll be on us.'

'Then we have to make sure he doesn't.'

'Well, I thought that was the point of being a vampire hunter in the first place,' Robert said, almost snapping. 'You kill them, so they don't kill innocent people.'

Juliet took another pause, breathing in and out, pressing her lips together, focusing on the road. She shook her head. 'Look, all I know is, Aaron doesn't want to hurt me. Okay?

He may have instincts now that he has to manage, but that's normal. We all have to manage our instincts, if we want to function.'

'Well some people can't manage their instincts, and those people go to prison. Only, Aaron can never go to a normal prison, because he'd kill everyone and probably burn to death because of the sun.'

'I'm not giving up on him,' Juliet said. 'He wouldn't give up on me. And I'm not giving up on him. I'll do it with or without you.'

'Jules ...'

'He needs me right now, to believe in him. To believe in his good character. He won't want to escape, and he won't want to hurt anyone. Okay?'

Robert sighed. 'I hope you're right,' he said, and looked out the window again.

There was another pause, before Juliet spoke. 'D'you wanna go and get a drink Rob?'

'What?'

'Let's not go straight home. Let's go and just ... not be doing all *this*, for an hour or whatever. We could get lunch?'

Robert swayed with the motion of the car, not really knowing what to say. So he just said, 'Okay.'

†

Tilly had gathered as many of the kids together as she could, which wasn't many, as the afternoon ran on. There was Laura, Harry, and Mark; there was Chrissie, who was there because Alfie had agreed to listen; and there was Gemma Read, Jenny Lewis and Tom Howard. The nine of them were gathered in the very spot where Jenny and Tom had burst into the crowd the previous Thursday night, bringing with them the vampire which had almost killed Harry.

'I reckon it came here because of the graveyard by St. Luke's,' Tilly said. 'I bet it rose, that night.'

'We think that there's something about Ecclesburn that brings them here,' Harry said. His voice was deep, and authoritative.

'Like what?' Mark said.

Tilly looked at Harry, smiling. 'Okay, either the grown ups here in town have some kind of ... dark, unholy alliance with them ...'

'À la Riverdale,' Harry said.

'I was thinking Pet Sematary,' Tilly said, looking to Harry.

'Or The Power of Five?'

'Hello, nerds?' Mark snapped.

Tilly was still smiling. 'That theory means the grown ups are happy to sacrifice us to them,' she said, 'probably in exchange for some kind of protection, or just so they get to walk around without fear of getting eaten.'

'That's not cool,' Chrissie said.

'And I don't buy it,' Alfie said, sitting next to her. 'There's no way my parents are okay with that.'

'So what's the second theory?' Laura asked, seemingly impatient.

'Okay,' Tilly said, 'so, maybe, there's some kind of secret magical, mystical reason that vampires are drawn here.'

'À la Buffy the Vampire Slayer,' Harry said. 'Hellmouth principle.'

Tilly gave him a solid, matter of fact nod.

'What the hell is Buffy the Vampire Slayer?' Chrissie said.

Tilly gave her absolute evils. 'I'll give you my iTunes password and you can educate yourself,' she said. 'By the end of season two, you'll be naming your cuddly toys after Spike and the Scoobies.' She turned to Laura now. 'Hellmouth principle's my own personal favourite for this thing.'

'Any other theories?' Mark sighed.

'Well, the third theory is that all of the towns, and villages, and cities, are like this, and the whole world is ... not what we think it is,' Tilly said.

'So, think True Blood,' Harry said.

'I'm not allowed to watch True Blood!' Alfie said, like the very idea of it was absurd.

'Or, like, a superhero movie then,' Harry said. 'The whole world knows about vampires, but they keep it from us until we reach a certain age.'

'If this is true,' Tilly said, 'then all of the towns are like Ecclesburn, and the grown ups just don't think we need to know about it yet.'

'It would make sense,' Harry said, 'if you think about it, because our parents aren't exactly hiding the fact we have to have garlic on us at all times, and crosses, and copious amounts of holy water knocking about. Even my mum—who thinks Catholics are, like, antichrists or something—even she has holy water she never tells anyone about.'

'But ... we'd have heard something, if the world was full of vampires, and everyone knew about it,' Laura said.

'Maybe we have heard about it,' Tilly said. 'I mean, we all know all the ways to kill one. Don't we? It's not like vampires are *unheard* of. We just ... we just never believed they exist, until we saw one. But our parents obviously did.'

'So what are we supposed to do about this?' said Tom. It was the first time he'd spoken in a while, and he was still shaken, like he was waiting to be attacked and chased again.

'Well'—Tilly looked to Harry for agreement—'if our parents are in on it, and they're happy for us to be bloodsucker food, we have to seek help from *outside* Ecclesburn. From vampire hunters. If there's something here, some magical, mystical convergence, or whatever, we have to try and ... shut it down, I guess? And if the whole world is, like, not what we thought it was? Well, then, I guess, we're pretty screwed.'

'So how do we find out?' Alfie asked. 'Like, how do we find out which it is?'

Tilly smiled proudly, and pulled her phone from her bag. 'I have a friend I can ask.'

'Oh, your twenty-five year old mate who definitely isn't a gross old guy?' Laura said.

'Her name's Sophie,' Tilly said. 'She's a vampire hunter, from Cheshire. We're friends on Facebook, and she said I could ask her anything.'

†

Jack's heart was racing, as he looked at the time on his phone for probably the thirtieth time in five minutes. He was so excited he couldn't help but smile, because Becky had said she'd be thirty minutes, twenty-nine minutes ago.

In front of him was his fourth beer. He'd switched to Victoria, a pale lager from the Bohem Brewery, because it was weaker, and he didn't want to be too hazy when Becky arrived. He'd bought her a large white wine, as per her request, and he couldn't wait to see her.

And then he did.

She came around the corner from the Nelson's front door, still wearing her seventeenth century outfit. She beamed a smile. It was like some kind of wild, intoxicating drug, and Jack stood up to greet her, overwhelmed by the passion that was under every inch of his skin.

'How do I look?' she said, as she joined him at the table.

He pulled a chair out for her. 'Beautiful,' he said.

She looked a little startled, as she sat, and he realised she was probably asking about her costume. Just as Jack was about to cringe, she smiled, her eyes meeting his, appreciating the compliment.

Jack felt like he could run a marathon. 'You're beautiful,' he said again, before softening into a more casual manner. 'And very ... authentic seventeenth century. Not that I'm really an expert.'

She sipped her wine, still holding her eye contact, and then said, 'So, Jack Turnbull. What would you like to do with me for the rest of the day?'

And now, Jack felt like he could run *two* marathons.

CHAPTER TEN
Entitlement, Overconfidence, and Aggression

Tilly let herself into her house, and was quickly followed by Laura. The two girls made their way through the hall into the kitchen, where Tilly's grandmother was, predictably, drinking wine and playing on her iPad. 'Hey grandma, where's dad?' Tilly said.

Her grandmother looked up, only mildly interested. 'In the pub I think.'

'The Crow's Feet?'

'How the bloody hell should I know? He's out, wasting his money, as always.'

'Okay,' Tilly said, before leaving the kitchen and running up the stairs for her room. Once inside, she let Laura in, quietly shut the door, and then she sat into her office chair, in front of her computer.

'Still nothing?' Laura asked.

'Not yet,' Tilly said, as she switched her computer on and began waiting for it to load. She turned to face Laura. 'She'll get back to me though.'

Laura still had her suspicious face, but that soon gave way to a mischievous smile. 'So. Any needle movement re Harry?'

'Needle movement?' Tilly repeated, trying to seem taken aback.

'Yeah, needle movement,' Laura said, still smiling. 'Progress. Anything?'

'Well, we vaped a little leaf, and ... he told me that he likes me,' Tilly said.

Laura's smile vanished. 'Wow.'

Tilly checked her computer screen, but it was still loading. 'Like, he just came right out with it. "I like you, Tilly Turnbull",' she said, putting on a deep, silly voice.

'Did he actually Romantic Full Name you?'

'What?'

'You know, when the guy in the movie uses the full name of the girl he's into, in that kind of squinty, intrigued, "I'm cray cray for you and this is my way of telling you" way?'

Tilly made a face. 'Again I say, what?'

'You know what I mean,' Laura said, folding her arms.

'I don't think he actually used my full name, no. But he did tell me he likes me.'

'So exciting.'

'He thinks I'm cool, apparently, and he wants to spend time with me. It was actually pretty sweet. Like, he wasn't too butt hurt that I didn't, like, fawn over him or something.'

'He could have, like, most of the girls in our year, you know.'

'Good God, Laulau, what a thing to say.'

'I just mean, like, he's a catch. He's dead good at football, he's good looking, he's fit, *and* he's nice.'

'Your priorities are absolutely all over the place, you know,' Tilly said, turning back to her computer. Prompted by the screen, she hit Control-Alt-Delete, and started entering her password. 'Nice should come first. Good at football should come, like, never.' She hit Enter, and waited while her computer loaded. 'What about you, and Mark?'

Laura smiled and playfully looked away from Tilly's eyes. 'We may have kissed.' She focused, leaning forward. 'His arms are so hard. I think you'd like his arms. They're ... *hard.*'

Tilly frowned, feeling kind of grossed out. 'Laulau, the way you talk to me sometimes, I wonder if you actually know me. Like, do you know anything, at all, about me?'

Laura gave a devilish smile. 'Hard arms,' she said again.

'Sick and wrong is what you are,' Tilly said, her voice shrill and formal. She turned back to her computer and opened Chrome. 'Anyway. Enough boy talk.' She smiled at Laura, the way she imagined a confident, tantalising demon fighter might smile. '*Vampires* are afoot.'

†

Juliet sat at her table in the Lord Nelson, on the red-cushioned sofa, while Robert waited at the bar for drinks.

She was exhausted.

The pub's locals had stared at her when she'd walked in. Her celebrity in Ecclesburn was huge, and she knew it. She normally didn't go to places like the Nelson, specifically because of this attention, and because inevitably a growing crowd of chronic alcoholics would attach themselves to her, hoping for any free drinks they could wring out of her.

But her fame wasn't really bothering her now.

It was annoying, but mostly irrelevant.

The thing that was really pressing on her was the weight of what she was doing. She had absolutely no peace about it. About trying to redeem Aaron.

Redemption.

When she framed it that way, it seemed such a pure and noble goal.

But then she thought about the boy, in Cleve Woods. The boy who Aaron had nearly killed. The intent was there. The only reason that boy survived that night is that she and Robert intervened. But for that, Aaron would have killed.

He would have killed a child.

That was his first thought. His first instinct.

To kill a child.

She let out a long sigh, realising that she'd been rapidly rattling her fingernails on the table, causing a couple of the locals to look at her irritably.

She smiled at them and stopped, and they got back to their drinks.

And she wondered if such a creature even deserves to be redeemed.

What would the boy's mother think? His father? What would they think of her, saving the monster that wanted to kill their son?

All of the anxiety, the dissonance, the internal conflict, she felt like it was manifesting in her blood, making her tense and impatient and angsty. It was like there was something rotten within her soul. Like everyone who saw her could see the corruption within her. Like they could see that she would put them all at risk, just to get her boyfriend back.

She let that thought fester a while, not resolving to do anything about it, one way or another, when she noticed Robert talking to a woman at the bar.

Juliet watched the exchange curiously.

The woman was dressed like she was from the past. It was the weirdest thing. She was pretty, full figured with long red hair, but Robert looked ... safe, talking to her. There was no desire in him, from what Juliet could see.

She raised her eyebrows and wondered, not for the first time, if he might be gay.

Juliet shook off the thought, while her friend nodded and smiled his goodbyes, and returned to her, carrying his lager and her wine.

'Here,' he said, sliding her the wine and her change while he sat opposite.

'Thanks. Who's your friend?'

Robert turned in the direction of the woman from the past. 'Oh. That's Becky. She's in my theatre class.'

'Why's she dressed like that?'

'She's been rehearsing. A bunch of the guys in the class are putting on a play. On Halloween.'

Juliet sipped her wine. 'You didn't wanna take part in that?'

Robert looked like the answer was obvious. 'I can't be in Lancaster, in a play, all night, on Halloween. Right after the clocks go back? First night of Allhallowtide?'

Juliet nodded. She was sad for him. 'That's a shame. Would you have liked to be in it? In the play?'

Again, Robert looked like he was stating the obvious, when he said, 'Well, of course.'

'So you're just gonna ... put your life on hold?'

'It's only these first few long nights,' Robert explained, drinking his lager. 'It's not like my ... my *life's* on hold.'

'Okay,' Juliet said acceptingly.

'Let me ask you something,' Robert said, shifting a little, focusing on her. 'And ... please, don't get mad.'

Juliet's eyes glazed over, just a little. 'Sure.'

'I'm being totally abstract here, okay?'

Juliet nodded, inviting him to go on.

'I've been thinking about this since the car. If we can redeem Aaron ... does that make us, I don't know, wrong, to just kill vampires, like they're animals?'

'I don't know ...'

'Does it change the way we should think about ourselves? I mean, we're hunters, right?'

Juliet was struggling to engage with this. 'Yeah.'

'If they're redeemable, if they're not inherently *evil*, are we just ... executioners? And shouldn't we try to do better? Shouldn't we at least ... I don't know, lament the fact that we have to kill sentient beings that are capable of goodness, capable of kindness, of sympathy?'

'Yeah,' Juliet said, looking up at Robert's eyes now. 'I think we *should* ... lament it. I mean, how many vampires have we killed? A hundred, each?'

'More. I'd guess over a hundred just last winter alone.'

'I mean, we've saved lives, right? Like, how many people—how many *kids*—would be dead right now if we'd let those vampires live?'

'Sure.'

'But ... those vampires ... they were people once. They were little kids. They were babies. Loved, by their mums and dads. Precious.'

'Precious ... like Aaron?' Robert said, sipping more of his lager.

'Exactly.'

Robert put his glass down and took a deep breath, but said nothing.

'I'm desperate to save him,' Juliet said, rattling her fingernails on the table again, before catching herself and stopping. 'But ... I don't want to put anyone at risk. I hate the thought of him hurting someone. I hate it.'

Robert settled into a steely silence. Finally, he said, 'We'll make sure he doesn't. One way or another. We'll make sure.'

'You mean ... we'll kill him?'

Again, Robert didn't seem to want to respond. But he did. 'Yeah. We will.'

Juliet had a drink, and ran her free hand through her hair, leaning forward. 'If this animal blood can, like, satisfy his cravings, we really might be able to save him you know.'

'I'm not gonna lie Jules, I've been pretty hopeless about this whole thing,' Robert said. 'I've never considered that a vampire could be ... saved, before. And ... even though I'm going along with it, I can't help feeling like ... we're gonna fail. Like ... we're gonna have to kill him eventually.'

'Can I tell you something I'm really ashamed of?' Juliet said. 'There's a part of me that thinks we *should* kill him, just out of ... mercy.'

Robert nodded grimly.

'But if this animal blood works,' she said, picking up her energy again, 'we really might save him. We really might get him back. God I hope so. I mean, we can afford to go for the blood every day. That's not really too much bother. If we pay enough we might even be able to have them ship it to us every day like the weekly shop.'

Robert let out a little, tired laugh.

'I just want this blood to satisfy him,' she said. 'And we can get back to keeping people safe. We can get back to saving lives. And ... hunting, the bad ones.'

Robert lifted his lager and took a couple of gulps. Then he set the glass down and eyed Juliet hard. 'And the ones that haven't killed anyone? The ones that have just been turned? We can't wait for them to take a life. And we can't fill the cellar with vampires.'

Juliet didn't know what to say. She pursed her lips and eyed him back. 'Okay,' she said, summoning positivity. 'We see how Aaron takes this blood. And then ... we slay the bad vampires. If we come across another vampire who's never killed anyone, we reason with him. Or her.'

Robert nodded, though he didn't look certain by any means.

'Let's stay positive,' Juliet said. 'Until we see what happens with this animal blood.'

Robert remained unconvinced.

'You with me?' Juliet asked, her voice soft and vulnerable.

And now he smiled, softening entirely. 'Always.'

†

'I still say it might be some gross, sweaty, old guy,' Laura said.

'No way,' Tilly argued.

The two girls were sitting at Tilly's computer. Tilly herself was in the control chair, which is the only way she would have it; and Laura was on the spare office chair, by her side.

'She doesn't talk like a guy,' Tilly said. 'You can tell when a guy's talking, no matter *how* old he is. The entitlement, or the ridiculous overconfidence, or the aggression *always* comes out.'

Laura raised her eyebrows, and inspected Tilly with her stare. 'Oh really? And you're having revealing conversations with guys twenty-four sevs, are you?'

'Look, the best guy I know?' Tilly said. 'My dad? He's adorable. But he too is bitter with the world because it didn't bend over for him and make him what he wanted to be. It didn't make him as important as he feels.'

'What about Harry?' Laura said, turning her head and smiling provocatively.

'Harry's sweet, actually. Like, he kind of has the overconfidence thing, but it could be worse. But'—Tilly shifted in her seat, focusing—'you need to be careful with Mark, because *that* is an aggressive boy.'

'He is not!'

'Seriously, he's got "Ecclesburnian Jailed For Murdering Girlfriend" written all over him,' Tilly said. 'He's angsty, he's twitchy, I bet his mum overindulges him and his dad's a royal scumbag.'

'Stop,' Laura said, no longer provocative, no longer smiling at all. 'Okay? Sometimes, the way you talk, I think maybe *you're* overconfident.'

Tilly reflected on this, going into her thoughts a little, and her feeling was that Laura was right. Tilly's perceptions of people had been wrong before. So, resolving not to be guilty of acting out her own pet peeves, she focused back on her friend. 'You're right. I'm sorry Laulau. I was talking about things I don't understand. I'm sorry.'

Laura twitched a little, as her frosty demeanour softened. 'It's fine,' she said, shrugging it off, before smiling again; a token of appreciation, Tilly assumed, for the apology.

The computer pinged, grabbing the attention of both girls.

'Is it a message from Sophie?' Laura asked, leaning in front of Tilly to see.

Tilly tensed up, put out by Laura's closeness, and positioned herself away so she could see. 'Yeah, it is,' she said. 'She wants to FaceTime with us.'

Laura sat back, her eyes wide.

'At least you might believe me when I say she's not a guy,' Tilly said.

†

As the sunlit portion of the day came close to ending, on that last October Saturday, the mood in Rayne Manor was becoming increasingly stressed. Robert and Juliet had finished their drinks, and made their way home. Juliet was downstairs, waiting outside the cellar door with two wine bottles full of animal blood, whereas Robert was busy in his office, creating folders and text files on his computer.

The biggest discovery he'd made during those first two hours of work concerned Bishop Powell, who apparently had a lovechild—a son, now an adult, called Timothy Kinghorn, who he never sees. According to the mother, he never even paid any child support.

Robert had found *nothing* on Father William.

But, as busy as he was, he was always aware of the *time*.

It was Saturday, the twenty-eighth of October, 2017, which would be the last day of the year before the clocks would turn back one hour.

This was huge, to a vampire hunter. Mainly because it gave vampires an extra hour to be out, in the open, free to hunt and to kill. Wintertime was, in general, peak season for a vampire hunter, and the last day of daylight saving time was colloquially referred to by the community of hunters as Hell's Eve.

Nautical dusk—the instant when the geometric centre of the sun lies twelve degrees below the horizon—was the event that brought vampires out. Before this, they were forced to hide in darkness; after this, they were free to roam the earth. And Robert's practice was always to memorise each day's nautical dusk time for months in advance, wherever he would be in the world.

And nautical dusk in Ecclesburn on Saturday, October 28, 2017, was at 7:04pm. Whereas, on Sunday, October 29, 2017, it was at 6:02pm. And it would continue to tick down, earlier each day, until mid-December, when it would blessedly start ticking back up again.

Robert sighed at the thought of six months of heightened vampire activity. He wondered how much time would be wasted trying to prevent Aaron from developing into his true self. How many people would die, because the Rayne Helsingers were not out there, protecting them, but were inside, trying to reform one of the monsters they were supposed to destroy.

And then he felt a prick of guilt, for thinking that the time would be wasted.

Because, while deep down *Robert* believed it was a waste of time, he was still aware that Juliet did not.

Juliet believed Aaron could be redeemed, and that he would remain a Helsinger, despite his new, dark nature.

A vampire with a soul, as it were.

'Angel was so much cooler than Spike,' Robert found himself saying aloud, before he put away his childish musings, and his mood sank once more.

He looked at the time in the corner of his computer screen.

6:59pm.

'Dinner bell's in five minutes,' he said with what felt like the hundredth sigh of the day.

†

When Sophie The Vampire Hunter From Cheshire's face appeared on the computer screen, Tilly couldn't help but feel a moment of relief that she had been right. Sophie *was* who she claimed she was. She was *not* a weird old guy.

'Hi,' said the wise and trendy looking woman on the screen. 'Wow, you guys look so young.'

'We're twelve,' Laura said, her voice blunt and awkward. 'I'm gonna be thirteen next month.'

Sophie nodded.

'Tilly here, she's thirteen next year.'

'February,' Tilly said, though she wasn't at all invested in the preliminary discussion about their ages.

'So, you girls wanna know how to fight vampires, huh?' Sophie said.

'We do,' Tilly replied.

'*She* does,' Laura said.

Sophie nodded. 'Listen, girls, I'm so sorry that you were attacked.' She shook her head now. 'It must have been terrifying.'

Tilly and Laura looked at each other, and then back at Sophie. 'It was, at first,' Tilly said.

'At first?'

'Well it didn't last long,' Laura said. 'The vampire chased two of our friends, to where we were all hanging out, and then it grabbed one of the boys, and it was about to, like, eat him, or whatever, when it was stopped.'

'Right,' Sophie said, nodding.

'I told her all that already,' Tilly explained to Laura.

'Listen, I can teach you guys some tricks, how to be safe, et cetera, but you shouldn't be going out by yourselves in Ecclesburn after dark.'

'Why is that?' Tilly said, leaning forward. 'I mean, what's so special about Ecclesburn? Like, is every town not like this?'

Sophie shook her head slowly. 'No, girls. Most towns are *not* like that.'

'Are we cursed?' Laura asked.

'That's one way to put it, yeah. Ecclesburn is one of a number of places that are renowned in the community of hunters. A hot spot. There are seven of them, in the North West. There's one here in Cheshire, there's you guys in Lancashire, and there are two in Greater Manchester, two on Merseyside, and one in Cumbria.'

'What are they?' Tilly asked. 'What causes it?'

Sophie eyed the two preteens cautiously through the screen. 'Do you girls know about the Depths?'

Tilly and Laura eyed each other. 'Are you talking about the sea?' Tilly asked.

Sophie smiled. 'No, no, not the sea. See, the Depths is what we call the Underworld.'

Tilly squinted curiously. 'The Kate Beckinsale movie series?'

Sophie seemed a little baffled. 'Um, no. The Underworld is the realm that lies beneath ours.'

'Like, Narnia?' Laura said. 'Only ... below?'

'Kind of,' Sophie said, nodding nonchalantly, 'if Narnia was a horrifying, distorted, vampire-riddled cesspit of rotting, derelict shithouses.'

Tilly laughed, and so did Laura.

'Honestly,' Sophie said, 'it's worse than Stockport down there. Now, you can only access the Depths at certain times during the day, and in certain places. And wherever the portals are, that's where your hotspots are.'

'So there's a ... a portal, here in Ecclesburn,' Tilly said, before nudging Laura. 'Hellmouth principle, see.'

Sophie looked a little confused, but shook it off. 'And not just in Ecclesburn,' she said. 'There are portals in those six other towns throughout the North West.'

'What about the rest of the world?' Tilly asked. 'Is the whole planet filled with these portals, these ... Depths?'

'Okay, all I know for sure is that there are eighty-eight portals, scattered about the British Isles.'

'That seems high?' Tilly said.

'It's not that high, really. And, for all I know, there may be more. I can tell you that there are fewer down south than there are up north. And Scotland and Northern Ireland are especially dense with them, and so's the north of England.'

'Why?' Laura asked.

Sophie shook her head. 'No idea. What we know is that they were colonised by vampires centuries ago, because of the distance from the sun. At least, here in the North West they were. I can't speak for the Depths in Ireland and Scotland, or down south. I hear in London there are pretty well organised little towns and cities underneath, but that might be a load of old horse sh'—this time, she stopped herself before swearing, cleared her throat, and said, 'it might be a load of old cobblers.'

Tilly was trying to get to grips with all of this new information in her head. She did not like being surprised, really. 'So, there are all these portals to a whole other realm, which is *beneath* where we are, and people know about this, but no one talks about it?'

'Well, Joe Average on the street doesn't know about it,' Sophie explained. 'Vampire hunting communities are mostly exclusive. And they're somewhat patriarchal too, although that's changing. The thing is, most of us found out about vampires from our parents, who were also hunters. Once upon a time, I could have been exiled from the community for talking to you guys right now.'

'So ... what's changed?' Tilly asked.

'Well, that's just it, times *do* change,' Sophie said with a shrug. 'There's greater freedom for hunters to share what they know. And the way I see it, you girls are gonna be safer if you have more information, rather than less.'

'Like sex education,' Tilly said, smiling and trying to sound grown up.

Sophie, though, looked a little put off, and swerved it, saying, 'Sure, I guess. But ... my point is, I don't mind helping kids like you guys, *especially* when you're from somewhere like Ecclesburn, where there's a portal to the Depths. You need to be safe. You need to not be going out into the woods after dark, for a start.'

'Okay ...' Tilly said, making herself *sound* acquiescent, while remaining otherwise internally.

'Grab some pens,' Sophie said brightly. 'I wanna teach you guys how to be smart, how to avoid being found by vamps and how to make yourselves unappealing to them if they do find you, and then I want *you* to teach all your little mates.'

Tilly still smiled, and to look at her you would assume she was fully on board with what Sophie was suggesting, but inside she was gutted. She did *not* want a safety first lecture. What she wanted was to be one of the hunters. To be part of their community.

And then she noticed something very odd.

This was the first time she'd wanted to belong to *any* community.

And as quickly as that thought arrived, it began to fade away, because being a part of the vampire hunting community meant adhering to the social laws of that community, which meant denying something true to who she really was, and what she really wanted, and what she believed was right.

That, she thought as she reached for a pen and a notepad, that sacrifice of self-determination, was too high a price to pay for any membership to any community.

†

Robert stood at the window of his office and stared out the window, at the fading sky above the Barrington Cliffs, and he felt rotten. He felt like there was a foreign substance coursing through his veins. Something dark and unpleasant and unforgivable. And he hated it. He despised it. He would have given anything, at that moment, to be rid of it—that ugly, almost ominous constant presence— and yet there was nothing he could conceive of that *would* get rid of it.

He scratched each of his arms roughly as he made his way back to his table, which is when he realised that there was an envelope sitting on the tray next to his monitor. It was where Juliet would put his mail. 'Huh,' he muttered curiously to himself, while he reached for the envelope and fingered it open.

He unfolded the letter, and read:

"1 Peter 3:17-18"

The writing was a firm, black ink, and the penmanship was elegantly rich. It was almost *proper*, Robert thought. He went to his bookshelf and took the Bible from it, flicking through to the latter pages, until he found the letter from St. Peter to the exiled early Christians in Asia Minor.

He scanned down, looking back at the letter for the reference, until he found the verses, which read:

"For it is better to suffer for doing good, if suffering should be God's will, than to suffer for doing evil. For Christ also suffered for sins once for all, the righteous for the unrighteous, in order to bring you to God. He was put to death in the flesh, but made alive in the spirit."

'What the hell is that supposed to mean?' he said, thinking aloud. He went to his phone, which had been resting on his desk, opened it up and called Bishop Powell.

There was a five second wait before the bishop answered. 'Hello?' he said.

'Bishop Powell, this is Robert Entwistle.'

'Of course. What can I do for you, my young friend?'

'Your Excellency,' Robert said, putting into practice the formalities he had spent a small portion of the evening committing to memory.

'There's no need for that, my son,' the bishop said.

'I, um,' Robert began, taking the bishop's permission, 'I received a letter.'

'Okay?'

'All it had on it was a Bible verse. One Peter, chapter three, verses seventeen and eighteen.'

'One Peter, three, seventeen to eighteen, you say?' the bishop repeated, his tone clear with fascination.

'Yeah, do you know what it is? I have it here, if you—'

'The just for the unjust,' Bishop Powell said, reciting slowly, 'that he might bring us to God, being put to death in the flesh, but quickened by the Spirit.'

'You just, know it, to recite it, off by heart?' Robert said. 'That's—'

'It is a contentious verse, young man, among the community of Christian vampire hunters.'

'Oh, right.'

'You say someone sent this to you?' the bishop said. 'In a letter?'

'Yeah, I just saw it, just now.'

'But you don't know who sent it?'

'No.'

Bishop Powell hummed thoughtfully. 'This is ... curious. Very curious.'

'Why's the verse contentious?' Robert asked.

'Well, St. Peter was talking about the resurrection of Christ, when our Lord was raised by the Holy Spirit. Quickened, you see.'

'Okay?'

'But Christians throughout the ages have searched the writings of the Apostles for doctrines, not just regarding faith, and salvation, and of the nature of God, but also regarding the unholy workings of vampires.'

'Right, so what does this have to do with hunting vampires?'

'Well, probably nothing. It is my reading of the text that St. Peter was merely repeating the doctrine of the Resurrection.'

'Fair enough,' Robert said, 'but what do people think it means? Regarding vampires?'

Bishop Powell took a breath. 'Vampires are dead men, and women,' he said, laying a foundation to build to his point. 'But they can be resurrected. Restored, to life.'

'What?' Robert said, stepping forward, his own soul *quickened*.

'Well, that's what they say,' Bishop Powell said.

'How? How can vampires be restored to life?'

'Well, by death, of course. Just as we will be resurrected because of the death of Christ.'

'Whose death?'

'Well, according to the doctrine, there are very powerful vampires, who are like ... the grandfathers of dozens, maybe hundreds of others. They are called Polysires. According to the tradition, of course. You must slay the Polysire to free all those who have been turned by him, or by the vampires he has already turned.'

Robert took a deep breath, and contemplated this. If it were true, he could save Aaron. He could save countless others as well. 'This is incredible,' he said.

'Now, listen, young Robert,' Bishop Powell said. 'In the twenty-five years I spent serving the Lord and hunting vampires, I never saw anything that made me believe this doctrine has any weight to it.'

'Right, right, sure. But—'

'I think you should think carefully about who sent you this letter, and what his intentions were,' the bishop cautioned. 'It is mostly a discredited doctrine. It is a wild, even spurious interpretation of God's holy word. That is not a small matter. You need to be careful. You are being called by Christ to serve his church, and that makes you a target for other forces that are not benign.'

But Robert couldn't focus on the bishop's warnings. His mind was away with the possibility of saving his friend.

But he would have to discover the identity of the ...
Polysire. Quickly, he focused on the concerned clergyman
on the other end of the phone. 'Thank you, Bishop Powell.
I'll, um, I'll be careful. I'll try and figure out who sent me
the letter.'

'Good,' Bishop Powell said, though Robert could tell by
his tone that he was still quite concerned. 'I shall be
praying for you, young Mr. Entwistle.'

'Thank you, Bishop Powell,' Robert said, and cancelled
the call.

His mind was alive with the news. He had barely even
registered the bishop's words of caution. All he could think
about was discovering who Aaron's Polysire was, and how
he could find him.

†

As Juliet made her way down the steps and into the
cellar of her childhood home, she was not afraid. She
perhaps should have been, she thought, but she was not.
Because the monster within was not some unknown
creature in the dark, but her own love. The man she'd
shared a bed with for over a year. The man she'd loved
when they were still children.

'Aaron, I brought you blood,' she said, stepping into the
cellar and letting her eyes adjust. 'Two wine bottles full of
the stuff.'

'No Entwistle?' came Aaron's familiar voice, as he
stepped into the faintest spot of light.

'He's upstairs. I just ... I wanted to spend some time
with you, one to one.'

Aaron made a low humming sound, which almost
sounded like a hungry growl.

It was disquieting, but Juliet silenced her fear, and reached for the light switch. 'Do you mind?' she said.

Aaron turned his head and stared at Juliet. 'Be my guest,' he said.

CHAPTER ELEVEN
Kiss

'I have pig, and cow,' Juliet told Aaron as she held the two wine bottles, one in each hand, with a messenger bag over her shoulder. 'I thought you could see which one you prefer?'

Aaron took a step towards her, his eyes fixed to the two bottles. Then, he looked up. 'Cow first,' he said.

Juliet smiled and nodded. 'Exquisite choice, sir,' she said in a posh voice, before walking to the hard wooden table against the wall and setting the two bottles down. She couldn't help but notice Aaron's dad's army bayonet, sitting there, on the table, but she chose to ignore it. She swung the messenger bag over her shoulder and placed it gently on the table. Then she pulled out another wine bottle, this one actually containing wine, and two glasses.

'What is this?' Aaron said.

'I thought we could drink together,' she said, as she uncorked the cow's blood bottle and poured. 'Like we used to.'

'We used to do this?'

As she topped the glass, she looked up. 'Don't you ... don't you remember?'

'I remember drinking wine,' he said. 'With you. And with ... Entwistle.'

'Right, well I have wine, and you have blood. It'll keep you from wanting to ... hurt me. I mean, you still ... you still don't want to hurt me. Right?'

'No,' he said. 'I do not want to hurt *you*.'

The emphasis on "you" sent a chill down Juliet's spine. 'Well, good,' she said, being chirpy, ignoring the chill. She put a bottle stopper in the neck of the blood bottle, and then opened her wine, and poured. 'Are you going to sit down?' she said, gesturing at the seat in front of him with her eyes.

He moved slowly, now that he was different. He pulled the chair out without looking at it, and sat.

Juliet corked her wine, and sat down too, next to Aaron. She was close enough to reach out and touch him, which is what she did, resting her hand on his thigh. 'Hey,' she said tenderly.

'I am not ready,' he said, 'for contact.'

Juliet pulled her hand off him. 'Oh. I'm sorry. Does it ... does that make it harder for you?'

Aaron closed his eyes with a look of earnest concentration. 'Impossibly, devastatingly hard.'

As well as moving differently, he *spoke* differently. He had more pain in his voice, and in his eyes. He had more depth about him. Juliet wanted to keep things light, so she lifted their glasses, and offered Aaron's to him. 'Here, take your blood.'

He opened his eyes, and took the glass.

Juliet offered him hers, to clink, and he did so, albeit somewhat reluctantly. 'To us, my love,' she said, as her voice let out a note of the heartache she was carrying.

Aaron said nothing, but drank. His face stayed human as he downed the entire glass, and set it down.

'How is it?' Juliet asked.

Aaron's eyes fell. 'It is ... empty, and meaningless.'

Juliet twitched, trying to remain positive. 'Okay, well, that's not the best review. Was the, um ... was the rabbits blood better? Or the deer?'

'Juliet, please, I cannot pretend that something stale is something abundant. I can sense your eagerness to please me, and to placate me, with this blood, and I am thankful to you for bringing it to me. Really, I am. But I cannot give you the response you want. This blood is foul. It is insulting. It is a vile and odious detritus.'

Juliet wanted to cry, but she didn't. She had tried so hard. She had done so much to give Aaron something that he might enjoy, something that might alleviate his pain and his hunger, and she had failed. 'Okay,' she said, nodding, forcing herself now to be upbeat. 'I'm sorry.'

He reached for the bottle, took the stopper off and poured another glass, to the top. 'Entwistle desires you,' he said.

Juliet was, to say the least, taken aback by this. 'Um, what?'

'Robert Entwistle harbours a deep and profound love for you,' he said. 'I was aware of it in life, I now realise, although I never understood it then. But now I see it. I see him. Everything at work within him is for you.'

'No,' Juliet said, 'no, that's not true. Rob isn't into me.'

He looked at her, narrowing his eyes. 'I see you, too, you understand. I see that you know how Robert feels. You know it in your gut, and in your heart, though you deny it in your head.'

Juliet took three long gulps of her Rioja, and put the glass down. 'Oh really. You can see all that with your magic vampire powers, can you?'

'It is not magic,' Aaron said. 'It is merely the movement of blood. His moves to you and yours moves to him, though you direct yours instead towards me. Why?'

'Look, just because you're a vampire and you need blood, it doesn't mean you know how I feel, or how Robert feels.

You're not a bloody mind reader.   You're just a'—she stopped herself.

'Just a what? An animal?'

'No. Not an animal. I just mean, you're not a mind reader.'

'It is not in your mind, Juliet, and it is not in Entwistle's mind either.'

'Would you stop calling him Entwistle. He's Rob. I'm Jules, you're Aaron, and he's Rob. He's not into me. He's thinking of becoming a priest, actually.' The moment the words passed her lips, she regretted them.

'He has no interest in becoming a priest,' Aaron said, lifting his blood and drinking, more slowly now. 'He wants to take you. He desires to possess you. And until he does, the lack of you will gnaw at him, the way the lack of blood—of *human* blood—gnaws at me.'

'What are you saying?'

'He will take you. I will take you. We will all take the thing we desire, the thing we lack.'

Juliet finished her wine, and refilled the glass. 'Are you threatening me?' she said, drinking again.

'No, Juliet, I am not. I am simply stating a fact. We all take the thing we want. Look at yourself, for example. You wanted me, though I have been reborn, a monster. You wanted me anyway, so you took me and now you keep me here, locked away from the world. I am your prisoner here.'

'You're *not*,' Juliet protested.

'I am clipped. Forced to remain. Neither a man, nor a monster.'

'So what do *you* want? What are *you* gonna take?'

He drank some blood, finishing his second glass. 'I don't know. I will not lie to you, Juliet, though you may kill me for my truth. I want to take you, to take your blood, and be full with it. And then I want to find another beauty to be full with.'

Juliet felt tears coating her eyes, but she locked them away.

'I want to become the monster that I am. I want it desperately.'

'Is that all you want?'

'Curiously, no,' he said, filling the glass again. 'I also desire to become once more the man that I was. I value my clean conscience. The fact I have not killed. I owe that to you, and I value it highly.'

These words now were like music to Juliet's ears. 'So, all you have to do, is prioritise,' she said. 'You have to choose what you want most.'

'Yes,' he said, drinking more of the cows blood he hated so much.

'I mean, we all want things we can't have,' she said.

'Indeed we do,' Aaron said. 'But you must understand something, Juliet. I am different now. I see things I did not see before, and I cannot go on with the charade of our previous paradigm.'

'Our what?'

'The way we were. Before. The ... three of us.'

'Rob doesn't ... desire me, or whatever it is you think. He's been by my side, helping me, helping me save you. He wouldn't do that if he ... had feelings for me.'

'He does this specifically *because of* his feelings for you. He cannot *bear* your pain. It manifests within him as it manifests within you, so besotted with you as he is. He would rather redeem for you the man you think you desire than see you suffer his loss.'

'I don't *think* I desire you, Aaron, I *do* desire you. Would you please stop presuming you know how I feel?'

'It is as clear as day,' Aaron said. 'You cannot hide it. He cannot hide it. It is pointless. The blood flows the way it flows, and that is that.'

'Stop it.'

Aaron made a fist and slammed it so hard onto the table that the wood splintered. 'I told you already,' he said. 'I will not pretend that something stale is something abundant, and neither will I pretend the opposite. Your feelings for each other are not stale, as your feelings are for me. Your feelings for him and his for you are beyond abundant. They are luminous.'

'This is nonsense, Aaron. I don't want to make you angry, but I need you to understand that my feelings for Robert are *not* ... luminous. They're ... neutral. I love him, sure, but it's the way you love a friend, or a brother. It's not the way I love you. It's not.'

Aaron was clearly not persuaded, at all. But he seemed to settle into a sort of calm about it. 'I do not see how we can move forward,' he said. 'My eyes are open, and I see what I see. It is not something that can be argued.'

'So you don't want to ... to come upstairs, out of this cellar? Because, what I thought was ... was that we could be hunters, together again. The Rayne Helsingers, back together.'

Aaron laughed. 'You want me to kill my own kind?'

'You can be a good vampire. You can drink animal blood, and slay evil vampires. You're stronger, and faster now. You won't be able to use holy water or garlic, obviously, but you can fight. You were always kind of the strongman of the group anyway.'

'I don't know how I feel about killing vampires now,'
Aaron said. 'It was the natural order before. But, now, it
seems ... apostate.'

'It seems what?'

'Wrong,' Aaron explained. 'I cannot say why, but it
feels like a betrayal. A terrible, unforgivable betrayal.'

'Right,' Juliet said. 'You know, Rob and me were talking
about it, just today. We figured that, vampires who kill,
who are, like, dead inside, and who have no guilt and no
sense of empathy, they need to die.'

'All vampires feel,' Aaron said. 'They feel all of those
things in ways you can never understand.'

'But they kill. Freely. They kill innocent people.
Children.'

'It is the hunger. You cannot understand what it is like.
It compels. It is a vicious, uncompromising master.'

'Right, sure, but you're going to master *it*. Right?
Because you're a good person. Vampires who don't, they
have to die, because they go into the world and take lives.
They're not entitled to do that. Those lives matter.'

'Life has no intrinsic value,' Aaron said, like a teacher to
a child. 'We all began with nothing, and we all return to
nothing. And whether we live for five years, or five
hundred, when we are gone, we are forgotten. As
irrelevant as we were before we were born. The pretence
that life has meaning, that it has value, it is the thing that
drives you, and that once drove me, but it is a lie, Juliet.
You should embrace this truth, for it will embrace you
whether you consent to it or not.'

'I don't get it,' Juliet said, putting her glass down and
forgetting about it. 'If you think my life has no value, and
you want to drink my blood, because all the animal blood is

meaningless and empty and insulting and foul, why don't you just do it?'

'Why don't I drink your blood?'

'Yeah? If you think my life has no value, why don't you want to hurt me, given that the other part of you, y'know, wants to hurt me?'

'That I understand that your life has no value is not to say that I desire to hasten your removal from this world.'

'What?'

'Ultimately, we are *all* irrelevant. This is the truth that alleviates my conscience, when I contemplate taking a human life. But I would still *feel* your absence. I would still suffer for it.'

'You'd ... miss me?'

'I miss you already. For you are entirely lost to me. I see it. And my indecision with regards your fate is entwined with my inability to determine just what it is that I desire most. The dream, on the one hand, that you and I might be restored to something recognisable to me; or, on the other, the moment's relief of taking you for myself, once, and for all time.'

'Drinking my blood, you mean?'

Aaron smiled, picked up his glass, and drank. As the cow's blood flowed into his throat, he winced a little bit. It was almost as though he was trying not to let his distaste of it show. 'I can wait for you, and hope that you will return to me. Or, I can kill you. Those are my paths. I must choose the wisest.'

'You know I won't let you kill me, right?'

'I am talking only of intent, Juliet. Not of practicality.'

'Great,' Juliet said sarcastically, letting her eyes drift from Aaron, down to her own glass, which she lifted and drank from. The wine was warm, and full, and sharp. It felt the way Juliet imagined human blood would taste to Aaron.

'You are wrong,' Aaron said, staring at her. 'The way you respond to your wine is *not* the way I would respond to the very lifeblood of *you*.'

'Can you read my mind?' Juliet asked, leaning back from him. 'Because that's ... a little too intrusive.'

Aaron laughed heartily. As he did, his sharp fangs glistened in the modest light. 'You do not understand. Of course, you cannot.' He settled, and straightened his face, though the amusement remained in his eyes. 'Juliet, I can see you. I told you already, you cannot hide from me. It is all in your blood. Every desire, every twitching ache.'

Juliet was losing the will to go on with the whole thing, and, as soon as she realised this, she realised also that Aaron was probably reading it in her body language, or whatever. She did not appreciate the way he presumed to understand her better than she understood herself.

'There is no presumption,' he said, before sipping more blood.

'See, now you're lifting specific words right out of my head. It's weird. Can you stop it, please?'

He straightened his face a second time. But, this time, there was absolutely no amusement in his eyes. 'I told you. I cannot unsee what I see. And I will not—'

'You will not pretend that something stale is something abundant,' she said, performing a fancy yet frustrated voice, before finishing the wine in her glass and reaching for the bottle. 'Christ, I get it.'

†

Jack's heart was racing with the eight or nine pints of beer he'd drank, and with the near half a pouch of Golden Virginia he'd smoked. But, mostly, it was racing with the sheer, intense beauty of the woman he was with. A beauty that was radiant, and incomparable. He couldn't help but wonder what lucky quirk of fate had led him to this moment.

He was walking her back to her home: her rented apartment above the Crow's Feet.

It was not a long walk, but it was late, and they were both quite drunk. It would have been the thing to do, even if they weren't Ecclesburnians. But, given that they were, it was a damned necessity.

'I'm really very proud of her,' Jack said, his hands in his pockets as he walked, his shoulder occasionally bumping Becky's. 'She's a smart little thing. I'll give her that. And, you know, she has this hard exterior, but, inside, she's my little softy. She's the little woman I'd read bedtime stories to. The little woman I'd sing songs to.'

'You sang her songs?' Becky asked.

'When she was little, yeah,' Jack said, remembering the times he'd sit with his guitar, singing to Tilly's wide eyes.

'That's really sweet.'

'Tilly and me have always had an affinity,' Jack said, as his head rolled with the alcohol in his blood. 'Don't get me wrong. She can be a right little madam. But'—he smiled—'she's my little madam. She's my little softy.'

'You said that bit already,' Becky said, turning to look at Jack. Her head bobbed drunkenly a little, as Jack's had.

'Did I?'

'You did. You said she was your little softy.'

Jack smiled, and continued walking.

'Can I ask you something?' Becky said.

Jack tried to disguise a burp. 'Sure.'

'It's okay if you don't want to answer.'

Jack lightly banged his chest with his fist. 'No, it's okay. What is it?'

'What happened with her mum?' Becky said, suddenly a bit more sober. 'I mean, where did she go? It seems weird to me, that you have custody of her. I don't mean that to sound bad. It's just, usually, the mum has the weekdays, and the dad has, like, every other weekend. If he's lucky.'

Jack tried to think of the best way to present the facts. In his younger years, he'd have put a lot of effort into packaging the details of his failed marriage, so as to optimise Becky's opinion of him. Now, as he neared the grand age of forty, he just wanted to show the naked truth. 'She left,' he said. 'I don't know where she went. One day, she left for work as normal, and, poof, I never saw her again.'

'Did you live ... here? In Ecclesburn?'

Jack nodded.

'So, do you think that she ... you know? Do you think she got ... taken?'

Jack took a deep breath. 'Do I think she was killed by vampires, you mean?'

Becky cringed, but there was a recognition in it. 'I don't like the V word.'

Jack let the moment breath. 'Nor do I,' he said.

'But, do you?'

'To be honest, I don't know,' he said. 'When she first disappeared, there was a part of me that believed it had something to do with ... the way this town is. But, as time went by, I just figured she got bored of the life we had, and went off to find something a little more interesting.'

Becky took his hand as they walked. 'I, um ... I'd be surprised. If she didn't find her life, with *you*, interesting.'

Jack stopped now, pulling on Becky's hand to do the same. When she looked back at him, with her long, red hair vibrant, even in the dim moonlight, he wanted to confess every desiring thought he'd ever had for her. Instead, he said, 'I've had a hell of a day.'

'Yeah?'

'Yeah. I'm real glad you text me.'

'Well, I, um'—she looked down, shyly, and then back up at his eyes—'I found myself wanting to see you.'

Jack held her gaze, studying every flicker in her eyes. 'You're ... beautiful, Ms. Brannigan.'

Slowly, Becky stepped towards him and wrapped her arms around his back. Her eyes were inches away from his. Her *mouth* was inches away from his. 'I can see where Tilly gets it from,' she said, her eyes rich with fascination now.

'What?'

She leaned forward and kissed him. A gentle, connective kiss. Her lips were closed, mostly, but she held him strongly. It was real, and vital, and electrifying. And then she pulled away, just a little. 'You're my softy,' she said, studying his eyes again with hers.

Jack never wanted to let go of her. Feeling her, pressed against him, as their arms locked them there, was possibly the most alive he had ever felt, in his entire life up until that point. He was close enough to see every freckle, and to smell her sweet mix of perfume and alcohol.

And she kissed him again. This time, it was more passionate than connective. He gripped her more tightly, and pulled her into his chest. The smell of her, the *feel* of her. It was ... everything. It was the sun, and the earth, and the sky, and more. There was no time before, and he felt there would be no time after.

All there was, was her.

†

Robert was exhausted from reading and researching. He had been at it for about three hours, he figured, when he looked at the clock on the wall of his office. His eyes were sore from focusing, and his mind was dull from thinking. So, when Juliet opened the door and came in, he was thoroughly relieved for the break.

She sighed and fell into an office chair.

'Hey Jules ... don't you think Angel was cooler than Spike?'

She looked at him, with tired eyes, which emphatically disagreed. 'Is that a joke?'

'Angel was deeper, and ... better.'

'Angel was *lamer*,' Juliet argued. She smiled. 'The only time Angel was legitimately better than Spike was, in one of the flashbacks, when he says—'

'Those were *my* nuns!' Robert said, performing an Irish accent as he quoted the line.

Juliet laughed loudly, and let her head fall back into the chair. 'Exactly.'

Robert laughed too. 'When him and Spike are running around Rome chasing the Immortal and getting blown up and stuff ...'

Juliet chuckled away. 'We should rewatch that.'

'We really should,' Robert said, before taking a breath, letting the humour of the moment pass. 'Hey, you wanna know something kinda gossipy?'

'Sure, I guess.'

'Bishop Powell has a son.'

Juliet looked at him, kind of vacantly.

'His name's Timothy Kinghorn. He's, like, twenty-eight. And the old Romeo never paid child support. Bishop Powell knew about him, but never saw him, when he was a kid.'

Juliet looked angry about this, but only a little, like she had other things on her mind. 'What a scumbag,' she said.

Robert looked at Juliet with concern now, increasingly aware of the sadness that was around her. 'You okay?' he asked.

'No,' she replied.

Robert nodded. 'How was he?'

'He's an arse.'

This took Robert a little by surprise. 'What do you mean?'

She looked at him, and became a bit more cautious and serious in her manner. 'Okay,' she said, leaning forward, 'I went to so much trouble, getting blood for him. I'm absolutely knackered from running around and getting bloody animals for him, and bottling two kinds of blood for him, and he says that it's, like, odious and foul and insulting.'

'He said it was insulting?'

'Like, he apologised for it, but yeah.' She fell back into the chair again and covered her eyes. 'Honestly Rob I wanted to cry.'

All of Robert's devotion returned to him at once, presented with her suffering. 'I'm sorry,' he said.

She ran her hands through her hair and shook her head, being strong. 'It's fine. I mean, he didn't ask me to do it. It's fine. I just ... I thought it might help him.'

'Did he drink it?'

'Oh yeah, the bastard guzzled it down well enough while he told me how insulting it was.'

It seemed odd to Robert. He wondered what Aaron might have meant, and none of his theories were comforting. 'Insulting ...?' he said, trying to get his head around it.

'I mean, that's kind of a brutal way of putting it, right? Like, fine, it's like non-alcoholic lager, or something? I get it. But ... when I've been running around bloody Lancashire, snapping at the butcher, and'—she sobbed, suddenly—'killing bunnies ...'

'It's a dick move, definitely,' Robert said. It felt kind of liberating, describing Aaron's actions as dickish. He'd always felt a sense of loyalty, to both of them, which had prevented him from calling out Aaron's dickishness before.

She looked at him with gratitude. 'It *is* a dick move. Right?'

Robert smiled sadly at her. 'Yeah.'

She shook her head again, like she was trying to shake away all of her pain, and then pressed her fingers into her forehead, rubbing the tension away. When she was done, she looked at Robert's desk, at the dozen or so books sitting on it, and said, 'What's all this?'

Robert's smile turned to a cautious wince. 'Okay,' he started slowly. 'Listen. I don't want to get your hopes up.'

Her eyes widened with curiosity now.

'There are people who believe it's possible to turn vampires back into humans.'

She didn't react. She just stared at him.

'It might be total bollocks,' he said. 'Okay? It probably is. So, like I say, don't get your hopes up, okay?'

The way she looked at him was hard to read. Robert wasn't sure if she was ... angry, or sad, or confused. 'Okay?' she said.

'I've been looking through these books of your mum's. There's all kinds of vampire lore in them. And it's all conflicting. Like, some hunters believed vampires were the devil's children, like Bishop Powell said, right? But others think they're, like, just a species like any other. They're metaphysically paradoxical, and—'

'Rob I'm real tired,' she said bluntly.

'Sorry. I mean, they shouldn't exist. Like, in nature. They shouldn't exist. But, the point is, there were these Catholics, in Germany, the'—he wheeled to his desk and sifted through the books, lifting one that was open— 'Andressites,' he said, reading from the page. 'They were from, like, the thirteenth century, and they believed that you could transform a vampire back into the human he was by finding the Polysire and killing him.'

Juliet took a deep breath and looked at Robert. 'What's a Polysire?'

'Right, so there are these, like, super vampires. They're more powerful, and they've turned, I dunno, like, fifty people or more, or something. They become kind of overlords of a certain place. If we find Aaron's Polysire— not *his* sire, but, like, his great, great grandsire—and if we slay *him*, all the vampires he's turned and all the vampires those vampires have turned, become human again.'

'I'm so confused right now, Rob. What are you saying?'

Robert straightened, excitement in his eyes. 'If we find the vampire lord here in Ecclesburn, and if we kill him, we might be able to save Aaron. To make him human again.'

Juliet seemed like she wanted to cry but didn't have the energy. She looked back at his pile of books, and said, 'You've just been up here working on this all this time?'

'Well, yeah.'

'It's Saturday night, and you could be doing ... anything. But you're up here, working your arse off, for me?'

Robert wasn't sure what to say to that. 'Well, you know, it's the right thing to do, yeah?'

She looked a little embarrassed now. 'No, no, of course.' She shook her head. 'I mean, no, it's not just for me. That's, like, super narcissistic of me to say. I don't think you were just thinking of me.'

The way she was acting confused Robert, and tempted him to believe that she was aware of the way he felt, and that she was trying to let him know it. 'Jules ...' he said, summoning courage, 'all of this'—he nodded at the books— 'it's not ... it's nothing.'

She looked at him, waiting for him to say more.

'For you,' he went on, 'I'd do ... more than this. I'd do ... anything. For you.'

She swallowed. 'Why?'

'Because ... you're everything.'

'What do you mean?'

Robert felt like he was falling. 'I mean ... that I love you,' he said, staggered by the words coming out of his mouth.

'Like a sister, right? Like a friend.'

'No. Not like a sister. Not like a friend. I love you with everything I have. I want to make you happy, more than I want ... anything else.'

Tears fell down her cheeks now. 'So, to make me happy, you'd spend all your time trying to save Aaron, so that I can be with him again? Even though you ... even though you love me?'

'I want you to be happy Jules. I'll do whatever it takes. Yeah, I'd save Aaron for you, to make you happy.'

She ran toward him, as though being pulled by an invisible, passionate force, and gripped him tightly.

And then she kissed him.

He wasn't in control of himself anymore. He gripped her back, and pulled her into him, as tight and as close as he could. Her lips were soft, and sweet with wine. The two of them fell into his chair, and she sat on top of him, straddling him, reaching with her fingers up his top, feeling his skin, kissing him still.

Robert was utterly out of control now.

He needed her.

She was everything.

She was vital.

She was life itself.

He kissed her, pulling her harder and harder. He felt her chest pressed against his own, and, in that moment, everything in the world that wasn't her fell away, and he couldn't care less whether it ever returned.

†

Down within the cellar of Rayne Manor, Aaron poured a glass of pigs blood, and turned a page of the book he was reading.

Anna Karenina, by Leo Tolstoy.

He could feel the movement of blood, far above him, where his former beloved and his former friend were taking each other, kissing each other, feeling each other.

He did not judge her.

She was in pain. She had fought hard to contain herself. But, he thought, we all take the things we want eventually.

But Robert, on the other hand, he *did* judge.

Robert was a hypocrite, and a coward, giving him books to read about love, and passion, and desire; all while he pursued Juliet for himself.

He looked up at the ceiling, towards Robert above. 'I will not always drink the blood of animals, Entwistle,' he said, sipping from his glass. 'I swear it. I will not.'

CHAPTER TWELVE
Dorothy and the Andressites

Juliet was wandering through what felt like a field. It was muddy, and misty, and cold—although she couldn't *feel* the cold. She just knew that it was. There was a house. Like an old, farm house, made of black stone, with a chimney, with frosted, dirty glass windows.

She started to walk toward the house, and suddenly found herself inside it.

'T'will draw you to any more cunning, that you might emboss him,' said an undressed girl, lying on a bed, to a man, standing and clothed. 'That you might front him. And that you might slay him.'

The man seemed pleased. 'I give you thanks, sister,' he said, eyeing her hungrily. 'But ... I wonder. If he is indeed more cunning than I, how shall I best him?'

Juliet watched, unable to move, as the girl smiled. 'T'is enchanted in more than one way, m'lord.'

'Pray, speak.'

The girl wrapped the object up in her quilt. 'I mustn't leave this about while I utter the charmed words, m'lord.'

The man raised an eyebrow.

Once it was away, she spoke. 'When you find him, you must only speak these words, m'lord: "Nocturnal terror, come by night; thou art in error, to know my sight; for, enemy, thou'd never best; thine sturdy foe, now evanesce".'

And again, just like the first time she'd had this dream, a third voice spoke.

'Others may have claimed my fame, but only I am worthy of it.' Again, the voice was everywhere, surrounding Juliet and pressing into her. There was such malevolence in it. Such contempt. 'And now, just as I consumed the lifeblood of your mother, I shall consume the lifeblood of you.'

Juliet opened her eyes.

She wasn't in the house with the man and the girl and the hateful detached voice anymore.

She was in her bed, in Rayne Manor. She was intertwined with Robert, both of them naked, while he slept. He was wheezing rhythmically as he breathed, and she didn't want to disturb him.

But her mind came to life with the dream. She remembered having it before, two or three nights earlier, she wasn't sure.

She didn't feel like she'd be able to sleep, so she decided to recite the words spoken in the dream by the girl, over and over and over, in her mind.

She would memorise those words, and Google them in the morning.

†

Tilly Turnbull was sick of hearing about crosses and garlic and holy water. She was absolutely done with it. She didn't want to just be safe. That wasn't enough. She wanted to find a vampire, and she wanted to kill it.

It was not that she was particularly violent. She tended mostly to shy away from even the suggestion of physical conflict. But ever since she'd seen that vampire on that frosty night in the woods, she'd been unable to shake off a terrible urgency within her, to find it, and to rid the earth of it.

They don't get to go around killing kids, she thought.

She would like to have said it aloud, but she could not. For, sitting around the breakfast table with Laura, and her oddly cheerful dad, and her typically cranky grandmother, it would have seemed a strange and alarming thing to say.

'Thanks again for letting me stay over, Mr. Turnbull,' Laura said politely as she lifted her toasted bacon sandwich to eat.

'Ah, you're incredibly welcome little Laura, you know that,' he replied.

Tilly eyed him with equal curiosity and suspicion. Something was going on with him. This was the second morning in a row he had been uncharacteristically chirpy.

'So what are the two of you planning on doing today?' he asked.

Tilly and Laura looked at each other. 'Um,' Tilly started, 'nothing, really.'

'Well it's another clear and beautiful day out.'

'Season two of Stranger Things is out,' Laura said, swallowing a bite of her sandwich. She looked at Tilly. 'We could blitz that?'

Tilly gave her friend a censorious glance. She didn't want her dad or her grandmother to know she'd watched the first season because they'd think it was too scary for her.

Laura seemed to take the hint. 'Or we could go see the new Thor?'

'I thought you were doing that yesterday?' Tilly's grandmother said, peering at the girls over her iPad.

'Well, we didn't,' Tilly said sharply. 'But, yeah, maybe we'll do that today.'

Tilly's grandmother redirected her attention to her little glowing screen, and muttered, 'Children today, they don't know they're born.'

Tilly wanted to scream, as she forced her breakfast down. She simply could not fathom why—given that they lived in a place where there's a portal to another world, below their own, where vampires live—she couldn't fathom at all why they weren't talking about it.

The grown ups clearly knew what was going on in Ecclesburn. The little regularly filled bowl of garlic that sat on the table by her front door was proof of that. The fact she'd been encouraged to smear the stinky little cloves over her neck and wrists since she could remember was further proof. So, why weren't they talking about it?

Was it all just too unseemly?

Too unpleasant?

Terribly un-British?

She scowled at the thought and resolved, deep down, not to live like this. She would master the art of vampire hunting. She would discover the nature of their vulnerability, and she would use it to fight them back. She would, if necessary, go through the portal to "the Depths", and kill every last one of them, so that a group of kids could go out and be kids and not fear for their lives the whole time.

†

Juliet slowly woke up.

And, as she did, she started to piece together the events of the previous evening. She was still lying next to Robert. They were still both naked, and intertwined. And he was still sleeping, breathing lightly and kind of contentedly.

She really didn't know how to feel.

There was a hell of a lot of guilt, obviously.

Guilt for Robert: for how her actions would impact him. She understood now that he was in love with her. He had left her in no doubt of that, both by the way he'd kissed her, and by the way he'd spent so much energy working to make her happy.

Lying in his arms, she could not deny to herself that she wanted this. She wanted him. She wanted to wake him, and to kiss him again, to feel him again. She almost cried at the thought of simply getting in her car with him and leaving Ecclesburn forever, leaving bloody vampires and never looking back.

She did not want to sacrifice animals.

She did not want ... she did not want Aaron.

And that was the second side to her guilt. She couldn't abandon him. He had done so much for her, through the years. He had suffered for her, and she had to suffer for him in return. It would be too cruel, to leave him to become a monster. To know that that same man was still in there, yearning for a clean conscience but being unable to have one.

She didn't know what to do.

She held Robert as he slept, his firm, hairy legs coiled around her own, and she tried not to cry. She simply clung to him, to his love, his boundless, openhearted love, and, though she knew it was a lie, she felt safe. She felt like she could ask him to fix things, and he'd do it. Regardless of what it took, he would do it. It was a powerful thing, to have someone's unconditional support.

He started to blink awake, and, as he did, he met Juliet's eyes and smiled. 'Hey ...' he said, his voice warm and light.

'Hey ...' Juliet said back. And then she saw the lights beginning to switch on in his eyes. 'Yeah ...' she said.

He looked at her and it was clear that he got it. He got it all. He was as naked inside as he was out. There was nothing between the two of them, except the lingering reality of Aaron, down in the cellar below.

'What are we gonna do?' Juliet said.

'I don't know.'

'Listen, no matter what,' she said, 'I want you to know that ... I love you. I don't know much, but I know that. And I just ... I don't want you to think I don't appreciate everything you've done. Because it means more to me than you could possibly understand.'

'Okay ...?' Robert said.

'You feel so good,' she said, clinging to him, squeezing him.

'You're ... everything,' he said, clinging right back.

'I would say that Aaron's gonna kill us, but I think it's a little on the nose right now,' Juliet said, allowing herself an achingly tired smile.

He took his time. 'We can still save him, you know? Or, at least, we can try.'

'I wanna hear all about that. I do. And I wanna talk to you about this dream I've had, twice now. But I'm way too hungry right now to start thinking about it.'

'Okay?'

'D'you wanna shower, then go get some breakfast? We can go to Viva? Make a plan?'

Robert closed his eyes and made a pleasure face. 'Their bagels ...' he said.

'Hey Rob,' she said, almost timidly. 'Before we shower, do you ...'

'Yeah?'

'Do you wanna ... do you wanna ...'

He kissed her, and she knew that he understood what she wanted. She kissed him back, pulling him with her hands, clinging to him, needing him. And, as she did, the rest of the world, with its pain and its horror and its confusion and its cruelty, all faded away, leaving only a pure and innocent joy in its place.

†

'So how do we find the Polysire?' Juliet said as she sipped her Coke.

'I have no idea at this point,' Robert replied.

They were in Viva, a trendy café for rich knobheads that was nestled on the high street by Ecclesburn's shopping centre, in between the Waterstones and an indie bespoke jewellery shop called Discretion. And as snooty and up themselves as Viva's customers were, the staff treated Juliet with tremendous respect, and it didn't hurt that the food was amazing either.

'Do you really think it could work?' she asked. 'I mean, if it's true, why haven't we heard about it before?'

'Look, I don't know. I think it's a long shot. But it's something we have to try. At the very least, we'd be killing a powerful vampire. That's no bad thing.'

Juliet nodded. 'How are we supposed to find him, though?'

'Well, it may mean going back into Undertown? We could go see the Cacolamia again, if we have to.'

'I thought you really hated it there?' Juliet said, guilt in her voice.

'I did, but that doesn't mean we shouldn't go. But there are other things we can try first. Reach out to people, other hunters, other Catholics, people who believe in this stuff.'

Juliet nodded again, thinking it through. 'Wait, tell me something. How did you even find about this?'

Robert's eyes widened as he sipped his coffee. 'God, I didn't explain,' he said, putting the drink down. 'I got a letter.'

'A letter?'

'Yeah, a letter, addressed to me, at Rayne Manor, and inside was a sheet of paper, right, with nothing but a Bible verse on it.'

Juliet furrowed her brow. 'You what?'

'I rang Bishop Powell, and he said that the Bible verse is used by some Catholics, to argue that the whole Polysire thing is real.'

'What's the verse?' Juliet asked. 'No, wait, I don't care. Who sent you the letter?'

'I don't know!' Robert said, his eyebrows high and his voice energetic.

Juliet wasn't sure how to react to this. 'Wait, so someone sent you a letter, with a reference to some theory that vampires can be turned back into their human selves, but you don't know who it was?'

'Right.'

'Well, Rob, that means that someone out there knows about Aaron. Someone knows what we've been doing this last few nights.'

Robert stopped to think. 'Yeah ... I guess so.'

'Because, whoever it is, they're not gonna just send you a Bible verse out of the blue, right? Whoever it is, they know, and they're trying to, like, nudge you towards finding this Polysire.'

Robert hummed thoughtfully.

'Could it be the bishop?' Juliet asked.

'No, we only talked to him for the first time yesterday. The letter had already been sent. It was delivered yesterday morning, so it must have been sent Friday?'

'The weird priest at St. Luke's? Father whatshisname?'

'Father William?' Robert said, mulling it over. 'I guess it could be. He said he doesn't believe in vampires, though ...'

'He said he doesn't believe in vampires? He just came out and said that?'

'Well, I'd asked him for holy water. He said he knew that the people here in town were kind of superstitious, re: the whole vampire thing. And he said that there were Catholics who do believe in vampires, but that he isn't one of them.'

'So, maybe he was just saying that?' Juliet said. 'Maybe because he's one of these, what did you call them?'

'Andressites,' Robert said. 'A Catholic sect of vampire hunters, who believe vampires can be turned back into people.'

'Right, maybe he's one of those, and he's just keeping it to himself until he thinks he can trust you. Like, maybe he's testing you? Trying to recruit you?'

'God I bet that's it. But if it is ... how does he know about Aaron?'

Juliet pursed her lips pensively. 'I don't know, but ... whether it's the priest or not, *someone* knows about Aaron, and that means he could be in danger. I mean, we really don't want the vampire hunting community finding out that we have a vampire in our cellar. So, what do we do? Should we go talk to the priest?'

Robert drummed his fingers while he thought it through. 'Maybe I'll go alone? He might get spooked if we both go?'

'Okay, fine,' Juliet said. 'I'll go to the slaughterhouse in Cockerham and get more blood for tonight.' She looked startled suddenly. 'Wait, the priest thinks you want to be a priest too, right? Won't he think it's a bit weird that you're not in his church on a Sunday morning?'

Robert looked around the restaurant. 'I guess. I'll just come up with something.'

A calm settled between them. And they took a moment, resting in the resolution they'd reached, to look into each other's eyes, in the way young lovers do, when they haven't a care or a worry in the world.

'Hi guys,' came the strong, well spoken voice of Trisha, the waitress, carrying their food. 'I've got two Scottish breakfasts, one with extra bagels?'

'Extra bagels over here,' Robert said, lifting his hand.

†

When Robert opened the church door, the worshipers inside were listening to Father William's closing announcements and his dismissal of them. When he was finished, they said as one, 'Thanks be to God,' and he smiled in a magnanimous sort of way which Robert found hard to read.

Robert sat, in a seat at the back, as the members of the congregation began slinking out of their pews and filing out of the building.

He waited as the building emptied, all the while watching Father William, who was shaking hands with some of the parishioners at the front, taking the time to speak and be pastoral with them.

And as the numbers within the church began to dwindle, Robert watched Father William, watching *him*. It was unclear, whether the priest was eyeing him because he indeed was the Andressite, or simply because Robert had said he wanted to become a priest. Nevertheless, Robert was sharp and alert, trying to expect the unexpected.

As the last of the churchgoers siphoned out of the building, Father William followed them down the aisle towards the back of the church where Robert was sitting. 'Mr. Entwistle,' he said, smiling cryptically.

He looked ... terrible. His forehead was sweaty, and he seemed pastier than he had before. 'Hello, Father. Are you ... okay?'

Father William coughed into his fist. 'I've been better,' he said lightheartedly. 'English germs, perhaps.' He straightened a little. 'I was expecting to see you this morning. After our discussion on Friday.'

'I had some personal issues to attend to this morning,' Robert said. 'I'm sorry.'

Father William nodded, not letting his eyes move an inch from Robert's. 'No penance is necessary, young Robert.'

Robert climbed from his seat and stood in front of Father William. 'Father, I wondered if I could ask you something.'

Father William offered a ceremonial wave to someone, and then gestured to Robert towards the front of the building. 'Of course.'

'Well,' Robert began, following him, 'I wanted to ask you about a passage, from the Bible.'

'Excellent,' Father William said emphatically, like he was reviewing his favourite beverage, and then coughed again.

'It's from First Peter,' Robert said. 'Chapter three, verses seventeen and eighteen.'

Father William lifted his head, like he was recalling the memory of the verse, as they neared the front of the church. He hummed for a second, deep in thought, took out a handkerchief and dabbed his forehead with it, and then turned to Robert. 'My dear, young Mr. Entwistle, would it trouble you deeply if I asked you a favour?'

'Um, no?'

'Are you squeamish?'

'What?'

Father William cracked a toothy smile. 'Are you a terribly squeamish soul?'

'No ...?'

'Then, I make my request of you this,' Father William said. 'Come out into the yard and assist me in the slaughtering of the Sunday chicken.'

Robert didn't quite know how to react, so he simply stood, with his mouth open. 'Assist you in the what-ing of the what?'

Father William laughed. 'I am entertaining a family this afternoon. The Smiths. Mrs. Smith has offered to cook, so I have offered to supply the food.'

'So you're going to kill the chicken? Right now? And you want me to help?'

The priest's eyes were warm and cordial, and he gestured with his hand towards the door at the far end of the echoey church. 'If you don't mind?'

'No, of course,' Robert said, a touch of neurotic sarcasm in his tone, 'let's go kill a chicken, why would I mind?'

†

The church yard was now doubling as a free range chicken farm, by the look of it. There were coops, which were open, as roughly twenty chickens wandered about the muddy grass. Robert couldn't help but sink a little, as he'd had of late, he felt, his share of being up close to animal death.

'Around here is the slaughter wall,' Father William said, gesturing with his arm towards the back of the church building, which was all set with a job lot of grim looking apparatus. 'Come along.'

'Ah, really, what is all that stuff?' Robert said, wincing.

'This is just the processing station,' Father William said, coughing again as he led the way.

There were four knives, resting on a table, which really drew the eye. They were visibly razor sharp, even from the short walk away. There was a rather sinister looking metal cone, pointing downwards over a tank, which was connected at the top by two wooden poles. Additionally, there were a few more tanks, and another table with gloves and other bits on it.

'Marvellous,' Robert said, summoning the necessary bravado.

'Would you like to choose the sacrificial fowl?'

'Would I like to choose the chicken that has to die?' Robert said, his eyebrows almost as high as the tone of his voice. 'Nah, you're alright mate, I'm okay, I'm sound, you choose.'

Father William laughed with a nod as he walked into the midst of the cluster of chickens, which were all pottering about. With one swift motion, he darted his arms down and scooped up one of the birds, which dutifully began flapping its wings about and squirming manically. 'Perfectly ... normal,' Father William shouted over the sound of squawking, while he spun the chicken upside down and held it by the feet, his arm fully stretched.

This seemed to calm the chicken, which became still and quiet.

Father William marched over, grinning. 'Young Mr. Entwistle, meet Dorothy.'

Robert crossed his arms and frowned as the memory of Henrietta Boffin the cat returned, accompanied by a fresh dose of guilt. 'Dorothy,' he said, an ironic pleasantry.

'Right,' Father William said, as he neared the great, big cone. Slowly, he lifted the chicken, still dangling it by the feet, and lowered it into the cone so that its head poke out of the hole at the bottom. 'Pass me the first knife, would you. On the far left.'

Robert looked to the wall, at the four sharp knives. He did as he was told, picking up the requested knife and holding it out for the priest, who was busy pulling some thick, blue gloves over his fingers.

'Now, this is the grisliest part I'm afraid,' Father William said, coughing as he took the knife and yanked sharply at the chicken's head through the cone. Next, he slashed at the chicken's neck, one quick slice on each side, and pulled its head down, allowing blood to pour out, pooling heartily in the tank below. The chicken started kicking and jerking.

'Ah, lord,' Robert said, managing to censor himself from saying the more instinctive "Jesus".

'Don't fret, young Robert,' Father William said, still draining the chicken. 'The creature is unconscious now. It can't feel a thing. Completely unaware of what's happening.'

'There's your blood,' he said, gesturing at it, still pulsing out of the bird, as it finally, mercifully started to slow down, coming to a mere drip.

'Now, you wanted to discuss a verse?' Father William said, looking up at Robert as he squeezed the last drops of blood out of the unfortunate Dorothy.

'Yeah,' Robert said through a wince. 'One Peter, chapter three, verses seventeen and eighteen.'

Father William squinted, as though deep in thought, then he lifted the now deceased chicken out of the cone and made his way towards one of the other tanks. 'Remind me?'

Robert squinted too now, trying to get the measure of Father William. 'It's better to suffer for doing good,' he began. 'If suffering should be God's will.'

Father William nodded, dunking the chicken into the tank, swirling it and dipping it. 'Go on.'

'For Christ suffered too,' Robert said, trying to get the words right, 'for sins, once and for all, the righteous for the unrighteous.' He worked to summon the rest of the words from the recent parts of his memory. 'He was ... put to death, in the flesh, but made alive by the spirit.'

Father William lifted the chicken out of the steaming water in the tank and started plucking feathers from it, before dunking it again. 'Well cited,' he said, with what looked like an almost proud smile.

'Thanks,' Robert replied, trying not to give anything away.

'What would you like to know?'

'What does it mean?' Robert said, without thinking through his words properly.

Father William seemed to pick up on it too. He looked mildly flabbergasted. 'Which part?'

'Um ... the um, the last part.'

Father William blinked, and continued plucking the chicken and coughed into his shoulder. 'Put to death and quickened by the Spirit?' he said, clearing his throat.

'Yeah.'

'Well, St. Peter is reciting sacred doctrine, first of all,' Father William said.

Robert recognised this interpretation from Bishop Powell's reading of the text.

'But it is a phrase dense with meaning, of course,' Father William went on. 'Put to death, *in the flesh*. Quickened, or, made alive if you prefer, by the Holy Spirit.'

'Yeah.'

'St. Peter was exalting the divinity of the Holy Spirit,' Father William said simply. 'Confirming his place within the Godhead.'

Robert was confused by this, but didn't want to let on.

'Within the Trinity,' Father William explained, evidently aware of Robert's ignorance. 'St. Peter was clarifying that the resurrection of our Lord was not accomplished without the power of the Holy Spirit.'

Robert was thoroughly disappointed. He'd wanted to see at least a flicker of something more from the priest, but all he'd had was yet more stale Christian theology. 'Okay.'

'Why do you ask?' Father William said, lifting the chicken out of the tank and walking back to where the metal cone was. He removed the cone with one hand, and hung the chicken where it had been, piercing its feet with little metal hooks. 'The next knife along, please.'

Robert turned again to the knives. 'Oh. Um, well someone recommended the verse to me,' he said. 'But ... they didn't say why, really.'

Father William stood by the dead, hanging chicken, with his arm out, his palm open, waiting for the knife. 'Curious.'

'So I just wondered if it was something I should, you know, put some research into?' Robert said, handing the knife over.

Father William pulled on the chicken's neck again and started scraping along the surface of its now half-bald, half-feathered skin. 'You say someone spoke a word to you?'

Robert couldn't keep the confusion from his face.

'Someone told you to read this verse, particularly?' Father William clarified.

'Oh. Yeah.'

Father William continued scraping the dead chicken's skin, but he didn't take his eyes off Robert's own.

There was something in his eyes that was dark. Robert was convinced of that much. But he wasn't at all convinced that the new priest was the one who'd sent him the letter, or that he was actually a particularly bad person. 'Why?' Robert said. 'Why would someone want me to read this, do you think?'

Father William stood, straight and tall. Then, he pointed the knife at Robert, and said, 'I don't know, but it's curious.' Now, with the knife still in his hand, he put his fisted knuckles on his hips, with his elbows turned outwards. 'Who is this mysterious fellow? Who spoke this verse to you?'

'I, um ... I don't actually know,' Robert said. And though he was being cryptic, he tried to tell Father William with his eyes that it was okay to come clean. That the priest could reveal himself, and it would be fine. He could admit it. 'Why do you think someone would do that?'

'There are a number of reasons,' Father William said, throwing the knife firmly into the ground and leaning into the chicken, inspecting it curiously. 'Perhaps someone in the town is taken with you. Someone is trying to share a sentiment with you, by this odd, even secretive method. It might be that he's confused about his feelings for you.'

Robert narrowed his eyes. 'Are you ... are you talking about a gay crush?'

Father William laughed again, a laugh which turned into yet another cough, as he pulled feathers from the late Dorothy. 'No. Male relationships needn't be sexually motivated in order to be complicated in nature.'

Robert was absolutely not comforted by this statement, from this man. 'Okay?'

'I'm saying that someone might be trying to establish a bond with you, Robert. Maybe someone from here in town, who knows of your earnestness, and your faith.'

'Do you think I should be troubled by this?'

'Well that's an interesting question,' Father William said, standing straight to think it through. 'I suppose, perhaps, yes, you should. For these facts are undeniable. One, someone knows where you live. Two, that person knows of your faith. And, three, that same person is trying to steer you in a certain way without presenting himself to you.' Father William leaned his head to one side and narrowed his own eyes. 'Yes, perhaps you *should* be troubled by this.'

Robert felt a chill go down his spine, which made him shudder. 'That's ominous.'

'Third knife along.'

Robert stopped in his thoughts, turning to the wall for the next blade.

'But whoever it is,' Father William went on, his voice becoming more formal, more performed, 'he wishes to bond with you over Scripture. This suggests a certain level of faith in him. This suggests that, though his motives may *seem* clandestine, may seem *disquieting* even'—he held Robert's eyes as he took the knife—'you can trust him.'

Robert let the moment hold, while he kept the priest's gaze and tried to figure out just what the hell was going on behind his eyes. 'Okay,' he said finally, content, at least, for now.

†

Tilly Turnbull looked out of her bedroom window as the sun began to set on another day in Ecclesburn. The changing of the clocks meant that it was getting dark way earlier than it had the previous night. Tilly had never thought about that before. It was just something that, kind of, happened. Now, though. Now, it just seemed to mean that the monsters in her town were free to come out an hour earlier.

She wondered what Juliet Rayne was doing.

She wondered what Sophie The Vampire Hunter From Cheshire was doing.

She sighed, and muttered to herself, 'Not bloody sitting around being *safe*, that's for sure.'

†

Juliet waited in the hall of her home, for Robert to return. She had been to Cockerham for Aaron's blood, and it was almost time to go down into the cellar and give it to him. But she wanted to see Robert first. She wanted to kiss him again. To feel his warmth, even just through his clothes. The thought made her shake, almost bouncing in her armchair.

She steadied herself, and looked at the three bottles sitting next to her bag by the cellar door. The door clicked, and the sound echoed through the wood of the room.

The door creaked open and Robert walked in, immediately smiling as he saw her. He looked tired.

'Hi,' she said.

'Hey.'

He walked straight toward her, and cautiously kneeled in front of her. Slowly, he reached out and put his hands on her knees, so she leaned forward and kissed him.

'I missed you,' she said, looking into his eyes.

His own eyes widened briefly as he adored her with them. 'I'm sorry. Father William invited me to have a bloody roast dinner with the Smiths. It was hard to get away.'

'It's okay,' she said.

'When you come back up I'll fill you in on everything he said.'

Juliet looked up at the clock on her wall. 6:02pm. Nautical dusk.

Robert's iPhone alarm went off, right on cue. 'Dinner time,' he said.

She nodded, kissed him again, and said, 'I'll talk to him, okay? I'll tell him ... about things.'

'Be safe.'

'I will.'

With that, she stood, squeezed his shoulder, and headed for the cellar.

†

And deep, within the dark safety of the Rayne Manor cellar, Aaron waited. He was aware of every stark and raw human emotion above him. He could feel each desire, and the completion of each desire. Again, and again, and again: the awakening of a need, and the satisfaction of that need.

Robert and his Juliet were giving themselves to each other.

They were taking peace in one other.

And as that knowledge settled over him, like a grim, itchy blanket landing on raw, burning skin, he heard the cellar door open, and footsteps descending once more.

CHAPTER THIRTEEN
Almost Transgressive

When Juliet entered the cellar this time, Aaron was sitting at the table with the dim light on. His hands were resting on the wooden surface, and his head was lowered. She couldn't tell what his mood was. He seemed like a robot, which had been switched off.

In front of him was his late father's army bayonet, still sitting on the table from the night before, only with menace now, which made Juliet take a sharp intake of breath.

His head moved in her direction, just a little. 'Hello,' he said.

'Hey,' she said, stepping in and pulling out the chair next to him, where she'd sat the previous evening.

'Blood and wine again, is it?'

'I have lamb, and cow,' Juliet said, trying to ignore the bayonet, while wondering whether the innocence associated with lamb would give him any pleasure at all. She tried to lock up her thoughts, aware that he could read her mind pretty well.

'I will have the lamb first,' he said. Then, he looked up at her. 'Please.'

She nodded, and took two glasses from her bag, before starting the corkscrew on the lamb's blood.

'How was your day?' he said, his tone flat and deathly, but with a hint of what seemed like genuine curiosity.

'I, um,' Juliet began, feeling her cheeks flush as she popped the cork out the bottle, 'it was fine. Yours?'

He stared at her. 'I slept.'

'Of course.'

'And read.'

Juliet placed his glass in front of him and poured. 'Right.'

'One of Entwistle's entirely randomly chosen works,' Aaron said, picking up the glass and wincing through his first long gulp.

'What?'

'The Great Gatsby,' Aaron said, setting the glass on the table. He smiled with contemptuous eyes, and then stared at Juliet. 'It is fascination itself, the books our friend chose for me.'

'Why's that?' Juliet said, putting the corkscrew to her Pinot Grigio.

'It doesn't matter,' Aaron said.

Juliet watched him curiously as he drank more, trying to figure out what he was thinking. 'Listen, I want to talk to you about something,' she began, cautiously. 'And I don't want you to get upset.'

'Yes?'

Juliet popped off her own cork now, and filled her glass to the top, before swigging liberally for the courage. 'I'm sorry I gave you a hard time last night,' she said.

'About what?'

'About ... what you said. You said Robert has feelings for me. And that I have feelings for him. And I was super harsh at you.'

'You were affronted,' he said. 'By my presumption.'

'Yeah ...' Juliet said, her mouth staying open. She drank again. 'But, listen. Aaron, you weren't wrong. Okay? And I feel ... I feel terrible.'

'Do you?' he said. There was no doubt in his voice. There was very little of anything, in fact.

'Yeah, I do,' she said. 'Listen, I don't wanna chicken out of telling you this. I ... I slept with him, Aaron. And I know that was a real shitty thing to do while you were stuck down here, and after everything that's happened to you.' Tears welled in her eyes at the guilt. 'I'm really sorry.'

He remained an utter mystery, giving nothing away. 'Thank you.'

'Thank you?' she parroted. 'Seriously, you're thanking me?'

He drank more of his lamb's blood, hiding the wince better this time. 'For the apology,' he said.

'Aaron, I just told you that I slept with Robert.' She jabbed him lightly with her her first and middle fingers. 'And you're *thanking* me?'

'Would you rather I responded furiously?' he said, flashing eyes that had started to become the same murky bright red they'd been in Cleve Woods, three nights before. The rest of his face was human. Only the eyes had changed. 'Is that it? You desire me angry, Juliet?'

'No, but ... I thought you'd feel *something*.'

'You have no comprehension the depths of my feeling,' he said, his voice lowering into something like a growl. 'You are utterly benighted, utterly—'

'Speak a language I understand—'

'You are ignorant, Juliet,' he snapped, leaning at her, 'you are a child in the dungeon palace of a philosopher king, and you come in here with your sorry and the smell of his

DNA on you, mewling into me of your guilt; well you can keep it, I do not want it, do you understand?'

The tears which had welled before, fell now. 'I knew the "thank you" was bullshit,' she said.

Aaron, gritting his teeth, grabbed his dad's army bayonet off the table and turned and threw it. With a thunk, it stuck into the wooden wall, and swayed a little, finally settling, still sticking out.

After this, he settled down, and drank.

'I deserve that,' she said. 'I deserve more. And, I know you don't want to hear it, but I'm still sorry.'

'Looking back,' Aaron said, his voice neutral again, 'I can see it all. I see Entwistle, staring over the water at your green light.'

'You made more sense before you were turned,' Juliet said, drinking her wine.

'He yearned for you,' Aaron explained. 'He stayed close, always nourishing his hope that you might be his.'

'He's not ... he's not been sneaky, if that's what you think. I don't want you to take this as some kind of thing where he's responsible and I'm not.'

'I don't.'

'And, like, one of the other things I need to talk to you about is proof of that.'

Aaron actually seemed surprised now. It was the first time he'd looked that way since he'd died.

'Robert's been working hard on something,' Juliet said. She felt excitement rising within her, as the hope grew. 'And, I don't want you to get your hopes up, okay?'

'What is it?' he asked impatiently. 'I cannot see it. What is it?'

'We *might*—and, like, "might" is the operative word here—we might be able to ... turn you back.'

'Turn me back?'

'Yeah. Into a man again. We might be able to save you from ... all this.'

Aaron laughed. 'So, we too beat on,' he said, eyeing her intensely. 'Boats against the current, borne back ceaselessly into the past.' A sadness came over Aaron's face now. 'Juliet ...'

'Just, go with me, okay?'

'Juliet ...'

'There are these vampires out there, called Polysires. They're old, and powerful, and they've turned dozens of people into vampires. If you can find the Polysire, and kill him, all the vampires he's turned turn back.'

'You think I was turned by one of these ... Polysires?'

'What? No. No, it's not just the vamps the Polysires turn who get saved. It's all the vamps turned by the vamps he turned. I know it's confusing, but—'

'You mean to kill my vampiric grandfather, as it were?' Aaron said.

'Exactly.'

'And you believe that this will undo what has been done to me?'

'We believe it might. And, while it's possible, we have to try.'

Aaron drank more of his blood. 'You believe it is possible to return dead matter to life?' he said. 'Because I *am* dead, Juliet. I am not sick. I do not have a virus. I am not under a spell. I am *dead*.'

'Well, look, I don't really get the whole Catholicism thing, but it's more or less *about* bringing dead people back to life. Right? And, like, we've always used holy water and crucifixes to fight ... um, vampires. So there's clearly a connection between church stuff and, like, the laws that govern vampire existence, or whatever.'

'My metaphysics are in some way tied to the church, you believe?'

Juliet took a moment. 'Well, yeah.'

'I used holy water, the night that I died. The church did not spare me then.'

'No, I know. And ... we think there's something off with Father William, the new priest. Rob's been with him all day, trying to figure him out.'

At the mention of Robert's name, Aaron flinched a little. 'I see,' he said.

'Does that sound ... does that sound, y'know, good?' Juliet asked.

He looked at her, his eyes deep and far away. 'Does it sound good?'

'Being saved. Being human again.'

'I will not lie to you, Juliet. I desire further death. I want to take you, and then I want to go upstairs and take Entwistle. After that, the town.'

Juliet's heart ached for him.

'That is what I want. And I do not want to be liberated of my want.'

'You're getting me all pickled,' she said. 'What?'

'Consider your feelings for Entwistle, glowing now as they do,' he said.

Juliet swallowed nervously. 'Okay?'

'Your need of him hurts me.'

'Yeah ...'

'You know that?'

Juliet drank more of her wine, trying to drink away the pain of her guilt. 'I do,' she admitted.

'The thing you desire causes harm to another,' he said. 'And yet, should I offer you some enchanted potion, to make those feelings go away, would you drink it?'

Juliet contemplated it. To be free of her love for Robert would mean being free of her guilt. And yet. 'No, I wouldn't drink it,' she said.

'Because you want to want him.'

'I do.'

'It is the same way with me,' Aaron said. 'I want to want your blood.'

She took a deep breath. 'Okay, but we went through all this last night.'

'There is a difference between a smoker giving up smoking,' Aaron said, 'and a smoker throwing away his Zippo.'

This actually made sense to Juliet. It was like an alcoholic pouring wine down the sink, rather than keeping it in a hidden cabinet for a bleak future, when it might become necessary again. 'I get it,' she said quietly.

'Yes,' he said, eyeing her intensely. 'You do.'

'So, do you not want us to do it?' she asked. 'You'd rather stay as you are?'

Aaron clenched his fist on the table in front of the last half an inch of lamb's blood in his glass. 'It is right, to try,' he said.

Juliet was filled with respect at these words. Even though she had come down with the smell of his friend on her, even though she had admitted to cheating on him when he was suffering and alone, and even though he was having to manage a crippling bloodlust, he still had the moral strength to agree to do the right thing.

She lifted her glass and held it out.

He read the gesture, lifted his own, and clinked.

And, as they drank to the plan, Juliet started to allow herself to feel a moment of relief, like everything might turn out okay.

†

'Polysires?' said Steve Fitzpatrick, the Liverpudlian vampire hunter, through the phone. He sounded a little taken aback.

'Aye,' Robert replied. 'Old, powerful vampires, who've turned, like, dozens, maybe hundreds of people.'

'Yeah, yeah, I've heard of them mate,' Steve said, 'I just don't really know too much.'

'Steve mate, just the fact that you've heard of them is more than I've had from the last fifteen people I spoke to.'

'You've been on the phone all evening, hey?' Steve said.

'You've no idea,' Robert said, sighing as he tried to rub away his stress headache. 'I'm well into my third hour here. But you've heard of them?'

'My arl fella used to say he'd fought one,' Steve said.

Robert could only blink at the possibilities opening up before him. 'Your father told you he'd fought a Polysire?'

'Aye mate,' Steve said, his voice grave with the memory. 'It's what got him binned from the community.'

Robert ran his hands through his hair and let out a deep breath. 'Okay,' he said, nodding. 'So, what was his story?'

'It was back in the seventies,' Steve began. 'Dad would've been about eighteen, nineteen at the time.'

Like me, Robert thought.

'The way he tells it,' Steve went on, 'or, I should say, the way he told it one time, and one time only, the vampire was called ... Etienne of Chécy.' He took his time over the words, as though remembering them after years with deep respect. 'A French bloodsucker, from a town just east of Orléans.'

'Okay ...'

'Etienne lived in the Depths below Liverpool at that time, and came up through the Williamson Tunnels, in Edge Hill.'

'The town in the Depths beneath Liverpool is called ...'

'Silverdock,' Steve said, clearly sensing Robert's uncertainty.

'Silverdock, right,' Robert said with another nod.

'Anyway, that's where Etienne lived, according to my dad. He got it into his head that if he killed Etienne he'd be able to save a mate of his. A guy called Dougie.'

'Was Dougie turned?' Robert said. 'By this French vampire?'

'According to my arl fella, yeah, he was,' Steve said.

'And did your dad save him? Did he save his mate?'

Steve paused at this. 'Nah, Rob mate,' he said, speaking like he was stating the obvious, but still with sensitivity. 'If he had, he wouldn't have been booted from the community, now would he?'

'I guess not,' Robert said. 'Wait, was your dad exiled permanently? I thought your parents were both hunters?'

'No, he had a five year ban from events, and gatherings, and conferences. Anywhere the community was organising, really. By the time I was born he was back in.'

'Five years huh?'

'Well you know how the community was,' Steve said. 'Way more religious back then. Way more bothered with Regs, with its orthodox thinking and its commitments.'

The truth was, Robert wasn't really familiar with the way the community had been, in the seventies, in

Liverpool. But he figured Steve's assumption couldn't hurt. 'Sure,' he said.

'But, even though he kept his mouth shut later on, he told me he'd never swerved from his belief, that his arl mate Dougie could've been saved, that he should've been supported by the community, rather than binned out of it.'

'He believed in the Polysire thing to the end?'

'To the very end, mate.'

'So ... Steve, can I ask ... do you believe in it?'

Another pause. 'Look,' the Liverpudlian hunter began, 'I had nothing but respect for my arl fella. The bastard was a tough, mean arl arse, but he'd have taken a bullet for me. He'd have taken being vamped for me. So, it doesn't sit nicely with me, having to say this, but no. No, I don't believe in it.'

'Okay,' Robert said, accepting Steve's words. 'Would you be pissed off if I asked why?'

'Because we've no record of a vampire becoming human, do we?' Steve said. 'If this were true, there'd be at least one person out there, someone who'd been a vampire once, but who'd been cured. That person, if he was out there, he'd have come forward. He'd have come and found the community.'

Robert didn't say anything, but Steve's words struck a chord within him. A powerful, fascinating rabbit hole of a chord.

'Because,' Steve went on, 'if this thing *was* true, it'd change everything. We'd be able to save ... hundreds of people, just by taking out one vampire. We'd be able to save thousands, tens of thousands, when you think about the spread of it all.'

'I guess.'

'Listen, my arl fella bought into it because he lost a mate. Right? That's the only reason he—'

'But you said he believed it until he died, that he—'

'Rob, mate, he wasn't all there. The life ... it takes it out of you. You're young, so maybe you don't fully appreciate this yet. But, when you've lost mates, when you've lost people you love, you lose a little part of your grip on things. I reckon you *have* to, just to stop from chucking yourself off the nearest high-rise.'

'What if your dad was right, though?'

'Look, I've thought about it,' Steve replied. 'Obviously, I've thought about it. I miss my arl fella, and I'd love it, I'd love to connect with his memory, by taking up where he left off.'

'Okay, so—'

'So, it doesn't work that way,' Steve said. 'The world isn't the way we want it to be. We can't force it to be the way we want it to be, no matter how much we might like to. At some point, Rob mate, we all have to grow up, and that means letting go of that thing we all think when we're little, that the world revolves around us, rather than the other way around.'

Robert scratched his nose with his free hand. 'Okay. But, like, okay, just because it's immature to run off and chase wild ideas about saving our mates, about saving the people we love, that doesn't mean that we shouldn't look into it, right?'

Silence came through the phone.

'And,' Robert went on, 'it seems to me that your reason for believing that your dad was wrong is based more on the fact that you don't actually *want* him to have been right, rather than on any actual proof.'

'Steady on, lad ...' Steve said.

'No, but, really,' Robert said, 'you're telling me that it's a good reason not to believe your dad, just because the *community* didn't? You're telling me that it's like, some kind of childish fantasy?'

'No—'

'Well it sounds that way,' Robert said, speaking louder now. 'It sounds like you're saying that, if someone like me, or your dad, believes that Polysires are real, and that they can be killed, and that people can be saved, that that's the same as a baby, thinking the world resolves around him. Right?'

'No—'

'Well it sounds that way,' Robert said again.

Steve took his time answering now, like he was setting himself. 'Why are you asking all this?'

After hours on the phone to suspicious hunters, Robert was prepared for this question. 'It's a no-brainer,' he said for the umpteenth time that evening. 'If we can take out dozens, maybe even hundreds of vampires, by killing just one? We have to do it.'

'And what about the poor bastards you change back?' Steve said.

'What about them?'

'They're stuck with God knows how many years of killing weighing on their consciences? Christ, if it was me, I'd probably want to top myself. Some of them will have spent, what, ten, fifteen times as long as a vampire than they've ever spent as a human?'

'So, what, your logic is that it's better to just kill them?'

Steve sighed. 'It's all academic anyway, mate,' he said. 'It's not possible. It can't be. We'd have heard about it.'

'Right,' Robert said, although he was already disengaging with the Scouser's cautions. His mind ran to the one thing he'd learned during this conversation: that the Polysire in Liverpool, in the seventies, had made its home in the Depths. That was a decent lead, and it made sense. 'Listen, there's something else I wanted to ask, while I've got you, if that's okay?'

'Of course, mate.'

'You ever had any issues with holy water glitching?'

'Glitching?'

'Have you ever attacked a vampire with holy water, only for it to have no effect?'

Steve took another pause, and then hummed thoughtfully. 'Personally, no. I haven't. But I've heard stories about failing holy water, for sure. We always get ours from St. Clare's, in Sefton Park. We've never had a problem. Neither did my mum and dad, as far as I know.'

'But you've heard stories?' Robert said.

'Yeah, always the same, too. Hunters were in a hurry and had some water blessed by some priest, some gobshite, and the water didn't work.'

'I see.'

'Why, have you had bad holy water? Community Regs are pretty clear, if you have. You have to declare where you got it, and who you got it from, and—'

'Yeah, I know the Regs,' Robert said, trying to sound casual. 'And, well, I'm not sure yet.'

'You're not sure? Whether your holy water works? It either kills vampires like hot acid or it doesn't. What's to not be sure of?'

'It's just ... there's nothing concrete, yet,' Robert said, a little awkward now. 'If there is, you'll hear about it.'

Steve's narrow eyed suspicion was practically coming through the phone. 'Okay, lad,' he said finally, while the office door opened.

Robert looked to see Juliet entering with a half full bottle of white wine in one hand, and two glasses in the other. He gave her a smile. 'Listen, I've gotta go,' he told Steve, not taking his eyes off Juliet's.

Steve was saying his goodbyes when Robert lowered the iPhone in his hand and cancelled the call.

Juliet walked toward him, saying nothing, and wrapped her arms around him. Robert felt the bottle and the glasses pressing lightly into his back. He held her, and waited for her to take the comfort she needed before saying anything, or pulling away from her.

'Given he's a vampire, he took it really well,' she said, turning her lips into Robert's neck.

'You told him about ... about us?'

'I did.'

Robert held her tighter still, and took a moment to appreciate what he had, smelling the combination of soap and perfume and wine on her. 'And he took it well?'

She pulled out, now, and looked into his eyes. 'Yeah,' she said. 'He got super angry at one point, but he was pretty good about it generally.'

'And the Polysire thing?'

'He's in,' she said.

Robert smiled. Things were looking up. 'Alright,' he said, nodding.

Juliet went to Robert's desk now, and started pouring wine into the two glasses. 'I missed you today,' she said, making her voice soft, and gentle, and pleasant.

'I missed you too,' he said.

Still standing with her back to him, she turned her head a little. 'Really?'

Robert thought back over his day. The killing of the chicken, the pretending to harbour a deep, Christian calling over a long, long roast dinner, and the unique oddness of Father William. 'Definitely,' he said.

She brought him a wine, and once he'd taken it, she slipped her free hand around his back, and kissed him. She was simply ... intoxicating. Robert wanted to drop the wine, and to lift her off her feet, and carry her to his desk—but he didn't.

'How did it go with the creepy priest?' she said, before sipping from her glass.

Robert gestured to his office chair, and Juliet took his lead, taking a seat.

'Well, he's not well for a start,' Robert said.

'Not well?'

'Yeah, he's sick. He looks terrible.'

'Getting used to the climate?' Juliet said.

'I guess. That's what he said, actually.'

'And the whole letter thing?'

'Well, he didn't come out and admit that he sent it,' Robert said, putting his glass down and lifting himself onto his desk.

'But ...?' Juliet said.

'He implied pretty heavily,' Robert said. 'Like, he made out that he didn't know anything. So, if it *was* him, I guess he's not sure he can trust me.'

'Okay?'

'But he said I can trust whoever sent me the letter. That was pretty much the big giveaway.'

'He said you can trust whoever sent the letter? How would he know that? If it's not him, I mean?'

Robert sipped some of his wine, and leaned back as he tried to remember the details. 'Well, he said that, given the sender used a Bible reference, that that means I can trust him.'

'Oh, right. I guess, yeah, he would think that.'

'But, you should've seen the way he looked at me when he said it. I mean, he's kind of an intense guy, generally. Like, I might be reading too much into it. But he definitely came off like he was saying, "I can't come out and say this, but it was me".'

'Okay, well that's ... probably a good thing?'

'Yeah,' Robert said, 'I think it is, I think it's a good thing. I mean, I don't know why he's being so cagey, and I don't love the fact that, if it's him, he knows about Aaron. Like, again, if the community finds out we're keeping him here, in the cellar, they'll show up, and they'll kill him.'

'I know,' Juliet said, caution and guilt in her eyes.

'And there's something else,' Robert said, squinting as his mind raced. 'Something Steve said.'

'What?'

'The whole, entire reason he doesn't believe in all the Polysire stuff is because, he reckons, if there *were* vampires who'd turned back into humans, we'd know about it, because they'd have sought us out.'

'Us?'

'Vampire hunters,' Robert said. 'The former vampires, would have sought out the community of hunters.'

Juliet wrinkled her nose as she looked up at Robert. 'Not really, I mean—'

'No, but then I thought, what if that's Father William?'

Juliet stopped, her face stunned. 'You think Father William used to be a vampire? That he was turned back?'

Robert leaned forward. 'Not necessarily, but think about it. His holy water doesn't work. Maybe it's because he's—'

'What, a former vampire?'

'Well, we've never had an issue before.'

'Sure ...'

'But then this guy rolls into town, and suddenly the holy water isn't so ... holy.'

'Right?'

'Maybe the priest who blesses it has to be pure, you know? And, no matter how good this guy's intentions are *now*, if he's killed hundreds, maybe thousands of people, as a vampire, is it really that surprising that his holy water doesn't work?'

'Rob, I've never given holy water a second thought, until the last few days,' Juliet said. 'I haven't got a clue why it'—she stopped a moment, looking for the right word—'works.'

'Okay, well, basically, things are looking up. Steve Fitzpatrick said his dad fought a Polysire, in the seventies. Some French vampire who lived in the Depths.'

Juliet raised her head. 'Oh?'

'Yeah, so that's another lead.'

Juliet, smiling now, nodded slowly. Then, she reached out and put her palm on Robert's thigh, squeezing him softly, but with an energy. 'You're not drinking your wine?' she said, her eyebrows high.

He put his hand on hers, and began running it up her bare arm. 'I'll get to it,' he said.

'Rob ... can I tell you something?'

Robert nodded.

'Everything's so crazy. I feel like I'm in the middle of ... some kind of, tempest, or something.'

'Right?'

'But you're ... everything, right now. I'm so sorry that I spent so long with'—tears coated her eyes, so she closed them and steadied herself. 'I'm sorry I took until now to open up to you about ... how I feel.'

'Me too. I mean, though, about how *I* feel.'

'You've ... you've loved me, for years, haven't you,' she said.

Robert smiled again. 'I've loved you, since the first day of high school, since the first time I saw you.'

'We were lost,' she said.

'Trying to find the E blocks,' Robert said with a laugh.

'Right, our first RE class.'

Robert nodded.

'It seemed so important then,' Juliet said. 'Like, I bet Mrs. Dunne wouldn't have given two shits if we'd shown up late.'

Robert's hand was still rubbing up and down Juliet's arm, and he squeezed again. 'Yeah, I loved you then,' he said. 'And every single day since.'

Juliet winced now, like she was in pain and trying to hide it. 'I'm so sorry. It must have killed you. Seeing me with Aaron, every day, for years. You know, he rode me pretty hard last night, saying that I was in love with you, all these years, and—'

'Hey, no,' Robert said tenderly, shaking his head.

She looked up, and her blue eyes had never been more perfect. 'I'm just, I'm sorry. He wasn't wrong.' She looked at the floor. 'I've always ... deep down, I mean, I've always ... wanted you. I've always wanted to touch you. To be touched by you. And I don't mean, just, like, with our hands. I mean, I've always treasured talking to you.'

It sounded like true and solid logic to Robert. 'Completely,' he agreed.

She looked up now. 'But, I swear to God, I'm so sorry, Rob,' she said, as tears welled behind her eyes again.

He shushed, and shook his head, and gripped her lovingly.

'There's no good way to say this,' she said, drying her upper cheeks with her knuckles, 'but ... I felt like being with Aaron was the right thing to do.'

'You don't have to say any of this,' Robert said.

'I need to,' she said, setting herself. 'Because ... it's eating me up.'

'You're worried about how Aaron's taken it tonight?'

'No,' she said. She didn't sound angry, or upset, or anything like that. 'No, I'm worrying you'll think I'm coming to you because I'm lonely, or because I'm in pain, or ... for any reason other than the fact that ... I want you. I need you. I always have.'

Robert did worry, though. He worried because she was clearly upset, and emotional, and stressed. He knew his own feelings. He'd nurtured them for years. He could trust *them*. And, though he fully trusted Juliet with his *life*, there was a cautious part of him that, right at that moment, couldn't help but hold back a piece of his heart.

Just in case.

'Okay,' he said.

Juliet took a breath and blinked away her emotional high, before reaching for her wine and taking three long gulps. She set the glass down hard. 'I love you,' she said.

'I love you too,' he said, before leaning forward and meeting her forehead with his own. 'We'll figure everything out, okay?'

She nodded, their heads still joined.

'And whatever you need, I'll be,' he went on. 'I swear it, Jules. I swear to God. You're ... you're safe, with me.'

'I know,' she whispered.

'I won't let anything bad happen.'

'Thank you,' she said, and looked at him intensely. 'Rob, take me to bed. Please. Take me to bed, and fuck me.'

The words, "fuck me", seemed so stark that they were almost transgressive. The raw, earnest, entirely compelling *truth* of them overrode every other impulse within Robert's psyche.

She reached out and pulled his head toward hers. 'I need you. I need you, now. I can't wait. I can't. Please.'

Robert wrapped his arms around her and pulled her, lifting her up, out of her chair. She stood, and straddled him, his arms still locked around her. He tensed his lean biceps, surrounding her, and forcing her even closer into his embrace.

He was in no doubt.

He would do anything she wanted.

Now, and forever.

†

Aaron had read Plato's Symposium, Tom Piccirilli's A Choir of Ill Children, Leo Tolstoy's Anna Karenina, Thomas Hardy's Jude the Obscure, and now F. Scott Fitzgerald's The Great Gatsby. All in the space of a few nights. And, though his body was dead, his mind was absolutely alive with the rich *humanness* of the stories found within those pages.

That thought fascinated him.

His mind, alive, stirred by humanness.

It made him wonder, as he put Fitzgerald's fictional treatise down and lifted his second bottle of animal blood off the cellar desk, just *what* he was.

He felt the need to put the thought into words. To externalise the sentiment. 'What am I?'

No grand response came. No revelation. And his question stayed.

'To what degree ... am I *human*?'

In life, he had been a dull, if impressively loyal young man. He'd enjoyed football, and cricket, and Call of Duty. He'd liked sex, and nature, and martial arts movies.

But, now, all he was bothered with was desire.

Desire.

It was, after all, he now realised, everything there *was* to be bothered with, really.

Desire.

And, he noticed, looking into his own thoughts: he was the same person in death as he'd been in life. He knew that. He knew it absolutely. He was the same creature, the same entity. Only, in becoming a vampire, he felt like he'd skipped about a hundred years of experience, and wisdom, and learning, and maturing. He felt now like an *old* man. Not young.

His mind was sharper. Doors to grand teachings opened easily now, where once they'd been locked and fortified on both sides.

He poured blood into his glass, and wondered, were he to return to life, to become human again, would he lose his newfound clarity of thought?

He did not want that.

He could not go back. Back to sport, to fantasy football, and Netflix, and the bland nothingness of human sex.

'All there is, is desire,' he said, letting out the truth within him again, as he lifted his glass and drank the weak, unsatisfying pig's blood. 'And I desire death.'

He closed his eyes and searched upward with his mind. He could feel them, betraying him again. He could feel their *blood*. The movement of human blood during sex was, he realised then, the closest thing in the living world to the desire he now knew, the desire that was now the cornerstone of his entire identity.

The realisation allowed him to sympathise with his friends.

They were, after all, merely doing what they had to do.

And at that moment a terrible, urgent resolution settled over him. He would kill. He would take. It was what he had to do. It was what he *existed* to do.

He could not go back.

An infant cannot go back into its mother's womb, and neither could he into *life's* womb.

And, with his new ability to identify the emotions and the motivations of the humans around him, with the profound precision of his clarity in this matter, he was quite ready to get inside Juliet's head, to create confusion and doubt, and pain and guilt.

His manipulation of her would come as freely to him now as catching a slowly arcing cricket ball had done before.

He smiled, and drank more blood.

'Until tomorrow,' he said, to the Juliet in his mind.

CHAPTER FOURTEEN
To Ecclesburn

Jack Turnbull's mood was still as high as a kite. True, it was Monday morning, which was usually a below average state of affairs, but today it didn't matter. He'd showered, he was in his work clothes, his phone had about ten football podcasts stored and ready for his day's listening pleasure, and, best of all, he was standing in his concrete garden, drinking a coffee, smoking a roll up, and texting with Becky.

His phone buzzed. 'If you want to do it, you should to it xx' read the text.

He'd told her his childhood dream: to sing, in a romantic, bohemian, alt-rock, post-punk, indie pop band. Well, he'd simply said, "a band", but that was what had been in his head. He inhaled from his cigarette, and then pinched it between his lips, and typed, 'Feels a bit daft, now.'

While he waited for the two grey ticks on his screen to turn blue, he heard a rapping on the window.

Rita was frowning at him.

She shuffled for the door and joined him outside, before sitting on one of his patio chairs, crossing her legs under her thermal dressing gown.

'Morning, Reet,' Jack said warmly.

She grunted, and took out one of her Marlboro Greens, lighting it with Jack's Zippo off the patio table. 'Have you thought about what we talked about?' she said, looking up at him with flat, pre-coffee eyes.

Jack's phone buzzed again. 'Have I thought about what?' he said, looking down at the phone.

The message read: 'Do you want to do it or not? Xx'

Rita said, 'Have you thought anymore about leaving Ecclesburn?'

Jack was busy typing. 'I don't know,' he wrote, and sent. Then, he looked up at Rita, and said, 'Oh. Um, well, no. I mean, I can't just find a job and buy a house and sell this house in the space of a few days.'

'I'm aware of that,' Rita said.

'Good,' Jack said, looking back down at his phone and taking another drag.

'But have you even started looking for work, somewhere else?' Rita went on.

Jack's chest tightened as he started to feel irritated by Rita. He didn't want to hear it. He just wanted to be outside, on his own, texting Becky and smoking his first ciggie of the day in peace. 'No,' he said. 'But, look, I'll do it tonight.'

'It's not safe here,' Rita said for the hundredth time. 'It's not safe for Tilly here.'

'Christ, I know that, Reet,' Jack snapped. 'What do you expect me to do about it now? I have to go to work. I have five minutes to myself to enjoy a smoke and you're up my arse about this?'

His phone buzzed again. 'You said you did,' read Becky's text. 'I'd love to hear you sing. Xx'

He smiled. He couldn't help it, despite his irritation.

'Who's that you're texting?' Rita said. 'The trollop from the pub?'

Jack sneered at her. 'Nice,' he said.

'You're still married, you know,' Rita said. 'Legally, you're still married. To *my* daughter. I think I get to call her a trollop if I want to.'

'I'm not talking about this,' Jack said, bitter in his mind, wanting to defend himself, wanting to defend Becky, but knowing it would be pointless. 'I'm not the one who left,' he muttered, focusing on his phone again.

'Just start looking for work,' Rita said, her voice hard, and fed up.

Jack breathed in the last of the Golden Virginia from his cigarette, and then exhaled soothingly, before stubbing it out in the patio table ashtray. 'Fine,' he said, and made his way for the door.

†

Tilly Turnbull was in her room, staring at the collection of religious symbols and artefacts she'd spent the previous day collecting. There were mostly crucifixes, which seemed deeply, unnecessarily gory, as well as holy water, Bibles, and rosary beads.

She'd hidden them in a Halestorm backpack, which she'd stashed under her bed.

It all seemed so bloody weird.

Why did all this stuff hurt vampires?

The question had been bothering her ever since she'd met her first vampire, days ago.

The theory she'd settled on, for now, was that the power wasn't inherent, but that it was bestowed upon the symbols by the vampires.

It was like a psychosomatic effect. The vampires believed the items were pure and holy, and therefore those items obtained their power.

She leaned this way because the alternative truth was that God exists, and he's Catholic, which seemed even weirder.

I mean, she thought, why would God bestow magical powers on this creepy collection of sticks and beads and liquids? What's he playing at? Why not have a vampire slayer, one girl in all the world, with super strength and all that? Why do *this*?

She sighed huffily.

It was no good, she thought. She would have to work with the tools at her disposal. She grabbed her phone off the bed and started to text Laura.

'Can you come over today?' she sent. 'I wanna talk to you about something.'

Still kneeling over her backpack, she took another breath and looked over her Catholic collection once more, clutching her phone with both hands, in her lap.

It pinged.

'Gimme half an hour xx' read the reply.

Tilly sent back a thumbs up emoji, and smiled to herself, as her busy mind, ever in overdrive, began to plan the best way to convince Laura to go along with her plan.

†

Bishop Powell was quite merrily reading the Guardian online—an opinion piece about Brexit talks—when his doorbell rang. He looked up, sipped some tea from his cup, and stood, before making his way for the door. When he arrived at it, he unlocked it and opened it up.

'Alright Basil mate,' said Steve Fitzpatrick, the Liverpudlian vampire hunter.

'Steven,' Bishop Powell said cordially, before turning to the pale-skinned woman who was standing next to the Scouser, who he didn't recognise. 'I'm sorry, I don't believe I've had the pleasure.'

'My given name is Anna-Marie,' she said. 'But please call me Iris.'

'Um, of course,' Bishop Powell said, a little bewildered.

'Look, Basil mate,' Steve Fitzpatrick said, 'we need to talk to you about something that's a little ... troubling. Can we come in?'

Bishop Powell was still a little flustered, but his curiosity was piqued, so he pulled his door open, invitingly.

†

'You *do* wanna go vampire hunting!' Laura said, sitting on Tilly's bed.

Tilly shushed her, and shut her bedroom door quietly. 'How can we *not*, Laulau?' she said. 'Kids are going missing. You know something, I heard that now the clocks have gone back the vampires come out more. They come out earlier, looking for people, looking for kids to ... eat, and to kill.'

Laura frowned, her lips squished to the side of her face. 'Yeah, but ...'

'*But* it's not okay,' Tilly said, making her voice firm and clear. 'We're talking about kids here, Laulau. Little kids, younger than us.'

Laura rolled her eyes, not in an arsey way, but in a kind of accepting-yet-begrudging way. 'I know,' she said.

Tilly raced to her friend and sat next to her. 'Holy water's like acid to them,' Tilly said. 'And so's garlic. And crucifixes burn them. Crucifixes make their skin blister and boil and—'

'I get it, okay Till? I get it. I just don't like it. I don't wanna do it.'

'Look, I text Harry about it. He's up for coming out and ...'

'And what?'

'And hunting,' Tilly said. Now, she smiled. 'Mark too.'

Laura's eyes widened with nervous optimism, before her face sank into a skeptical frown. 'Did you tell him I was up for going?'

Tilly's smile turned a little guilty. 'Listen, we'll be totally safe,' she said. 'The chances are we won't even find one. But we need to go out and protect the kids who live here. We do.'

'*Why*, though?' Laura moaned, and climbed to her feet, like she wanted space away from Tilly's closeness. 'Why do *we* have to do it?'

Tilly steeled herself, and looked up at her friend. 'Because ... it isn't right. Like, my mum just vanished. Like, years ago. And, given what we know now about this town, where do you think she went?'

Laura didn't answer.

'She must have been killed,' Tilly said, still sitting on the bed, looking up at her best friend. 'And I bet she was scared. I don't believe she'd have just disappeared. I don't believe she'd have left me and just chosen not to see me. So ... she must have died. And I ... I miss her, Laulau.'

Laura nodded, listening sensitively.

'Look, maybe no one else in this town wants to do anything about the way things are here, but I do. I want to change things. So that ... so that kids stop going missing. So that mums stop going missing. Is that so crazy?'

It was Laura's turn to feel a prick of guilt, judging by the look in her eyes. 'But why do *I* need to come? Why does it matter so much that I come?'

Tilly stood. 'Look, if the four of us load up, if we carry all the stuff we need, we're safer. Okay? Say I go out on my own—which I'm willing to do, by the way—'

Laura winced.

'Say I do that,' Tilly continued, 'and I run into, like, more than one vampire, I'll be way more likely to get hurt.'

'That is true.'

Tilly stepped toward Laura. 'But if we all go, it'll be safer.'

Laura's wincing half-smile seemed to thaw a little. 'And Mark will be there? Like, you're not bullshitting me about that?'

'I swear to God, I'll show you Harry's texts,' Tilly said, speaking urgently, before gesturing towards her phone on her bed, sensing Laura's impending agreement.

'How much holy water do you have?' Laura asked.

'Loads,' Tilly said. 'And so does Harry. He had to hide it from his mum because she's, like, pentecostal or something, and she thinks that Catholics are the antichrist or whatever, and—'

Laura's eyebrows shot up with a naughty curiosity. 'You've been texting Harry a lot, huh?'

Tilly twitched. 'Um, yeah. For, you know, the vampire thing.'

Laura smiled. 'I saw you'd liked his new profile photo on Facebook as well.'

'Well, it was kinda funny, with the way he was flaunting his vaporiser.' Tilly shook herself straight, standing properly and avoiding Laura's eyes. 'I just ... I admired the ballsy-ness of it.' She sighed, dropping her proper facade.

'You know, your constant Hally shipping is super creepy and, kinda makes me wonder about you in general.'

'Hally shipping?' Laura said.

'You know, Harry and Tilly, smushed together,' Tilly said, frowning. She pulled her sleeves over her fingers and crossed her arms.

'You've put some thought into that, huh?'

Tilly took a deep breath, and let the question go. 'So you're in for tonight, yeah?'

'Do you think me and Mark should be Lark, or Maura?'

'Are you in for tonight or not?' Tilly said stiffly.

Laura smiled, focusing now, but, as she did, the hint of fear returned to her eyes. 'Look, yeah. I'll come. But I wanna be, like, the most garlicky, holy watery, crucifixy girl that ever wandered around this town.'

Tilly smiled. 'I wouldn't have it any other way. And, just so you know, Lark and Maura are both terrible.'

†

Bishop Powell placed a tray of hot drinks down on his living room table. Two teas, and one strong, black coffee. 'All I have is instant, I'm afraid,' he said to the young woman who identified as Iris Oceanheart, and who looked like a character from an Anne Rice novel, with her long, black dress and elaborately gothic make up.

'Thank you,' she said meekly.

Steve Fitzpatrick leaned forward and picked up his tea, before blowing into it. Then, he looked at Iris, and said, 'Go ahead, love. Tell him what you told me.'

Iris squirmed a little, and turned from Steve to the bishop. 'It was Thursday morning, last week,' she began. 'My partner Mars and I had been called to cleanse the body of a girl who'd been killed by vampires, to prepare her, for her transition into the Summerland.'

Bishop Powell didn't want to offend the young pagan. He was particularly sensitive about this. Vampire hunting had always brought together Catholics and Celtic pagans, so it was nothing new to him. Juliet Rayne's parents, for instance, had been one half Catholic and one half Celtic pagan. 'Of course,' he said finally, nodding respectfully.

'Juliet Rayne came to the Expanse, our Tearveil, and—'

'Um,' Bishop Powell said, 'she came to the what?'

'It is our place of cleansing, and preparation,' Iris explained. 'It is where the bodies of victims are to dwell, where Mars and I treat them, and give respect to them.'

Bishop Powell had plenty of respect for rituals regarding the treatment of the dead, of course, so he nodded.

'Juliet came with her friend,' Iris went on. 'I described him to Steve.' She nodded at the Liverpudlian, who was watching her considerately. 'His name was Robert, apparently.'

'Robert Entwistle?' Bishop Powell said.

Iris nodded. 'Juliet said she needed'—she winced a little, and put her knuckles to her eye, as though fighting away tears—'she said she needed the ears of a girl called Sara Bradshaw.'

'She *what?*' Bishop Powell said, leaning forward suddenly.

Steve cleared his throat and sat up a bit. 'Sarah Bradshaw was a girl, who was killed by vampires, the previous night.'

'She had this huge dagger on her,' Iris went on, her voice breaking completely from the memory, 'and she went and chopped off Sara's ears, and took them.'

'Why?' Bishop Powell said. 'What on earth could she have possibly wanted with a dead girl's *ears*?'

Iris shook her head. 'I don't know.'

'And you say Robert was with her at the time? That he went along with this ghastly business?'

Iris nodded now.

'Speaking of Robert Entwistle,' Steve said, sipping his tea, 'he called me last night.'

'Why?' Bishop Powell said.

'He was asking me about Polysires.'

'I see,' the bishop said, growing concerned.

'I told him about my arl fella,' Steve said.

Bishop Powell sipped his tea. 'I remember,' he said, turning to Iris. 'There are some Catholic sects who believe in the existence of a kind of patriarchal super vampire. The belief goes that if you kill the Polysire, you free all of its victims from the vampiric curse.'

Iris didn't respond. She merely listened.

'Steven's father was a member of one of those sects, for a time,' Bishop Powell said, turning to Steve. 'What year was it?'

'Seventy-five,' Steve answered. 'And he got a five year ban for it.'

Bishop Powell nodded. 'Of course.'

'So what do we think of all this?' Steve said, setting his tea down. 'Because, like, I don't know why young Julie Rayne needed the ears off some poor lass. But I got the impression talking to Robbo last night that he's lost a mate.'

'There were three of them,' Bishop Powell said. 'Three Helsingers in Ecclesburn.'

'Aye, that's right,' Steve said. 'Young Julie, who lost her parents, what four, five years ago? And Robbo, and then there's the lad Aaron.'

'Aaron, of course.'

'I knew his dad,' Steve said. 'Arl Gordy McLeary. Beast of a fella.'

Bishop Powell laughed a little. 'Yes, fond of his knives, as I recall.'

'Is it right Julie and Robbo came to see you the other day?' Steve asked.

'Um, yes, that's right.'

'And Aaron wasn't with them?'

Bishop Powell took his time. 'No,' he said slowly, picking up his teacup and taking a sip.

Steve turned to Iris. 'And there was just Juliet and the lad Robbo who came to get the ears off your lass Sara?'

She nodded.

Steve turned to Bishop Powell. 'Well, are you thinking what I'm thinking?'

Bishop Powell sighed. 'Yes, I think I am. Aaron McLeary has been turned into a vampire, and Juliet Rayne and Robert Entwistle are scurrying about, trying to save him,' he said, placing his cup of tea down and leaning back into his armchair.

'I'm almost certain,' Steve Fitzpatrick said.

Iris Oceanheart was being quiet, for the most part. The fact was, she had been well and truly shaken when Juliet Rayne had come down into her Tearveil and put a knife to her ear. She'd felt its harsh edge, and she had put her own wellbeing over the wellbeing of the late Sara Bradshaw. She couldn't lose her sense of guilt, over that.

'This is terrible,' Bishop Powell said. He sounded distraught.

'Look, they're just kids,' Steve said. 'I think the community put too much confidence in young Julie, just because of who her parents were, and because of how strong she is, how strong she always was.'

'Steven, did you ever meet her parents?'

'A couple of times, aye. Never for very long, really.'

'They were such *loud* people,' the bishop went on. 'They'd fall out, they'd have these blazing rows, but they were always *touching* each other. Frankly, I was always astounded that they only had the one child, as passionate as they were.'

'So ... what do you think we should do about this?' Steve said.

Bishop Powell took a long breath and then sighed it out. 'If we're right, we have to slay the vampire.'

Iris wanted to join in, to speak more, to help. 'Where do you guys think the vampire is? Like, is he out there, killing, and eating?'

'I'd like to think that Robbo and young Julie wouldn't let that happen,' Steve said. 'When my arl fella was out trying to save his mate Dougie'—he turned to Iris to explain— 'Dougie had been turned by this French vampire, you see. Anyway, my dad had Dougie chained up in my gran's pantry. After the Scouse elders found out, they showed up, they staked Dougie, and booted my arl fella out of the community.'

Bishop Powell nodded, and then leaned forward. 'Rayne Manor is a huge building. If memory serves, there's a fairly solid cellar. Thomas and Amelie used to keep wine down there.' He looked at Iris, and then back at Steve. 'No sunlight in that cellar.'

'You think the Helsingers are keeping a vampire, chained up, in the cellar?' Iris said.

'Well, at this point, we don't think anything with any certainty,' Steve said.

Bishop Powell lifted his cup and downed his tea, saying, 'I think we're clear on what we ought to do next, though.'

Steve nodded.

Bishop Powell put down his empty cup and slammed his palms onto his thighs, readying to stand. 'Let's go to Ecclesburn.'

†

Robert and Juliet were still in bed, though the morning was passing on and on. They were face to face, still naked, head to toe, and their arms and legs were intertwined, like the inosculated branches of a pair of sycamore trees. Robert thought about that, as he looked into Juliet's eyes, and could have happily stayed, intertwined with her, for years, as a pair of sycamores do.

'What should we do?' Juliet asked.

'Well ...' Robert started, getting his mind into the game, 'I don't know. We can't just go up to Father William and say, "Hey, were you a vampire before?".'

'No.'

'But ... if he was, he must know who the Polysire is around here.'

'And you think that the Polysire lives in the Depths?' Juliet said.

'I do. Or, at least, that's my working theory right now.'

Juliet nodded her head, as Robert's stomach growled hungrily. Juliet's eyebrows raised. 'You want me to make you something?'

'I guess,' he replied. 'We should probably get moving. I just'—he closed his eyes and kissed her, breathing her in, and then looked at her again—'can't we stay like this all day?'

She smiled.

'Okay,' he said, 'why don't we go out for breakfast? We can figure out how to handle the Father William thing over bagels?'

'We need to go to the slaughterhouse too.'

'I hadn't forgotten,' Robert said, trying to sound reassuring rather than narcissistically petty. 'We'll go after breakfast, and then onto Father William's.'

She squeezed him gently, with her arms and with her legs, and kissed him again, before saying, 'Perfect.'

†

Tilly and Laura, Harry and Mark were gathered in Cleve Woods on that late, chilly Monday morning. It was nearing midday, and Tilly was disappointed that only the four of them had shown up. The rest of the kids who'd seen the vampire, back on that Thursday night in the woods, had one by one started to shy away from Tilly, with her plans and her ambitions.

She figured they'd rather pretend that the danger didn't exist, than tackle it.

'We all need to tell our parents we're meeting at Tilly's house, right Till?' Harry said.

She smiled. 'Right. Say we're having a Netflix session or something. And then, once the sun goes down'—she smiled again, wickedly this time, and made her voice deep and dramatic—'we go kill ourselves some motherfucking vampires.'

She was very proud of herself. Harry seemed equally impressed, eyeing her like she was some kind of perfect and enchanting superhero, and even Mark let out an excited grin.

Laura, however, didn't seem too keen at all.

'Too much?' Tilly asked.

Laura nodded, wrinkling her nose. 'A little too much.'

†

The trip to and from the Cockerham slaughterhouse had gone without incident. The staff there seemed to be getting used to the two youngsters showing up every day for a couple of blood bottles, and they didn't seem to mind too much.

Robert's stomach was full and he had caffeine in him, and he was holding Juliet's hand as he walked from the Asda car park toward the bridle path down to St. Luke's. He was filled with a sort of contentment, despite everything, which he'd literally never felt before, with her hand in his own.

It made him swell, and he felt like the blood pumping around his body was stronger and more alive and sweeter and *joyous* even, than he'd ever known. That was the way it felt, though the thought made little sense. He felt like he could conquer the world. Like he could fight a hundred vampires at once.

Frankly, in the end, he was *happy*.

'You're sure you don't mind me tagging along?' Juliet said.

'Hell no,' he replied. 'The truth is I'd rather not get sucked into another day long session, talking, like, the Bible and Jesus and stuff.'

She squeezed his hand and nuzzled her forehead into his shoulder a little as they walked. And then Robert noticed four kids, walking towards them, away from St. Luke's. Two boys and two girls. He wouldn't really have noticed them at all, except that one of the girls was staring at Juliet and, to a lesser extent, at him.

He gave her a questioning look, but she just looked back at her friend, like she was trying to be nonchalant as they passed by.

'That was weird,' he said, looking over his shoulder at the quartet of little people, who'd now passed him, to see the nosy girl staring back at him.

'What was?' Juliet asked, turning.

The curious little girl turned away, faking again.

'That kid was staring at us,' he said, stopping to look properly.

'What, one of those kids?'

'Yeah, the girl with the dark brown hair.' Robert and Juliet waited a moment, before he sighed away his curiosity. 'Never mind. She probably just knows who you are.'

Juliet smiled like it was nothing new. 'Apparently they still call me the Orphan Princess of Ecclesburn in school.'

'Jesus, still?'

'That's what Rosie Townsend said.'

'To Ecclesburn, you're kind of a big deal. I forget.' He nodded. 'Okay. That must be it.' Now, he turned, facing forwards. 'Come on, let's go.'

†

Bishop Powell climbed out of the back seat of Steve Fitzpatrick's Nissan X-Trail SUV, while the timid, young Iris Oceanheart climbed out of the front passenger seat.

'Are these all hers?' Bishop Powell said, nodding at the row of fancy, posh cars that lined the long drive.

'She's worth over fifty million quid, you know,' Steve said.

Bishop Powell sucked air in through his teeth. 'That's such a lot of power for a young girl with no parents.' He looked at Steve. 'Why's there not an elder living here with her? That would have been the practice in my day.'

'Well, mate, she didn't want one. She's an adult. And, more than that, she funds half of our spending.' Steve shrugged, as he started to make his way for the door. 'Kinda makes it hard to enforce Regs, which have been slipping for well over ten years anyway.'

Bishop Powell frowned as Steve pulled the great door knocker and gave it a good, hard slam. The three of them waited for a response, but when none came, Steve took a step back and spied a doorbell to the right of the entrance. He pressed it in and waited as the dull bing bong echoed through the walls from inside.

More time passed, and finally Steve turned to the bishop, and then to Iris, and said, 'Maybe there's no one home?'

†

Father William opened the door to his home, connected to the back of St. Luke's, and flashed Robert and Juliet a slow, toothy smile. 'Greetings, young Robert.' He turned to Juliet. 'And the most lovely Ms. Rayne.'

'Miss,' she said.

'Noted,' he replied. 'To what do I owe the pleasure?'

'Can we come in?' Robert said. 'There's some stuff we need to talk to you about.'

Father William looked like like he needed to be in bed, especially when he pulled a handkerchief to his mouth and coughed into it. 'Of course,' he said, pulling his door open. 'What can I do for you?'

Robert was a little apprehensive as to how best to proceed. But, as he stood there, hoping to at least get into the house before tipping his hand, he couldn't have predicted what Juliet was about to say.

'Basically,' she said, 'we wanna know one thing. Did you used to be a vampire?'

CHAPTER FIFTEEN
Carfentanil and Remifentanil

Father William had not offered Robert and Juliet any hot drinks, or any biscuits, or much at all beyond a very serious and seemingly concerned demeanour. Because, after Juliet's somewhat unexpected "Did you used to be a vampire?" while he had invited them in, all of his ordinarily odd yet chirpy behaviour had evaporated.

'Father William ...' Robert began, trying to sound diplomatic, 'we talked, the other day, about ... vampires.'

'Yes,' Father William replied, giving nothing away.

'We've been looking for'—Robert stopped, concentrating on choosing just the right words—'since Saturday evening, we've been looking for someone who might have, once upon a time, been ...'

'A vampire?' Father William said, coughing into his fist.

'Yeah ...' Robert replied.

'I see.'

'What do you think?' Juliet said. 'Just so you know, if you were, you can tell us.'

Robert blinked irritably.

'If I was a vampire, once upon a time, I can tell the two of you, can I?' Father William said, staring at Juliet.

She looked at Robert for support, and then back at the priest. 'Well, yeah.'

'Father William, I'm sorry to burst in and spring this on you,' Robert said. 'And, I know how outlandish we must be seeming right about now, but—'

'Do you?' he said.

'But … it's important to us. I told you on Friday, when I came to see you, that we use a lot of holy water in this town.'

'Yes …' Father William said, leaning back into his chair and rubbing some sweat off his forehead.

'Look, mate,' Juliet said, 'it's pretty straightforward. I don't know whether you're the guy we're looking for or not, but, if you are, you can tell us. You don't need to go sending letters and being all cryptic.'

Father William narrowed his eyes like he was trying to size Juliet up.

'And we can take you out tonight and show you, if you're not the guy,' Juliet continued. 'We can prove to you that vampires are real. Hell, Ecclesburn will prove that to you if you don't know it already.'

Father William looked like he was utterly baffled, and the amusement seemed to return to him a little.

'Father …' Robert said, taking his time. 'Did you send me the letter, with the Bible verse, on Friday, after I came to see you?'

Father William looked at Robert for what felt like an awkwardly long time. Then, he turned to Juliet and seemed to sharpen a little. 'No,' he said, looking back at Robert, and seemed about to speak again when Robert's phone pinged.

Robert took the phone out of his pocket and looked at the screen as it lit up. It was a text, from Steve Fitzpatrick, which read: 'I'm at your gaff lad. With Basil Powell and a pagan lass from Clayton.'

Robert's heartbeat quickened, and his eyes widened.

'Something wrong?' Father William said with a sniff.

Another text came through, from Steve again: 'Where you at, lad? When will you be back?'

Robert turned to Juliet, who was inquisitively examining him with her eyes. 'Steve Fitzpatrick's at ours, right now, with'—he checked Father William with his eyes, before turning back to Juliet, and leaning forward with a whisper—'the bishop, Bishop Powell.'

Juliet's eyes expanded with nervousness, just as Robert's had done.

Robert, still whispering, said, 'And I think Anna-Marie Gregory is with them.'

'Iris Oceanbrain?' Juliet hissed back. 'God, Rob, *why*?'

Robert glanced once more at Father William, who now had a terribly quizzical look across his face.

'Father,' Robert began, 'I'm really sorry, but, we need to go.'

'Is it an emergency?' Father William asked, inclining his head a little to one side. 'Is there'—he coughed—'anything I can do?'

Robert blinked a few times, his face stiff, while he tried to think of an answer. 'Um, thank you. No. We just ... we have to get home.'

'We have some unexpected guests is all,' Juliet said.

'Can we try this again later?' Robert said.

Father William's eyes were tiny thin slits now, they were so narrow. 'Can we try ... you asking me if I used to be a vampire, and if I sent you a cryptic reference by post?'

Robert smiled awkwardly, and climbed to his feet. 'Yeah.'

Father William stood as well, though it seemed to pain him. 'Of course,' he said.

†

'Well that cleared nothing up,' Juliet said to Robert, as they paced frantically, towards the north end of Lockwood Mews. 'And that guy's definitely not right. Guy needs to be in bed with chicken soup and hot lemon.'

'I know,' Robert replied, almost skipping into a run.

'I think he might be the guy though,' Juliet said. 'Did you see the way he looked at me? Like I was bloody Eve in the garden of Eden or something?'

'Yeah ...' Robert said.

'If it's him, he might trust you, but he definitely doesn't trust me.'

'Okay ...' Robert said, as Juliet's words began to settle in his mind, making perfect sense. 'But ... all of that aside, Jules, what the hell are we gonna do about Steve Fitzpatrick and the bishop and the pagan girl being at our bloody house right now?'

Juliet shook her head as they walked. 'I guess we just ... bat them away.'

'Avoid the cellar ...'

'Definitely,' Juliet said.

'Jules ...' Robert said grimly, 'what do we do if they want go down there?'

'Why would they want to do that?'

'Just ... what if they do?'

'They're probably pissed off with us because of what we did in Clayton, taking Sara Bradshaw's ears.'

'Yeah, that was *us*, wasn't it,' Robert said pointedly. '*We* did that, didn't *we*.'

Juliet looked at him, a little sadly.

Robert felt her sadness, and started feeling guilty for causing it. 'I'm sorry. It's not like I stopped you. We did do that.'

Juliet took a moment, and said, 'But that's gotta be why they're in town, right? They don't know about ... I mean, they couldn't know about Aaron. Could they?'

Robert shook his head and took a deep breath to settle his heartbeat a little. 'I don't know. I don't know, Jules.'

'We could say we're out of town?' Juliet said. 'We could say we can't get back. They can't get in to ours. It's not like they have a key. And they're not gonna sit about waiting outside forever, right?'

'Nah, it needs dealing with. They may go away but they'll come back. We'll take our lumps for the ear thing, say our sorries, promise never to do it again, and accept any punishments they dole out without arguing. Yeah?'

'They need us more than we need them,' Juliet said as they entered the Asda car park. 'Who'd they think'll fund all their boozy trips to Morecambe if they push us out? That Steve Fitzpatrick guy had about five bottles of red wine to himself last time, at hotel prices, and didn't put his hand in his pocket once.'

Robert laughed. 'They won't push us out. Like I say, let's just play along and get them out of the house as quickly as we can.'

Juliet clicked the car key in her hand and her Audi beeped dutifully. 'Fine,' she said, and headed for the car.

†

Juliet pulled into the grounds of Rayne Manor, and turned towards her mum and dad's collection of cars—all of which she was insured to drive. As she neared a spot, she saw a giant, black people carrier, which she didn't recognise. 'That'll be them I guess,' she said, nodding at the SUV as she span the steering wheel into the parking spot.

Robert was watching the people carrier cautiously, when the three people inside began to climb out. Once Juliet had parked, Robert opened his door and stepped towards the SUV, with his hands in his pockets and his shoulders hunched forward.

He felt Juliet at his side, though she kept a civil distance.

Steve Fitzpatrick walked straight for Robert, and reached out to shake his hand with a grin.

Robert shook Steve's hand and half smiled, half winced at him. 'Alright mate,' he said uncertainly.

Steve nodded. 'Hope you don't mind us popping in on you unannounced?'

Robert looked over Steve's shoulder, at Iris Oceanheart. 'Nah ...' he said.

'It's fine,' Juliet said, standing at Robert's side, but with her hands on her hips.

Robert could almost sense her there. Her strength, her immeasurable flair for improvisation—he adored it.

'Come in, all of you,' she went on, leading the way.

†

'Can I get you all something to drink?' Juliet said, leading their three guests out of the Rayne Manor hall, and into the big living room adjacent to the kitchen.

Bishop Powell cleared his throat and took off his glasses to wipe them. 'Miss Rayne,' he said, walking to one of Juliet's big sofas, 'your mother always used to keep at least one Château Margaux, in her wine cellar.'

'Oh aye?' Juliet said, settling into her armchair, resting her forearms on its faux leather sides.

'Yes ...' Bishop Powell said, as everyone who wasn't already sitting sat. 'I don't suppose you have any now?'

Robert was wide eyed and anxious now. Why was Bishop Powell hinting at getting into the *cellar*, straight away?

'Aye, we've got two Grand Vins,' Juliet said, peering at the bishop fearlessly.

Steve Fitzpatrick puffed a breath out of his mouth at the easy luxury of it.

'Would you ... consider uncorking one?' Bishop Powell asked, a little gingerly.

'Absolutely,' Juliet said, though she didn't move.

'Shall I ...' the bishop began, still unsure of himself, 'shall I go down to retrieve it? Will it be where it ever was?'

Juliet climbed to her feet now and rested her hands on her hips. 'No need.'

'Really, I don't mind.'

'Nah, it's not that,' Juliet said. 'They're both in a rack in the kitchen.' She smiled at the bishop. 'No need to go downstairs for that.'

†

Juliet poured a full glass for herself, and another for Robert, before holding the bottle over Steve Fitzpatrick's glass. 'Steve?' she said. 'You like a red wine, don't you?'

He smiled. 'Just a little one for me, love. I'm driving.'

Juliet nodded and poured an inch into his glass, before moving onto Iris Oceanheart's. 'Large?' Juliet said.

Iris nodded, and Juliet obliged.

'Will you have a large too, Bishop Powell?' Juliet said, moving on.

'Given the wine,' the bishop replied, 'I feel I must. If you don't mind.'

'Not at all,' Juliet said, pouring the wine into his glass generously. When she was finished, she left the cork off and set the bottle down in the centre of the table, before returning to her chair. 'Now. What's going on?'

No one answered.

'What she means,' Robert said, 'is ... why are you here?'

Iris looked at Steve Fitzpatrick to explain, but he just eyed Robert guardedly.

It was Bishop Powell, who took up the responsibility of speaking first. 'Aaron McLeary lives here with you, does he not?'

'He's visiting his mum,' Juliet said without skipping a beat.

'Of course,' Bishop Powell said. 'She's in Dunfermline now, is she not?'

'Kirkcaldy,' Juliet corrected him.

Bishop Powell nodded.

A terrible thought went through Robert's mind at this. Mrs. McLeary had lost her husband, a decade or so ago, and now she had lost her son—and she didn't even know it.

His resolve to save Aaron was only fortified by this thought.

'Look,' Steve Fitzpatrick said, 'you'll notice that we've brought young Iris with us. I'm sorry but I have to ask the pair of you. Why did you want Sara Bradshaw's ears?'

Juliet turned her harsh eyes on Iris, and then on Steve. 'That's none of your business.'

Steve glanced sideways at Iris, and then back at Juliet. 'I think we can all agree that it's *her* business.'

Iris's eyes were glued to the floor now.

Juliet rolled her head and sighed, before picking up her wine and sipping it elegantly. 'Look, I wasn't happy doing it. But I had to.'

'Why?' Bishop Powell said, and Robert thought he could hear in the bishop's voice that he wanted to believe.

'Look,' Juliet said, 'in order to keep the peace in this town, we make bargains, we make deals. We don't love it, but we do.'

'What deals?' Steve said.

'In the Depths, there's ... witches,' Juliet said, bristling a little at the word "witches".

'We're aware of that,' Steve said.

'And some of them have a lot of power, and they're not always super good people,' Juliet went on.

'And?' Bishop Powell said.

'*And*, sometimes, we have to deliver a tribute, to certain people down there.'

'Nah, nah, nah,' Steve said, leaning forward, 'the Regs are crystal on this, love. You don't make deals with dark witches. You come to us, and we seek support from—'

'I'm aware of the Regs, Steve,' Juliet snapped, 'My parents had me memorising the bloody Regs before I started *school*. But real life isn't Regs, is it? In real life, sometimes, you have to make a choice, and you don't always like it.'

'Why did the witch require the tribute?' Bishop Powell asked, still coming off as a friend, rather than an accuser.

Robert eyed Juliet over his wine glass as he drank, waiting to see what story she was about to spin, almost admiring how convincing a liar she was.

'She had a sister, here in the world above,' Juliet said. 'The sister was killed by vampires, at the beginning of the month.'

'So ... the witch needed ears?' Steve said. 'That doesn't make sense?'

'The witch called a meeting with us after she found out about her sister,' Juliet said. 'She blamed us because we "let it happen".'

'That makes sense,' Bishop Powell said, giving Steve a mildly optimistic look.

'I didn't really ask why she wanted the ears. I figured, she's a witch, she wants them for, like, some scroggy spell or something.' She smiled mischievously. 'Maybe human ears are an aphrodisiac? Maybe she was planning a little Netflix and chill with some young, well hung—'

'Jules!' Robert hissed.

She smirked at him, and then looked at Bishop Powell. 'See, that's Internet slang for—'

'Jules!' Robert hissed again, firmer this time.

'Look, we're not just here about the ear thing,' Steve said, shifting awkwardly. 'As disconcerting as that is.'

'Indeed,' Bishop Powell said. 'No, we also need to—'

Iris, who had been sipping her wine, coughed suddenly, and proceeded to pat her chest with her palm. 'Oh my God, *that's* what Netflix and chill means?' she said, to no one in particular.

Bishop Powell frowned, and tried to go on. 'We need to talk to you about your recent interest in Polysires.'

'I just thought people were binge watching Orphan Black and The OA,' Iris said, still talking mostly to herself. She took a big gulp of wine, and looked terribly embarrassed.

Bishop Powell cleared his throat, becoming irritable. 'The Polysires,' he said seriously, looking straight at Robert. 'Why are you investigating this? Why now?'

Robert wanted to play innocent, inspired by Juliet's flawless deceit. 'Because I only just found out it was possible,' he said casually.

'D'you know something,' Steve said, 'when my arl fella was running up and down, in and out of the Depths, chasing the vampire he believed to be a Polysire, he was doing it to save a mate of his.'

'Is that right?' Juliet said, affecting her voice with a show of compassion.

Steve looked at her suspiciously. 'Yeah ...' he said slowly. 'Anyway, his mate's name was Dougie Gibbons.'

'You told me all this last night on the phone,' Robert said.

'Well, I'm mentioning it now because'—Steve looked at the Bishop cautiously—'we're a little worried, about young Aaron.'

'Young Mr. McLeary,' Bishop Powell said. 'You say he's with his mother in Dunfermline?'

'Kirkcaldy,' Juliet said. 'I said Kirkcaldy.'

'Of course,' Bishop Powell said.

'My arl fella had Dougie chained up, in my gran's pantry, you see. While he tried to save him.'

Robert's curiosity got the better of him, and he said, 'What happened to him? What happened to Dougie?'

'The community elders slew him, of course,' Bishop Powell said. 'Once they'd identified the problem. Once they'd ... figured out what was happening.'

'Dad was binned from the community because of all this,' Steve said, directing his words at Juliet more than at Robert now. 'For five years.'

'Wow,' Juliet said, her eyes sarcastically wide. 'Five whole years huh?'

'Hey,' Steve said sharply, 'don't take the piss.'

She flashed him a defiant glare.

'My dad loved his mate,' Steve went on. 'That's what drove him to go to such lengths. And being part of this community meant something to him. It was *dear* to him. D'you understand me? Maybe it's not too important to you, Miss Rayne, but it was important to him, and it's important to me.'

'I must agree with Steven,' Bishop Powell said. 'Juliet, your parents were sworn members of the community. Your mother's great-grandfather was a *founder*. A little respect, eh? It goes a long way.'

Juliet feigned sincerity. 'Look'—she turned to Steve—'I'm sorry, for being facetious.'

Steve nodded, settling his sternness a little.

'Well, we all appreciate that, young lady, we really do,' Bishop Powell said. 'But there's something I'm going to have to insist on, before we draw a line under this.'

Robert was sure he could feel the beginnings of sweat on his forehead.

'What's that?' Juliet asked.

'Well, while we're here ...' Bishop Powell said, 'I want to take a long, hard look around your mother's wine cellar.'

The beads of sweat on Robert's forehead began to descend onto his eyebrows now.

'Why?' Juliet said. 'You're after more of my wine?'

'Not exactly ...' Bishop Powell said.

'I can't say as I blame you,' Juliet went on. She smiled. 'You should definitely try a glass of the Krug Vintage Brut I've got down there.'

'No,' Bishop Powell said, standing to his feet. 'I'll be frank with you both. There's been some concern that Aaron McLeary has been turned. That the two of you have been keeping him chained up somewhere, probably here, in the house.'

'That's ridiculous,' Juliet said.

'Perhaps you'd like to get him and his mother on the phone?' Bishop Powell said.

Juliet paused, still sitting, looking up at Bishop Powell. 'He's unreachable actually,' she said, just a hint of panic in her voice at last.

'Convenient,' Steve said, climbing to his feet too.

Iris, who had been nursing her wine, set it down and followed the example of the men by standing, though she kept her eyes low.

Bishop Powell lifted the briefcase off the floor. 'Is the entrance to the wine cellar still on a latch, or do you have a lock and key nowadays?'

Robert was panicking now, so he stood. 'Bishop Powell, you can't go down there right now,' he muttered feebly.

Bishop Powell ignored this, and started for the door out of the living room that led to the Great Hall.

Robert looked down at Juliet to do something, but she was staring in no particular direction and she looked beyond tense. 'Jules ...'

Bishop Powell stopped before leaving the room, and turned to Juliet. 'I'm sorry, Miss Rayne,' he said, and he clearly meant it. Then, he turned and made his way out of the room, and was swiftly followed by Steve, while Iris sheepishly made her way too.

'Jules ...' Robert said again, whispering firmly, 'they're gonna kill Aaron!'

Juliet took her phone out and started swiping and typing at it, occasionally looking up at the five glasses on the table and back down at the phone.

'Jules, they're gonna go down there right now, and they're gonna kill Aaron. We have to ... we have to tell them about the Polysires, about Father William, we have to ... we have to ...'

'Okay ...' Juliet said, still typing something into her phone. 'Rob, hold your breath, okay?'

'What?' Robert hissed.

'Just *do* it,' Juliet snapped, looking at him fiercely.

He finally did as he was told, after taking a deep breath. He pinched his nose, and looked at her desperately for an explanation.

Juliet, however, marched out of the room after their guests.

The only way Robert could tell she was holding her breath is that she looked a little tight, a little still in the chest. He wanted to sigh, but he didn't. He just kept his breath held and followed, almost not daring to go into the hall, almost wanting to pretend that none of this was happening.

He entered the hall, to the sound of three people collapsing gracelessly onto the hard floor.

He'd had a kind of grim expectation, after Juliet had told him to hold his breath, but seeing Bishop Powell, Steve Fitzpatrick and the sweet and innocent Iris Oceanheart land on the floor, obviously poisoned by the woman he loved, he couldn't help but feel a terrible sting of shame and self-loathing.

Juliet paced straight for front door and made her way out into the fresh air outside, so Robert ran after her.

They made their way past the line of Juliet's cars and onto the tarmac at the top of Ragged Stone Road.

Finally, Juliet started to breath, so Robert did likewise.

'Jules ... what the hell?'

'They were gonna kill Aaron. You said it yourself.'

'What did you do?'

Juliet winced. 'Carfentanil and remifentanil,' she said.

'What and what?'

'It's a knockout gas. An aerosol mist.'

'You just have that, like, in the house, ready to go at a moment's notice?' Robert said. He looked at the building, the door still standing open. 'Are they gonna be okay?'

'They'll be fine,' Juliet said, taking out her phone. She quickly entered a series of instructions and commands.

'Is that how you did it? With your phone?'

She nodded but didn't look up from the screen. 'We'll need to get them out of their clothes, once the air's safe again.'

'What?' Robert said, becoming more and more upset. 'Why?'

'The gas gets into the fabric,' she said, still looking fixedly at her phone. 'I only pumped it into the hall. It'll be safe to go back inside in about five minutes.'

Robert was breathing fast, so he tried to settle himself, to slow down a little. 'How long will they be unconscious for?'

'Depends,' she said. 'But we can wake them whenever we want.'

'Oh Jesus, Jules.' Robert shook his head. 'How are we gonna explain this? This is ... this has to be super illegal.'

She looked at him patronisingly. 'Of course it's illegal. That's not the point.'

'We'll be kicked out of the community. That's for sure. No question about it.'

'I really couldn't care less about that,' Juliet said, looking at the house now. 'I mean, do you? Do you care about being a member of the sodding community?'

Robert took a moment, but found the truth within him. 'No,' he said simply. 'I don't.'

Juliet nodded, and even allowed herself the slightest of smiles.

'All I care about is being with you, and saving Aaron. After that'—he shook his head—'nothing else matters.'

Juliet fell toward him at that.

She buried her head in his chest. She wasn't crying, or even breathing erratically or anything. She just rested. 'I love you,' she said.

He wrapped his arms around her, and let her settle in his embrace. 'I love you too,' he said.

†

Tilly checked the time on her phone, sitting in the park to the north of her house, half a mile's walk from St. Luke's graveyard, and Cleve Woods. 'Sun sets in one hour,' she said, her heart beating fast.

Laura, who was busily checking her own phone, said, 'The boys are on their way.'

Tilly lifted her backpack off the floor and slid the phone into the front pocket, before unzipping the main bit and eyeing the contents within for the tenth time that hour. 'Okay I'm nervous now,' she said, before looking up. 'Are you?'

Laura held out her hand, which was shaking terribly. 'I think that's an understatement,' she said. She seemed tense and twitchy. 'You know ... we could ... we could just not go?'

'Do you want to back out?' Tilly said, unable to keep the beginnings of despair off her face at the thought.

Laura stepped closer instinctively. 'No, no, I won't leave you to do it alone. I just ... I'm just saying ... this isn't our responsibility. We're not ... we're not bloody Schildmaids. We can literally just go home and put the TV on and have toast and listen to music.'

Tilly considered it. The thought of going home, getting into her pyjamas and hiding from the world was normally her favourite. But the counter-thought of leaving monsters—easily killable monsters, for that matter—out in town, to hunt her friends and her family was too terrible, too awful. 'No,' she said. 'We'll do all that after. TV, and toast, and one point five litres of fizzy Vimto. Yeah?'

Laura nodded with a smile. 'Yeah,' she said. 'How long do you wanna give it? Say, we see no'—she shuddered—'vampires. How late do you wanna stay out?'

'I hadn't really thought about it. I guess ... about nine?'

'Okay,' Laura said. 'That's cool. It helps me, in my head, to know we have a time limit.'

Tilly smiled. 'This is gonna be good. I promise. This is gonna make the town a better place. For everyone. For the pikeys and the trendies, for Gemma Read and the cool kids. For you and for me, and for Harry and for Mark. For ... everyone.'

Laura's lips were pressed together in an uncertain but brave semi-smile, and she gave a dutiful nod. 'Okay. You're right. You're totally right.' She held out her hand again, which was now still. She brightened. 'Oh my God!' she said, her eyebrows up. 'Would you look at that.'

Tilly, still smiling, and growing in courage, took her friend's hand, and pulled her into a cuddle.

'Badass pep talk,' Laura joked.

Tilly held her friend, and said, 'Badass pep talks are one of my features.'

CHAPTER SIXTEEN
A Broken Compass

Juliet was beyond exasperated. She was sitting on her kitchen surface, a glass of Apothic Dark at her side, while Robert leaned back against the fridge, holding a bottle of San Miguel. Bishop Powell, Steve Fitzpatrick and Iris Oceanheart, however, were still unconscious, and were tied to various pieces of her living room furniture.

Juliet rubbed her forehead. 'So ... the sun sets in'—she looked at the time on the microwave display—'what, thirty minutes?'

'Thirty-two, to be exact,' Robert said.

'And if we can't find—and slay—the Polysire, soon, then what?'

Robert sipped his lager, an impotent look across his face.

'We can't leave those guys tied up in our living room forever,' Juliet said.

'No.'

'But if we can cure Aaron, soon, we can untie them, and let them go. I mean, what are they gonna do?'

'Well, being chucked out of the community is really the best case scenario at this point,' Robert said. 'I mean, they can't exactly go to the police. Right?'

Juliet looked up at him and shook her head. 'Nope.'

'But ... now they know what we've done,' Robert said, 'we really are kinda stuck. If we can't cure Aaron, they'll kill him. You said it yourself, we can't leave them tied up. We have to let them go at some point. We can't just keep them here like bloody slaves until we find the Polysire. What if it takes weeks?'

Juliet swigged from her glass, soothed as ever by the warmth of the wine. Then, a thought occurred, and she flashed her eyes at Robert. 'What if we just go?'

'What?'

'What if we leave Ecclesburn?'

Robert shook his head, confused.

'I've got cash. And I can take out more. We'll find someone, somewhere, to hide us until we can … I dunno, find new identities or something.'

'And take Aaron with us? While he's still a vampire? How will we avoid the sun? And what if he kills someone? We'd have to—'

'Do you have a better idea?'

Robert looked vacant for a minute, and then sharpened. 'We could hide in Undertown?'

Juliet looked at him for a minute, taking in the thought.

'There's no sunlight down there so Aaron'll be safe,' Robert went on. 'And when we went down last week we were safe enough.'

Juliet sighed. 'Oh I don't know,' she said, breaking a little. 'I don't know what we should do.' For what felt like the hundredth time that week, tears coated her eyes. 'I just … I just wish my mum was here.'

Robert put his lager down and paced over to Juliet, rubbing her shoulder, inviting her to embrace without forcing it.

Juliet toughened herself, and forced her eyes closed, willing them dry. 'You know, she'd always tell me what to do. Dad was always … he was always tough, and righteous. He had his code. Right was right and nothing else was important.'

'Okay?'

'But mum understood that there are challenges in life, and that ... morality is fluid. The right thing to do today'—she shook her head—'it may not be the right thing to do tomorrow.'

'Sure.'

'She'd have understood what we're doing. Dad wouldn't have.' She nodded towards the living room. 'He'd have been tied up in there with them lot.'

Robert laughed gently.

'But mum would have helped us. She understood that ... you don't just turn your back on the ones you love. You can't. If you do, you never love anyone. Not really. You just love ... law.'

'I get it.'

'But without her, it's like someone's ... it's like someone's robbed off with my moral compass.'

'Yeah ...' Robert said.

The word "compass" made her think of the actual compass her mother had left her. The compass in her purse, behind her on the kitchen surface. She reached around and took it out. 'You know, mum said she'd explain to me what happened to this when I turned eighteen.'

'I didn't know that,' Robert said.

'And now ... this is all I'm left with of her isn't it. A broken compass. Something that doesn't point north. So I'm ... I'm alone to figure out my way, by myself.'

Robert took his time, and said, 'I get what you mean, but I just ... I wanna say this because it needs saying. You're not alone.'

Juliet looked up into Robert's eyes, and smiled appreciatively. 'I know,' she said. 'And ... I appreciate the hell out of it.'

Robert was still offering himself, so Juliet took up the offer, and jumped off the kitchen surface and fell into his arms. She loved his blend of strength and love. But what she craved most was wisdom. And as that wisdom eluded her, as she reached out for it, with her heart and mind ...

'You don't deserve that compass ...' came the faint voice of Bishop Powell, from the living room, through the open door.

†

Jack Turnbull pulled his phone out of his pocket and thumbprinted it on, as he left work to the chill of the early evening. There were three texts from Becky, all within the last hour. The built up stress and irritation he'd been carrying melted away, as he headed out of the gate and onto Corporation Street to start his walk home.

The first text read: 'So I've been thinking xx'

The second read: 'Would Tilly's gran watch her overnight, d'you think? Xx'

And the third: 'Because... if she will... after the play tomorrow, do you wanna stay behind, come to the party, and then come home with me? Xxxx'

Jack noticed that he'd started skipping every few steps. Actually skipping. He smiled, stopped walking, and sent back: 'That sounds amazing. I'll talk to Rita tonight.'

And with that, he plugged his headphones into the phone, opened up Amazon Music and shuffled his latest playlist. "Close To Me" by The Cure came on. He smiled at the appropriate precision of it, dropped the phone into his pocket, and reached into his coat for his tobacco and Rizlas.

†

'What do you know about it?' Juliet said as Robert followed her from the kitchen through to the living room.

Bishop Powell, who was roped to one of Juliet's faux leather armchairs, and whose head was rolling wearily, said, 'That compass was your mother's.'

'I know that,' Juliet said.

Bishop Powell laughed hazily, like a man waking from a drunken stupor. 'You don't know what it does. You don't know where she got it. What she had to go through to win it. You don't know anything ... you wicked, foolish little child.'

Juliet sat on the sofa, opposite Bishop Powell, and stared at him. 'Wicked? Me?'

'I wanted to ... believe in you ... out of respect for your parents, but ... you've gone too far.' He glanced over at Steve, and then at Iris, who were also bound, but who were still unconscious. 'You ... threatened that poor girl. You desecrated a body under her care. And now you've poisoned her. Are you proud of yourself.'

'No!' Juliet snapped. 'No, I'm not *proud* of myself. I'm trying to save an innocent life, that's all.'

'You ... can't ...'

'How do you know that?' Robert said. 'With respect, how do you know that we can't? Because it seems to me that the only reason you don't want to try this is because of your faith, because of your bloody Regs, your precious community's ... orthodoxy.'

Bishop Powell's eyes closed and he shook his head. 'There's no evidence that Polysires exist,' he said, pulling his head up and eyeballing Robert. 'For centuries, we've fought back the forces of evil, and for centuries we've written down all of our struggles.' He turned his attention to Juliet. 'I believe there are tomes upon tomes, here in Rayne Manor, passed down by your ancestors. Scour through them. You won't find even an oblique reference to anything about blasted Polysires, in any of them.'

'That doesn't prove anything,' Robert said. 'The books were curated by the community. I mean, the writings that were passed down were the ones that were approved by the elders. You don't know that there weren't loads of writings that were burned, or that were dismissed, specifically *because* they included those references.'

Bishop Powell looked confused, through his intoxicated demeanour. 'Why on earth would the elders withhold accounts from the community? Are you a conspiracy boffin, Mr. Entwistle? I think you must be. Do you ... think that ... the moon landing was faked as well? Or that the earth is flat?'

'No, don't be ridiculous,' Robert said, leaning forward. 'But this is how the Catholic Church acts. Isn't the Bible itself just the collection of writings that Rome approved, back in the day? Like, isn't there a Gospel of Thomas out there, and a Gospel of Judas? Maybe the accounts about the Polysires are like those? Forbidden by stuffy, doctrine-obsessed wankers like ...'

'Like me?' Bishop Powell said.

Robert started to climb down a little. 'No. Not you.'

Bishop Powell scoffed. 'I guess your calling to the priesthood was a mistake, no?' he said sarcastically.

'Listen mate,' Juliet said, 'I don't give two shits about whether you believe in Polysires or not. Okay? I don't respect you, because you've closed your mind. I'm willing to try. To try to save ...'

'Ah yes ...' Bishop Powell said, nodding, still hazy. 'Young Aaron McLeary. I take it we were right? He is ... in your mother's cellar?'

'He's not killed anyone, you know,' Juliet said.

'When Steven and I theorised that you were keeping a vampire in your cellar I hoped ... so dearly that we were wrong. I never suspected for a moment though the lengths to which you'd go to protect an evil, soulless demon.'

'You're wrong,' Juliet said. 'He's not evil. He's not ... soulless, whatever that means. And he's not a demon. I told you, he's not killed anyone.'

'Oh, because you've got him chained up down there.'

Juliet shook her head.

'Believe me, young lady,' the bishop went on, 'if he were loosed, he would kill. It is what he exists to do.'

'You're wrong ...' Juliet said, growing angry and trying to contain herself.

'You think I'm wrong because of your love for him, and I understand that, but—'

'I think you're wrong because he isn't chained up,' Juliet snapped, leaning forward in her chair.

The bishop suddenly looked very pale, and after a moment he settled, then strained to glance towards the window.

'He's not tied up down there,' Juliet said. 'He's been *loosed* for four consecutive nights.'

'Oh my lord, what have you done?' Bishop Powell said, still straining. 'What time is it?'

'It doesn't matter,' Juliet said. 'At sunset I'll go downstairs and take him two bottles of animal's blood. He'll drink it. Like he did last night, and the night before that. Hell, I take wine down there and drink with him!'

Bishop Powell turned to face her now. He looked so scared, and he seemed old and small all of a sudden. 'You've been ... *socialising* with the demon?'

'He's not a demon! He's Aaron. Okay? You get that you old freak? He's him. He's never hurt anyone. He doesn't *want* to hurt anyone. He's *good*. He's managing things, and he wants to be human again.'

'He *can't* be human again, you stupid, foolish girl!'

Juliet screamed, 'I'm not the one who's tied up so I don't think I'm the stupid one you fucking twat!'

Bishop Powell took his time, absorbing the verbal assault. And, after what seemed like an age, he smiled. And the smile almost seemed fond. 'You are so much like your mother,' he said with a laugh.

It was Juliet's turn to take her time to respond. Eventually, she ran her hands through her hair, and said, 'What did you mean before?' she said. 'About the compass. You said I don't know what it does. What *does* it do?'

Bishop Powell laughed again, but this time his hostility seemed to have come back a little. 'Why would I tell you that now?' he said. Then, he strained once more to see the window. 'Please, what time is it? You *must* slay the vampire. You cannot let it escape. Not while young Iris is here, helpless as a babe.'

Juliet opened her mouth to argue, but—

'Bishop Powell,' Robert said, 'please ... what does the compass do?'

'I said that the two of you are unworthy of it, and I'll—'

'No, no,' Robert interrupted. 'See, you tell us what the compass does, or maybe I'll have to tell your archbishop about Timothy Kinghorn.'

Bishop Powell looked at Robert with a mix of curiosity and panic.

Juliet smiled broadly. 'Yeah, maybe we tell the pointy-hat brigade about your secret little lovechild?' she said.

'You're ... blackmailing me?' he said finally, his voice empty and resigned.

'We're trying to save a life,' Juliet told him.

'The compass won't do that,' the bishop said. 'I mean ... it only works in the Depths. It's not—'

'What do you mean?' Robert said.

'What does it point to?' Juliet asked.

Bishop Powell pulled his head back in his seat, as though trying to keep his silence.

'What does it point to?' Juliet repeated. 'Tell us or I'll Google the archbishop's email address right now.'

'In the Depths ... it points to ... the most fearsome, the most powerful vampire.'

Juliet and Robert looked at each other, and then back at the bishop.

'In the world above it spins pointlessly,' the bishop said. 'But down there ... it takes you straight to the strongest demon.'

Juliet looked at Robert and shared a look of excitement. 'Are you thinking what I'm thinking?' she said.

'It'll take us to the Polysire ...' he said, smiling.

'What?' came the voice of Bishop Powell. 'No. No, it won't. It'll get you both killed. Now, please, untie me, and untie Steven and Iris. We must slay the vampire *now*.'

But Juliet wasn't listening to him. She clicked open the compass and looked at its needle, spinning as it always did, without any pattern, without any purpose.

She reached for Robert's hand and squeezed it tight. 'This is it,' she said. 'This is the key.'

Still smiling, and equally as excited, he leaned forward and kissed her firmly on the lips. 'It is ...' he said, pulling back just enough to meet her eyes with his own. 'We're gonna save him.'

†

'Rita?' Jack shouted as he walked into the kitchen, noticing she wasn't sitting at the dinner table as she would normally be. He looked through the back door window, to see her outside smoking. He pushed open the door and joined her. 'Is Tilly upstairs?'

'Out with that brat friend of hers I think,' Rita said.

'Out?' Jack said, reaching for his tobacco.

'She has a phone, you know,' Rita snapped. 'You could text her yourself.'

'Steady on, I know,' Jack replied, trying to soothe Rita's ire a little.

'She said they were going to her friend's house to do *young person* things I couldn't *possibly* comprehend,' Rita said bitterly.

Jack tried not to laugh, as he pinched a clump of tobacco and placed it neatly on his liquorice Rizla. 'Okay. I'll text her in a bit.' He licked the paper and rolled the cigarette neatly. 'Listen, I wanted to ask you about tomorrow.'

'You already asked me about tomorrow.'

'No, I mean, I was thinking about staying at a mate's, if you're okay to watch Tilly overnight?'

Rita exhaled smoke with a long, frustrated sigh. 'You do take the piss, don't you.'

'I mean, you're gonna be here anyway, right?' Jack said, lighting his cigarette.

'What if I wasn't? What if *I* had plans? What if *I* wanted to go out every night. Do you ever think about that? No, you just take it for granted that I'll be here to do your babysitting for free while you go out getting drunk and chasing girls half your age.'

'Half my age? I'm thirty-eight. I'm not chasing'—he did the maths in his head, and stumbled a little when he reached the answer—'nineteen year olds.'

'You'll be thirty-nine in a few weeks.'

'October to December isn't a few weeks.'

'Look, the point is, you don't appreciate me. You take advantage of me. And you're getting worse. Do you ever think about Tilly? She lost her mother, and she needs a father. And you're out every night so she's all alone.'

'Don't give me that, Rita, you don't care about Tilly. You *hate* Tilly. You never stop *moaning* about Tilly.'

'Well she's an ill disciplined little shit at the best of times,' Rita snapped. 'Maybe you'd know that if you ever looked after her yourself.'

'Okay, look, I'll spend a few nights with her. I won't go out. I'll stay and watch movies with her, she likes that.'

Rita gave him a look of something almost resembling respect, and then dropped it. 'I'll believe it when I see it.'

'I will,' Jack promised. 'After tomorrow night.'

Rita rolled her eyes. 'What's so important about tomorrow night?'

Jack suddenly felt a bit self-aware. He scratched his nose, and his cheeks. 'I'm just meeting some old uni mates in Lancaster, that's all,' he lied. 'Everyone's staying there, rather than worrying about making the last train or paying a fortune for a taxi.'

Rita peered at him suspiciously. 'You'll make it back in time for work in the morning?'

'I'll take a bag. Drive won't take long.'

'Fine,' Rita finally agreed. 'But I want a decent bottle of wine for my troubles. None of this less than four quid bollocks you've been picking up.'

Jack smiled. 'Rita, I'll but you that fancy Campo Viejo you like. Not the yellow labelled one, the fancy copper one.'

Rita looked a little surprised at this, and stubbed her cigarette out. 'A fifteen quid bottle of wine? That's actually pretty impressive for you, you great tight arse.'

Jack was still smiling, and still high off Becky's offer. 'Nothing's too much trouble,' he said, unable to keep the giddiness form his voice.

'Hmmm ...' Rita said, watching him, trying to figure him out. 'Don't forget, as well. You said you'd look for work. Somewhere else. You said we'd be able to leave this town.'

And suddenly, Jack's irritation returned, and his smile faded. 'Fine,' he said, rolling his eyes. 'Yes, I'm gonna look for work. I'm gonna try and sell the house. I'm on it. Okay?'

Rita stood, and made her way back inside, stopping just to say, 'Make sure you do. Before something terribly *Ecclesburn* happens. Before something terribly Ecclesburn happens to *Tilly*.'

Jack said nothing. He simply let Rita go inside, and smoked his cigarette.

†

Tilly was clutching her bag more tightly than she had ever done before. Harry and Mark had arrived, and together with Laura the four of them had made their way past the church, and were clustered together where the graveyard met Cleve Woods.

Tilly was watching the sun, shining through the misty evening, and she thought it had never lowered so fast in her life. She was pretty sure she could actually *see it* going down over the western horizon.

'Me and Mark are gonna take a walk,' Laura said. She was staring at him like he was the second coming.

'No, you're not,' Tilly said. 'We're hunting vampires. This is, you know, prime horror movie stuff. No one's doing any dumb, stupid shit.'

'What the hell are you talking about?' Mark said.

'Oh please, you go off together to get off with each other and you get yourselves killed. Or at least attacked. I mean, it literally happened to Jenny and Tom, less than a week ago.'

'She's right,' Laura said.

Harry nodded, and then tossed his fringe off his forehead with a flick of the head. 'Once the sun sets, I'll keep my eye on the graveyard, in case any vampires, you know, rise, or whatever.'

Tilly grunted approvingly. 'I'll watch the woods. Make sure they don't attack us from there. Laulau, you focus on the west; Mark, the east.'

'Which is west and which is east?' Mark said.

Harry sighed. 'Mark you absolute knobhead, the sun rises in the west, and sets in the east,' he said.

'So ... that means ...'

'How did you ever even learn to talk?' Harry said. 'The sun's over there. That's the east.'

Tilly couldn't believe her ears. 'You're *both* knobheads!' she yelled. 'The sun sets in the west.' She pointed at it. 'That's the west.'

'It's a good job no one's doing any dumb, stupid shit, right Till?' Laura joked.

'Boys,' Tilly said, 'I swear to God if we all die because of your intense stupidity, I'll kill you both.'

Mark shot Tilly a condescending look. 'You can't kill us if we're already dead.'

'That's the point, you total divvy,' Tilly said, fixing her gaze on Cleve Woods. 'Jesus I'm jealous of the people who don't know you.'

†

Robert looked out of the kitchen window of Rayne Manor, as the low sun almost disappeared over the distance. He sipped his lager and checked the six slices of cheese on toast bubbling under the grill. It looked good. 'They may be prisoners right now but at least they're eating well,' he muttered under his breath.

He went to the cupboard and collected three plates.

And although he was growing accustomed to Juliet heading down to the cellar with two bottles of animal's blood and a bottle of wine, he was not feeling any easier about it.

Everything they were planning rested on the assertion that Aaron could overcome his impulses.

But, more than that, now that Robert and Juliet were together, all of Robert's hopes for happiness rested on that assertion too. He just wanted to make it through the night, to go down into the Depths and find the Polysire, and to save Aaron, without anyone else getting hurt.

And, as he prepared mentally to deal with the three angry, confused and frightened people in his living room, he pulled their dinners out of the oven and started sliding the half dozen slices of cheesy toast onto the three plates.

He took a deep breath, and said, 'Be safe, Jules ...'

†

Juliet reached for the light switch in the cellar, and flicked it on.

'Oh, hey,' she said.

Aaron was sitting at the table, where the two of them had sat together the previous couple of nights. He smiled, and he looked like his old self. Softer, and less cutting. 'What did you bring me?' he said.

'Two lamb,' she said, holding her bag up and making her way to the table. 'Is that okay?'

He grimaced, just a little bit, and then nodded slowly. 'Thank you.'

'You're welcome.' She set the bag down on the table and started uncorking the first bottle from inside.

'Who are your guests?' Aaron said, eyeing the ceiling with his still, hollow eyes.

Juliet wasn't sure how best to proceed, so she eyed him cautiously as she popped off the cork of his first bottle of lamb's blood, and said, 'There's a Catholic bishop who used to hunt with my parents,' she said.

'Oh?'

'His name's Basil Powell. D'you remember him? He knew your dad.'

Aaron smiled. 'Yes,' he said, as though pulling the memory, long lost, from an obscure part of his mind. 'He had more passion than he let on. He carried hidden shame.'

Juliet poured blood into his glass. 'How did you know that?'

'My memories are all in tact. And I can visit them as I wish. And I can clearly see in them now things I couldn't have ever seen before.'

'Well, he has an illegitimate son,' Juliet said, going for her wine now. 'Some fella called Timothy Kinghorn.'

Aaron was still staring at nothing, as though still in the recesses of his mind. 'I would be surprised if he has only the one.'

Juliet smiled, applying the corkscrew to her bottle. 'Great big crossdressing hypocrite, he is.'

'Who are the others?'

'There's a Scouse hunter called Steve Fitzpatrick, and a pagan Celt called Iris Oceanheart.'

'Oceanheart?'

'Well, her real name's Anna-Marie Gregory,' Juliet said, pouring her wine.

'A cleanser?'

'Yeah, from Clayton.'

Aaron stared at Juliet now, and she could feel him reading her mind, or her blood, or whatever. 'You feel guilty.'

'Pretty much endlessly at the minute, yeah.'

'About the cleanser, was my meaning,' Aaron said.

'Oh.' Juliet thought about it. 'Well, I threatened her with your dad's bayonet, and I took the ears off a corpse she was purifying, and then I drugged her and tied her up, so yeah.'

'Whose ears?'

'Sara Bradshaw's.'

'Why did you need her ears?' Aaron asked. He seemed fascinated, in his now intense and creepy way.

Juliet took a gulp of wine. 'Well,' she said, swallowing, 'after you were turned, I figured I could find you by going to see the Cacolamia.'

'The Undertown witch?'

'Yeah. She told me where you were. But she doesn't dish out help like that free of charge.'

'And her payment was—'

'Sara Bradshaw's ears,' Juliet said, finishing his sentence for him.

Aaron drank, slowly. 'You went to all that trouble to save me?'

'Of course.'

'You didn't think me lost?'

Juliet looked at him, and she couldn't prevent some of her feelings for him returning. 'I knew it was a long shot. But I had to try.'

'Why?'

'Because I ... loved you.'

'Loved?'

'Well, in a way, I'll always love you,' Juliet said, taking another long gulp of wine. 'I mean, you were my ... first love. And we've been through so much together.'

'You couldn't let me go?'

Juliet couldn't look at him, because she found herself wanting to touch him.

But it was he who touched her. He shifted in his chair to face her, and took her hand. 'Juliet ...'

Her heart was in her throat, as she looked up into his eyes. 'Yeah Aaron?'

'You should not feel any guilt on my account.'

Juliet was taken by surprise by this. 'What?'

'I can hear your feelings. They dance about your head and your heart. I see the terrible despair in you. I see how it calls out for comfort.'

'What are you talking about?' Juliet said, pulling her hand from him now, leaning away from him.

'You cannot be alone. You hate it. To you, solitude is as the dark. To be alone is to fade away. It foreshadows the state of death. The state of nothingness which awaits you.'

'What are you saying?'

'You give yourself to the nearest set of broad shoulders,' Aaron explained. 'You took refuge in me from your fear, and as soon as I was unavailable to give you shelter you turned to Robert. If you were to lose him too you would go and find the next pillar of flesh and strength, and you would not have to search long, as sweet and as lovely as you are.'

Juliet looked absolute daggers at him, and topped up her glass. 'D'you know what, Aaron? Fuck you.'

'Ah, you are angry again.'

She nodded. 'It's a real gift you have there.'

'Why do you resent your truth?' he asked.

'Because, sometimes Aaron—and this may be a foreign concept to you—sometimes people like to choose for themselves how they feel, rather than being vamp-splained at.'

Aaron grinned, as though tickled. 'Vamp-splained?'

'Yeah, you, with your bloody mind reading, or ... blood reading, or whatever it is, thinking you're the sodding Sigmund Freud of the undead community.'

'The point is that feelings are not chosen, Juliet. You cannot force desire. It takes you wherever it wishes. And your desire is not for me, or for Entwistle. It is to avoid solitude. *That* is your greatest, most governing need. And it has been, ever since your parents left you.' He looked at her curiously for a moment. 'No, not your parents. Your *mother*.'

Juliet's teeth were pressed together so tightly that it hurt. She wanted to absolutely scream. 'Jesus Aaron, can't you just be your old self. Can't you just bore on about your bloody cricket or something?'

'It's almost November, there is no cricket.'

'You're killing me here,' Juliet moaned. 'Like, I'm not looking for a sodding diagnosis. I just wanted to have a drink with you and keep you up to date with where we're at.'

Aaron sat absolutely still for a moment, and then seemed to soften his devilish side a little. 'And where *are* we at?' he said.

Juliet was still huffy, but she appreciated the opportunity to change the subject. 'Okay. Well, you know my mum's old compass?'

He nodded.

'Well Bishop Powell says it points to the strongest vampire.'

'What?'

'He said it only works in the Depths. Me and Rob think that the strongest vampire means the Polysire. So the plan is, tomorrow, we go into Undertown, we find him, and we kill him.'

'And you believe that this will return me to life?'

She shuffled and leaned into him now, resting her warm hand on his cold one. 'You could go outside again. You'd be free of the hunger. We're pretty sure we'll be booted out of the community but frankly, at this point, I pretty much think they're a bunch of freeloaders sucking dry my mum and dad's money anyway.'

'Well ...' Aaron said, lifting his glass. 'I will drink to that.'

Juliet clinked, and drank. But when she put the glass down, she was left with a niggling doubt about her feelings for Robert, and about her feelings for Aaron. 'Listen,' she said, 'do you mind if I get out of here and head back upstairs?'

'I won't read your blood again,' he said, obviously understanding exactly why she wanted away.

She watched him cautiously. 'You can turn that on and off then can you?'

He smiled. 'I will ignore the movement of your blood, and focus only on the movement of your words.'

She wanted to touch him again. To *feel* him. And ... even though she had no intention of doing so, the idea of being close to him didn't suck. 'Okay,' she said. 'Until I finish the bottle.'

And, with that, still smiling, he emptied his glass of lamb's blood, and reached for the bottle to refill it.

†

'Um ... guys ...' Harry said.

Tilly spun around, and she saw it. A dark, shadowy figure in the distance, by the church. She was certain that it had seen them, and that certainty was confirmed when it began walking straight towards them.

'Oh Jesus ...' Laura said.

'Is that ... one of them?' Mark said.

Tilly felt like she might vomit, though she tried to be strong. 'Don't worry guys. It's picked a fight with the wrong kids.'

And, while Laura, Harry and Mark stood absolutely still, Tilly walked through them, past them, away from the clearing into Cleve Woods and towards the church, towards ... the vampire.

She unzipped her bag, and reached for the weapons inside, as it moved closer and closer still.

CHAPTER SEVENTEEN
Friends

Tilly's hands were trembling. She was terrified. Defiant, and determined, but terrified. She could feel her three friends huddled behind her, quiet as mice, yet following her lead; and the faith they had in her gave her strength, and confidence.

The vampire was close now. So close that she could hear it growling. So close that she could see the glowing yellow of its eyes.

It looked like it had just risen. It was dressed like a corpse might be dressed, in a cheap black suit, which was stained, Tilly assumed, with the wood and earth it had clawed its way through to escape.

Its face was contorted, like a demonic animal, and as it neared her it growled again, more scarily this time, and bared its impressive teeth.

Tilly straightened her back and lifted her head, determined not to show any fear.

And when the vampire was a mere few feet away, she stepped towards it, plunged her hand into her bag and pulled out a water balloon filled with holy water from St. Luke's.

She gritted her teeth, pulled her arm back, and threw the balloon at the vampire's face.

It seemed to hurtle through the air forever.

And then it landed.

It burst, and the holy water inside soaked into the vampire's face, and began to run down its neck, into its suit.

Tilly waited, her heart in her mouth, for something to happen.

The vampire looked confused, but ...

Nothing happened.

Tilly felt like she was going to throw up.

The vampire grinned, and wiped its face. 'I see you ...' it said, its voice a scratchy, throaty snarl.

Harry ran from behind Tilly and swung his baseball bat towards the vampire's face, but the monster grabbed the bat with a swift arm movement. It snatched the bat out of Harry's hands, and tossed it behind him into the distance.

'Shit ...' Harry said.

Still trembling, Tilly seemed to regain control of herself, and grabbed a big, ornate crucifix from the bag. She steadied herself, lifted her head again, and held the crucifix up in front of the vampire.

'Demon ...' she muttered. 'I command you ...'

The vampire peered down at Tilly curiously. It grabbed the crucifix in its cold hand, and, while Tilly still held onto it, the vampire snapped the symbol with one hand.

Tilly felt like her hand had been crushed too, and she jerked forward, towards the vampire, unable to wrestle herself free as the separate pieces of crucifix fell onto the crunchy leaves below.

'I am not a demon,' the vampire said, as it pulled Tilly closer.

She let out a shrill yelp, and tears fell down her cheeks as her shoulders heaved. And still she couldn't pull her hand free. Then, the vampire crunched her fingers together even more harshly, and she cried out in pain again.

'I am not a man either ...' the vampire said, lifting Tilly now.

It pulled her up, so that they were face to face. Tilly's hand fell loose, so she batted at its face with her fists, flinching away from its horrible teeth and rotten breath.

'I am more god than man, more angel than demon,' the vampire snarled into Tilly's ear, and then threw her.

She felt like she was flying.

She wondered if she'd ever land, and then she *did* land. She hit something, or someone, and fell to the ground in a tangle of clothes and panting breaths.

She heard Harry, letting out something like a war cry.

Now, Tilly gathered her senses, and looked around. She had landed on Laura. They locked eyes, lying side by side.

'We have to get out of here Till ...' Laura whispered.

Now, Tilly heard Harry's scream fly through the air, and saw him land about five feet away, beyond Laura.

'Tilly please, get up,' Laura said.

Tilly was about to speak, when Laura began to shoot away from her, as though dragged by the feet. Laura screamed and clawed at the floor with her fingernails, but it was no good. Tilly rolled onto her side, and sat up on her knees, facing the vampire.

It was holding Laura now.

She was facing Tilly. The vampires's hands were on her shoulders. She looked so tiny.

And then it bit her.

It wrapped its massive arms around her little torso and plunged its teeth deeper and deeper into her neck.

'Ow ...' Laura said quietly. 'Ow ...'

Tilly felt like she might pass out, the pain in her was so intense. She felt like her stomach had been ripped open. She wasn't really sure that it *hadn't* been.

And still, Laura's eyes were open.

Her eyes were fixed on Tilly's.

'Ow ...' Laura said again, as tears fell down her increasingly pale cheeks.

Tilly had to act.

She had to.

She climbed to her feet, ran to her bag and took out the wooden stake inside. She nodded, trying to be strong, and ran at the vampire, lifting the stake as she went, but as she closed on the monster eating her best friend, it dropped her and lifted Tilly off her feet, throwing her again, in the other direction this time.

When Tilly landed on crunchy dry leaves, she rolled and looked back at the vampire.

It was on top of Laura now.

She was on her back, and the giant, monstrous vampire was on top of her, eating her.

Tilly wanted to die.

She wanted to die.

'No, stop!' she cried.

Harry and Mark ran to her side.

'Tilly we have to go now,' said one of them. Tilly couldn't tell which.

'No ...' she said, trying to get back to her feet, trying to run to Laura.

But the boys lifted her and started carrying her away.

'No!' she yelled, wrestling for freedom. She spun in their arms, and saw Mark's face. She swung a fist at him, hitting his chin. 'Let me go!' she shouted. She swung her fist again, hitting his nose.

He shook it off.

Tilly kept fighting but she couldn't get free, and she was getting further and further away.

Further away from Laura.

Laura, who was alone, in the dark, being eaten by a monster.

'Oh God ...' Tilly moaned. 'Oh God, oh God ...'

She began to lose her mind.

Her stomach felt like it had been stabbed, and her heart felt like it might explode. 'Oh God ...' she said again, though the words were coming out all by themselves now.

And when the storm of her senses and searing emotions got the better of her, she mercifully faded out of consciousness.

†

When Tilly came to, she tried to figure out where she was. She was on a mattress, for a start. She looked up to see posters of footballers and bands. She groaned, 'Where am I?'

'Hey ...' came a voice.

She rolled onto her side and sat up.

Harry was sitting by the side of the bed. He looked tired and stressed and pale, and sad.

And then images began to return to Tilly.

Her best friend. Her oldest friend. On the ground. Being eaten.

'Oh God no ...' Tilly said without thinking.

Harry wrapped his arms around her, and let her nuzzle into his chest, into his warm, soft jumper.

And she cried, her shoulders heaving with every sob.

'You passed out,' Harry said softly.

'I have to go back ...' she said, though she wasn't ready to leave the safety of Harry's arms.

'I'm so sorry Till, but ... we can't go back. It's so too late for that.'

Tilly still didn't try to pull free from his arms. 'How long was I asleep for?'

'It's half ten now, so about ... what, two and a half hours?'

'I'm so sorry Harry.'

'No, shh ...'

'I'm so fucking stupid ...'

'Don't ...'

But Tilly couldn't not. She hated herself. She loathed herself more fully and more completely than she'd ever loved or loathed anything or anyone. 'I'm so sorry Harry. I'm so stupid.'

He didn't reassure her again, at first. He just held her. 'You wanted to make the town a safer place. So did I.'

Tilly thought about those words. 'There are no safe places are there?'

Harry took a deep breath.

Tilly rested in his chest as it got bigger, and then smaller. 'I guess not,' he said.

'I got her killed,' Tilly said. 'I got my best friend killed. She must've been so scared, Harry. She was in pain, and she must've been so scared. And it's all my fault. It should've been me to die, not her. That's what *I* deserve. Not her.'

'I don't think anyone deserves that,' Harry said. 'Not that.'

She pulled away from him, just enough to look up at his eyes. 'Can I stay here? Can I stay here with you? Tomorrow, I'll ... face whatever I need to face. But, for now, can I please stay here?'

Harry looked nervously at his bedroom door. 'Clothes on, yeah?'

'Yeah, please.'

'If my mum comes in it'll be bad. But not as bad as if we ... didn't have our clothes on. You know?'

'I can't tell you how much I don't want to take my clothes off Harry.'

'Okay,' he said. 'Good.'

She settled in his arms again.

'I won't tell you that everything's gonna be okay, Tilly,' he said. 'But ... however bad things get ... as long as I'm still, like, alive, or whatever, I'll be here for you.'

Tears poured from her eyes at Harry's sheer kindness. 'Thank you,' she said, before lifting her arm and rubbing her eyes with her sleeve. 'Did Mark get home okay?'

'Yeah. You gave him a nose bleed,' Harry said, with a little laugh.

'Oh. I'm sorry.'

'It's okay. It was ... a crazy situation.'

'But he's safe?'

'Yeah. He's totally shitting his pants and he doesn't wanna leave the house ever again, but yeah.'

Tilly nodded into Harry's chest, and then clung more tightly to him. And then she tugged him to lie next to her.

He pulled his duvet out from under them and rested it over them.

And as she closed her eyes, still pressed into the soft warmth of his chest, he stroked her hair, until she slept.

†

It was Halloween morning, and Robert Entwistle felt like his circumstances suited that fact. One of his best friends was a vampire. And he had three people tied up in his living room, which after over twelve hours was a messier and smellier affair than he'd really expected.

He and Juliet had tried to make them as comfortable as possible.

They weren't mortal enemies, or anything.

They were just locked in a conflict with particularly high stakes.

For, if loosed, they would kill Aaron without mercy.

That knowledge comforted Robert a little, when he tried to justify his actions to himself. After all, Aaron wasn't tied up, but he had not killed anyone. Aaron wasn't the one intent on murder. No, that was the hunters.

So, as the kettle came to the boil, rumbling away, he nodded to himself, sure that the people who were tied up were the ones who *needed* to be tied up.

Juliet walked into the kitchen, and stood a few feet away. And that was the other thing bothering Robert that morning. Ever since she'd been down in the cellar with Aaron, the previous night, she'd been acting weird. She'd been keeping a distance—both physical, and emotional.

'Are you making one for me?' she asked.

'Yeah,' Robert replied. 'Of course.'

'Rob ... can we get out of here for a bit?'

Robert looked towards the living room, his mind going to the three captives within. 'Um, okay?' he said, made anxious by her detached manner. He nodded at the door. 'What about them?'

'Aaron's asleep, and mostly they're just playing "Who Am I?" to stop from getting bored.'

'It's horrible,' Robert said. 'Isn't it. Keeping them here.'

'It really is,' Juliet agreed. 'But—'

'Oh, there's nothing we can do about it,' Robert said. 'I'm just saying.'

'Okay.' Juliet took a breath and focused. 'I've got the compass. If you could grab as many weapons as we can carry?'

'Sure,' Robert said, looking round at the kettle, 'I, um—'

'Thanks,' Juliet said, and went straight out of the door to the back halls of the manor.

Robert, left alone, merely said, 'What about your coffee?'

†

Tilly put her key in the front door of her home and let herself in, followed glumly by Harry. The house was warm, and Tilly almost felt it trying to console her, but, deep down, she was inconsolable.

'Are you sure your dad isn't here?' Harry asked.

Tilly slid out of her shoes and gestured at Harry to do the same. 'He text me. He left for work, like, over an hour ago.'

'Oh.'

Tilly made her way towards the kitchen. 'Grandma?' she said.

But when she turned into the room, her heart sank. 'Mrs. Durkin?' she said instinctively.

'Oh,' Harry said. 'Mrs. Durkin.'

'Hello Tilly, sweetheart,' said Laura's mum.

'What are you doing here?' Tilly asked, blunted by the anguish of the last twelve hours.

Mrs. Durkin blinked a few times, startled. 'Well, Laura told me she was staying here. I came to pick her up. Your father said you'd stayed at a friend's house and were heading home. Where's Laura?'

'You spoke to my dad?'

Mrs. Durkin looked at Tilly's grandmother. 'Well, yes,' she said. 'I came to pick Laura up when he was getting ready for work. Why, where's Laura?'

'Um, Mrs. Durkin,' Harry said, stepping in front of Tilly a little, 'Till and me were watching Netflix all last night, but we haven't seen Laura since'—he looked at Tilly—'what, about four o'clock, yesterday afternoon?'

Tilly realised what Harry was doing. 'No ...' she said quietly.

Laura's mum looked pale at once, and, yet, like she didn't believe it. 'What?'

'We haven't seen Laura since yesterday afternoon,' Harry said again.

'No ...' Tilly repeated, still quietly.

'Who are you?' Mrs. Durkin asked Harry, raising her head to look down her nose at him.

'I'm friends with Laura and Tilly,' Harry said.

Tilly's grandmother cleared her throat and sat forward. 'I thought you said Laura was staying here with you?'

'When we left her she was heading for—' Harry began.

'No!' Tilly said, grabbing Harry's arm and pulling him back. 'Mrs. Durkin. I'm so sorry.' Her voice broke and she started to cry.

'Why?' Mrs. Durkin said, still sombre, still anxious, like she didn't want the answer.

'We went out last night,' Tilly said.

'Tilly, no,' Harry said.

Tilly pushed past him. 'We went out to hunt vampires,' she said.

The room fell into silence.

'D'you hear me?' Tilly went on. 'We went vampire hunting. And we found one.'

'Is this a ... joke?' Laura's mum said.

'No, it's not a joke,' Tilly said. 'We attacked it, but it was too strong.'

Mrs. Durkin's hand began to shake, making the cups and saucers rattle on the breakfast table. 'Where is Laura? You tell me.'

'Laura died,' Tilly blurted out. 'She died. The vampire ... it bit her. It drank her blood. And it killed her.'

Mrs. Durkin wept. 'Why would you say something like that?' she said, staring at Tilly with disgust. 'Do you think this is funny?'

'No!' Tilly shouted, as tears welled and fell from her eyes again. 'No, I can tell you, without a shadow of a doubt, I do *not* think this is funny. I watched my best friend die. I watched some *thing* eating her.'

'Tilly, stop,' Harry said.

Tilly's grandmother stood, and marched over to Tilly. And she slapped her on the cheek, so hard that Tilly was sent flying, crashing into a chair and falling over. 'You're a little shit, do you know that?' Tilly's grandmother said. 'Fancy saying something like that. You really do have evil in your heart, don't you.'

Tilly looked up at her grandmother and climbed to her feet. 'Don't you ever do that to me again, d'you hear me grandma?'

Harry was standing in front of her, between grandmother and granddaughter, like a guard dog.

Indeed, Tilly's grandmother looked at Harry like he *was* a dog, and said, 'Believe me, lad, you can do better for yourself than *her.*'

Tilly didn't care about her grandmother's barbs though. She looked at Laura's mum, who was still sitting, still shaking. 'Mrs. Durkin,' she said. 'I'm sorry but it's true.

Laura's gone.' She broke again. 'And she's not coming back.'

'I don't want to hear your fairytales,' Mrs. Durkin said, staring back at Tilly. 'I just want to know where she is.'

'Fairytales?' Tilly snapped bitterly. 'Seriously, fairytales? I've been to your house, I've seen your crucifixes and your little pots of garlic by the door. You know as well as I do that vampires are real, and yet you're passing it off as fairytales?'

'Stop it ...' Mrs. Durkin said.

'I mean, my God, what is *with* the people in this town? It's like you're happy to go along being picked off one at a time. D'you know how many kids are in my year at school? One hundred and fifty. And d'you know how many joined in September last year? One hundred and eighty. Okay? That's thirty kids who've gone missing since we started high school. Thirty-one now! And the grown ups are still gonna lie to us about why a sixth of my year group's vanished in the last year?'

'For God's sake, you little brat, would you please shut your mouth!' Mrs. Durkin cried. 'And tell me where—'

'You know, I've spent the last twelve hours blaming myself,' Tilly said. 'I even dreamt about it. I dreamt about *her*. Watching me as that *thing* bit into her and took her away from me. But you don't, do you? You don't blame yourself. Even though if you wanted you could just pack your bags and move to another town where there *aren't* any vampires. But *we* can't, can we? We're just stuck here, living where you choose. We don't get to—'

Harry placed his hand on Tilly's shoulder. 'Till, stop,' he said. 'It's not gonna help. Come on, please.'

Tilly looked around at him, a little annoyed at first that he'd stopped her mid-flow; but when she saw the kindness in his eyes she thawed, and turned back to Laura's mum. 'Fine ...' she said.

And, with a huff, she turned and made her way for the stairs, while Mrs. Durkin shouted something shrill and inaudible behind her.

†

Upstairs, Harry closed Tilly's bedroom door and said, 'I can't believe you told her the truth.'

But Tilly was already on her knees, her hands under her bed, pulling out her collection of Catholic so-called weapons.

'That's your church stuff?' Harry said.

'A load of total bollocks is what it is,' Tilly said, lifting it all onto her bed, wrapped in one of her old Hannah Montana blankets. She clenched her fists as she looked down at it, and she wanted to scream. Instead, she grabbed the a couple of the vials of holy water and paced towards her window.

'What are you doing?' Harry said.

Tilly opened her window and began pouring the first holy water out, into her back garden. 'I'm getting rid of this,' she growled. She held the vial until it was completely empty, and then she started on the second.

'For what it's worth, I think you're doing the right thing,' he said.

Tilly dropped the two vials in her bin and marched to the bits on her bed, taking the crucifixes and dumping them in the bin too. Then, she turned to Harry. 'Doing what right thing?'

'Chucking all your vampire hunting stuff.'

Tilly sighed and looked down at her bed. Mostly there were just stakes and garlics, and a few more crosses and mini Bibles. 'Just the Catholic stuff,' she said.

'What do you mean?'

'I mean I'm not getting rid of the stakes.'

'You're not thinking of going out again?' Harry said. He sounded stunned.

'Someone has to stop them,' Tilly said.

'Someone *else* can stop them!'

'Who? Because no one stopped that one last night. I won't let it keep happening. I won't.'

Harry stepped forward a little. 'You're just hyper after last night. Tilly you can't go out there again. They're way too strong. The garlic bat did nothing. Your holy water did nothing. It straight up snapped your cross into bits.'

'They must have a weakness Harry, and I'll find it.'

'You'll die, just like—'

Tilly waited for him to finish the sentence, but he didn't.

'Look,' he said, sighing away the pressure that had built up in him, 'I just want to keep you safe, Tilly. What happened last night was straight up horrifying. Like, something from a bloody nightmare.'

'I know that,' Tilly muttered.

'So let's not do that again. Okay? We couldn't stop it. It threw you through the air, and then it did the same to me, and ... what it did to Laura was ... well, I don't think I'll ever forget it, even if I live to be a hundred and fifty.'

'Look, just go, if all you're gonna do is try and talk me down.'

'Tilly—'

'I don't wanna hear it Harry. Just go. I have work to do.'

Harry didn't move at first. He just looked at her with a sadness. 'I said I'd be here for you and I meant it.'

'So you're gonna stop trying to talk me down and get with what I'm doing here?'

He cringed. 'Till, we can't go back out there. We're lucky we made it away the first time.'

'So, when you said you'd be there for me, you meant only as long as I do what you want me to do?'

'No, I meant that ... I meant that, like ... well'—he stoped, and sighed. 'I didn't think you'd wanna go back out there, that's all.'

'Well I do, Harry. So if that's too much for your pretty little head to get around, please, leave.'

'You know what?' Harry said, a little angry now. 'Fine.'

And, with that, he turned and left, leaving her bedroom door open as he went.

Tilly heard his feet clopping down the stairs, so she marched over and pulled her door closed.

And once alone, she regretted sending him away. Because in the silence that was left by his going, she was now free to realise how many little reminders there were of Laura, all over her room. Bracelets they'd made, photo collages they'd made, grungy music magazines they'd read together and laughed at, make up they'd stolen.

Her entire room was a treasury of memories, and all of them were either about Laura, or they included her.

She heard her grandmother shouting something, and then she heard her front door slam.

And then the silence returned.

She picked up her half of the friendship necklace Laura had given her, the half with "Friends" written on it, and began to cry.

†

Robert and Juliet were in Viva, drinking coffee. The air between them was tense, which was to be expected, given the circumstances; and yet, Robert was completely anxious about it.

'What time is it now?' Juliet said, nodding at Robert's phone, sitting on the table between them next to his coffee.

He clicked it on. 'Ten.'

'Okay. We have an hour and a half.'

Robert nodded. It wasn't new information, so he wondered what Juliet was getting at.

'Listen, Rob ... we need to talk.'

At those words, Robert's anxiety threatened to turn into panic, so he kept a lid on his feelings, and said, 'Oh?'

'Last night, when I was down in the cellar with Aaron, he ... said some stuff.'

'Right?'

'Like, you know how he has this whole blood-detective thing going on?'

'He thinks he can read your mind?' Robert said, sipping his coffee and trying to calm his nerves.

'It's more like he can read my feelings, and translate them into words,' Juliet explained. 'Like, on Saturday night, when I was down there with him, he told me I had feelings for you.'

'And then you came upstairs and ... we kissed.'

'Yeah,' Juliet said meekly. 'Well, last night, he said some stuff and it's really stuck with me. It's kind of rattled me.'

'Okay ...' Robert said. 'So what did he say?'

Juliet pursed her lips tentatively. 'He said that I'm ... scared of being alone.'

Robert frowned.

'And,' Juliet went on, 'he said that ... I was with him because he made me feel safe. And that ... when he stopped being available, I gave myself to you. Again, so I could feel safe.'

'Do I make you feel safe?' Robert asked.

She brightened a little, lifting her head. 'Well, you do, yeah. And, like, I do love you. Like you wouldn't believe. I want nothing but good things for you, you have no idea.'

Robert shook his head. 'So ...'

'So I'm ... a little shaken. That's all. Because ... it's not cool of me to have used him. And it's not cool of me ... to use you, now.'

Robert winced, not really getting the problem. 'What are you saying? Are you saying you don't want to be with me?'

'I'm saying that I ... I haven't not been in a relationship since my parents died. I'm saying that I don't want to be with you just because you're someone to be with.'

'Look, Jules, I think you're overcomplicating things. I mean, do you want to be with me or not? If you do, do. If you don't ... well, say so.'

She smiled sadly. 'It *is* complicated though.'

'Why?' Robert demanded, a little resentment escaping him. 'It doesn't need to be. Does it?'

'Don't be angry.'

'I'm not angry!' he shouted.

She withdrew a little, and her sympathy faded. 'I'm trying to explain to you that I need a little space in my head right now,' she said. 'I mean, the last week has been absolutely insane.'

'I'm aware of that Jules—'

'I'm not saying that I don't want to be with you,' she said. 'I'm saying that I can't be with you right now.'

Robert made fists with both hands and tried to control his breathing. 'I knew something was off when you got back upstairs last night.'

'I'm sorry. I needed to process what I was feeling, what was in my head, before I said anything.'

'In the meantime I'm just sitting about wondering what I've done, wondering why you're being weird, and—'

'God, Rob, would you just grow up?' Juliet said. 'I'm telling you respectfully that I need space, that I can't be more than friends right now. When things have calmed down, when Aaron's better and we don't have prisoners tied up in our living room, maybe I'll have the emotional bandwidth to revisit some of this stuff, but, right now, I don't.'

Robert rubbed his head firmly, down his cheek and around his chin. He was utterly bristling inside, and couldn't seem to calm down.

'I need to figure out what I want,' she said. 'I need to face some dark shit inside me. Can't you just accept that? Can't you be mature ab—'

'Are you taking the piss, Jules? You bring me here to dump me and then have a go at me and expect me to be all calm and rational and cool and stuff? It doesn't work like that. You don't get to—'

'Well, make it work,' she snapped, talking over him, 'because I've said I'm sorry and I've told you what I need and you're not respecting that. Okay? You're not entitled to me Rob.'

'I don't think I'm *entitled* to you, I just ... I don't get it. I don't understand why being alone is any better than being with me.' He looked at her, and a horrible thought occurred. 'Is it me?'

'What?'

'Is it me?' he repeated. 'Is this just because you don't want to be with *me*? You're gonna be back with Aaron when we get back from Undertown?'

'What?' Juliet exclaimed shrilly. 'No!'

'So you don't still have feelings for him?'

'Of course I have feelings for him, he's been in my life for more than ten years!'

'You know what I mean!' Robert shouted. 'You're saying you don't have romantic feelings for Aaron?'

Juliet stopped in her tracks a little now. 'Okay, look,' she began, 'last night, when I was in the cellar with him, I did have some ... feelings.'

Robert was furious. He nodded.

'But I don't want to be with him. I wasn't lying when I said I want *space*.'

'Fine,' Robert said bitterly.

'Listen, I've told you. My feelings are all over the place. And you might not like it but it *is* complicated.'

'Well my feelings for you aren't complicated,' Robert said, leaning forward. 'I only want to be with you. There's no one else in *my* heart.'

'Well I'm sorry Rob but you're not the only person whose feelings are relevant!' she shouted.

He nodded again, still fuming, breathing heavily. And when he didn't answer, the two of them let the silence have its moment. Robert looked away, out of the window, over the rooftops of Ecclesburn.

'Look ...' Juliet began. 'I'm sorry.'

He didn't look at her. 'Okay.'

'I shouldn't have kissed you. I shouldn't have slept with you. I knew how much you wanted me, and I took advantage of that.'

He still wouldn't look at her. 'Okay.'

'But we still have work to do,' she said. 'Are you gonna be able to do it? I didn't want to go down into Undertown without talking to you first.'

'No, I mean, why let me go around feeling happy when you can make me feel like this instead,' Robert said, his eyes still out the window.

She didn't respond at first. Finally, she said, 'Look, if you're gonna be a baby about it, my sympathy's gonna run out real fast.'

He flashed furious eyes at her, and said, 'A baby?'

'A baby,' she said, staring back at him.

He sighed, and scratched at the top of his head. 'No. I'm not gonna be a baby.'

'Good. So ... how long do we have?'

He clicked on his phone again to check the time. 'Still over an hour.'

She nodded. 'Okay. Listen, we should get moving. I'll go pay.'

'No,' he said, imagining the day ahead, in Undertown with her at his side, wanting to hold her hand, wanting to kiss her, and not being free to. 'I'll go to Undertown by myself.'

'What?' she said. 'No—'

'It's better than us both going,' he said, avoiding her eyes again. 'Look. I'll give you space. I'll ... do what you want. But you have to throw some respect back at me, right?'

She settled a little. 'Right?'

'So'—he took a breath—'you've just dumped me. It'll be hard for me. Being by your side all day.'

She stared at him a moment, sympathy returning a little.

'I'm not asking you to feel sorry for me,' he said. 'I get it. You need space. I just ... I'll go and kill the Polysire, and then I'll come back.'

'Will you be able to do it by yourself?'

'I've killed loads of vampires by myself,' he said.

'This one might be stronger than the average, though.'

'Look, I can do it,' Robert reassured her. 'You go back to the house, and make sure Aaron doesn't come out of the cellar after sunset.'

'You think he'd attack Bishop Powell and the others?' she asked. She sounded a little betrayed by the suggestion.

'Well, he was gonna kill that kid last week,' Robert said. 'Best not to take the risk.'

The look of betrayal settled into a deep sadness. 'Okay,' she said quietly.

'And, you never know,' he went on, 'if the Polysire thing works, you might be able to bring him up out of the cellar and into the sun before it even sets.'

'Yeah,' Juliet said, still sad.

'Okay, that's settled then,' Robert said. He looked at Juliet, held out his hand, and said, 'The compass?'

She looked back at him, taking him in, feeling for him despite his hostility, and then reached into her purse for the compass. She pulled it out and held it out for him to take. 'This was my mum's.'

'I know,' Robert said, taking it.

'I'm just saying ... bring it back. Whatever happens, you bring it back to me.'

'I will.'

'Swear it, Rob.'

He nodded gravely. 'I swear it. I'll bring it back to you.'

CHAPTER EIGHTEEN
Labyrinth

Jack was practically bouncing as he made his way from his desk at work to the break area. For, it was Halloween. He would drive to Lancaster, he would maybe grab a quick pint in a pub somewhere, and then he would go to Becky's uni to watch her perform in the student-managed production of Vinegar Tom.

After that was the after show party.

And after *that* ... well, that was the part that had Jack bouncing giddily around the building.

For, Becky was a singularly beautiful woman.

She was a star, shining brightly in an otherwise dark and grey sky.

He wondered how it was possible that she had seen fit to be interested in *him*, of all men. And the fact that there wasn't a line of suitors beating her door down on a daily basis baffled him. It utterly baffled him.

Who else was worthy of any man's attention, after all?

He couldn't think of anyone.

Every woman he saw, day to day—it was as though they were all sisters, and as though Becky was the only *woman*.

He'd felt like this for a while, but it seemed to have sharpened over the last few days. He felt like a man possessed now. Drawn as though by magic to *her*.

He smiled to himself as he landed into the break area sofa, and pulled his phone out of his pocket. He'd been eagerly anticipating seeing texts from Becky, but most of the ones at the top of the screen were from Rita.

He glanced down the list at them.

'You need to talk to Tilly,' read one.

'Anne Durkin has only just left,' read another.

'Tilly told her that her daughter was killed by vampires.'

Jack wasn't sure if he'd read that right at first, so he swiped open WhatsApp to have a proper look. And he had read it right. 'What the hell?' he said to himself.

'The poor woman's beside herself thanks to Tilly,' Rita went on in another text. 'Fancy saying that. She's been hiding in her room ever since.'

Jack scrolled down to the next message, from about a half hour later.

'She's gone out. Didn't say a word. Not a sorry, not a please. Nothing.'

Jack frowned, and let out a sigh.

'She's back,' read the next message, an hour or so later still. 'Still hasn't said a word. You can talk to her. I am not going to waste my time.'

'Oh for God's sake ...' Jack muttered, and closed his phone. He took a deep breath and then let it out again, choosing to roll a cigarette rather than look at his phone. 'Killed by vampires ...' he said, bewildered by it and not daring to believe it might be true. He sighed again, and focused on rolling the cigarette.

†

Robert was at the top of the snakelike tunnel slide, within the decrepit Play Shed, where once upon a time parents would bring their kids to play, and occasionally disappear into The Hidden Borough—the vampire-ridden slum-town within the Depths.

He had a bag tied to his ankle. Inside were weapons, and a compass, and *food*.

After his previous visit to Undertown, he'd realised that bringing food along was a necessity.

He checked his phone, which was the last item to go into the bag.

It was time.

He dropped the phone in with the rest of the contents in the bag and fastened shut the watertight seal.

'Okay,' he said to himself with a deep sigh. 'Here I go.'

He leaned forward, and dove headfirst into the slide.

†

Juliet was about to put her key in the door, when she stopped. The truth was, she didn't want to face Bishop Powell, Steve Fitzpatrick and Iris Oceanheart. She didn't want to face up to what she'd done. She just wanted Aaron to be human again, so that she could bring him out of the cellar, untie her slay-happy guests, and get rid of them.

She wanted a break from it all.

She wanted to get on a plane, by herself, and leave it all behind. She could go anywhere. She could go to New York, or Paris, or Rome, or Madrid. No one would be able to find her, and she wouldn't be responsible for anyone but herself.

She could read, and eat nice food and drink expensive wine, and visit beautiful scenic places she'd never seen.

She just wanted to be free of *hunters*.

Free of *vampires*.

And free of *conflict*.

She sighed and really felt like she might cry, but she was sick of crying, so she lifted her head, took a deep breath, gritted her teeth, and put her key in the door.

†

Robert climbed out of the putrid, clumpy brown water that made up the Undertown River, and rolled onto his back.

He had not missed the smell of this place. There was the strong, unmistakeable smell of shit, which he understood came from the river. There was also the smell of piss, which was deeply unpleasant too, and which also seemed to come from the river. There was also the smell of *dirt*. Like a wet dog. And mixed into it all was the smell of cooking meat. That part by itself would have been nice, had it not been for the rest of the foul odours drifting about.

He rubbed his hands vigorously through his hair, trying to rub it as dry as possible, and then sat up in front of the bag that was still tied to his ankle.

He opened up the bag and took out the compass.

He clicked the release catch and the lid flipped open.

The needle was still, pointing very firmly in one direction. He followed the needle's destination with his eyes, seeing that it led towards a cluster of run down houses, with lanes running through them, between them.

Now, Robert moved the compass in his hand, testing the needle, and it stayed true, pointing still in that same direction, towards the houses.

'I guess you're that way,' he said, and climbed to his feet.

'What do you have there?' came a voice from behind him.

He turned to see a mucky, grey little man, with a huge rucksack on his back that towered over him by a clear foot, and was clearly stuffed to bursting.

'What did you say?' Robert said.

The grey man peered down at the compass in Robert's hands. 'Is that ... m'lord's enchanted lodestone?'

'What?' Robert said.

'M'lord Aliester's enchanted lodestone,' the little man said, creeping towards Robert. He looked up at the sky, and then back at Robert. 'You just came from Eglesborne, did yer not?'

'Ecclesburn, you mean.'

'Aye, Eglesborne.'

'So what if I did?' Robert said, swinging behind him the bag that was still tied to his ankle.

The little grey man narrowed his eyes and smiled wickedly, as he stared at the compass. 'I'll have an entire leg to feast on, I bring that to m'lord,' he said, licking his lips and advancing on Robert with his hands out like claws.

Robert stepped backward, and tripped over the bag that was behind him. 'Jesus,' he said, rolling onto his side, still clutching the compass. He turned to face the grey, little man, who was right on top of him now, baring his teeth and wielding a dirty pen knife. 'For fuck's sake, Jesus!' Robert yelped, and knocked the knife-wielding hand away.

'Maybe an arm *and* a leg ...' the little man said, coming again.

Robert rolled backwards and flipped up onto his feet, and, as the man lunged at him, Robert swung his free leg and kicked the pen knife out of his hand and into the river. 'Now back off, you freaky little weirdo,' he said.

The man had no intentions of backing off though, it seemed, as he growled giddily and ran at Robert, who met him square in the chin with a meaty fist.

The little man's head jerked back and he began to fall forward, so Robert stepped out of the way while the horrible man landed clumsily in a heap on the floor.

Robert waited for the man to stir, but he simply lay there, completely still, and still grinning with his eyes open.

'God, are you ... are you dead?' Robert said, kicking at the man, turning him onto his back.

He wasn't breathing.

'Wow,' Robert said. Then, he looked in every direction to make sure no more Undertowners were about to attack him. The street was clear, so he pulled the bag off his ankle and swung it over his shoulder, before refocusing on the compass that had nearly got him killed.

'This way ...' he said to himself, following the needle.

†

Juliet fell onto her living room sofa, and faced the three bound people staring at her. Well, Bishop Powell and Steve Fitzpatrick were staring; Iris Oceanheart had her eyes on the floor.

'I brought you guys some bakes from Greggs,' she said. 'Two chicken, two steak, and two cheese and onion. And I got four slices of pizza. Two Margherita and two pepperoni.'

'That's a lot of food ...' Steve said, hungrily eyeing the greasy bags next to Juliet.

'Guilty conscience, is it?' Bishop Powell said.

'Of course it's a guilty conscience,' Juliet said dryly.

'Can I ... have one of the pizzas?' Iris said sheepishly.

Juliet frowned sorrily at her. 'Of course,' she said. She grabbed one and took it to Iris, who reached for it, slowly sliding it out of its paper bag.

'Look, if I untie you guys, will you promise not to kill Aaron?' she said.

Bishop Powell and Steve Fitzpatrick looked at one another, but said nothing.

'You'll notice that he didn't hurt any of you last night,' she said. 'And he could've done, you know. I didn't chain him up. The cellar isn't locked. If he was a demon, if he was some ... child of Satan, or whatever, he could've come up and done anything he wanted.'

'I'm sorry, Miss Rayne, but I for one will slay the creature if you free me,' Bishop Powell said. 'I'm not going to lie.'

'I'm with him,' Steve said.

'I just want to go home ...' Iris said, biting a tiny piece off her pizza.

Juliet turned to her and nodded.

'I wouldn't know how to kill your friend, even if I wanted to,' Iris went on.

'Okay ...' Juliet said.

'Okay?' Iris responded.

'Okay, I'll untie you.' She looked at the men. 'But not you two. Not until Robert kills the Polysire. Not until Aaron's safe.'

'Then you'd better get used to our company, I'm afraid,' Bishop Powell said.

'Yeah, we'll see,' Juliet said, walking behind Iris and grabbing the ropes that were binding her. Then, a worrying thought occurred. 'Hey, Oceanbrain,' she said.

Iris waited a moment, and then meekly said, 'Ocean*heart*.'

'What are you gonna do when you get out of here?'

Iris turned her head a little to one side. 'I'll just go home and shower. That's all. I swear.'

'You're not gonna tell your mates about ... what's happening here then?'

'No, I won't, I swear to Caireen and to Coventina. I'll go home, and keep my mouth shut.'

Juliet wasn't buying it. Her hands were still resting on the rope, but she hadn't yet loosened it one bit. 'Tell me something,' she said. 'Did Steve and the bishop here come to you? Did they just call you and say, "Hey, did Juliet Rayne come and see you the other day in an ear-chopping mood"?'

'What?'

'Did they come to you, or did you go to them?'

'Why does it matter?' Bishop Powell said harshly. 'Do the right thing, Miss Rayne. Young Iris won't hurt the demon you're so worried about. But, this way, she will at least be safe.'

Juliet poked Iris on the back of her shoulder. 'Did they come to you or did you go to them?'

'Mars saw a conversation on Facebook,' Iris said. 'Steve was asking about you and Robert, and I ...'

'You contacted them?' Juliet said. 'You went out of your way to get back at me for what I did to Sara Bradshaw?'

'Julie, love,' Steve said, 'she was worried, and so was I. She was doing the right thing.'

Juliet sighed. 'Yeah, well, that's as maybe, but ... I'm sorry. I can't take the risk that you'll run and tell your mates about this.'

'I *won't*,' Iris said desperately, her voice breaking a little. 'Please, I hate this, I hate not being able to move, I hate sitting in my own—'

'Dammit Julie,' Steve said.

'Let her go,' Bishop Powell said.

But Juliet's mind was made up. Aaron's life wasn't worth the risk. So she climbed to her feet and walked back to the sofa. 'No. No one leaves.'

'Despicable ...' Bishop Powell said.

'Listen. I'm gonna go and have a sodding drink. D'you guys want this food or what?'

Bishop Powell and Steve Fitzpatrick said nothing. Iris was still clutching her pizza.

'Fine, suit yourselves,' she said, heading for the door to the kitchen. She stopped, turned, and said, 'You know, Aaron doesn't wanna hurt *any* of you. But you still want to hurt him. Think about that.'

And with that she left them to their stubborn hunger.

†

Robert had been following the enchanted compass's needle for about thirty minutes. Most of the journey had been uphill, and yet when he looked back the grimy town looked flat. That had not been the case when he and Juliet had visited Elspeth the Cacolamia, so Robert assumed that the path to the Polysire's layer was also enchanted.

He'd learned quickly to hide the compass. For, the residents of Undertown, with their unwashed peasant looks, seemed like they were obsessed with it.

He'd had to fight off a boy whose enthusiasm more than made up for his lack of upper body strength; but the public demonstration of Robert's energy and brawn had seemed to ward off any further aggressors.

And now he was looking up at a massive cliché of a vampire castle, which, he figured, was where the Polysire could be found.

The castle was tall, and made of what looked like black stone up close. There was a tower with a pointy top. There were huge stained windows. And there was a shallow moat of filthy water running around it.

'I wonder if that runs into the river,' Robert said to himself.

He took a deep breath and looked up at the castle. And then, with a nod, he set off over the bridge towards it.

Once outside the huge stone door he was struck by the size of the building. The houses in Undertown were mostly small, cottagey things, dank and shabbily constructed. So this castle was, by comparison, actually quite impressive.

What struck Robert most sharply, though, was the sign above the door, which read:

THE RAYNE FAMILY FORTRESS
Come Ye Who Seek Righteousness

'Okay I'm gonna talk to her about that when I get back,' he muttered, as he grabbed the bell rope dangling at the side of the door, and yanked it.

The bell chimed noisily, and he took a step back, awaiting a response.

Nothing happened.

'Hello?!' he shouted. 'Any vampires home?'

Still nothing, so he walked towards the bell rope, but before he got there, the door started to creak open towards him.

He waited. 'Okay ... here we go,' he said.

He gripped a flask of holy water in his hand—some of the still working holy water that had been blessed by Father McMahon—while the door continued to creak open. The noise of it was like nails scraping up a blackboard. But when it stopped, the entrance agape, Robert loosened his grip on the flask a little at what he saw.

'Oh ...' he said.

Standing in the doorway was a boy. He looked about ten.

'Are you a ... vampire?' Robert asked.

'No, m'lord,' the boy said.

'You just ... work for one? You're like his ... kid-butler?'

'M'lord?'

'You ... serve the master of this house?'

'Aye, m'lord.'

'And the master of the house is a vampire?'

'Aye, m'lord. The noble Baron Aliester.'

'Great, super,' Robert said, nodding. 'Aliester. And is he ... here?'

'He sleeps, m'lord.'

'Great,' Robert said. 'Listen, do you mind terribly if I ... kill him?'

The boy didn't answer, or show any emotion on his little face.

'Because, you see,' Robert went on, stepping in a little, 'I have a friend, in ... the world above, who I might be able to save by killing your master.'

'You would kill my lord and master?' the boy said.

'Well, that's what I do, see,' Robert said, stepping a little further. 'I'm a vampire hunter. And I can't imagine he's a *good* master. Is he?' Robert looked at the boy's neck, and at his wrists, both of which were covered in sore red spots. 'See, I can see that he feeds off you. That can't be good, having an old perv biting you all the time?'

The boy shook his head. 'I don't follow, m'lord?'

'Look, can I come in and kill the old bastard or not?' Robert said, cutting to the chase.

But before the boy could offer a word in response, he was flanked by three pale and tall creatures, in full vamp-face, who landed on the floor and gracefully adopted attack poses.

'Oh here we go ...' Robert said, still gripping his holy water, and reaching for more weapons from his bag while the little boy ran to the side to get clear of danger.

He pulled out his garlic-infused chakram and with a swipe of his left arm tossed it at the vampire to his left. The semicircular blade took off the vampire's head in one go, causing it to dust at once, while the chakram lodged itself into a grandfather clock by the far wall.

Now, the vampire in the middle, snarling horribly, ran at Robert.

Robert doused it with holy water. The creature's skin hissed and grisly steam rose, and its bones cracked as it crumpled into a heap on the floor, before also bursting into dust.

The final vampire, to Robert's right, edged nearer but more cautiously. It threw its shoulders back and jutted its evil face forward, hissing bitterly at Robert.

'Bring it on, dickhead, I don't need holy water for you,' Robert said.

The vampire was fast. It was a blur when it moved. It hit Robert in the chest and sent him flying out of the castle door, back onto the bridge over the moat.

His bag of weapons had gone flying. He didn't know where it was.

'God I hate the speedy ones,' he said, and rolled onto his side.

He looked down at the bridge. It was made of wooden slats, so he made a fist and punched hard into one of them. The slat broke under his force and he pulled free a yard long shard and rolled onto his front.

The vampire leapt into the air and was about to land on Robert, so he lifted up the broken slat, ragged edge up, and shoved upward when the vampire landed.

The wood went through the creature's heart, and after it made an anguished face it burst into dust, which landed on Robert.

He blinked for a moment, and then started to cough.

He stood, and banged his chest to settle his tickling throat.

Victorious, he took a deep breath and headed back inside, picking up his bag, which was lying on the floor by the door, inside. He marched over to the grandfather clock to retrieve his chakram, which he dislodged and dropped into the bag, and then looked around for more vampires.

There were none.

There was only the boy.

'How many more are there?' Robert asked him.

But again the boy didn't speak. Instead, a voice came from ... up, somewhere.

'Very impressive,' spoke the voice, dry and thick.

'Thanks,' Robert said, turning to face his next enemy.

'But they were merely infants,' the voice said. 'I believe you will find *me* ... somewhat more vexing.'

'Oh yeah?' Robert said, stepping towards the voice, which led to a stone spiral staircase. 'Do I seem vexed to you, Count Duckula?'

The voice became a laugh. A slow, maniacal laugh, which seemed a little on the nose to Robert, but he shrugged it off; he was used to that.

And then the vampire revealed himself. He was pale, of course, and had long white hair slicked back into a ponytail. He wore a light black shirt and a loose pair of also black trousers.

'You're Aliester, are you?' Robert said.

'Child, the Baron Aliester sleeps. I ... am Lionel Casimir, the Death-Bearer.'

Robert laughed. 'Lionel? That's your scary vampire name?'

Lionel Casimir the Death-Bearer narrowed his eyes, an attempt at menace. Then, he pulled a long sword from behind his back.

Robert couldn't help but give an impressed look at the sword. It was big. 'Nice sword,' he said.

'I will split your skin from your bone and sell your flesh to the residents of this Hidden Borough ...'

'Enough!' came another voice. This one came from ... a blazing torch, which was propped up against the far wall, not far from the grandfather clock.

Robert turned to it. 'Who's that then?'

'It is I, the Baron Aliester, of Undertown ...' boomed the fire.

Robert firmed his jaw and nodded. 'Good!' he shouted.

'And you ... are Robert Entwistle of Ecclesburn.'

'You know why I'm here?'

'I do ...'

'You up for a fight?'

'I live to fight ...'

'Good ...' Robert said. 'So ... where are you? Let's go.'

'Lionel ...' the fire boomed, 'bring the upsider to the Halls of the Wise.'

'Of course, my master,' Lionel Casimir said.

'We shall see if he possesses the requisite speed of thought to gain access to my Inner Sanctum.'

Robert rolled his eyes. 'Great.' He turned to Lionel Casimir. 'Come on Lestat. Let's go.'

†

Robert had followed Lionel Casimir the Death-Bearer up through the many halls of the Rayne Family Fortress, and it had not been pretty. There were rooms where female vampires were performing depraved acts on male vampires; there was blood literally everywhere, staining walls and floors alike; and there were dungeons, where dozens upon dozens of humans were being kept as slaves.

'Entwistle ...' said Lionel thoughtfully.

'Yeah?'

'I knew an Entwistle.'

'Is that right?'

'In 1522,' Lionel said. 'Her name was Cecily.'

'I see,' said Robert, unsure how to take the Death-Bearer's tone as he followed him through yet another dark and unpleasant corridor.

'She was an extraordinary beauty,' Lionel went on. 'I was of two minds, whether to turn her or simply devour her.'

Robert pursed his lips into an apprehensive wince, disquieted by the story.

Lionel stopped and turned around. 'You see, in those days, to turn a human without sanction was worthy of execution, in Lancashire.'

'What a predicament,' Robert said.

'Yes,' Lionel agreed, missing Robert's muted sarcasm. 'But she was *such* a rich beauty. I would have risked execution, to have preserved that face.'

'But you didn't?'

Lionel smiled wistfully. 'Alas, no. I took everything she had to offer, and finally, with a heavy heart, I took her life.'

'Lovely story.'

Lionel peered at Robert curiously. 'She looked like you, you know.'

'Look, can we get back to you leading me to the ... to the Halls of the Wise, or whatever?'

'I wonder ... perhaps she was an ancestor of yours,' Lionel said. 'She was of your name, and of your town, after all.'

'Seriously, you're being dead weird and I'm not into it.'

Lionel smiled, and tilted his head as he examined Robert up and down. 'Have you ever given yourself to a man?'

'I'll give you a flask of holy water to the face if you don't back off, you bloody freak.'

Lionel laughed, and turned his back on Robert, readying to lead the way once more. 'We will see ...' he said, with a sideways nod. 'I think that I shall petition the Baron Aliester for your stewardship, once he's done with you.'

Robert sighed. 'Bloody vampires ...' he said.

†

'Here,' said Lionel, gesturing at the locked door in front of him.

'This is it?' Robert asked. 'Aliester's in there?'

'This is the entrance to my master's Halls of the Wise.'

'Great. What does that mean?'

'You will see.' Lionel turned to the door, unlatched the lock, and spoke, as though into the door, 'Limina tua disrumpam.'

The door opened, shuffling from right to left with a gravelly rumble.

'Enter, Robert Entwistle of Ecclesburn ...' Lionel said formally.

'Yeah, thanks,' Robert said, and made his way in.

Once across the threshold, the door slammed shut in one swift movement, much faster than it opened.

Robert looked back at it, took a deep breath, and turned to face forward. There was a font, filled with water in the very centre of the room. On either side were two pewter jugs, one bigger than the other.

'Okay ...?' Robert said.

He walked around the font to the far end of the room, where there was a wooden door with a nasty gargoyle's face mounted on it. Beneath the gargoyle were the words:

> *Four gills, if you would,*
> *If more or less, I'll have your blood.*

'Right ...' Robert said, and turned to the jugs.

The first of them was bigger. "5g" was etched onto the front. The second was smaller, and had "3g" etched onto it.

'Okay, so ... I need to use these to get four gills, or I'm dead,' Robert said. He nodded. 'I can do that. Didn't John McClane have to do this?'

He looked at the two metal jugs and thought it through, with a sigh.

'Okay ...'

He filled the three gill jug from the water in the font, and then poured it into the five gill jug. Then, he looked at the three gill jug and tried to figure out what to do next.

A terrible rumbling from above distracted him, and he looked up to see what was causing it.

'Holy shit!' he said.

The ceiling, which was covered in rusty-looking daggers pointing down at him, was lowering.

'Okay.' He filled the three gill jug again, and used it to fill the rest of the five gill jug, which he then emptied into the font.

He looked at the three gill jug and said, 'So this has one gill in it.'

The rumbling was getting closer and louder.

He quickly poured the remaining one gill from the three gill jug to the five gill jug.

'Alright, alright, alright,' he said, as he filled the three gill jug from the font again, then poured the contents into the five gill jug, which should, if the etchings were accurate, contain four gills of water.

He carried it over to the gargoyle on the door and poured the water in.

The daggers were right on top of him now, so when the door creaked open he jumped through it, and rolled onto his back.

'Jesus ...' he said.

He blew a long breath out of his cheeks, and pulled himself up, climbing to his feet.

There were two cats, one white and one black.

'Hi there ...' Robert said.

'Hello,' said the white cat, who sounded like an old Scottish man.

'Hello,' said the black cat, who sounded like a girl with a northwest accent.

Robert just blinked down at them. 'Of course.'

He looked around. There were two doors, one on either side of the room, one on the left side wall, one on the right.

'I am Jeremy McAllister,' said the white cat.

'And I'm Anastasia,' said the black cat.

'Of course,' Robert said. 'No last name, Anastasia?'

'Nope.'

'Right.'

'I speak only truth,' Jeremy declared, 'and *she* speaks only lies.'

'False!' Anastasia cried. 'For *I* speak only truth, and *he* speaks only lies!'

'Wait, wait, wait,' Robert said, 'I know what this is. You're gonna tell me that one of these doors goes where I wanna go, and that one leads to, like, my doom, or something. And I get one question, right, to figure out which door is which?'

The two cats looked at each other.

'Is that your question?' said Anastasia.

'No.'

'So ...' Jeremy said. 'What is your question?'

'Remember,' said Anastasia, 'if you ask the cat who speaks in truths, you can trust the answer; if you ask the cat who speaks in lies, you cannot.'

'So, traveller,' Jeremy said, 'what is your—'

'Hey, moggies, I've seen this before. It's in Labyrinth.'

The cats looked at each other again.

'I take it you've never seen Labyrinth?'

'Are you talking about the construction of Daedalus and Icarus?' Anastasia said. 'The dwelling of the Minotaur?'

'What?' Robert said. 'No. No, the movie Labyrinth. With David Bowie?'

The cats looked up at him, blinking strangely.

'I saw my baby ...' Robert sang, 'crying hard as babe could cry ...'

The cats didn't respond.

'Nothing?' Robert said. 'Look, the point is that I know what to do.' He looked at Anastasia. 'If I asked Jeremy which door leads to Aliester, what would he say?'

Anastasia looked at Jeremy. 'He would say that it was'—she looked to her left—'that one.'

'Right,' Robert said, nodding. 'So. If you're telling the truth, that means he'd be lying, which means its'—he pointed to the other door—'*that* one.'

'Okay ...' Jeremy said.

'But, Anastasia, if *you're* the liar, that means he *wouldn't* say it's that door, which again means that the door I want'—he pointed again—'is *that* one.'

'You seem very sure,' Jeremy said.

'Literally never thought an encyclopaedic knowledge of that film would come in so handy,' he said, and marched for the door.

And as the cats bickered, he pushed the door open, and stepped through it.

†

The room was pitch black.

'Hello?' Robert said.

'You bested my servants, and you solved my riddles,' came a detached voice, echoing in the dark.

'I know right?' Robert said. 'Where are you?'

'I am everywhere ...' the voice said.

Robert sighed. 'No, you're not everywhere. You're somewhere. Same as me. So, are you gonna show yourself and we can get this over with?'

The detached voice became a laugh. The room instantly lit up, blinding Robert a little. He covered his eyes and waited for them to adjust, and then had a tentative look around.

And everywhere he looked, all he could see, was a man.

There were hundreds of him. Thousands maybe.

He was grand, as Robert expected. He wore a black and red robe, and had long, pale hands, with long, sharp fingernails.

Typical vampire overlord.

'Wow,' Robert said. 'So, okay, you *are* everywhere.'

CHAPTER NINETEEN
She

'I have watched you,' said the vampire overlord known as Aliester, the Baron of the Hidden Borough. There were hundreds of him, perhaps even thousands, and they all moved at the same time, in the same way; and his voice seemed to come from none of them, but rather seemed to fill the room.

'Can I ask ... why the riddles?' Robert said.

'I would be found only by the wisest and strongest of men,' Aliester explained.

'Yeah but I only solved those riddles because I'd seen Die Hard with a Vengeance and Labyrinth.'

'Your mind is sharp,' Aliester said. 'Which qualifies you for my company. But it is your *pain* which qualifies you for my gift.'

'Oh aye? And what's my pain?'

'Juliet.'

The name was like a knife. 'How do you know that name?'

'Your blood sings it to me,' Aliester said. 'She is an elixir to you, isn't she. The sweat of her love is still on you. The running of her passion is still within you.'

'Gross.'

'You see, I understand your suffering better than you think,' Aliester said. 'For I understand the anguish of want.'

'The anguish of want?'

'The clawing, desperate, pressure, that builds up within you. It is present now, is it not? You needn't lie, for I feel it in you.'

'Yeah, but, see, the thing is—I'm not here about her,' Robert said.

'You are in all places, and at all times, about her.'

'What does that mean?'

The army of Aliesters smiled. 'It means that she is the thing that drives you. It is all dance, and foreplay, young Entwistle of Ecclesburn. Your strife, your efforts, your ambition—it is all for her; it is all to be *worthy* of her.'

Robert thought about it. He couldn't deny the dark cancerous feeling inside him, which had plagued him, though he'd ignored it, ever since Juliet said she wanted "space".

'Yes,' Aliester said, 'space.'

'Are you reading my mind?' Robert asked huffily.

'No,' Aliester said, with a tilt of the head. 'But I *can* see you. She said she wanted space, didn't she. And, even though your blood boiled at the notion, you denied yourself and accepted it. Why?'

'What do you mean?' Robert said. 'One person wants to break up, you break up.'

'But you still want her.'

Robert took a deep breath, and blew it out irritably. 'Well, you can't always get what you want.'

'That is your way?' Aliester said. 'You wish to go on, but you are told you may not, so you accept it?'

'Well, what would *you* do?' Robert said. He'd intended it to sound rhetorical, but then he realised who—or what—he was talking to, and understood that he was going to get an answer.

'I take what I want,' Aliester said.

'Is that right?'

'You adapt to your environment. I dominate mine.'

Robert gritted his teeth. He'd been goaded into this conversation, and he knew it. 'Adaptation's necessary, mate.'

'Adaptation is compromise. It is the acquiescence of the weak, the pitiful, the empty.'

'Listen, I get that you're doing your big spiel here, but I'm really not interested. Can we please fight?'

'Tell me ... how it felt, when you were inside her. When her legs were either side of your tongue.'

'Jesus Christ, mate, tone it down.'

'Tell me how it felt.'

The fact of the matter was that Robert didn't *want* to remember how it felt, because it aroused a pain more intense than any he'd felt before. His whole body ached. He felt full of it, this cancer, this torment, this ... *space*. To have had her, and to have lost her so quickly, seemed ... cruel.

'The world *is* cruel,' Aliester said, still reading Robert's mind. 'And this is precisely why we mustn't adapt to its will. Why we must instead force it to adapt to ours.'

'I ... can't do that,' Robert said.

'Because you are afraid,' Aliester said. 'You worry that she will hate you.'

'No, that's not it, that's not—'

'But she hates you already, does she not? She gives herself to you, so that she may be full of you, and when she no longer needs your fullness, she casts you aside.'

Robert shook his head, trying to resist the vampire's logic.

'She hates you already,' Aliester said again. 'She takes from you, and she casts you aside.'

'Stop it.'

'Make the world adapt to *your* will, Entwistle of Ecclesburn. Make *her* adapt to your will. Do not adapt to hers.'

'I said stop it.'

'This is the truth, which vampires understand, and which humans hide from. There are masters, and there are slaves. The choice before you now is clear. You can either be a master, or a slave.'

Robert made fists with his hands, and swung a left hook at the nearest Aliester. His knuckles struck glass, which shattered.

Aliester laughed. 'Good ...' he said hungrily.

'I'll kill you ...' Robert growled, and hit another Aliester. Another pane of glass shattered.

'She hates you, Entwistle,' Aliester said. 'Her need and her want is on your skin, and in your stomach, and it sings to me. She will not seek space from *men*. She will seek space only from *you*.'

'Stop it!' Robert screamed, and struck another Aliester.

'Picture her ...' Aliester said. 'Picture her face, taking pleasure from another man's fullness.'

Robert couldn't get the image out of his head, and the rage inside him flared up like a forest fire at night. 'I'll kill you!' he screamed, and hit another Aliester.

'She will climb onto another man's unworthy frame, Entwistle ...' Aliester said. 'As surely as the sun rises. As surely as the snow falls in winter. As surely as the dew drops in spring.'

He hit another Aliester.

'Her dripping, pink lips will be parted by the dullest, and most dreadfully unworthy of men. Men who are unaware of how singular she is, how rare and divine she is, because they're too busy looking at themselves. And you will stand outside her chamber, howling like a hungry dog.'

'It's not fair!' Robert shouted, and hit another Aliester.

'Yes ...' Aliester said, grinning.

'It's not fucking fair!' Robert shouted, attacking another. 'You're right!' He hit another. 'She'll fuck anyone but me!' And another. 'Absolute meatheads like Aaron, who care more about cricket than her!' He hit another. 'When I would *worship* her! I'd do anything she wanted. I'd give myself a thousand times over!'

'*Yes* ...' Aliester hissed.

Robert fell to his knees, exhausted, while his heart raced in his chest, and he wanted to attack the very universe itself.

'*Yes* ...' Aliester hissed again, even more excitedly now.

Robert was about to hit the black floor, when he felt a shape position itself behind him. He felt like he should fight, but he couldn't summon the willpower. 'Do it ...' he said.

And then he felt lips press against his neck. He felt teeth tear his skin open, tear a vein open, and he felt his blood, flowing out of him and into the creature behind him. And it was ... peaceful. Being poured out. Because the pain and the frustration went as the blood went.

It seemed to take forever.

He couldn't believe how *much* of him there was to lose.

And he felt his skin tightening, all over his body, wrapping over his bones, tighter, and tighter.

And when he had no life left within him, the creature behind him dropped him to the floor and rolled him onto his back.

Robert saw him now. The real him. His perfect invulnerability was ... *beautiful*, as his eyes glistened in the dark like little flickering lamps.

'Robert Entwistle of Ecclesburn ...' he said. 'If I leave you now, you will die.'

Robert groaned, trying to speak.

'But if I feed you, you will live, forever.'

Robert tried to groan a "yes", but he couldn't, he didn't have the energy.

'So tell me,' the vampire said. 'Would you die a slave, or rise again, a master.'

'Y...'

'Would you return to the lady Juliet, and *take* her, and keep her from unworthy men?'

The mention of her name gave him strength, and summoning every ounce, he said, 'Yes ...'

Aliester grinned wickedly, and used his long, sharp nails to puncture two holes in the skin of his neck. And as blood began to run out of them, he lowered himself onto Robert's lips.

Each drop made power surge through Robert's frame.

He reached around the vampire's back, and pulled at him, clinging to him, snarling as his blood poured into him.

It was ecstatic.

The power.

And yet it was incomplete. The ecstasy, for all that it was wonderful, was unfinished.

There was something in the world that he did not possess, and which, until he did, would make him suffer.

And as he began to fill, and overflow, with the blood of the Baron Aliester, he swore to himself, that he would not rest until he possessed that one thing.

The blood of Juliet Rayne.

And all of the treasure that came with it.

†

'I'll always love you,' Juliet said, while Aaron listened. 'You were my first love. We've been through so much.'

Robert could see her saying it, and he could hear her saying it, but he could not affect her in any way. It was as though he was frozen in time, forced to witness the thing of which he was most afraid.

Juliet's love for another.

'I'll always love you,' she said again. 'You were my first love. I'll always love you. You were my first love. I'll always love you. You were my first love. I'll *always* love you. I'll always love *you*. I'll—'

'No,' Robert said, and opened his eyes.

He was not in the cellar of Rayne Manor anymore.

He was in the Inner Sanctum of the Baron Aliester's castle, in Undertown, lying on a hard slab of stone.

'Welcome, Entwistle of Ecclesburn,' Aliester said. 'Sit up.'

Robert did. Then, he swung his legs off the side of the stone, and jumped down.

'I'm strong ...' he said.

'Yes. Tell me,' Aliester said, inclining his head curiously, 'what did you see, while you slept?'

Robert looked at his sire. 'I saw *her*.'

Aliester closed his eyes as though enjoying rich, warm blood. 'Of course you saw her.'

'She was confessing her love for one who is unworthy,' Robert said, as his senses raged inside him, adjusting to death, adjusting to the profound vampiric strength that was now his.

'It is what she does, Entwistle. She confesses her love in exchange for companionship.'

Robert nodded.

'Entwistle, hear me,' Aliester went on. 'My soul danced when you entered my Sanctum. My spirit *soared* ...'

'Why?'

'Because of your desire. Some men are'—he shook his head dismissively—'divided, in their wants. They desire sport, and games, and alcohol, and industry—as much as they desire women. Other men desire women, but they cannot settle. They go through women as you will go through victims.'

Robert watched Aliester with interest.

'But you,' the baron said, 'you are like me.'

'Yes?'

'Your love is pure. *She* is all. All there is. All you can see.' Aliester stroked the side of Robert's face lovingly. 'It is ... beautiful.'

'I will kill her ...' Robert said.

'Of course,' Aliester replied.

'I must kill her,' Robert said. 'I will taste her, first.' The very thought began to overwhelm him. 'Oh my God, I will taste her.'

'Yes ...'

'And I will give her this gift you have given me,' he said, looking up into Aliester's eyes. 'I understand everything now. I see it all. The joyful song and dance of wanting and taking. I see the liberty one can possess, when he takes what he wants without compromise.'

'Yes ...'

'I will make her beg for me,' Robert said, his tone hard, as though making a promise. 'She will crave me. She will reach for me. And I will satisfy her. Forever.'

Aliester merely nodded happily.

'Tell me this ...' Robert said. 'Is it true that, should I kill you, your gift would be withdrawn?'

Aliester grinned, and excitement flickered in his eyes. 'I see you've been reading your Bible?'

Robert gave Aliester a curious look.

'Received any interesting letters recently?' Aliester said.

'It was *you*?' Robert replied. '*You* sent me the Bible verse? Why?'

'To draw you to me, of course,' Aliester explained. 'I wanted you.'

'How did you know of me?'

'You visited my kingdom. Paid a visit to a witch.'

'The Cacolamia ...' Robert said as it started to make sense. 'She told you why we came?'

'One of your three was turned. And the two that remained desired to undo what had been done. I gave you the push you needed, to do your reading, your investigating. I knew you would come.'

'So ... the Legend of the Polysire ... is a lie?' Robert said.

'Of course,' Aliester replied with a dramatic shrug. 'My death will undo nothing—not that I intend to die now, or ever.'

Robert narrowed his eyes, and said, 'Good.'

Aliester smiled. 'There are considerations you must make now,' he said. 'In life, your people hunted mine. Your ... community. And, our weaknesses being so well documented as they are, those hunters have had terrible successes.'

'I will kill all of them,' Robert said. 'Every one that stands in my way. I am not afraid of them.'

'Good ...' Aliester said. 'Now, come. Eat. For your first taste of human blood, I have every kind of flavour you could want. I recommend—'

'No,' Robert said sharply. 'Thank you, no. I will wait.'

'For your strength, Entwistle, you must eat.'

'I said no. My first taste of human blood will be of Juliet's vein.'

'You will die ...'

Robert made fists and felt the power within him. 'No. I will not die. I will return to the world above. I will kill Aaron McLeary if he resists my will. And then I will take my satisfaction from her.'

Aliester seemed impressed. 'I will come with you,' he said. 'And so will Lionel. Once above, I will find every vampire, every lost and hungry creature, and together we will take the town. We will take it back. Starting with Rayne Manor.'

†

Tilly was sitting at her computer, in her room. Her webcam was switched on, and was recording, while she tried to figure out where to start.

'Hey Sophie,' she said, her voice monotone and empty. 'I just wanted to tell you that ... your *community* is a joke.'

She sniffed, her lips pursed bitterly while she tried to decide what to say next.

†

With a heavy heart, Juliet looked out of Robert's study window as the sun set over the Barrington Cliffs. She didn't really know what to expect. She'd been and checked on Aaron, not ten minutes ago, and he was still a vampire. He'd been sleeping, but he was cold, and decidedly not breathing.

Sleeping vampires, she'd discovered, essentially looked like corpses.

It was so weird, not seeing or hearing breath.

She wondered how Robert was getting on, and deeply regretted not going with him.

What if he'd failed? What if he'd been killed?

She would never see him again.

The thought was like a knife in her belly.

She really didn't want to keep Steve, Iris and Bishop Powell tied up in her room another day. She was contemplating taking Aaron somewhere safe, after sunset, and then returning home to free the trio—but she didn't want to leave Aaron out in the world, where the risks of temptation were everywhere.

And then a terrible thought came over her.

She hadn't gone to the slaughterhouse in Cockerham! With everything that was going on she had forgotten. The sun was about to set and she had nothing to give Aaron, no blood. And she couldn't exactly go and get some now.

'Oh God,' she sighed, and ran her hands through her hair. 'Come on Rob ...' she said. 'Please ... get it done.'

†

Rita was looking in the fridge as Jack came down the stairs and into the kitchen. 'How do I look, Reet?' he said, a nervous tension well and truly settled in his chest.

She looked up from the fridge. 'What?'

'Do I look okay?'

'You look fine,' she said, and then got back to inspecting.

Probably choosing her booze, Jack thought.

'Have you spoken to Tilly about this morning?' Rita said, not looking away from the fridge.

'Yeah, we've been texting all afternoon, and I've just had a good chat with her.'

'She still talking openly about vampires, is she?'

Jack grimaced a little. 'Yeah. Look, I'll talk to her.'

'Fat lot of good it'll do ...' Rita muttered.

'Dad?' came Tilly's voice from behind him.

He turned. 'Hey, baby,' Jack said softly, leaving the kitchen and leading Tilly through to the lounge.

She sat on the sofa, and Jack sat on the coffee table in front of her.

'Don't go out tonight,' she said.

'What?'

'Look, I know you have plans to go out, but ... don't.'

Jack felt sick at the thought of not going. 'But, baby, I've got ... I've got stuff I can't cancel.'

Tilly nodded, and looked at the floor.

'I promise, baby, tomorrow, I'll stay in and we can do anything you want. If you wanna talk to me about this whole ... vampire thing, you can. Or if you wanna just do normal father daughter stuff, we can do that.'

She nodded again, and tears rolled down her cheeks. 'Okay,' she said.

'Oh, darling, don't cry,' Jack said, rubbing her cheeks.

She pressed her forehead against his arms, as her shoulders started to bob up and down.

'Oh my love,' he said. 'Come here.' He fell to his knees in front of her and wrapped his arms around her. 'It's gonna be okay. Everything's gonna be okay.'

'Nothing's okay ...' she said, her voice nasal and wet and sad.

Jack held her and let her feel whatever it was that she was feeling.

'Please don't go out daddy,' she said. 'Please.'

Jack didn't know what to say. So he waited, leaving a moment of silence, and then said simply, 'I have to, baby.'

She nodded again, but firmer this time. She pulled out of his cuddle, and dried her eyes with her sleeve. 'No, sure,' she said. And then she got up and marched towards the hall.

Jack followed her.

She grabbed her red coat off the rack and picked up a wicker basket that was sitting next to the radiator by the stairs, before opening up the front door.

'Tilly, wait, where are you going?' Jack said.

'What do you care, dad?'

'Of course I care!'

'Nah, you don't.' She put the coat on, and said, 'I'll go be with a guy who actually gives a shit about me.'

And with that she left.

Jack simply stood staring at the door, opened mouthed, when Rita opened the door from the kitchen.

'Have you had my vodka?' she said.

'What?' Jack said, not really interested, still worrying about his daughter.

'My Russian Standard?' Rita went on. 'Have you had it?'

'No I bloody well haven't Reet,' he snapped, while he stood there trying to decide what to do.

†

The walk from Tilly's house to Harry's took about fifteen minutes, and Tilly was about half way there. There had been a whole bunch of kids trick or treating, supervised by anxious-looking parents. Well, mostly, they were supervised by anxious-looking *mothers*. She'd actually seen zero fathers.

She realised that in her thigh length, hooded red coat, and carrying an actual wicker basket she could be mistaken for a trick or treater herself, but she was really past caring, as it started to rain, lightly at first.

She pulled her hood up, turned onto Lockwood Mews and made her way southwardly, toward Harry's.

†

Jack was driving up the M6, as a dreadful rain beat down on his windscreen. He was completely uneasy about it, about the way he'd left things with Tilly, but he would text her, as soon as he arrived in Lancaster, and make sure she was okay.

He was listening to Darklands, by The Jesus and Mary Chain. Currently playing was Happy When It Rains, and, indeed, as the rain landed on the bonnet of his car and ran onto the motorway, he couldn't help his mind wandering.

Away from Tilly.

Towards Becky.

He was in the fast lane. Going eighty miles an hour. In the rain. On his way to see *her*. To see her act, to see her dressed up, performing.

His skin was tingling at the very thought of it.

He'd been daydreaming about this night all day.

And, yet, there was that niggling worry.

That guilt, trying to get in.

He shut it out, and thought again about Becky. About the way she felt, the way she smelled, the way her lips tasted.

And he let himself wonder how the rest of her might taste, as Jim Reid sang, 'You were my sunny day rain, you were the clouds in the sky, you were the darkest sky, but your lips spoke gold and honey, that's why I'm happy when it rains.'

†

'Hello Mrs. Fox,' Tilly said, shivering from the wet and the cold. 'My name's Tilly. Is Harry in?'

Harry's mum held the door open, invitingly, and the warm smell of roasting meat, boiling potatoes and green vegetables wafted out. 'He is, my love,' she said. 'Come in and get dry.'

'Thank you,' Tilly said, walking in before wiping her feet on the welcome mat that had the words "Jesus is Lord" written on it.

'Harry!' his mum shouted upwards. 'There's a girl here for you!' She turned. 'Tilly, did you say?'

She nodded.

'It's Tilly!' Harry's mum shouted, and then turned again. 'Come in, please, let me take your coat, love.'

Tilly took off her red coat and handed it to the tall, slim, blonde-haired woman, but held her basket tight to her side. 'Thanks.'

She led her through the hall and into a kitchen, which was tidy and clean, despite all of the cooking. Tilly couldn't help but notice that Harry's mum was drinking water. Her dad and her grandmother would have been well into a second bottle of wine by now.

Harry's mum looked at Tilly's vest top curiously. 'Defiant af?' she said, as Harry came bouncing down the stairs towards the kitchen.

Tilly looked down at her vest as the door opened.

'What does "Defiant af" mean?' Harry's mum asked.

'Defiant as fuck,' Tilly said flatly.

The tall woman looked stunned for a moment, before the slightest smirk appeared on her face. 'I see,' she said, before walking to the kitchen surface and picking up some kind of leaflet.

'Hey mum,' Harry said. 'This is Tilly. We, um, well, we've had kind of a mad twenty-four hours.'

'I've no doubt,' Harry's mum said. Then, she made her way to Tilly and presented her with the leaflet.

'What's this?' Tilly said.

'Mum ...' Harry moaned.

'It's for Tilly,' his mum said.

Tilly examined it. It had "youthalpha" written in a funky, slanted red font over a graphic-heavy blue background. 'What is the meaning of life?' she read off the front page, flicking to the next. 'Dare to be different!' she read, in a mocking tone.

'It's about Jesus Christ,' Harry's mum said. 'Open your heart. Don't rush it. Just take your time, have a read through it, and see what happens.'

'Mrs. Fox,' Tilly said, looking up at her, 'does your religion think it's okay to be gay?'

Harry's mum smiled patiently. 'Well, the apostle Paul was very clear,' she said, taking a deep breath. 'And, no, homosexuality is a perversion. You can't be saved and have homosexual relationships.'

'Then I don't think it's okay to be whatever kind of Christian you are,' Tilly said, and threw the leaflet onto the kitchen table. 'Harry,' she said, turning to him, 'can we go upstairs?'

'Um ... yeah,' he said, leading the way.

†

Jack was sitting in a uni bar called The Herdwick with a pint of Lancashire Stout. Not too strong or heavy, he thought, as he sipped it and took a seat in the busy pub.

He took out his phone.

He had several texts from Becky, but none from Tilly.

He thought he'd check in with Becky first, as she'd sent so many. He took a few gulps of the stout ale, and started to type.

†

'What do you have in here?' Harry asked as he began to lift the blue and white tea towel up.

'Medicine,' Tilly said, dropping her coat onto his floor, and shoving the tea towel back down, in place.

'What does that mean?' Harry said.

Tilly didn't answer. She just looked around the room.

Harry was a little embarrassed, as his room was a little messier than it had been when they'd left there that morning, but she didn't seem to care about that. She was just marching about, her head jerking this way and that.

'Where's your vaporiser?' she said.

'Why, d'you wanna get a little wasted?' Harry asked, brightening at the thought.

'Where is it?' she said. 'Where do you keep it?'

'I think that's an amazing idea,' he said, making his way towards his sock drawer. He sifted through the bunched socks inside, until he found the right one. Then he unfurled them over his bed, causing the vaporiser to fall out onto it.

Tilly grabbed it.

'Did you bring leaf with you?' he said keenly.

But she just shoved it in her basket. Then, she turned to him. 'You wanna come with me right now?' she asked.

'What?'

'You wanna come with me?'

'Come ... where?'

'I wanna go and see Juliet Rayne. And the other hunters here in town.'

'What?' Harry said. 'No. No, Tilly, that's insane. Okay, you're lucky you made it from yours to mine in the dark without getting bitten. And now you wanna take a walk up Ragged Stone Road, after dark? In the rain? On Halloween?!'

'I'm going,' she said.

Harry sighed, almost growling. 'Jesus, Tilly. You wanna get yourself killed, is that it? You actually do, don't you? Mark said you did, and I didn't believe him, but it's true, isn't it?'

Tilly didn't speak. She just stood there, holding the basket. Her face was rock hard, her lips all bunched together, like she was in some kind of pain.

Her phone pinged, and she ignored it.

Harry snatched the basket out of Tilly's hands and turned his back on her, while he lifted the tea towel up, exposing the contents.

He lifted a bottle out of the basket, when a hard foot kicked him in the small of his back, knocking him forward, onto the bed.

'Never snatch anything out of my hands!' she hissed.

He looked at the bottle in his hands. 'What's this? Vodka?'

'That's mine,' Tilly said, and grabbed it back.

'That's your *medicine*, is it?' Harry said.

Tilly stuffed the bottle back into her basket and covered up the contents again, before grabbing her coat off the floor and heading for Harry's bedroom window. She opened it up.

'Tilly, wait,' he said. 'Don't go. Seriously, you could get hurt.'

She hoisted one leg out, and looked in. 'You can come if you want, but I'm going either way.'

Harry stood there, wanting to think of something clever to say to persuade her to stay—but nothing came. 'I love you, Tilly Turnbull,' he said finally, desperately. 'Please, don't go.'

'Don't Romantic Full Name me,' she said, and disappeared out of the window.

†

Juliet was sitting outside the cellar door, absolutely out of her mind with worry. She had practically no fingernails left at all. She looked at the time on her phone, and her heart sank. It was five to seven. That meant that Robert, down in Undertown, had just twenty minutes, to kill Aaron's Polysire and get back to Ecclesburn.

'Oh God, oh God, what am I gonna do?' she muttered.

She contemplated checking Aaron again, but she had been down about ten minutes ago, and she was beginning to piss him off, pestering him over and over again.

And, she felt like she'd rather live in hope, that maybe he was human down there, than face the miserable reality that he was not.

She sighed.

It was no good. If he was human again, he'd come upstairs, he'd knock on the door, and come out.

No.

He was not a human.

He was still a vampire.

Which meant Robert hadn't been successful. And which meant she would have to decide whether to let the bishop and the others out, or leave them tied up for their second night.

'Oh God ...' she said.

Guiltily, she opened the Dominos app on her phone, and started ordering her prisoners some pizzas.

†

Rita was playing SCRABBLE Mattel on Facebook, when a message notification popped up. She ignored it at first, as the little banner showed at the top of the screen, but out of the corner of her eye she caught the words, 'URGENT MESSAGE your granddaughter is in danger ...' and clicked the message.

It was from a young woman, called Sophie O'Hara.

Anxiously, she started to read.

†

Time was almost up.

Juliet was close to despair. If Robert was going to be successful, he wasn't going to return for another twenty-four hours; but, if he was about to come back, that meant he'd killed the Polysire and it hadn't worked.

Because Aaron was still a vampire.

And she still had nothing to feed him.

'Oh fuck, oh fuck, oh fuck ...' she muttered.

She felt, at that moment, a profoundly dark temptation, to simply untie her captors and leave.

To pit hunter against vampire.

To let them sort it out amongst themselves.

'God dammit Rob ...' she said.

†

The vampire Robert Entwistle of Ecclesburn stood before the Undertown River, with the Baron Aliester, Lord of the Hidden Borough, and Lionel Casimir, the centuries old Death-Bearer.

Robert checked the time on his phone—one of the few useful functions the little black slab performed for him now—and turned to his fellows.

'It is time, my friends,' Robert said. 'We go. And when we arrive, we kill.'

And with that, the unholy trio dived, one by one, into the river, and began to swim to the bottom.

CHAPTER TWENTY
Now Evanesce

Robert Entwistle led Aliester and Lionel Casimir out of the abandoned Play Shed in Ecclesburn, and out into the rainy night. He had left his vampire hunting weapons in the Undertown River, for he had no need of them now, and no desire for them to be in the world.

The only thing he still held was Juliet's mother's compass.

For he had sworn to return it, and he would keep his word.

'I do *love* this town,' Lionel said, as he marched forward, towards Seven Sisters Road. 'I have not revisited the upside since 1943.'

'You've been in the Depths for seventy-four years?' Robert asked.

'We do not visit the land of sun without cause,' Aliester said. 'We send servants to bring us our quarry, and to populate my world.'

'There has been a Rayne keeping us away for over a century,' Lionel explained.

Aliester put his arm around Robert, and stood next to him, as the rain beat down upon them both. 'You intend to return that to the Lady Juliet?' he said, nodding down at the compass in Robert's hand.

'I do.'

'Do you understand that it belongs to me?'

Robert was actually surprised by this. 'What?'

Aliester smiled. 'It was enchanted for me, by a witch of extraordinary comeliness. I unburdened her of her innocence, and she repaid me with this. That I might find any pretender to my kingship, and destroy or subjugate him.'

'I had no idea,' Robert said.

'That was in 1704,' Aliester said. 'Amelie Rayne, your Juliet's late mother, she fought me and took it in 1997, when Juliet was but a seed in her womb, no bigger than a fingernail.'

'You survived a battle with Amelie Rayne?'

Aliester grinned proudly. 'I did one better.'

'You *killed* her?' Robert said. 'It was you?'

'Amelie *and* her husband. Fifteen years after that first fight. But the harlot didn't have the compass on her.'

Robert looked down at it. 'I swore to Juliet that I would bring it back to her,' he said. 'And I've no wish to—'

'My friend,' Aliester said fondly, squeezing his shoulder, 'I am in a state of celebration, and of revelry.' He nodded. 'I insist that you have it, a token of my amity. Go, and give it to your sweet lass. But'—he raised a finger with his free hand—'do me this service: when you return with her to Undertown, if it points to any but me, you tell me.'

'I shall, my lord.'

†

Tilly was sitting in the bus shelter on Horseferry Street, at the bottom of Ragged Stone Road, taking a moment of reprieve from the rain. She fiddled with the friendship necklace resting on her chest—the necklace she had no desire to lose, or put away, as long as she lived.

The evening was getting on, but all she wanted to do was hide in that shelter, listening to her music through her earphones, and cry.

But that wouldn't save anyone.

She would go back out, into the rain, and make her way up the hill towards Rayne Manor.

She would.

But ... not yet.

†

It was the intermission, so Jack walked out into the Lancaster evening for a cigarette, huddling under a nearby overhanging roof to keep out of the rain. There were a few others there, smoking too. They looked like parents, and Jack was struck by shame, that they probably thought he was there to watch his adult child in a play too.

He kept to himself, and started rolling the cigarette. When it was ready, he lit it and grabbed his phone out of his pocket.

There were ... dozens of messages, all from Rita, and a bunch of Facebook messages from someone whose name he didn't recognise, someone called Sophie O'Hara.

'Bloody hell ...' he sighed, exhaling smoke into the drizzly night air.

He opened the Facebook messages first, and, as he scrolled through them, reading with increasing urgency, he began to feel overwhelmed by a sense of sheer, cold blooded panic.

He threw the cigarette on the floor, and began to run, away from the theatre, into the rain, towards his car, parked a quarter mile away.

†

'This is where we part, my lord,' Robert said to Aliester, who had Lionel standing behind him.

Aliester lifted his head, as though to the wind, and rain landed on his face and ran down onto his clothes. 'There are many of my children here,' he said. 'I will give you the time and the intimacy that you require, and I will go and find our brethren.'

Robert was still getting used to Aliester's gothically formal way of speaking, and desired to show due deference, so he nodded. 'Lionel is to come with me?'

'Juliet Rayne is still a Rayne,' Aliester said. 'Lionel will ensure that you cannot be bested by her. When I have provided the vampires of Ecclesburn with purpose, I shall come to you.'

'Very well, my lord,' Robert said, imitating that formal way of speaking as well as he could.

And with that, Robert and Lionel set off, up Ragged Stone Road, towards Rayne Manor.

†

Jack was going sixty miles per hour—twice the speed limit—along the A6, towards the entrance to the M6, all the while trying to read and reply to the messages that were appearing on his phone, one after another.

He wanted to find out who the hell Sophie O'Hara was, and what she'd been filling his daughter's head with; and he wanted to tell Rita to get some bloody garlic on her neck and wrists and get out there looking for Tilly. But it was not easy, texting while trying to drive in the rain.

He had one hand on the wheel, and one on his phone.

He opened his conversation with Rita and started thumbing, 'Get out and find—' when bright lights flashed and a car horn blared. He dropped the phone, and pulled the steering wheel to avoid the car heading straight for him. His back wheels skidded out and he lost control, and the car spun backwards and crashed into the bushes at the side of the road, right at Jack's window.

'Jesus fucking Christ!' he yelled.

There were no cars around, and his own vehicle was fine. Slowly and sheepishly, he started up the engine and swerved to the correct side of the road, before doing a U-turn in a pub car park, and getting back on track, heading south.

†

Juliet checked the Dominos app on her phone. The four massive pizzas she'd ordered were apparently out for delivery, so at least Bishop Powell, Steve and Iris could eat.

Juliet was sitting in the hall, waiting, and hoping that Robert would return, while trying to decide what to do about Aaron, when the door from the cellar began to slowly open.

Her spirit soared in that moment, and she turned to face the door, full of hope that Aaron's face would be back to the way it was, that he'd be breathing and smiling—but when he appeared through the darkness behind him, he was in full vamp-face.

'I'm sorry Jules ...' he said, 'but you said they want to kill me, and I have to eat ...'

Juliet jumped to her feet and blocked him with her hands. 'No, Aaron, please, don't do this.'

His eyes were bright red, and though there was hunger in them, there was such pain and regret as well. 'I have to ...' he said.

'No, Aaron, my darling, you don't ...'

'Your *darling*?' he snarled. 'I am *not* your darling.'

'Please, Aaron ... I love you. You can't kill them. You can't.'

'Not them, just one,' he said, eyeing the door to the living room where they were bound. 'The girl.' He focused on Juliet. 'Oh, God, I want the girl.'

Juliet stepped to her right, between where Aaron was standing and the door to Iris. 'No,' she said firmly. 'No. I'll kill you, Aaron. D'you hear me? I'll kill you if you try.'

Aaron stepped forward and grinned. 'I *told* you I'm not your darling,' he growled.

†

Billy Corrigan, the Dominos delivery guy, pulled over just inside the grounds of Rayne Manor. He climbed out of the car and looked up at the famous house, before going to the back seat and taking out the four large pizzas.

'Rich pricks may have ordered online but they'd better tip better than—'

He felt hands around his chest, pulling him backward, and as he dropped the pizza boxes he felt a searing pain enter his neck.

He tried to scream, but he couldn't, as the world began to fade.

†

Iris was screaming, while Bishop Powell and Steve Fitzpatrick shouted various religious threats at Aaron, now standing in the doorway.

'Aaron, *please* don't make me do it,' Juliet pleaded. 'Please!'

He growled, and inched further into the room.

'I swear to God I'll kill you darling!' she shouted. 'I'll do it. I'll fucking well do it!'

He trained his eyes on her. His red, demonic eyes. He looked so angry.

And then he moved at her, so fast she couldn't stop him, and pulled at her, pressing her chest against his. He yanked at her hair, exposing her neck, as she wept, all while Bishop Powell and Steve shouted.

'Aaron McLeary!' came a familiar voice. 'Put her down!'

It was Robert.

Juliet's heart lifted.

Aaron dropped her, and she looked up at the door.

Robert stood before her, but he ... he was ... he was *vamp-faced*.

'No ...' she whispered, as her skin tingled with the overwhelming horror of it.

Aaron walked slowly towards him. 'Of course ...' he said.

Robert lifted his head. 'Follow me, Aaron.'

'What?'

'Follow me. Serve me. Do this and I will spare you.'

Aaron laughed. 'Is this a joke?'

Robert took a step towards Aaron now. 'No.'

'This *has* to be a joke? You think I'd serve *you*? Serve the kid who cried when his dad died? Serve the sad piece of shit who perved on my girlfriend for years instead of finding one of his own?'

'You were never worthy of her. You used to ignore her texts so you could play FIFA. I would have killed you then, had I seen what I have seen now.'

'You *are* a sad, pathetic coward,' Aaron said. 'You think that just because I don't drop everything the minute she calls, like *you* do, that I'm unworthy of her? Relationships don't work like that, you little whipped bellend.'

'I'm done with this,' Robert said. 'If you won't follow me, I will kill you.'

Aaron jutted his head forward, readying for the fight, and growled, 'You'll try ...'

†

Tilly clicked the time on her phone, ignoring all the texts. It was almost eight. And the rain wasn't so heavy now. It was more of a fine mist. 'Okay ...' she said, nodding to herself. 'Now or never.'

She pulled up her hood, slid her phone back into her inside coat pocket, and stepped out of the bus shelter into the night, and began the slow walk up Ragged Stone Road towards Rayne Manor.

†

Aaron grabbed Robert by the throat and pushed him backwards, through the hall of Rayne Manor, towards the cellar door.

When the two vampires hit the door, it broke open inwardly, and they tumbled to the bottom of the stairs and into the cellar below.

'I think maybe I'll leave *you* down here,' Aaron said, climbing on top of Robert and slamming his head into the floor. 'I'll go up, into the world, and *I'll* take Juliet, in all the ways *you* want her.'

Robert was only strengthened by this threat. 'You won't,' he said, before slashing Aaron's throat with his solid, sharp fingernails.

The cut wasn't too deep. A thin line of blood trickled out of the wound and ran into Aaron's black shirt.

Aaron hissed, and head butted Robert, cracking his nose with his forehead.

The nose bone broke, and pointed down into Robert's upper lip. But Robert sniffed, and scrunched his nose, allowing the bone to heal in moments, shifting back into place.

'I knew you wanted her, you know,' Aaron said. 'I always knew.'

'Good,' Robert growled back.

'And if this had never happened to me, you'd have never had a chance with her. You'd have been dancing at our wedding and babysitting our kids while she went down on me in the back row of the Odeon.'

Robert growled again, even more angrily this time, and wrestled Aaron onto *his* back. 'That's not the way she tells it, *mate*,' he said. 'The way she tells it, she was only with you because she felt bad for you, because she owed you one for looking after her when her parents died.'

'And yet, just last night, she told me that she loves me, that she's *always* loved me,' Aaron hit back.

Robert couldn't help but let out a little anxiety at that. The words were so similar to what he'd dreamt, while he slept, in between life and death.

'Ah ...' Aaron taunted, 'you heard that, didn't you?'

Robert peered down at his enemy with nothing but hatred left for him.

'You did!' Aaron said, laughing. 'She's always loved me. Let's face it, when we were both available, did she ever come to you?'

'Shut up!' Robert snarled.

'Did she ever give herself to you when I was alive?'

'Shut up I said!'

'She didn't,' Aaron said, still grinning, still taunting. 'Because, even now, you're weak, Robert Entwistle. You could never keep a woman like her, with your whiny, needy shite.'

Robert lifted Aaron and threw him at the wall.

And then, he raced at him, and pressed his forearm into his throat. 'What's the matter?' Robert said as Aaron squirmed to get free. 'I thought you were gonna leave me down here and take Juliet in all the ways I want her?'

'I'll ... kill ... you,' Aaron said, as he failed to break free from Robert's grip.

'Oh yeah?' Robert snarled, and leaned his head forward so their brows were almost touching. 'How are you gonna do that?'

Aaron clenched his teeth and strained with everything he had, but it was no good.

Robert looked to the right of Aaron's head.

His late father's army bayonet was lodged into the wood.

'Well isn't that handy,' Robert said, and yanked it out of the wall. 'Any last words?'

'She'll ... never ... want you ... the way you ... want her,' Aaron spluttered.

Robert spat on Aaron's face, then put the bayonet to his throat, and growl-whispered, 'That won't stop me from possessing her though, will it, dead man?'

And with that, Robert put the blade to the wall.

Aaron's eyes widened, and his body dropped, while his head stayed. And then both head and body burst into dust, which fell to the floor.

Robert stepped back and grinned, taking slow delight in the death he'd wrought.

'No ...' came Juliet's voice.

Robert turned to her.

Her hands were over her mouth, trembling. Tears filled her eyes, and soaked her cheeks.

'Rob ...' she said. 'What have you done?'

†

Lionel Casimir walked into the living room of Rayne Manor, where three humans were sitting, bound by ropes, to chairs. And when he saw this, he smiled. For he could sense the profound animosity in the two men of their number, as they shouted their Christian curses at him.

He went behind the first of the men. He was the younger of them. And Lionel snapped his neck, and left it hanging down in front of his chest.

The second man, the older of them, shouted even louder, even more passionately, so Lionel walked in front of him, and grinned.

'Be gone!' the man said. He was wearing a Catholic's collar. 'Evil fiend, leave this place!'

Lionel simply smiled at him, and said, 'Why would I leave this place, this orchard of opportunity, when the fruit hangs so low?'

'Evil one, I command you, by the power of Christ, be *still*!' the man protested.

Lionel leaned closer to the man's face, and said, 'Christ has no power in this room, old man,' and palmed his face backwards, exposing his neck. Then, with two fingernails, he slit his throat, and watched while fat old blood ran down over his collar, and while the life slowly faded from his eyes.

It was now that Lionel became aware of the screaming of the third member of the party.

She was female, and quite lovely.

She wore the pain within her like a sign, with her black clothes and creative cosmetic artistry.

'Who are you?' Lionel said.

She didn't answer. She merely panted, between sobs, between heightened wails.

Lionel moved in front of her and shut her mouth hard. 'Who ... are you?' he said again, letting go of her mouth so she might answer.

'I ... ris ... O ... cean ... heart ...' she gasped.

'A sobriquet, surely,' Lionel said, running his thumb over her throat while he gripped the back of her neck.

She closed her eyes and shook her head as tears made black marks of her mascara down her cheeks, like sorry, miserable trails.

'What was your given name?' Lionel said.

'Anna ... Ma ... rie ... Gregory ...' she said.

'Anna Marie ...' he said, leaning his head to the side now, speaking with such desire, such want. 'Why would you want to change that?'

Again, she didn't speak. She closed her eyes, and sobbed.

Lionel allowed his face to change, inspired by her beauty, inspired by her pain. 'Do you know why a woman changes her name?' he said, running both hands now behind her neck, pulling her closer to him. 'Why she resents the world, for failing to see her as she sees herself?'

She opened her eyes, just a little. 'No ...' she managed, shaking her head.

'She does this because she has a wildly exaggerated sense of self-importance,' Lionel said.

She shook her head again, and flinched away from him.

'Anna Marie,' he said, gripping her more tightly still. 'Do you want me to give you the importance you lack?'

Her face was still, just for a moment.

Lionel, sensing her keenness, read this as a tacit offering of consent, and plunged his teeth into the milky softness of her neck. He tore a vein open, and sealed his lips around the wound, swallowing, again and again, as the life poured out of her and into him.

And then Lionel felt her pleasure at being taken, at being needed, and it made him bite harder still.

She clawed at his back, and pulled him into her with all the strength that she had.

He plunged still deeper, and wrestled her from her bindings, pulling her onto the floor on top of him, all the while lapping and swallowing at the lifeblood that spilled out of her.

And when there was barely anything left, he licked at the wound like a hungry dog, before rolling her onto her back, and placing his own neck between her teeth, offering himself to her.

He sensed her blend of confusion and desire, for just that moment—and then he felt her bite into him.

He pressed his neck into her mouth, pressed his skin over her teeth, forcing it to break, forcing his flesh to open to her.

And then he fed her.

And while she took him into herself, he pulled at the back of her head, pressing her into him, as life itself passed between them.

He felt her desire, her want, and it enraptured him.

He pressed his neck deeper still into her mouth, while she clung to him as though her life depended on it.

†

Jack turned off the M6 and onto the Clayton Road, the gloomy boulevard which led into Ecclesburn. The rain wasn't so bad now, but he was still anxious after the near crash. He went as fast as he felt he could, and he focused on nothing but the road ahead.

†

Tilly stood outside Rayne Manor, her hood still up over her head, and her basket of "medicine" resting in the crook of her elbow. She'd had some of her grandmother's vodka—for Dutch courage—back before she'd left her home, but she'd not had much. Mainly it just warmed her up and made her breath taste weird.

There was a Dominos Pizza delivery car, sitting in the drive. There were about fifteen other cars lined up as well, but they didn't seem so ... abandoned.

The pizza car was just sitting there, in front of the house, at an angle, with two of its doors open.

'Hello?' she said, lifting her head towards the car, as she stepped nearer to it.

†

'Juliet,' Robert said, in the cellar of Rayne Manor.

She looked like she was going to faint. 'What ... have you ... done?'

'He attacked *me*, Juliet,' Robert said, keeping his distance cautiously, sensing her absolute desperation, coming off her in waves.

'What the hell happened to you down there?'

Robert raised his head proudly. 'The compass took me to the strongest vampire,' he said. 'Just as Bishop Powell said it would. But there was no truth to the Legend of the Polysire.'

'How do you know?' Juliet said. 'Did you kill him? Did you kill the strongest vampire?'

Robert flinched at this. 'It was he who sent me the letter. He who wanted me to believe in Polysires.'

'What?' Juliet said, still keeping her distance, and still quivering with shock and horror. 'Why?'

'To bring me to him,' Robert said.

'That makes no sense ...' Juliet said. 'That's'—and then she stopped, as though understanding. 'Wait. It was about us? It was about ... defeating us?'

Robert shook his head. 'No, it was not about defeat. It was about destiny. It was about *my* destiny. And yours.'

'What the *fuck* does that mean?'

'There are masters and there are slaves ...' Robert said, trying and failing to explain. 'There—'

'And what does *that* mean?'

Robert stiffened his gaze, sensing in himself that softness in her company, which he had resolved to control. 'I'm going to take you,' he said, his head raised again.

She seemed to focus now. She stopped quivering, and clenched her fists at her sides. 'The *hell* you are.'

†

'Rita?!' Jack yelled as he ran into the kitchen.

She was standing, smoking inside the house. 'Jack, I'm sorry. I couldn't go out. I couldn't.'

'It doesn't matter. Where's Tilly now? Do we know?'

Rita exhaled smoke and shook her head.

'Okay, well she was going to Harry's house,' Jack said, 'so that's where I'm going. Will you call his mum and let her know?'

'Call her, how? I don't have her number?'

'Well text her on Facebook then!' Jack yelled. 'Her name's Selina Fox.'

Rita nodded dutifully, and Jack left.

†

'Hello?' Tilly said, pushing forward the already open door of Rayne Manor.

She made her way in. There was a creepy sort of abandonment to it.

She heard noises coming from a door to her right, so she crept towards it. It was open too, so she pushed it a little, peering into the room.

Her heart began to beat like a drum in her chest.

There were two figures, lying on the sofa, and they were ... biting each other. Their faces were all contorted, like the two vampires she'd seen before.

And in the centre of the room there were two men, tied to chairs, and while one of them's head was hanging horribly in front of his chest, the other was ... covered in ...

She gasped, and started stepping backwards, away from the room.

There was a creak, which came from another room somewhere, and it took all her willpower not to scream.

'There are vampires here ...' she whispered with barely a sound, and looked around, trying to stay calm.

†

The Baron Aliester saw his fellow creatures of the night, taking shelter in the Grosvenor Family Crypt, at the back of the graveyard at the church of St. Luke's.

'Brethren ...' he said, announcing himself with a loud, theatrical voice. 'I bring glad tidings, on this most unholy All Hallows' Eve night.'

The creatures began leaving the crypt, eyeing him with curiosity and fascination.

'You need not hide,' he went on. 'For our enemy is defeated. Come with me now, to Rayne Manor!'

'Are you mad?' one vampire said.

Aliester tolerated this defiance magnanimously. After all, they had been subjugated for so long. 'Do not fear, my friend,' he said with a smile. 'For the Family Rayne has fallen to my will. The Rayne Helsingers are vanquished, forever.'

Excitement began to grow among the undead group.

'Come with me,' Aliester repeated. 'For this is our night. Our Halloween. The darkest and most corrupt Halloween, to which this town has ever borne witness. Follow me now ... to glory in the death ... of Juliet Rayne.'

†

Jack rapped on the door of Harry Fox's house.

The door opened. 'Hello?' said Selina Fox.

'Yeah, hi. Is your son here? Can I talk to him a minute?'

Selina Fox seemed a bit surprised, but not unwilling. She held the door open for Jack to go in.

†

'I won't let you give yourself to unworthy men!' Robert said, and dodged a knife as it hurtled past his head.

'That is *so* not your call!' Juliet yelled, chucking another knife at him.

'I will make it my call!' he yelled, dodging it and racing at her, colliding with her and landing on top of her.

She gritted her teeth and pressed with her arms against Robert, against the man she'd known and loved since they were children. 'I can't believe what you're saying ...' she hissed.

He roared, and pressed her down. 'You don't get to beckon me and then send me away, as though I am nothing but a sack of emotional comfort, to be consumed and put away.'

'Oh we're way past that you absolute freak,' she said, flinching her head each way, avoiding his face, avoiding his eyes, his breath. She lifted her knee and struck him hard between the legs.

He rolled off her and clutched his groin in pain. 'You're not even sorry, are you ...' he panted. 'You really do hate me.'

'I never hated you Rob, you twat, until now ...'

He launched and landed on top of her, and when she tried to hit him, he grabbed the arm and pressed the wrist down. Then, he grinned, as his hungry saliva dripped out of his mouth and onto her chin.

She batted at him with her free hand, but he pressed that down too, and sat up, on top of her.

She couldn't move. All she could do was squirm her head this way and that, trying to resist, and failing.

'I will give you the gift that the Lord Aliester gave to me ...' he said. 'And we will be together ... forever.'

And with that, his fangs extended, and he lowered down towards her, drawn to the blood coursing through her veins.

And then he bit into her.

It was ... everything.

He lost himself to the absolute ecstasy of her, as he took possession of everything he had ever wanted, drinking the blood of Juliet Rayne, which flowed out of her and into him—when a voice out of nowhere distracted him.

'Hey, vampire ...'

High on the blood, he looked up.

It was a little girl.

In a red coat.

Carrying a wicker basket.

'Get the hell off of her, right now ...' the girl said, and stepped towards him.

He grinned, and hissed menacingly.

The girl reached into her basket and pulled something out, some kind of little white gun. She pointed at him, and, said, 'Trick or treat, asshole.'

And then she pulled the trigger.

A misty vapour covered his face—and as it did, Robert felt a pain more dreadful than any he'd known.

He fell to his knees, and jerked his back, and reached out his arms, while the skin on his face hissed and burned. His skull began to crack, and cave in on itself, while his body jerked and contorted.

And then, without ceremony, the undead body of Robert Entwistle burst into dust, which landed lightly on the cellar floor.

†

'What's this?' Harry asked.

Jack Turnbull hovered over the play button on Harry's computer screen, in his bedroom, while he sat, ready to watch. 'It's the video Tilly sent to Sophie O'Hara,' Jack said. 'You should watch it ... but tell me, where is she?'

Harry looked nervously at his mum, who was standing in the door.

She nodded, a serious look in her eyes.

'She's gone to Rayne Manor, up on Ragged Stone Road.'

'Thank you,' Jack said, and left.

Harry leaned forward and clicked play.

In the video, Tilly sat, staring at the screen with a ghostly look on her face. She sat forward, and said, 'Hey Sophie, I just wanted to tell you that ... your *community* is a joke.'

She sat there, staring. 'Last night, I went out, with my friends, and we found a vampire.' She nodded, pressing her lips together, keeping her emotions in. 'I used holy water, just like you said. But it didn't work. It just ran off the vampire, like it was nothing.' Tears welled in her eyes. 'The vampire killed my best friend,' she said, as those tears fell down her cheeks.

'But ... I figured out why the holy water didn't work ...'

†

'Tell old Lionel what you've got in the basket, little girl ...' came the voice of another vampire, from the next room.

Tilly was in the kitchen of Rayne Manor, with her back to the wall, by the door.

The door burst open and the vampire raced through it. Tilly flung the contents of the vodka bottle over his face.

'I call it Unholy Water,' she said, stepping backwards as the vampire hissed and writhed in pain, and collapsed into itself on the floor, before bursting into dust.

†

'I figured out why your community's been using holy water all this time,' the Tilly on the computer screen said, in the video she'd sent to Sophie O'Hara. 'See, I went to see the priest at St. Luke's today. Father William. He's got diphtheria.

'See, here in the UK, we get vaccinated while we're kids. But in South Africa, where he comes from, they don't.

'He came here a week ago, and started renovating the church.'

Tilly dried her eyes, and laughed, and then sat forward. 'It's the bacteria in the holy water fonts that's toxic to vampires, you absolute gang of dickheads. It started causing diphtheria, like a hundred years ago, because it breeds, in your holy water fonts. It's no secret. Google it for God's sake. From the nineteenth century, through to, like, a case as recently as 1995.'

She laughed again, and shook her head. 'And you lot go about saying it's because it's been blessed by a priest, as though God's got anything to do with it. I used holy water blessed by Father William, and it didn't work, but not because there's anything wrong with *him*; it's just because he'd replaced the *fonts*, so the bacteria had been cleared out.'

She smiled bitterly. 'I knew it was nothing to do with the Catholic Church.'

†

'You killed the one who made me ...' growled a demonic, gravelly female voice from the living room.

'That's the way it goes I guess,' shouted Tilly through the wall, waiting for her to come through and attack.

But while she was waiting, strong grown up arms surrounded her, as her attacker hissed and snarled.

Tilly shrieked, but then there was a sharp slicing sound, followed by a thunk, and the vampire let her go.

She fell forward and turned around, to see a vampire wearing a Dominos uniform, whose head came off.

He burst into dust, taking his blue and black outfit with him.

Tilly looked to her left, to see Juliet Rayne, holding her neck.

'You okay, kid?' Juliet said.

'Yeah. Thanks.' She turned. 'There's another. In there.'

Juliet marched to the wall on the other side of the kitchen and pulled some kind of circular blade out of it.

'Did you ... throw that?' Tilly said, impressed.

Juliet smiled grimly and held it up, pressing her other hand into her neck, clearly in pain. 'Not my first. Now ... let's kill the one in there.'

†

'Father William was good about it,' the Tilly in the video said. 'Gave me all kinds of gross infected stuff. Tissues, napkins, and a "lappie", which is apparently some kind of face cloth. And I made some stuff.'

On the screen, she lifted Rita's bottle of Russian Standard onto her computer table, off the floor. 'Take this for example ...'

†

The female vampire ran out of the living room, into the hall, and then straight out of the front door of Rayne Manor.

Juliet and Tilly followed her out.

But, once outside, they found a gang of vampires walking up the road towards the house. There was ten of them, once the vampire who had been Iris Oceanheart joined their number.

And at the front was one who looked like their leader.

He was grandly adorned, wearing a black and red robe, and had long, pale hands, with long, sharp fingernails.

One of the vampires ran at Juliet, and she lowered her body, ready for battle. When it reached her, she swerved, and jumped up, and sliced its head clean off with a great, big knife, moving onto the next one before it had even burst into dust.

Another ran at Tilly, but she still had the Unholy Water stored in the vodka bottle. She splashed the last of its contents in the vampire's face, and it began hissing and contorting, and turned to dust.

†

'And I made this,' the Tilly in the video said, pulling a pink and white aerosol of deodorant and holding it in front of the camera. 'I'm not gonna show you what I'm gonna use it for, because it'd be a total waste, but it's gonna do a hell of a lot more than a bloody crucifix. That's for sure.'

†

Another vampire charged at Tilly, so she pulled one of her dad's lighters and the deodorant can from her basket. She dropped the basket and clicked on the lighter, before aiming the aerosol at the flame, and squeezing the trigger.

A jet of bright yellow fire roared out from the lighter and exploded into the onrushing vampire.

The cocktail of fire, butane and Klebs-Löffler bacillus, the pathogenic bacterium supplied by Father William, erupted when it hit the body of the vampire, which writhed and flailed, and was consumed in moments.

Tilly charged at the vampires, as fire raged in front of her, and took out another two of them before the others dispersed for safety.

She checked Juliet, to see if she was okay, catching her just in time to see her thrusting a wooden stake into the chest of another.

And then Tilly was pushed to the ground by something that felt like a train.

She looked up.

It was ...

'You ... you killed Laura ...' she said, looking up at the vampire.

He grinned down at her. 'You brought her right to me,' he said. 'I should say thank you. She was sweet and rich and warm.'

Tilly gritted her teeth while absolute fury consumed her. 'You killed my Laulau, you absolute bastard!' she yelled.

The vampire launched into the air towards her.

She'd lost the lighter when she'd been shoved, but the aerosol was still in her hand. She pointed it at him and, as he was about to land on her, she sprayed.

The creature landed on top of her, flying through the mist she'd sprayed, and she squirmed underneath him while his skin began to blister. She pulled the aerosol tight into her chest and sprayed again, covering his face.

He rolled off her, and landed on the floor, writhing in torment, before bursting into dust.

Tilly took a deep breath, and sat up.

'I got him Laulau,' she said. 'I bloody well got him.'

†

'Juliet Rayne ...' the vampire leader said. He was the last one standing. 'You look so much like your mother.'

'What do you know about it?' she said, trying to stand tall. Her neck was throbbing where Robert had bitten her, and her left arm had been battered scrapping with two vampires at once.

'I wonder if you taste of sugar and cherries, as she did,' he said.

'Who are you?' Juliet said, lifting her head.

'Oh,' he said, 'my apologies, I thought you knew. I am Aliester, the Lord and Baron of Undertown.' He grinned wickedly. 'And the slaughterer of Thomas and Amelie Rayne.'

'You know how many times I've heard that?'

'Oh I think you can trust my word,' said the vampire, stepping towards her, in the gardens at the front of her home.

And then he moved at her, in the blink of an eye, and shoved her backwards, as her heels dragged underneath her. He pushed her back inside her house, and then landed on top of her, in the hall of Rayne Manor.

He restrained her there, on the floor.

She struggled with all her might to get free, but she could not.

'Kid?!' she yelled, hoping that she might again be saved.

'I'm afraid that your industrious little companion is not invited.'

Juliet could hear the kid banging on the door.

Aliester grinned wickedly. His face seemed permanently distorted, so that even when he wasn't about to feed you could see clearly that he was a vampire. 'Now ... watch my memories ...' he said, and closed his eyes.

Juliet saw it.

She saw her father, running, as though for his life, through what seemed like long, warped corridors.

He had nothing, no crosses, no stakes, no holy water.

He panted for breath, and put his hand on the wall for stability, when Aliester appeared out of the shadow behind him, and snapped his neck.

'No ...' Juliet said. 'Don't show me ... please ...'

But the vision continued. Juliet's eyes were closed but it was no good. She opened them, but it was still no good. All she could see was her mother, finding her father's body, and weeping over him.

Amelie Rayne screamed something, but Juliet couldn't hear it—she could only see.

Amelie stood and pulled a stake ready, glancing in each direction, for Aliester.

And then the life seemed to drain from her eyes, and she dropped the stake.

Slowly, a long sword jutted out of her chest, soaked in deep red blood.

'Mummy ...' Juliet whispered, as tears welled in her eyes, and all the anguish of her mother's death overwhelmed her.

In the vision, Aliester, still holding the sword, slithered around her, and licked the blood off the sword, before pulling it out of Amelie and wrestling her to the ground, and devouring her.

'Oh mum ...' Juliet said.

'So you see,' Aliester said. 'Others may have claimed my fame, but only I am worthy of it. And now, just as I consumed the lifeblood of your mother, I shall consume the lifeblood of you.'

'What did you just say?' Juliet said, struck by the words.

'I shall consume your lifeblood,' Aliester said, a note of confusion in his voice now.

The words took her back to her dream.

The dream with the girl, and the man, and the voice.

Aliester's voice.

Juliet put her hand to her belt.

The compass was there.

And she finally understood.

She pulled it to her chest, underneath Aliester, and said, 'Nocturnal terror, come by night; thou art in error, to know my sight ...'

'No ...' Aliester muttered, gritting his teeth.

'For, enemy,' she went on, 'thou'd never best; thine sturdy foe, now evanesce.'

Aliester's eyes lit up, and blinding, warming sunlight shot out of them, and out of his ears, and mouth. He cried out, and rose into the air above Juliet, still lighting up the room.

She rolled out from under him and stood up, taking backward steps, and watched.

She watched, as fire exploded within the vampire that killed her parents.

She watched as the monster burned to dust, which drifted harmlessly to the floor of her family home.

Once it was over, she slowly became aware of the kid, still banging on the door.

She raced over and opened it up.

The kid was standing there, with her basket over the crook of her left arm, and with her little Unholy Water mist gun thing in her right hand, poised to attack.

'Are we good?' the kid said. 'Is that all of them?'

Juliet smiled, bewildered by her tiny companion. She swung the door all the way open and gestured to the pile of dust in the centre of the hall.

'Oh thank God,' the kid said, walking in. 'He was the leader right? I mean, he had the scary robes, and he was faster than the others. How did you kill him? Stake?'

'Compass,' Juliet said.

The kid looked flatly up at her. 'Can you show me how to kill vampires with a compass?'

'I think it only works with this one,' Juliet said, looking down at the ornate copper artefact in her hand.

'Oh. Well, can I borrow it?'

Juliet, who was emotionally exhausted and out of strength, merely laughed, as a car raced onto her drive and parked in front of the open door.

A guy jumped out and ran into the house, yelling, 'Hello?!'

'Dad?' the kid said, surprised.

'Holy God in heaven Tilly,' the guy said, running to her and falling down onto his knees, cuddling her, pulling him into his chest.

'What are you doing here?'

'Oh thank God you're okay ...' he said.

'I killed five vampires, dad,' she said.

He didn't speak, he just rubbed her hair.

'I killed five,' she said again, proudly this time.

The dad looked up at Juliet confused, asking her with his eyes if his daughter was crazy.

Juliet simply nodded that her words were true.

'Come on ...' the dad said. 'I'm taking you home.'

EPILOGUE
Mermaid Scales, a Fae's Wing, Vampire Dust, and the Stolen Chippings of a Wizard's Staff

It was the next day. Wednesday, the first of November. And Jack Turnbull was waiting for Becky Brannigan to meet him for lunch in the Lord Nelson.

It had been a wild twelve hours or so.

He'd gotten a message that his daughter, his only child, intended to go vampire hunting in Ecclesburn. That she'd been vampire hunting once already, and that it had got her best friend killed.

Jack had always accepted the existence of vampires.

It was impossible to live in Ecclesburn and not accept it.

But it was not something that people talked about.

They just followed the rules. Garlic, holy water, crucifixes. It wasn't too much trouble, really, and it was the way it had always been.

But his daughter didn't seem too keen on following rules. He should have known, really. Tilly was never one for the rules. She had always tried to find the wiggle room. She had always tried to exercise her own authority over a situation, even when she'd been a toddler.

He sipped his Guinness, and wondered what lay in store for him and his daughter, when Becky arrived. She smiled at him and made her way over, so Jack slid over the wine he'd bought for her.

'Are you okay?' she asked.

'I'm so sorry I had to run out on you,' he began. 'I got this message that Tilly was in trouble and I had to go.'

She seemed to understand. 'Of course,' she said. 'I get that. What happened? Is she okay?'

'Well, no thanks to me, yeah,' Jack said. 'She's fine.'

'What do you mean?'

'Well, by the time I found her she was out of danger.'

'What was it?'

'She went ... hunting. For vampires.'

Becky's eyebrows raised and she looked around, to see if anyone was listening. 'I see.'

'She went out the night before, apparently. Her best friend died, and she watched it happen.'

'Jesus.'

'Yeah. She asked me not to go out, last night. She was so upset and she asked me to stay with her. But I'—Jack looked at the table, ashamed—'I wanted to see you.'

She drank some of her wine, and then put the glass down. 'You put seeing me in a play before your little girl?' she said.

Jack nodded, still sombre. 'I did.'

'I see.'

Jack didn't really know what to say, so he just drank some more of his pint.

'Did you know about her friend?' Becky asked. 'Did you know her friend had died?'

'I knew she was missing, which, in this town ...'

'And you still didn't stay with her?'

Jack felt awful, and he couldn't pretend otherwise. He shook his head. 'No.'

'I see,' Becky said a third time, and drank some more wine, leaving less than an inch in the glass. 'Can I ask why?'

Jack looked up, and took a deep breath. 'I wanted to see you. I wanted to be with you. I wanted ... to sleep with you.'

Becky nodded. She emptied her glass. 'Okay,' she said. 'Look, Jack, I like you, but ... I don't think you're who I thought you were. And I don't wanna be the reason you're such a shit father.'

Jack's heart sank.

'Listen, I think I'm gonna get out of here,' Becky said.

'What about lunch? I thought we could—'

'Jack, please. I feel so icky with all this. I just wanna get out of here. We can be friends, and I won't go around badmouthing you or anything. I just'—she shook her head—'I don't think I'm into it anymore. I don't think I'm into this.'

Jack felt absolutely rotten. 'Okay,' he said simply.

Becky stood, with her gorgeous hair down over her perfect shoulders. 'I'll see you around,' she said, and left.

†

Tilly was still in bed, though it was about noon.

She was going over the events of the previous week, in her head.

But mostly, she missed her friend.

She was resolute. She would continue to fight monsters. But she wouldn't get anyone killed again. She wouldn't take anyone along who didn't have the same conviction that she had.

Never again.

'Matilda ...' came the voice of her grandmother through the door. 'Can I come in?'

Tilly tensed up a little. 'Yeah,' she shouted.

The door opened, and Tilly's grandma came in, and sat in her computer chair.

'Your dad told me what happened.'

'Okay ...' Tilly said.

'And ... I know we've had our issues. But ... I wanted to say ... I'm sorry that I hit you.'

'Oh,' Tilly said. 'Good.'

'Your dad gave me hell for it. And I've not been able to stop thinking about it.'

'Why?'

'I ... I miss my daughter, Matilda. And I resent her for leaving. But I've grown resentful of you. Because you look like her. And that's not fair. I mean, you are staggeringly defiant, and you don't listen to me, and you've never listened to me, but—'

Tilly smiled. 'But what?'

Her grandmother almost smiled back, and then looked guilty. 'I'm sorry. For hitting you. And for hating you. There's a lot of'—she winced, as though discomforted by the vulnerability—'there's a lot of pain in my heart, girl. But I think I'm passing that pain onto you. And I don't want to do that anymore.'

'Wow,' Tilly said. 'Okay.'

'Can we ... spend time together? Did you go and see your film?'

'What, Thor: Ragnarok? You wanna go see Thor: Ragnarok with me?'

'Would I enjoy it?'

'Honestly? I have no idea.'

'Would you enjoy it?'

Tilly almost felt tears coming. She had wanted to see it with Laura. 'I would,' she said simply. 'I would enjoy it, yeah.'

Her grandmother smiled. 'Would you let me take you today?'

Tilly smiled back. 'Yes,' she said. 'Yes please, grandma.'

†

Two more days had passed. Friday the third of November. And Juliet Rayne was waiting for a visit from The Five Patriarchs—the five leaders of the North West vampire hunting community. Despite her family funding most of the community's exploits since the days of her grandfather, Juliet, the sole heir to the Rayne family's wealth, had never met a single one of the Patriarchs.

She knew she had done wrong.

She had no intention of lying about it, or blaming anyone else.

She would take whatever sanction they imposed—save for the seizing of her wealth. That was her mother's, and her father's. And frankly, she had more trust in herself to use it for good, than she did in the Patriarchs.

There was a rapping at the door, so she made her way from the living room through to the hall and to the door, which she opened.

'Hi Ms. Rayne,' chirped a small woman with a bonnie blonde pixie cut. 'I'm Jenna. The driver.'

'Juliet,' said Juliet.

'The blokes are in the minibus,' Jenna said, with a backward nod towards the multi-purpose vehicle in the drive behind her.

'Minibus?' Juliet said. 'That's a Mercedes-Benz Viano. It cost twenty-five thousand quid.'

Jenna turned to look at it and whistled. 'I probably shouldn't go so fast round these old country lanes then,' she said.

Juliet shrugged. 'Nah, don't worry about it,' she said, while the Patriarchs began climbing out, one by one.

†

'Basil Powell and Steve Fitzpatrick were good men,' said Cumbria.

'And Anna-Marie Gregory's grandfather wants you made an example of,' said Manchester.

The Five Patriarchs apparently went by the name of the county they represented. It seemed a little hoity-toity to Juliet, but not important. They were old, and white, and male. Rich, powerful, white guys. Dressed in smart suits, and difficult to tell one from the next, but for the accents.

Merseyside nodded. 'The old git wouldn't stop bleating on about it on the flight back from the Barbados golf trip,' he said.

'Made an example of ... how?' Juliet asked.

'He favours a ritualistic flaying,' Cheshire said, 'although we managed to talk him down to permanent banishment to the Depths.'

'Is that right?' Juliet said. 'Cheers for that.'

'Do not nurse a provocative tone, Ms. Rayne,' Lancashire said.

Of the five, Lancashire seemed the most protective. Juliet figured it was because, of the five, he represented *her*. He was her patron, of sorts.

'You kept a vampire in your home,' Lancashire went on. 'You drugged members of the community. Men who'd served for years, for decades. You bound them, and you got them killed.'

'I know that.'

'Then watch the lip, young lady,' he said.

'Yes,' Cumbria said. 'We must also account for the losses of Aaron McLeary and Robert Entwistle.'

'These men's fates, though not your fault directly,' Merseyside said, 'still bear witness against you.'

'So ... what's the plan then?' Juliet said. 'Do you boys really think I'm gonna go into the Depths for the rest of my life?'

The Patriarchs looked at one another, somewhat uneasily.

Finally, Cheshire raised his head, and said, 'Tell us about this ... holy water substitute.'

Juliet shrugged. 'It's not my story to tell. You wanna talk to Tilly Turnbull about that. She's the one who figured it out.'

'We're talking to *you*,' Lancashire said.

'Well, the kid figured out why the holy water stopped working after Father William replaced Father McMahon. It wasn't that there was anything evil or sinister about the new priest. It was because he had the church renovated.'

'Well that's still up for debate ...' said Manchester.

'Oh it's way past debate, mate,' Juliet said. 'The stuff Tilly brought with her, on Halloween, it'd never been blessed. It'd just been contaminated with this bacteria, this toxin. And it worked like holy water on steroids.'

The Five Patriarchs looked uneasy at this.

'See,' she went on, 'it was never God, hurting the vamps. It was never *faith*. It was just science.'

'But vampires are ... evil,' Cheshire said.

'Aaron McLeary ...' she said. 'After he'd been turned. He wasn't ... *evil.*'

Merseyside raised his head. 'You said he tried to kill a child, the first night, and that he wanted to kill Ms. Gregory on Halloween, and—'

'He did,' Juliet said. 'I'm not gonna lie. He did. But ... I think it was the *hunger.* He kept going on about the hunger. But, see, there were times, when I gave him animal blood, where we could ... sit together. And he didn't want to hurt me. If he was just *evil,* that wouldn't have happened. Right?'

'So ... you're saying you believe that vampires can be redeemed?' Cumbria said, an eyebrow raised.

Juliet's face was sorrowful, and her heart was heavy. 'No,' she said, shaking her head. 'I don't. I think they're lost. But ... I don't hate them. I don't think they're evil. And I do think they need to be put down.'

Lancashire nodded. 'Good girl.'

'We don't want to banish you, Ms. Rayne,' Manchester said. 'But your rehabilitation is going to cause us some issues. Steve Fitzpatrick left behind a family. And we've already explained Clarence Gregory's feelings on the matter.'

'Yeah, ritualistic flaying or lifelong banishment to the Depths were my choices, right?' Juliet said.

'But, we don't want that,' Cumbria said.

'No,' Cheshire agreed. 'Again, we do want to know more about this holy water substitute.'

'I told you already, you should speak to Tilly Turnbull.'

The Patriarchs looked at each other awkwardly.

'Oh ... you've already tried that?'

'That young lady is ... incredibly intransigent,' Cheshire said.

'She's what?'

Cheshire winced. 'Hostile. Aggressive. Belligerent.'

Juliet laughed. 'What did she say?'

Cumbria cleared his throat. 'She told us we could'—he coughed again, embarrassed—'go and ... suck each other's dicks.'

Juliet snorted a laugh.

'Those were her exact words, you understand,' Manchester said with a frown.

Lancashire leaned forward. 'We thought that maybe you could—'

'Sorry guys, I'm not gonna put any pressure on her.'

'But, Ms. Rayne, we—'

'I said no. She lost her best friend. And she saved my life. If she doesn't want anything to do with you, I'm not gonna try and persuade her otherwise.'

'Then ... would you at least find out what you can about her holy water substitute, and—'

'Unholy Water,' Juliet said.

Three of the five Patriarchs rolled their eyes at this.

'That's what it's called,' Juliet said firmly. 'You create it, you name it. And she created it, and that's what she named it.'

'Yes ...' Cheshire muttered disapprovingly, 'well, would you? Would you consider helping us to'—he shook his head, looking for the right words—'oh, I don't know, *manufacture* this ... Unholy Water?'

'Well, sure,' Juliet said. 'It'll save lives. Of course I will.'

Cumbria nodded. 'Well, that is good news.'

'There is one more thing that we're curious about,' Cheshire said. 'You said in your emails that you killed the Baron of Undertown with your mother's compass?'

'Yes,' Juliet said.

'Can you explain to us how that occurred?' Lancashire said. 'We were to understand that the compass was merely an old Underworld charm, a guide, which leads to the deadliest vampire?'

'It was more than that,' Juliet said. 'The witch who made it, she made it for Aliester.' She shook her head. 'I don't know how long ago it happened, but ... the witch made it as a gift for him.'

'A gift?'

'It was supposed to take him to any vampire stronger than him. And there's a magic word. You say the magic word, holding onto the compass, and the strongest vampire dies. She did it so that he could always be the strongest vampire, see.'

'How did you possibly discover all of this?' Cumbria said.

Juliet winced a little. 'I dreamt it.'

'You *what*?' Lancashire said, bewildered.

Juliet shrugged. 'I dreamt it. I saw it happen. I saw the witch. I saw Aliester. I didn't get it at first. But it all made sense when Aliester was on top of me, saying the words I'd heard in the dream.'

Merseyside leaned forward and eyed her cautiously. 'Have you had ... prophetic visions before?'

'Nope.'

'I see.'

'This is no small matter, Ms. Rayne,' Lancashire said. 'Prophetic visions ... have a source. They come from somewhere. They come from one who has knowledge of past, and present, and future.'

'Okay?' Juliet said.

'Will you contact us, if you have more?' Lancashire said.

'Sure,' Juliet said casually. 'No worries.'

'Good,' Lancashire said, though he remained pensive.

'We voted on this in the car,' Cumbria said. 'If you were willing to work with us, and to help us utilise this Turnbull girl's creation, we would smooth things over for you to return to the community, and—'

Juliet raised her hand. 'Um, guys?' she said. 'That's nice of you and all, but ... I'm not sure I want to return to the community.'

The Five Patriarchs stared at her.

'Is that right?' Lancashire said.

'That's right.'

'What do you want to do?'

Juliet took a deep breath. 'Well, to be honest, I want to get the hell out of Ecclesburn for a while. I want to see the world. By myself. I want to read. I want to travel.'

'We will need to position someone here, to monitor vampire activity in your absence,' Merseyside said.

'Fill your boots,' Juliet said. 'But I don't want anyone living in my home.'

'Very well,' Manchester agreed.

Juliet smiled a sad and wistful smile. 'I really am sorry. For everything.'

Lancashire nodded. 'The world is full of complications, Ms. Rayne. And each of us understands the risk that accompanies our every action.'

'You *have* transgressed, and there were *real* consequences,' Cheshire said.

'But are we right to assume that your conscience will remain ever pricked by the events of this last week?' Merseyside said.

Juliet looked into Merseyside's grey, old eyes. She nodded. 'God yeah,' she said.

'Then I think we can move forward,' Lancashire said. 'As long as you contact us, should you experience any more prophetic visions.'

She nodded.

Lancashire looked at his fellows. 'Are we agreed?'

'Aye,' said Cumbria.

'Aye,' agreed Cheshire.

'Aye,' said Manchester, with a nod.

'Aye,' said Merseyside.

'Good,' Lancashire said, turning to Juliet. 'Ms. Rayne, may God the Father of Christ, and the goodwill of all the gods of the Celts, be ever with you.'

She smiled awkwardly. 'Yeah. Thanks. And, um, the same to you.'

†

Tilly Turnbull rested under her father's arm, as the two of them watched fireworks screaming up into the sky above the Barrington Cliffs, at the annual bonfire night bonanza at Barrington Fields. There were fairground rides, there were vendors selling crepes and hotdogs and pancakes and donuts—all of which smelled amazing—and, for the first year in Tilly's memory, there were lots of people there.

Two more days had passed.

It was Sunday the fifth of November.

And word of Tilly's creation, Tilly's Unholy Water, had spread.

Loads of people had been pestering her for help with it. Father William, while being treated for diphtheria, had been super generous, offering his germs to the cause. And while absolutely no one had come right out and said the V word, or talked openly about what had happened on Halloween, there was a tacit understanding that things were safer now.

Not completely safe.

But safer.

And, as she rested under her dad's arm, that fact made her smile.

She smiled as she looked at all the families there, enjoying the festivities, as she saw kids from her year going on rides and snogging in quiet spots.

'There's Becky,' Tilly's dad said glumly.

Tilly looked. She was with some old guy, eating a burger.

'That's her father,' Tilly's dad explained.

'Oh right,' Tilly said. 'I figured, given she entertained the notion of going out with you, that it was, like, her new boyfriend or something.'

'You little madam.'

Tilly smiled, and sighed.

'I'm gutted, you know,' Tilly's dad went on. 'I can't stop thinking about her.'

Tilly frowned. 'Is that right?'

'I know it sounds ... a bit sad. But I can't help it. I don't think I've ever felt like this before. I don't think I'll ever feel like this again.'

'You know, dad, there was a time when I suspected you were, like, nothing more than an overgrown man-child, pathetically trapped by a desperate desire to be young and vibrant and relevant.'

'Okay. And?'

'And now, after what you just said, I'm certain of it.'

'Oh ...'

'I think you just put too much importance on the idea of being with her,' Tilly said, relaxing her head into his chest.

She felt him looking down at her. 'Oh aye?' he said.

'I just think you're restless. You do a boring job. You never play your guitar anymore. I think you just kind of bought into this idea that she was the answer to all your troubles. And you wanted her too much.'

'That's an interesting thought.'

'Beware desire in excess ...' Tilly said, making her voice grand and wise-sounding. 'If you want my advice, you need to find something to work for. Write some songs. Start a band. That's what you used to say you always wanted to do, when you used to sing your songs to me.'

'You remember that?'

'I thought you were so cool. I thought you were the most amazing guy in the world. Now I have to sit here and give you relationship advice—it's very unfair.'

He held her. 'Maybe I will,' he said. 'Maybe I will start playing again.'

'You go out too much,' Tilly said, her tone more serious now. 'I mean, we could hang out. We could watch movies, or, even, I could sing with you?'

He kissed the top of her head, and held her still. 'What a girl you are,' he said, with wonder in his voice. 'You know something. I'm so proud of you.'

'Yeah?'

'Yeah.'

'I got my best friend killed, dad,' Tilly said solemnly.

'Oh my love.'

'And I miss her so much,' Tilly went on. 'She was looking forward to coming to this, you know.'

'I'm so sorry, my darling,' her dad said. 'I shouldn't have left you the way I did. I'll never do that again. No matter what's going on. I swear it.'

She sniffed, and toughened herself. She was kind of annoyed that he was talking over her pain with his guilt, but she could sense that he was trying his best. 'Thank you. I don't hate you for it, if that helps.'

'I'm here for you,' he said. 'I wasn't, before. But I am now. If you need to talk, if you need a cuddle, I'm here.' He gripped her more tightly. 'I'm gonna be better—'

'They have mulled wine,' came Tilly's grandmother's voice. 'And a non-alcoholic one for you Tilly.'

Tilly's grandma sat down with them and looked up at the fireworks display, shooting and popping and cracking away.

'Thanks Reet,' said Tilly's dad.

'Thanks Grandma,' Tilly said.

And, together, the three of them sat and watched the display. And Tilly was kind of happy. She missed Laura terribly, and she felt sick with guilt. She fingered the necklace gingerly, and thought about her.

She could see Harry and Mark, juggling a football to each other, to the side of one of the crowds.

She could see Jenny and Tom, the couple who'd been chased by the vampire, that first night in Cleve Woods. They were holding hands and eating donuts, lit by the light of the bonfire.

And she could see Gemma, and Chrissie, and Alfie, and Grace, and Mr. Willis, her form tutor.

They looked ... safe.

And then she saw Juliet Rayne, standing with her hands in her coat pockets, looking back at her.

'Dad, grandma, I'm gonna take a walk if that's okay?' she said, climbing to her feet.

'Of course, love,' said her dad.

Tilly walked towards Juliet, who smiled her sad smile at her.

'Hey,' Tilly said.

'Hey,' Juliet replied.

'How's you?'

'I'm okay,' Juliet said, looking around. 'Big turn out.'

'Yeah.'

'That's your doing, you know. This Unholy Water thing's caught right on.'

Tilly smiled. 'We're gonna have to figure out a new way to make it when Father William gets better.'

'Well, I've no doubt you will.'

Tilly nodded proudly.

'Listen,' Juliet said, 'I know that the Patriarchs of the community came to see you.'

'Oh, yeah,' Tilly said, her irritation flickering at the mention of them.

'They wanted me to pressure you to join them.'

'Oh.'

'I said I wouldn't.' Juliet pulled her hair behind her ear. 'But, listen, they won't stop coming for you. They'll pursue you until you join them.'

'I'm not worried.'

Juliet nodded. 'I'm going away for a while. But I was wondering. Are you gonna keep hunting?'

'That's the plan.'

'Do you want some funding?'

'Funding?'

'Well, you know I'm rich, right?'

'Yeah?'

'I can set you up. I can have a workshop built for you. Or a lab, or whatever. You can have Unholy Water by the gallon.'

'Wow. Thank you.'

'You saved my life. I owe you.'

Tilly blushed a little. 'Nah ...' she said.

'I'm gonna give you my personal email addresses and stuff. Keep in touch with me. And, look, this hunting thing, it's ... kinda toxic. It can warp you. Make you do stuff you wouldn't normally do. Bad stuff. So ... if you ever wanna get away from it, and come hang with me somewhere, just let me know. Look after *you*, and don't feel guilty for doing it. Okay?'

'Yes, Ms. Rayne.'

'D'you do hugs?' Juliet said.

'Not really.'

Juliet nodded. 'That's cool.' She held out her hand. 'Handshake?'

'Yeah,' Tilly said, and took her hand.

'Good luck, Tilly Turnbull.'

'Thank you.'

And with that, Tilly turned to head back to her dad and grandma. They were drinking, and bickering, but there was a familiarity to it that was comforting. They were bickering in the safe way that *family* bickers. And, despite their flaws—despite their many, many flaws—Tilly knew that she would indeed be safe, with them.

She laughed as she neared them, ready to judge whichever one of them was wrong for whatever they had done.

For, the terrible curse of being right all the time was, in this family at least, Tilly's, and Tilly's alone.

†

Down, in the Depths, in Undertown, Elspeth the Cacolamia was looking down at her enchanted quilt, resting flat on her augury table. Projected, by magic, onto the quilt was a scene, playing out in the world above, in Ecclesburn.

'Aliester has fallen,' came the voice of Annie Reed, Elspeth's pet cat, who hopped onto a chair at the side of the table.

'Indeed he has,' Elspeth said. 'What a terrible shame.'

'Do you mind if I ask you something, m'lady?' Annie Reed said.

'Of course not, dear.'

'I have been checking our stocks.'

'*That* is not a question, Annie.'

'There are some items that are ... missing.'

Elspeth raised her eyebrows, a showing of sweet innocence. 'Oh?'

'Powerful items too. Mermaid scales, the wing of a Fae, stolen wizard's bark ... and even some vampire dust.'

'Oh dear,' Elspeth performed.

'It sounds to me like someone has been projecting visions,' Annie Reed said, staring curiously up at Elspeth.

'Yes, I would say that it does.'

'And I hear that Juliet Rayne used the Baron's compass to kill him. Now, how would Juliet Rayne know how to use that?'

'Perhaps she has a prophetic gift?' Elspeth said.

'Or perhaps a witch with an augury table and a shop full of charms *gave* her a prophetic gift?' the cat said. 'With mermaid scales. And the wing of a Fae. And vampire dust and the stolen chippings of a wizard's staff.'

Elspeth smiled devilishly.

The cat nodded. 'It *was* you?'

Elspeth walked to the door and clicked it locked. Then, she laughed. 'I told him the vampire dust was an aphrodisiac.' She looked down at the cat. 'I could not kill him myself. His drones would have burned my shop to the ground, with me inside.'

'Why kill him at all? He was no threat?'

Elspeth raised her head. 'I want Undertown. I want to *rule* Undertown.'

'I see. I never figured you for the power-hungry type.'

'Well ... I wish to leave something of worth for my daughter, you see,' Elspeth said, looking down at the enchanted quilt.

The cat hopped up onto the table, and looked down at it too. 'Right,' she said, nodding. 'Fair enough. This is her, is it?'

Elspeth looked down at her. At the girl she'd carried and delivered into the world, on the tenth day of February, in the year 2005. 'It is,' she said, rubbing the girl's image on the quilt.

'She's pretty,' Annie Reed said. 'What's her name?'

Elspeth raised her head and looked at the cat. 'Her name is Matilda. We called her Tilly. And, if I have my way, before she turns eighteen years old, she will be the queen of this realm, and the commander of all its people. She will be worshiped by all.'

Annie Reed peered up at Elspeth with fascination in her little green feline eyes. 'Do you ever *not* get your way?'

Elspeth smiled again, her devilish smile.   'No, Annie Reed,' she said. 'As Aliester would attest, were he here to do so, I always get my way.'

The End

Read More
Siren Stories: The Ultimate Bibliography

Lilly Prospero And The Magic Rabbit (*The Lilly Prospero Series Book 1*)
By J.J. Barnes

Lilly Prospero And The Magic Rabbit is a young adult urban fantasy exploring the corrupting effects of absolute power on a teenage girl. When the unpopular and lonely Lilly Prospero is given a talking pet rabbit, her life begins to change. She is thrust into a world of magic, mystery, and danger, and has to get control of a power she doesn't understand fast to make the difference between life and death. The first in a new series by J.J. Barnes, Lilly Prospero And The Magic Rabbit is a tale full of excitement, sorrow and mystery, as Lilly Prospero shows just how strong a girl can be.
Available in Paperback and for Kindle.

Alana: A Ghost Story
By Jonathan McKinney

Alana is a ghost, trapped in the New York Film Academy dorms, where she died. She has friends, fellow ghosts, with whom she haunts the students living there, passing her time watching whatever TV shows and movies the students watch.

But she is restless. She wants to move on. And when a medium moves into the dorms, Alana gets a nasty shock, which turns her mundane afterlife upside down.

Alana is a light yet moving short story about a miraculous love that travels many years and many miles to save a lost, trapped and hopeless soul.

Available in Paperback and for Kindle.

Emily the Master Enchantress: The First Schildmaids Novel (The Schildmaids Saga Book 1)
By Jonathan McKinney

Hidden, veiled behind the compressed wealth of New York City, is a dank underbelly of exploitation and slavery, which most people never see, or sense, or suffer. A cruel, expanding world.

And when Emily Hayes-Brennan, a proficient enchantress with a good heart and a tendency to overshare, is recruited to the world renowned crime fighters, the Schildmaids, she will find that that cruel world threatens to expand around her, and everyone she cares about.

She will be confronted by conflicts of fate and choice, as she seeks to find her place in the world.

Available in Paperback and for Kindle.

After the Mad Dog in the Fog: An Erotic Schildmaids Novelette
By Jonathan McKinney and J.J. Barnes

Emily Hayes-Brennan wants to get through a simple night out in her home city of New York, introducing her new boyfriend Teo to her friends, so she can get him home and have sex with him for the very first time. But when an obnoxious admirer and old flame shows up, she begins to fear that her plans are going awry.

After the Mad Dog in the Fog is a wild and energetic novelette about love and desire, and about the free joy that comes from prioritising the one you love before all others.

Available in Paperback and for Kindle.

Lilly Prospero And The Mermaid's Curse (The Lilly Prospero Series Book 2)
By J.J. Barnes

Lilly Prospero And The Mermaid's Curse is a young adult, urban fantasy following Lilly Prospero and her friend Saffron Jones on a magical adventure to Whitstable.

Whilst on a family holiday, Lilly and Saffron meet mermaids under attack from a mysterious and violent stranger, work with a powerful coven of witches, and fight to save not only the lives of the mermaids, but their own lives as well.

Available in Paperback and for Kindle.

The Inadequacy of Alice Anders: A Schildmaids Short Story
By Jonathan McKinney

Alice Anders can summon vision of the future, which guide her heroic friends through heroic acts. Sometimes she'll see vulnerable people in danger; sometimes she'll see her superhero friends in places where they can help those who can't help themselves.

But, for the last three and a half weeks, she's not been able to summon a single vision—and given that she started working for the superhero team of her dreams, the Schildmaids, exactly three and a half weeks ago, she's becoming anxious about her worth. And to figure out why her power has gone away, she'll have to push herself, and face some hard truths.

The Inadequacy of Alice Anders is a light and bittersweet short story about the pain of loss, and about facing that pain when it threatens to hold you down and hold you back.

Available in Paperback and for Kindle.

The Fundamental Miri Mnene: The Second Schildmaids Novel (The Schildmaids Saga Book 2)
By Jonathan McKinney

Miri Mnene is the Syncerus, a warrior, and the strongest of the Schildmaids, the New York team of legendary crime fighters. But she was not always the Syncerus. Once, she was the Xuétú Nánrén Shashou, the final student of the man-hating, man-killing Guan-yin Cheh.

And when she is sent to South Dakota to investigate a mystical brothel, which has been kidnapping women, kidnapping girls, and forcing them to work, she is confronted by the darkness that lives within her when her past and present collide.

The Fundamental Miri Mnene is a powerful novel about the lengths to which you should go, the lengths to which you must go, in order to see justice in the world.

Available in Paperback and for Kindle.

The Relief of Aurelia Kite: A Schildmaids Novella
By Jonathan McKinney

Aurelia Kite is a young New Yorker at Christmas, trapped in an abusive relationship, dreaming of escape. And when her controlling boyfriend Trafford takes on a new job, her path crosses with two highly serious female crime fighters, causing her to make a big decision about what she will and will not tolerate.

The Relief of Aurelia Kite is a harsh novella with a soft centre, about hope in the face of toxic romance, and about the salvation that can be found just by talking to a sympathetic stranger.

Available in Paperback and for Kindle.

Not Even Stars: The Third Schildmaids Novel
By Jonathan McKinney

Teo Roqué is journeying through Europe with Emily Hayes-Brennan, the woman he loves, when ancient hostilities give way to a war between powerful, clandestine organisations. A war which puts the young couple's lives in danger, as well as all those they care about.

And as a new threat emerges, fanning the conflict's flames, Teo and Emily must work together to end the war before it leads to a disaster much, much worse than they'd imagined.

Not Even Stars is an incredibly intense novel about all-consuming love, about awe-inspiring heroism, and about the cost of making the right choice when the fate of the world hangs in the balance.

Available for Kindle, coming soon in Paperback.

The Mystery of Ms. Riley: a Schildmaids Novella
By Jonathan McKinney

Alice Anders and Rakesha McKenzie are members of the Schildmaids, the legendary New York crime fighters. And when Alice sees visions of Nina Riley, a young New Yorker carrying a deep, hidden pain, the two heroes fight to determine what has caused that pain, and how to save Ms. Riley from a prison she cannot even see.

The Mystery of Ms. Riley is a harsh yet hopeful story about self-doubt, about ordinary, everyday oppression, and about the kind of love that defies the testimonies of everyone around you.

Available for Kindle, coming soon in Paperback.

Unholy Water: A Halloween Novel
By Jonathan McKinney

In the misty Lancashire town of Ecclesburn, kids go missing. But no one talks about it. Everyone knows why, but they don't talk about it. The grown ups smear garlic and holy water over their necks and wrists while walking the dog after dark, but they never say the V word.

And when one of the local pubs is taken over by a group of undead monsters, and a trio of vampire hunters is called to clear them out, a terrible series of events begins to play out, which will change the way Ecclesburnians live forever.

Unholy Water is a dark and bloodthirsty novel about desire in wild excess, about whether you should defy your circumstances or adapt to them, and about the kind of inflexible determination that can save or destroy those that matter most.

Available in Paperback and for Kindle.